PISSING IN A RIVER
LORRIE SPRECHER

THE
FEMINIST PRESS
AT THE CITY UNIVERSITY
OF NEW YORK
NEW YORK CITY

Published in 2014 by the Feminist Press
at the City University of New York
The Graduate Center
365 Fifth Avenue, Suite 5406
New York, NY 10016

feministpress.org

First printing June 2014

Cover design by Herb Thornby, herbthornby.com
Text design by Drew Stevens

Library of Congress Cataloging-in-Publication Data
Sprecher, Lorrie, 1960-
Pissing in a river : a novel / by Lorrie Sprecher.
   pages cm
ISBN 978-1-55861-852-7 (pbk) — ISBN 978-1-55861-853-4 (ebook)
1. Lesbians—Fiction. 2. Punk culture—Fiction. I. Title.
PS3569.P674P57 2014
813'.54—dc23

                                                    2014010815

To Angela Locke
and my two Kurts
—soul love.

And if I cried, who'd listen to me in those angelic
orders? Even if one of them suddenly held me
to his heart, I'd vanish in his overwhelming
presence. Because beauty's nothing
but the start of terror we can hardly bear,
and we adore it because of the serene scorn
it could kill us with. Every angel's terrifying.

—RAINER MARIA RILKE, *DUINO ELEGIES*, "THE FIRST ELEGY"

 **A SIDE**

I promised the women in my head that I would get to England even if it killed me. I knew that they were watching over me. Despite my mental glitches, I applied to do a year abroad in Britain and was awarded a place at an English university starting the fall term of 1980.

I'd been listening to Heart's debut album *Dreamboat Annie* when I first heard their voices. They started as a murmur, but then I could make out two distinct female voices with British accents talking inside my head. Who were they? What were they doing in there? It was like listening in on someone else's conversation on an extension phone.

I didn't freak out because I was used to hearing noise inside my head due to the obsessive-compulsive disorder I didn't know I had. I endlessly repeated prayers of protection to erase my own bad thoughts before they could hurt someone. I performed mental rituals to keep my hands from falling off for no reason. At seventeen, all I had was the diagnosis of major depressive disorder to explain why I wasn't coping well with my life.

Even though I was swept up in the punk revolution, I remained loyal to Heart because I was in love with Ann and Nancy Wilson, the two sisters in the band. In 1977, I bought the Sex Pistols and the Clash imports and *Little Queen* by Heart. Even after Heart became a big-name stadium rock band, I still listened to them and could get "corporate rock sucks" and "I joined the Heart fan club" into the same sentence. I had pink-and-green hair and my biggest secret wasn't that I was a lesbian, at a time when that still had maximum shock value. It was that between "London's Burning" and "Anarchy in the UK," I still listened to "Magic Man" on my stereo.

I believed the two women in my head were punks too, because whenever I entered a punk club, I felt their approval. Soon, instead of just hearing them talk to each other, I sensed them having feelings about me. Sometimes I could even see them, these women in my head. The older one had brown hair, shiny as wet tree bark, and her name was Melissa. The other one had dark hair, and I didn't know her name. I couldn't see their faces clearly. By looking up the places they mentioned, I figured out that they lived in London.

I felt like I was Moses being pen pals with God on Mount Sinai. I didn't go to punk clubs just to hear the music. I went to pray. Sometimes I thought I caught glimpses of my two women in the dark corners between the leather jackets, safety pins, and secondhand clothes. This was our sacrament, and I raised my bottle to them when I drank my consecrated beer. My new world was populated by people with punk noms de guerre like Lucy Toothpaste, Pat Smear, Donna Rhia, Becki Bondage, Tory Crimes, and Billy Club. I thought about changing my name to Amanda Mayhem.

Now I was getting ready to study English literature at Exeter University in Devon. As I packed my Sex Pistols T-shirt into my suitcase, I couldn't believe I'd actually gotten this far. My previous year had not been a good one. The biochemistry in my brain had completely run amok, and I'd succumbed to a full-fledged mental breakdown, which I'd somehow managed to hide from everyone. I'd almost flunked out of school. But one incident in particular got me through my affliction and out of bondage into the Promised Land.

I had just finished reading *The Bell Jar* for the tenth time. I was so depressed I thought about eating the thirty-two codeines I'd been hoarding since junior high school when I'd broken my leg and had my wisdom teeth removed. It might sound nuts, but I've always blamed segregation for screwing up my brain chemistry. I was born in a segregated hospital in Prince George's County, Maryland in 1960, off I-95, near the big Pepsi billboard, and was stuck in the white-babies-only room with all the other white babies shining in their cribs like light bulbs. You can't tell by looking, but half of my genes are olive skinned. Being born is becoming who you are according to what they say you can be.

When I was five, we'd moved to a southern California town where there were hardly any black people at all, and it was here, as a young adult, that I wondered how Sylvia Plath had waited thirty long years to kill herself. The need for me to do so now seemed urgent, but something was sitting on my chest and preventing me from getting up, a physical force, born of anxiety, pushing me into the bed. Lying there, unable to move, I had an out-of-body experience. I saw myself float into the bathroom to retrieve my codeine pills. I watched myself pour them into my hand and get a Diet Coke to wash them down. I'd been suicidal and survived before, but this time I was afraid I was really going to kill myself.

"Jesus Christ," the voice I recognized as Melissa's suddenly demanded, "what kind of person kills herself with a Diet Coke? At least drink a regular Coke. It's not like the sugar's gonna kill you." I felt Melissa's presence in the room. I kept my eyes shut to see her better. She was wearing torn blue jeans and a fuzzy gray sweater. I swear I could feel her weight on the mattress as she sat beside me. "Don't kill yourself, love. It'll be alright." When she put her cool, delusory hand on my forehead, the pain just stopped. When she left, I could sit up. The gargoyle pressing on my heart had gone. I felt a clear-headed, fragile happiness. I picked up my acoustic guitar and played for several hours. Then I fell into a deep, uncomplicated sleep.

I don't know if you'd call that a religious experience, but when I woke up in hell again, I knew I was going to live through it. I got myself together enough to stay in school. Then I discovered that the one black woman in my Jane Austen seminar had been born on the same day in the same hospital as I had on the babies-of-color side. And here we were together, even though the whole of society had conspired to keep us apart. I wondered if I would ever meet the women in my head. Surely stranger things had happened.

TRACK 3 DANCING BAREFOOT

I walked to the record store to get some blank cassette tapes for my trip. "Erase that thought. Erase that thought. Erase that thought," I said to the beat of my Converse high-tops to protect myself and my family from intrusive thoughts about spontaneous combustion. "Healthy, whole, and safe. Healthy, whole, and safe. Healthy, whole, and safe," I whispered to myself, trying not to move my lips. I taped my favorite punk albums and Heart so I could take them with me on the plane to England.

When I landed at Heathrow and stepped onto British soil for the first time, I felt a lightness in my head. Dazzled by the sunlight, I searched myself for signs of depression, but my depression had retreated. The voices outside my head, speaking in British accents, suddenly resembled the voices inside, and I achieved equilibrium. *I'm here*, I silently told the women in my head. *I've come all this way to find you.* I never once bothered to ask myself if I was crazy to have come this far for two voices. Women communicating with me from inside with no separation between our thoughts felt intimate, and our connection ran deeper than blood.

Exeter is two-and-a-half hours southwest of London by British Rail, and Devonshire is the greenest, rainiest borough in the country. The day I arrived with my guitar and suitcases at Exeter St. David's train station and saw the surrounding green hills and hedgerows full of brilliant flowers, I thought I'd died and landed in paradise.

I lived on the university grounds in Duryard Halls in a women's residence house called Jessie Montgomery. My room, B320, complete with an electric fire, wardrobe, desk, and single bed, was on the top floor. The grounds had once been botanical gardens and these had been preserved as much as possible. To get to school, I walked through woods full of wild blackberries. To reach the English department, I passed beautifully kept gardens with different flowers each season. I luxuriated in the richness of daffodils, violets, tulips, bluebells, rhododendrons, azaleas, primroses, and crocuses. A statue of Cupid was poised for take-off against the balustrade in front of Reed Hall. In winter, a dusting of snow on his wings kept him earthbound.

I got on well with the other girls in Jessie Montgomery House and made friends right away. I was always in someone else's room drinking tea because I didn't have an electric kettle. And I was a hit with their boyfriends down the road in Murray House, the boys' residence, because they liked the assertive way I played guitar. The two women in my head were always with me, and as I became more knowledgeable about regional accents, I could tell that the younger one was from the north of England. My OCD static faded to the background.

The walkway from my residence hall to the refectory was lit up with pink autumn leaves. I loved English food—chips with every meal—and the customs at Jessie Montgomery House. By rotation, we were invited in pairs to sit on the dais at the high table with the warden and her guests. It was supposed to be an honor and quite formal. Before tea, there was sherry at the warden's house. When the girl who lived next door to me at Jessie Montgomery House and I went, we dyed our hair blue with bottles of ink and left blotches on the walls of the warden's sitting room by accidentally leaning our heads against the white paint. Later we sorted out some proper hair dye, and for a change I wasn't the only person with punk hair at my school.

On the first afternoon of the school term, I lugged my green-and-white Exeter University book bag up the hill to the university coffee bar on my way to an E. M. Forster tutorial. The town of Exeter and the river Exe were shining below me, and I looked across at the neon-green hills and pastures of grazing cows and sheep. Later I took a bus into town in the afternoon drizzle. In the city center was a billboard I loved advertising meatballs. It said "Surprise 'em with Faggots for Dinner!" I thought, *Yeah, that's right. Put that billboard up in America and everyone will be surprised.*

I walked past the small shops lining the High Street and a big indoor market with fresh-cut flowers, fish, and vegetables. I had fish and chips at a nearby chippy. Sitting in the orange plastic booth, I thought about the women in my head as I always did when I had an idle moment. I imagined Melissa's brown hair smelling of rain and petunias and the other woman's dark hair curling softly against her collar.

After eating, I headed toward Marks and Spencer, the department store people called Marks and Sparks. Boots Chemists had pink flowers in window boxes and baskets hanging over the pavement. The local buses were bright green. I sprinted up the High Street and caught one back to campus. I liked to ride on the upper level so I could watch the countryside and look down on the traffic.

In between my mostly neglected studies and lectures, I went to London and looked up the places I'd been told about by Melissa and her friend. Everything was where they said it would be, like the roses in Queen Mary's Gardens at Regent's Park. Like a detective, I searched for traces of them all over the city. On the rare occasions when I was alone in my room at Jessie

Montgomery House, I wrote songs to them. And when I played guitar, it was for them because they inspired me.

Exeter was my Eden, and I was the lesbian Eve. There was even an apple tree outside the window of my room. Of course I knew that the forbidden fruit of the Torah was not an apple in Hebrew, but I enjoyed the symbolism anyway. With my OCD and ritualistic thinking, the universe was constantly sending me messages, and the apple tree was only confirmation of what I had already known. This was my home. And when I lay down to sleep, instead of grotesque OCD images of body parts falling off, grisly car accidents, and bodies mutilated by explosions filling my head, I saw pretty things, like the way the sunlight sometimes bounced off the hills turning them an almost unreal lime green.

TRACK 4   **AWAY FROM THE NUMBERS**

Annie was my best friend. We met when I volunteered to work on Gayline, a weekly counseling service for gay students that Annie ran with a guy called Mark. They said they'd never had another woman volunteer for it before. Thursday was the one night a week the university's telephone help-line and drop-in counseling service guaranteed that an authentic gay person would be available to deal with "gay" issues. I sensed that the younger, dark-haired woman inside my head was gay and had some kind of pain or conflict because of it. I felt like I was doing this for her, that it would bring her comfort. I fantasized about picking up the phone and recognizing her voice.

Annie was a second-year student and lived in a private flat behind Cornwall House, one of the university's pubs. It was very convenient. We could walk down when the pub opened and totter back up when it closed. We would sit on the yellow carpet of Cornwall House with pints of bitter and shrimp-flavored crisps.

Annie would take out her packet of tobacco and roll her own cigarettes. She had short, brown hair and wore a red leather jacket that zipped up diagonally across her prominent, nicely shaped breasts.

Echo and the Bunnymen played in the pub one night before they were famous. We got their first tape because I liked the guitar riff on the song "Rescue" and wished that I'd written it. We saw a lot of bands we liked that year.

I took a bus packed with mods in green parkas and T-shirts with the mod symbol—blue, white and red concentric circles—to see the Jam play in Dorset. We sang the entire *This Is the Modern World* album on the way there and *All Mod Cons* on the way back. At the venue, waiting for the Jam to appear, I sang along with the crowd, *"We are the mods, we are the mods, we are, we are, we are the mods."*

And when Ian Dury and the Blockheads came to Exeter, Annie and I even sang back-up vocals to "Fuckin' Ada." We were in our hard-won places at the front, clinging to the stage by our fingertips, withstanding the tide of the crowd. Ian Dury's security posse grabbed us and brought us up on stage. We droned *"Fuckin' Ada, fuckin' Ada, fuckin' Ada"* to give the audience something to look at until Ian Dury, who was small and fragile, could make it safely offstage. I had purple hair then and a corduroy leopard coat. The crew gave us special Ian Dury and the Blockheads badges. They said "Ian Dury &," "Sex &," "Drugs &," "Rock &," "Roll &" on five separate multicolored buttons.

One night when we were hanging about down at Cornwall House, I bet Annie that the university police who patrolled the campus grounds wouldn't react if I walked out of the pub with one of the chairs balanced on my head. Annie dared me to do it, and soon I was trudging up the hill with a pub chair for a hat. The campus cops outside Cornwall House watched us leave. The cold air slapped me sober, and I realized I'd stolen a chair and didn't know what to do with it. Annie and I decided we'd take it to Jessie Montgomery House and put it in the common room.

Suddenly a police car pulled up. Before I knew what I was doing, my legs ran me down the other side of the hill. Annie stayed behind and confronted the two cops so I could get away. There was no chance *she'd* be deported if she got arrested.

I threw the chair, which was the bright orange of a traffic cone, behind a tree. Then I slipped on the dewy grass and rolled all the way to the bottom of the hill. I landed on my face in a patch of soaking-wet daffodils behind Reed Hall. I lay motionless until I decided it was safe to move. Then I crawled out of the tall grass toward the beds of vibrant wallflowers and the ornamental chimney.

I sprinted down terraces of stone steps and through tall trees, saying *"sorry, mate"* to a statue I mistook for another student in the dark. I paused at the open stretch of road I had to cross before plunging for cover into the blackness of the woods. Everything was quiet, and I took off running. A waiting white patrol car snapped on its headlights and lit me up. I dove into the woods and legged it all the way to Jessie Montgomery House, my heart beating in my throat.

When I got upstairs, Annie was waiting for me in front of my room. "Where've ya *been*, mate? I was getting frantic, me."

"That was close," I said, breathing hard and unlocking my door. Annie sat on my bed and I tried to warm myself up in front of the orange bars of the electric fire. "What did you say to the cops?" I asked, still panting.

Annie leaned her head against the wall and rolled herself a ciggy. She wore a dangling silver earring in her right ear—it was *right-side-if-you're-queer* then—and a red-and-white-checkered Arab keffiyeh around her neck.

"Calm down, Amanda," Annie told me. "They asked me my name and I said, 'Dick Damage.' Then they asked me where the woman with the chair on her head had gone, and I said, 'What woman with a chair on her head?'"

In the Gayline office, Annie and I slept—or didn't sleep—in bunk beds, answered the phone, and gave tea and biscuits to

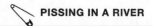

anyone who dropped in for a chat. Mark stopped by once a night to check on us. He also ran the "regular" helpline on the other six days of the week. Two students always worked together, and now he didn't have to do the overnight gay shift with Annie. I had the upper bunk. Sometimes I made Annie pretend our beds were a ship and the floor was the sea. Other nights, I brought my guitar and we sang Clash songs. Annie always said she admired the way I played, and that made me feel proud.

A sweet guy who lived outside of Exeter in the Devonshire countryside used to call me every Thursday around midnight to say goodnight. He liked to dress in women's clothing and couldn't talk to his mates about it. He would tell me what he'd worn that week and how he felt when he could be himself— exhilarated but lonely. He confirmed my belief in people's desire to express the essence of themselves and the longing for at least one other person to truly know them. I wondered if that was why we yearned for a personal God. I wondered if finding it somehow *was* God.

Gayline is how we met Neil. He came round because he was Catholic and guilt ridden about being gay. Annie and I, as we were pleased to discover, were both unrepentant, non-practicing Jews. We made him drink five cups of tea and fed him biscuits as though we'd decided that being Catholic, gay, and guilt ridden translated into being thirsty and hungry. Neil asked us about biblical passages that appeared to condemn homosexuals. Annie and I pointed out that in every case, the offending passage was about homosexuality in the context of sex without love, as in Sodom and Gomorrah.

"Remember that when David and Jonathan fell in love, God smiled on them," I said. "Plus, there's the fact that the Bible was written by men who reflected the culture of their time."

Neil stared at me as though the fist of God were going to smash through the ceiling and smite me. "But it's the word of *God*," he insisted.

"Not really," I said. "The one time God actually writes down something is when Moses goes up to receive the Ten Commandments. The Torah says that the Ten Commandments were written on stone tablets with the finger of God. But when Moses comes down from Mount Sinai or Mount Horeb and sees that the people are worshipping a golden calf, he breaks them. Then he has to go back up and tell God what he did. Can you imagine that conversation? God says, 'Make two more tablets and I'll write it down for you again.' But this time, God changes his-or-her-genderless-mind and dictates the Ten Commandments while Moses writes them down in his own handwriting. That leaves room for interpretation. Personally, I think God is over the moon about homosexuality."

"Hey, that's really good," Annie said incredulously. "What are you, some kind of biblical scholar?"

"Well, I've read it," I said.

"So have I," Annie said, "but I never thought of that."

"What about the New Testament?" Neil sounded frustrated. "It's alright for you, but I'm a bloody Christian."

"Haven't read that." Annie shrugged. "It wasn't compulsory in Hebrew school."

"I have. I'm a literature major," I explained to Annie, who gaped at me like I was going to betray her by suddenly turning into one of those Jews for Jesus or something. "At lot of stuff refers back to it. It's kind of an important document in Western culture. There's that whole thing about the gospel of Mark," I told Neil. "Mark was written first, and it's the only gospel that mentions the scantily clad young man who was with Jesus."

"What?" Neil laughed incredulously, shaking his head of dark curls, close cropped like a helmet.

"The man runs away naked when Jesus is taken away. None of the other gospels mentions him." I raised my eyebrows indicating conspiracy. "Then there's the part that was left out. A letter was found in a monastery near Jerusalem that mentions a secret gospel of Mark, an expanded, more spiritual version. In the part of the gospel that was left out, Jesus raises a young man

 **PISSING IN A RIVER**

from the dead. The man falls in love with Jesus and beseeches him to let him stay with him. After six days, Jesus tells him to come that evening. The man arrives wearing a linen cloth over his naked body. He spends the night, and Jesus teaches him the mystery of the Kingdom of God."

Neil, who had once considered entering the seminary, called the thurible he used to swing that billowed out clouds of incense during Mass, "me burnin' 'andbag" and showed us how he'd mince up the cathedral aisle. Then he and Annie performed skits from *Monty Python's Flying Circus* for me. Doing this well was a talent I noticed many English people had, like a birthright.

By morning Neil was gay and proud, and we were all best mates.

Neil had a car. That put an end to any chance that we might attend morning lectures. We were too tired from roaming around the countryside all night searching out every gay pub from Plymouth to Torquay. I loved Torquay at night with its fairy lights strung like candy necklaces across its main streets. It was peaceful there by the sea with all the boats. Bright shops ringed the harbor reflecting pink, yellow, and blue lights in the water. We sat outside the chip shop surrounded by seagull shit. Green lights illuminated a fancy hotel and fountain.

There was a secret gay club, mostly frequented by older men, up the hill on a nondescript street away from the lights. Going there was like a journey back in time. Neil rang a bell, and someone peered out of a tiny window in the heavy wooden door. We had to convince him we were gay before he would let us in. "Now really," Neil said, in his campiest voice, "do I *seem* straight to you? I'm as bent as a nine-pound note." Neil was slender, well-dressed, and very beautiful. That and the fact that we didn't look big enough to be threatening didn't hurt. When Annie put her arms around me and kissed me on the lips, the door opened, and the three of us minced inside.

Annie and I ordered a couple of pints, and Neil drank orange squash because he was driving. He was slightly older than we were and quite responsible. Half the girls in my residence hall were in love with his soft, heavily lashed, dark eyes and black, angelic curls.

Sometimes we stayed in Exeter and sat outside the Ship Inn, the pub in front of Exeter Cathedral. Drinking our pints, we'd look at it across the dark grass. Its huge, illuminated steeples made it look like a giant ghost ship rising against the sky. It was there that we joked about creating the Exeter Gay Women's Ball. But after closing time, as we lay peacefully on the grass outside the cathedral, the idea solidified.

Neil, Annie, and I decided to hold the first-ever Annual Gay Women's Ball in my room. Everyone was invited, but we called it the Annual Gay Women's Ball to shock people at our conservative red-brick university. Writing it on posters made us hysterical, especially the part about how anyone who attended would be an honorary lesbian for the evening.

We were certain no one would show up, but the point was to make a statement. The environment in Exeter was still really intense for gay people in 1980. If you wanted to get yourself beat up, all you had to do was hang around outside the Acorn, the local gay pub.

We were almost delirious at six p.m. when women started arriving from all over Devon. Somehow word had spread about our ball. We gave the women cans of lager, shandy, and Maid Marian cola we had chilling on my window ledge. As the night wore on, the Gay Women's Ball expanded to include our straight friends and closeted gay-male friends who had originally turned down our invitations. We ran out of beverages in the first ten minutes. As soon as we reached the end time specified on our posters and the ball was officially concluded, we shepherded everyone down to our local, the Red Cow. When the pub closed, we moved on to a one-night-a-week gay disco on the quay.

At two in the morning, when the club shut down, Annie and I bought soggy chips and warm Coca-Colas from a hamburger van that parked on the quay at closing time. The combination

of grease, caffeine, and cold air was great for absorbing alcohol. The bags of chips kept our hands warm. We staggered through the rainy streets away from the river. I zipped my bag of hot chips into my leather jacket to heat my body as the wind picked up. We were halfway up the hill when we collapsed on the curb, too pissed and tired to move.

I sang a verse from the Clash song "All the Young Punks," rain falling in my mouth. *"'Hanging about down in Market Street, I spent a lot of time on my feet / when I saw some bums and yobbos, and we did chance to speak. / I knew how to sing, you know, and they knew how to pose. / One of them had a Les Paul, heart-at-tack machine.'"* It reminded me of how Joe Strummer met Mick Jones and being in the Clash together just felt right. That's how I felt sitting in the rain with Annie. I felt the rightness of everything. I lived for those seconds when the warmth of well-being surged through my stomach. I fell against Annie's shoulder and kept on singing. *"'Face front, you got the future, shining like a piece of gold. / But I swear as we get closer, it looks more like a leprechaun.'"*

"Lump of coal!" Annie shrieked. *"'It looks more like a lump of coal.'"* She brushed my wet hair out of my eyes.

"Oh," I said. "It's like 'In the Crowd' by the Jam. I always thought it went, *'I fall into a trance at the supermarket. / The noise flows me along as I catch falling cans of babies on toast. / Technology is the most.'* Later I discovered it was really *'baked beans* on toast.'" I toppled over laughing, knocking my head against the pavement.

Annie lay on her back beside me, and we looked up past the tall trees at the stars. She sighed. "You know what? This is the best our lives will ever be. We're best mates, we're dead pissed, and I just found a dog-end in me pocket." She lit the soggy last bit of a hand-rolled cigarette. She took a long drag then passed it to me. "This is dead romantic."

I pretended to smoke Annie's fag. I didn't inhale. I just blew out smoke into the rain because I wanted to be like her. "Shit." I put my arm around Annie's sodden black peacoat. "I feel like I'm living in a Clash song."

We started singing "Cheapskates." *"I have been a washer-up, an' he has been a scrubber-up, / an' I seen him picking up dog-ends in the rain."*

"Come on, luv." Annie grabbed my arm and hauled me to my feet. "Stay at mine tonight."

"An' he has never read a book, though I told him to take a look. / He lifted his pool hall cue for another game."

In Annie's flat, we peeled off our wet clothes. Annie chucked me a dry sweatshirt and hung our socks on the radiator. She opened her window and took a bottle of milk off the ledge. We drank large mugs of instant coffee and listened to music. "We have to play only important songs to remember this night," Annie said. I nodded. It was our sacred obligation.

We listened to "Dreams of Children," "Strange Town," "Eton Rifles," and "Private Hell" by the Jam; "Stay Free," "Protex Blue," "Deny," "Remote Control," "The Prisoner," "City of the Dead," and "Police & Thieves" by the Clash; "Private Life" by the Pretenders and a Bob Marley cover, "Johnny Was," by Stiff Little Fingers. Those songs were the way we communicated and understood each other. We lived our lives according to how we felt when we listened to them.

Annie put on "Stay Free" again, and we sang along. *"We met when we were at school. / Never took no shit from no one. We weren't fools. / Teacher says we're dumb. We're only having fun. / We piss on everyone in the classroom."*

We snuggled under Annie's soft duvet. We were young. Neither of us wanted anything from the other except closeness and warmth. It gave me a feeling of purity. I felt safe with Annie's arm flung around me. And whenever I thought about my two best friends, Annie and Neil, my mind kept repeating, *"go easy, step lightly, stay free."*

 **PISSING IN A RIVER**

When Reagan was elected president, Annie and I walked to the university mental health center so I could ask for political asylum. I heard the women in my head telling me, "Stay in England. Stay in England." We were informed that Great Britain did not have a policy of extending political asylum to Americans. Of course Maggie Thatcher was just as bad, but I tried to argue that she wasn't as personally humiliating. Then I asked for citizenship based on being a member of a former colony, but that didn't work either.

We went to an "end-of-the-world" party in town given by a friend of a friend of Annie's. Music blared, and the house was crammed with people dancing. Annie and I fought our way to a bit of space in a corner, trying not to knock into anyone's cigarette ash or beer. "You wanna drink?" Annie shouted over "Ant Music" by Adam and the Ants. We were smashed up against a keg of Scrumpy. She handed me a plastic cup of the alcoholic cider and said, "Watch that. It goes down easy, but it's a killer."

We couldn't move, so I kept refilling my cup. The cider was sweet like apple juice. I was sweltering inside my red leather jacket. The first two things I'd bought upon arriving in Exeter were a pair of black Doc Marten boots and a jacket with zippers across the sleeves like the one Chrissie Hynde wears on the cover of the first Pretenders record. Those were my two essentials. Of course I didn't realize then that hers was probably not actually leather but made out of some cruelty-free substitute. The collar of my Day-Glo pink-and-black striped shirt stuck to my neck.

"You know, I don't really like most Yanks." Annie rolled a cigarette as I filled my cup again. "But you're not a real one, are ya?" She pulled a stray leaf of tobacco off her tongue. "You've got to stop sounding like them. We have to work on your accent and vocabulary. First off, the British 'R.' Not *arr*," Annie said, exaggerating the contortion of her jaw to sound American. "Say *aah*. Week*end* not *week*end. And for fuck's sake, stop saying garage.

It's *gair*-edge." But of course since Annie's accent was Mancunian, she didn't pronounce the "A"s the way they did in London and the south. "I want to smoke." Annie gestured at me to go outside for some fresh air. She threaded through the crowd, but when I tried to follow her, the room pulsated and my legs felt too weary to walk. Annie said later she'd got all the way outside before realizing I wasn't behind her. She had to fight her way back to the corner where I was still leaning against the wall.

"Oh, crap. What did I tell you about Scrumpy?" Annie put her arm around my waist and dragged me. I remember being poured into someone's car. The next thing I knew, I was lying on Annie's bed and she was handing me a mug of coffee.

I drank the coffee, and Annie put the kettle on to boil again. She had run out to get Cornish pasties and chips while I was passed out. Now she handed me the food and told me to eat something.

My red leather jacket hung on a chair, and I noticed a small tear at the elbow. "What happened?" I asked.

Annie said, "I dropped you," and we both started laughing.

By the spring, the tear had swelled and I finally got round to having my jacket repaired. The man with the leather stall in Exeter market noticed the badges pinned all over it: "Don't Do It, Di!," "Lesbians Unite," "Women United in Armed Snuggle." Because when I returned to pick it up, he offered me a hundred pounds to go to bed with him. He fingered the purple "PUNK DYKE" button on my lapel. "I've been thinking about you since last Saturday," he said. "Are you really like that?"

"Of course," I said. "You don't think I dress in meaningless slogans, do you?"

He began to ask those exasperatingly stupid questions unenlightened straight men ask about how two women could possibly have sex "*all alone.*"

"For Chrissake, read a book," I said.

"I'll tell you what I'll do," he said. "I'm going to take you out, buy you a meal, and then I'm going to go to bed with you. And I

 **PISSING IN A RIVER**

won't use my fingers. I'm going to change your life. I'll give you a hundred pounds. If I can't bring you to climax, you keep the money. Well?"

I stared at him, trying to work out how his enormous ego could fit inside a normal-sized head. I put on my jacket and pointed to a yellow-and-black badge that said "Piss Off." "Do you know what that means?"

"Yeah."

"Then do it."

When I got back to Jessie Montgomery House, I immediately rang up Annie. She and Neil drove directly to my residence hall. Neil had a garment bag full of clothes. "This tie will look smashing." He held up a green tie to the gray "Eve Was Gay" sweatshirt I was wearing. I'd had it made when we were in Cornwall. Neil had snapped a photograph of me pointing to the bright-red, blasphemous letters with an entire Salvation Army band marching behind me, staring. I put on Neil's baggy white shirt over a black thermal-underwear top. I put on his suit, and Annie rolled up the trouser legs. Neil knotted the tie around my collar, and Annie tucked my hair into a trilby hat. "You're Jeremy Lesbian," Neil pronounced.

As we left the car park in town, Annie took out the eyebrow pencil she sometimes used to underline her dark eyes and drew a mustache under my nose. Neil stepped back and eyed me critically. "As a gay man, I will say that I could be very attracted to Jeremy Lesbian."

Laughing, we walked down the High Street, holding our scarves over our faces against the strong wind. We were nervous and ducked into a wine bar for a quick half-pint to fortify ourselves. Neil drank tonic water. He was worried that the man at the leather stall would take a swing at me when I made a pass at him, and he wanted to be alert enough to pull me out of the way.

At the indoor market, Neil had a look at our target and said, "Christ, he's bigger than the lot of us. If he hits her, he'll knock her bloody head off."

"Don't be ridiculous," Annie said.

While they argued, I said, "I'm going to catch myself a real man."

"Sorry?" Neil acted like he was offended, running his hand through his hair.

Annie said, "A *real* man, missus," and put her hands on her hips. "Not some bloody poof."

I walked up to the leather-stall guy. "Listen," I said. "I'll tell you what I'm going to do. I'm going to take you out, buy you a meal, go to bed with you and change your life. I'll give you a hundred quid to have sex with me. You need a real man."

His face went completely red. Neil and Annie jumped out from behind a fruit and vegetable stall. Then he recognized who I was and calmed down. "Okay, I get your point." He held out his hand, and I shook it.

We ran out of the market feeling liberated. We believed that every little victory counted. I took off my hat before it was whipped away by the wind. Pink and white blossoms from the cherry and almond trees swirled around us like confetti. I felt like I was inside one of those plastic globes you shake to make it snow. I had one of Exeter Cathedral, and when I shook it, snow-flakes fell around the plastic steeples.

Neil started the car, and Annie wiped the eyebrow pencil off my face with spit and a Kleenex. I looked out the windscreen at the big drops of rain that plopped down, mashing blossoms into pink-and-white mud on the pavement as people trod on them. It was getting dark, and the yellow streetlights came on. Neil drove through the familiar roundabout to his flat.

Neil lived on Monk's Road in a sea of terraced houses with brightly painted woodwork and drainpipes. His flat was red brick with white brick around the bulging, ground-floor bay window. We walked toward the orange "THE CANTON FISH BAR" sign for some takeaway, then strolled back along the blue, black, yellow, and green-painted terraces, eating hot, mushy chips out of paper bags.

 **PISSING IN A RIVER**

Neil's room was in front on the ground floor. We dried our scarves and gloves on the radiator. I unwrapped the newspaper from around my piece of fried battered fish, and Annie pulled back the white, lacy curtains, letting in the light from the street.

I woke up the next morning to a cup of tea being set on the floor near my head. "Mornin' sunshine," Annie said. "Sleep well?" It was Sunday. We drank our tea and went to a nearby café for a proper English breakfast—a "fry-up," as Annie called it. I had a plate of fried eggs, chips, beans, sausage, tomato, mushrooms, and fried bread. Afterward Annie and I walked leisurely back to the university. A gray cobblestone lane led through blackberry vines, daffodils, and purple crocuses and alongside an overgrown hedgerow. I decided that the real Garden of Eden must be full of daisies, Queen Anne's lace, primroses, bluebells, white snowdrops, ornamental garlic, and cowslips.

That evening at Jessie Montgomery, it was regular Sunday tea—roast beef and Yorkshire pudding. I worked on a long-overdue E. M. Forster essay and had a hot bath. In my little room in Exeter, I felt insulated and safe. I had almost forgotten what it was like to have OCD-induced insomnia. I'd fall asleep listening to the rain beat against the window, surrounded by green hills that were so bright I almost thought I imagined them, tucked in among the glistening hedgerows.

TRACK 6   ENGLISH CIVIL WAR

Annie, Neil, and I were appalled when we read in *Gay News* that the mayor-elect of the town of Trafford, Stanley Brownhill, had announced that homosexuals were "sick" and that their "sickness could be cured by a .303 in the centre of the head." When Annie and Neil explained that a .303 is a bullet from an army-issue gun, I was even more outraged. That he made the remark in April, which had been designated "courtesy month" in Greater Manchester, was too much to take.

Annie grew up there. Her parents lived in an Orthodox Jewish neighborhood in Salford, which, like Trafford, had merged with the city of Manchester. Neil and I went with her to protest at a gay-rights demonstration that was going to take place on the day Brownhill took office. By now I was sounding pretty English and most people couldn't tell I was American.

We got off the train at Manchester Piccadilly. The local buses were orange. Annie navigated us through oceans of red-and-brown brick terraces to the one she'd grown up in. Her parents were reformed Jews, but they kept a kosher home because her grandparents, who lived with them, were "Orthos," as Annie called them.

Annie's mum and dad were lovely and welcoming. Her grandparents were rather off the grid and didn't understand why we were there. They inhabited a world where being gay was a concept that barely existed. But they were obviously proud of Annie, the first member of their family to attend university.

Annie's grandmum made us tea. We were standing in the kitchen chatting with her and Annie's mum when Neil put his teaspoon on the counter. We heard a gasp and saw Annie's grandmum point a shaking finger.

"Oh, Neil," Annie chided, "you've accidentally placed the spoon you used to stir milk into your tea on the counter reserved for meat and thrown the earth off its orbit."

"I'm so sorry." Neil quickly removed the spoon and placed it on the dairy counter. "I'm a Catholic, you see."

"Now, now, Esther." Annie's mum put a calming hand on the older woman's shoulder and ushered her into the sitting room, giving us an amused, conspiratorial smile. "Good luck protesting tomorrow, you lot."

Annie's dad was a lively bloke with a humorous gleam in his eyes. He kicked around a football with us in the field behind the house as the evening light faded, all the while making wisecracks with Annie. "Her grandmum wanted Annie to marry a nice rabbi. Imagine her surprise when the rabbi was a woman."

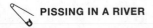 **PISSING IN A RIVER**

"You mean rabbit," Annie said. "I'm going to marry a nice *rabbit*."

"Christ," Neil said anxiously, "I thought she was going to collapse when I put the spoon on the wrong counter."

"Now you see why I'm a vegetarian," Annie said. "It's far less complicated."

Annie's dad was a fare collector on a bus. The next day, we rode around Manchester with him for several hours until it was time to go to the demonstration. We hopped off his bus in the city center and caught a crowded one to Trafford. BBC Radio One was blasting the new, sexist pop single from Sheena Easton. "*My baby works nine to five*," her voice oozed over the seats.

"Turn off that crap music," I yelled, weaving in the aisle and grabbing the overhead bar to steady myself.

"Oi, you." Annie pushed me toward the stairs to the upper level at the back of the bus.

I stood with my big cardboard sign proclaiming "No .303 for Me—Lesbian and Proud" wedged in the aisle. Over the radio noise, I gave a speech to the other passengers about why we had to stop the bullet-in-the-head mayor from taking office. Annie grabbed my arm when it was our stop. I thanked everyone for listening to me. "We now return you to your regular programming," I said, as I jumped off the bus behind Annie. The long black police coat she'd got secondhand at a surplus shop in Liverpool flapped against the ass of her blue jeans. Her grandmother had helped her sew a large pink triangle on the back.

We demonstrated in front of Trafford's town hall where the new mayor was being sworn in. A cop from Stretford took away another protester's megaphone as he was shouting, "A bullet in my head would make me dead, but it wouldn't make me straight!" A bunch of people kissed to annoy the police, so Annie and I started doing it. The cops surrounded us and told us to move off. I stood in front of the one giving the orders. I only came up to the middle of his enormous blue coat, staring into the silver buttons.

I said, "There's no law against kissing. I'll kiss her if I want to."

Neil and Annie practically lifted me off the ground they dragged me away so fast.

"Listen, you," Neil said. "You cannot get arrested. They'll deport you."

"Arrested for *what*?"

"He'll give you the riot act."

"Like the Elvis Costello song?" I asked, confused.

"'Insulting behavior likely to cause a breach of the peace,'" Annie said. "They can arrest you for doing anything they don't like."

"You mean they can arrest me for my behavior before I've actually *done* anything?"

We took a bus back to the big square near Manchester Piccadilly to get a transfer back to Salford. It started raining gray shivs. Annie smeared drops of rain off the black metal statue of Queen Victoria. "There's no law against lesbians, but gay men can be arrested for having sex with any bloke under twenty-one. Queen Victoria refused to sign lesbians into the law making homosexuality illegal because she didn't believe we existed. Stupid old cow." She kissed the statue on the head, shivered, and wiped her lips.

"Like in *Gay News*," Neil said. "That article about a thirty-two-year-old man getting nicked for having a nineteen-year-old boyfriend next to the picture of Prince Charles and Lady Di. He's thirty-two and she's nineteen, but you don't see him going to prison for it."

I caught Annie's eye in a way that meant we had unfinished business.

"The police can't arrest you for being a lesbian," Annie said, "so they nick you for 'insulting behavior.' That includes kissing and anything they want."

"Two women kissing is behavior likely to cause a breach of the peace?" I asked.

"God, I hope so," Annie said. "I hope it causes the downfall of civilization as we know it."

I walked to the Esso garage at the bottom of the hill to get chocolate and fizzy drinks for my trip to Ireland and bunged them in my book bag. I wrapped my long, green-and-white-striped Exeter University scarf around my face and tried to warm myself up. I was freezing when I got to Exeter St. David's train station. I sat on the train, watching green pastures and back gardens swoosh by, drinking cups of British Rail tea. Annie had spent the weekend in Manchester, and we were meeting in Liverpool to catch the ferry to Dublin. I bought a secondhand British Rail coat at a surplus shop near the docks.

The ferry wasn't full, and Annie and I were the only people in the on-board cinema. We watched a Peter Seller's film and slept in the red-carpeted aisle. Annie shook me awake in the morning. "I need a cuppa. I'm parched." We had tea, and one of the sailors let us climb out onto the slippery bow with him to see Ireland coming closer.

In Dublin, we looked for a cheap bed and breakfast. They got lower in price the further we walked away from the river. We found a room, dropped off our gear, and roamed the rainy, gritty streets. Music floated out of the pubs, and I tried to drink a pint of Guinness Stout. The murky, black liquid reminded me of the La Brea tar pits in Los Angeles where dinosaurs sank to their death. We bought some cans of lager, got fish and chips, and went back to our room.

It had stopped raining, but the air felt frozen. Our room overlooked a busy intersection to the west of the Liffey. We'd got water pistols to play with at a corner shop in Liverpool in case we got bored on the ferry. Annie found them in her bag when she pulled out her dry black sweater, or jumper, as my mind now automatically translated. We leaned out the window, spraying the buses below us until the drivers thought it was raining and turned on their windscreen wipers. Annie called it "playing God."

After another day in Dublin, we decided to take a train to Belfast. It was April 1981, and the civil war, aka the Troubles, was escalating in Northern Ireland as Provisional Irish Republican Army volunteer Bobby Sands led a hunger strike against British authorities in Maze Prison. There was no escaping the violence as IRA and Ulster-loyalist paramilitary groups engaged in armed conflict.

Annie and I didn't have a particular agenda in mind. I was just curious to see Belfast for myself, loved the Belfast punk band Stiff Little Fingers, and didn't realize that specific day would have any significance. As soon as we crossed the border into Northern Ireland, the train stopped, and British soldiers in green fatigues and flak jackets flooded our compartment waving giant automatic guns. We showed them our passports. Inadvertently, we had arrived in Belfast on the day Bobby Sands was elected to parliament from his prison cell.

We stepped into a city smothered by rioting.

"What's going on?" I asked, just as Annie and I heard an explosion. The people around us scattered.

"I don't know. Oi, mate," Annie caught the arm of someone running past us, "what's happening?"

"Bobby Sands was elected to parliament!" he shouted.

"Are we happy or mad?" I looked around and couldn't tell.

Four bombs went off in the city that day, and it looked like the entire British army was there. Every time I turned a corner, I found myself staring down the barrel of an M-16. Annie said that was because the soldiers fixed their sites randomly on people who were passing, looking for terrorists. After a few blocks, I stopped worrying about getting my head shot off by mistake. "Guns in my face" was the situation, and I quickly adjusted my sense of reality to normalize that. Sometimes I think our adaptability might be a bad thing.

The soldiers kept snapping our pictures. "I feel like a rock star," Annie said.

"'The British army is waiting out there, an' it weighs fifteen-hundred tons.'" I repeated that one line of the Clash song "White Man in Hammersmith Palais" until Annie gave me a jab in the shoulder.

We were riot-hopping, following the noise from one riot to another, when some soldiers stopped us for interrogation. The soldier who searched me was suspicious when he saw my American passport. He said that Belfast was a strange place to come on holiday. I said if he thought that was strange, I was going to Iran and Afghanistan next. I thought Annie was going to bite off my head. She gave me a solid punch in the arm. "Jesus fucking Christ, this is not Disneyland."

I rubbed my arm. There was a woman with the pinkest hair I'd ever seen sitting in the rain on a bench in front of the city hall with its blue-green domes, her hair clashing with the nearby bright-red phone box. All of the shopping precincts had checkpoints where we were searched and asked to show our passports. Soldiers stopped Annie from taking a photo of tanks in the street. They didn't want us photographing their equipment or them. I guess no one was supposed to know exactly what the British army was doing or how much of it had taken over the city. Soldiers cruised past us pointing submachine guns out the backs of their green Land Rovers.

Everywhere we went on the Catholic side of Belfast, we heard bombs going off as Protestant royalists protested Bobby Sands' election to parliament. On the Protestant side, pictures of the royal family stared out of every shop. Lady Diana and Prince Charles engagement mugs hung in the windows and their souvenir tea towels flapped in the breeze in eerie outdoor displays. The brick walls were spray-painted with Union Jack graffiti.

We were making our way back to the Catholic side of town when I looked behind me and saw a battalion of soldiers and police in riot gear. They held shields in front of their faces. I tapped Annie's shoulder, but she was staring straight ahead at an angry mob marching toward us wielding stones and bottles. I went speechless and tugged on Annie's sleeve.

"Get out of the fucking way!" Annie grabbed my arm and yanked me off the street. We dove into a doorway as rocks exploded against the brick wall behind us and bottles rocketed past our heads and shattered. We were trapped between the demonstrators and the law. It was pissing down bricks like rain. People scurried off the street like cockroaches surprised by light. We ran out of the doorway to help a young woman push her baby's pram out of the line of fire.

"Pick a side," Annie said.

"No contest." I looked over my shoulder at the advancing army. "If I'm going to die, they're gonna find my body on the Catholic side of town."

We got on our hands and knees and crawled beneath the flying debris toward the protesters. A few of them saw us trying to reach them and waved us on.

When we were safely behind the front lines, a bloke in the crowd took us into a leftist café and bought us cups of tea. Posters on the walls said "Troops Out" and "Free the H-Block Prisoners." I figured the "H" stood for "hunger," as the slogan referred to the IRA hunger strikers who wanted to be treated as political prisoners in an occupied country and not as criminals. We'd all heard Maggie Thatcher in her flat, bloodless voice talking about Bobby Sands on the telly, *"There can be no flexibility. Crime is crime is crime. It is not political. It is crime."* I wondered if she read Gertrude Stein.

When it got dark, we decided it was time to get out of Ulster, or "Ulcer," as Annie had begun to call it. Annie said she was bored dodging rubber bullets and tear gas, but I knew that meant she was nervous. There had been another bomb scare in the shopping precinct we'd just left with chips that were still too hot to eat. The pubs with their pro-IRA graffiti had elaborate fencing around the entrances that you had to weave through

 **PISSING IN A RIVER**

so no one could toss in a bomb and run away. The soldiers snapped our photos one more time. "Smile, you're a terrorist," I said. Annie wrapped her red-and-black Manchester United scarf more tightly around her neck and blew on her fingertips sticking out of black, fingerless gloves. I put my chips inside my green army-surplus jacket to warm myself up.

At the station, we discovered that we'd missed the last train to Dublin. Suddenly our tiny bed-and-breakfast room where we slept crammed into a single bed seemed like Eden. All we wanted to do was get back to it. There was only one more train leaving Belfast that night. It was a local one that would only take us as far as Portadown, about twenty-three miles to the southwest. We jumped on it anyway to put some distance between our bodies and the explosions. In Portadown, we asked a mother and daughter sitting on a bench how to get to the bus station. They smiled at each other. "It's in the city center," the mum said.

"How do we find it?" I asked.

"You can't miss it." The adolescent girl looked like she was trying not to laugh. "It has a bomb in the middle of it."

"Sorry?" I said.

"There's a bomb in the city center," her mum explained. "The whole area's cordoned off. You won't get near the bus station tonight, love."

"Brilliant," Annie said.

We walked to the motorway and tried to catch a ride south. The yellow motorway lights barely illuminated the trees behind us. No one would stop. We were freezing, and it was spooky. "Maybe it's 'cos there's two of us," Annie said.

"Maybe it's because it's dead stupid," I said.

"Maybe it's 'cos there's two of us," Annie repeated. She hid in the thicket, and I stood on the road alone.

Oh good, I thought. *Here I am, rape bait.* Almost immediately, a car stopped. I ran to the driver's side window. "Cheers, mate. Can you take my friend, too? She's over there." When I pointed,

Annie came out onto the road and waved. "I swear on my life we're harmless," I said, my breath blowing out in white gasps. "No one would stop for the both of us, and we're really cold and desperate."

Annie approached the car. "Sorry, mate. We hadn't wanted to fool you, but no one would stop."

"We're really, really sorry," I said.

The bloke hunched inside his green anorak. "Just the two of you? No blokes? Right, get in. Hurry up, it's freezing. I want to close the window." Annie climbed in back, and I sat on the passenger side, fastening my seatbelt and thanking the driver profusely. The heater was on, and as the car sped down the motorway, I felt my feet thawing inside my black-and-white Converse high-tops.

"I can take you as far as Newry," the man said.

"Ta very much," I said. "We really appreciate it."

"You're lucky I'm a decent bloke," he said. "It's dangerous hitchhiking out here. Don't you young ladies know that?"

"We got stuck in Belfast," I explained. "The train would only go as far as Portadown. There was a bomb in the city center, and we couldn't get to the bus station. We just want to get back to Dublin."

We were still caught in County Armagh, an IRA stronghold. On the motorway outside Newry, Annie said, "That geezer scared the shite out of me. As soon as he said that, about being a decent bloke, I was sure he was a serial rapist."

I said, "I couldn't decide if he was worried about us or if he wanted to give us a false sense of security before he murdered us."

From Newry we got a ride to Dundalk, right on the border. It also had a bomb in it. Then we got lucky and caught a ride with an older man who took us over the border and all the way to Dublin. He said we reminded him of his daughter, and I prayed to God it wasn't the daughter he'd raped regularly until she was sixteen. But he turned out to be a decent chap and dropped us

 **PISSING IN A RIVER**

off in front of our bed and breakfast, warning us not to accept rides from any lorry drivers.

The sky was cold slate. Nobody else was on the street.

"Crikey." Annie rocked back and forth in her black monkey boots, hands in her pockets. "What a relief."

"Yeah. We handled that really well. I'm proud of us," I said. "I mean, the whole time the bombs were going off and that, we had nerves of steel."

Someone's car backfired on another street, and both of us hit the pavement and rolled behind the nearest vehicle.

"Well," Annie said, standing up and dusting gravel off her trousers, "better safe than sorry."

We had a cheap bottle of red wine in our room and sat on the bed to drink it. I was pretty sloshed by the time we finished it and lay down. "Aren't you gonna even take off your baseball boots?" Annie asked.

"I'm too pissed." I pulled the yellow duvet over my clothes.

"They're wet, you lazy sod." Annie pulled off my sneakers and socks and threw them by the radiator. She rummaged around in my bag for a pair of dry socks and put them on my feet. She put her own shoes, socks, scarf, and gloves by the radiator and squeezed into the small bed.

I shivered and snuggled against her jumper for warmth.

"Why haven't we ever had sex?" Annie said.

"Because we're not each other's type."

"I know, but *why* aren't we? If you think about it logically, we're perfect for each other."

"It never *occurs* to me to have sex with you. You're my best mate."

"Aye, I can't get me own head round it. But isn't it kind of *mental*? We don't have a girlfriend between us. We should be having sex."

"Why?" I squinted at her. "Why should we be having sex?"

"Isn't it what we're supposed to want? Are we freaks?" Annie smacked me on the arse. "Kiss me."

"My head hurts."

Annie leaned back and said dramatically, "Take me."

I started laughing too hard to do any such thing.

"Take me, Amanda. When a woman says '*take me*,' you must take her. C'mon, give us a snog."

I laughed myself into tears. Annie and I sang the Stiff Little Fingers' song "Alternative Ulster" straight through five times. Then I played two Gang of Four songs in my head about the situation in Northern Ireland, "Ether" and "Armalite Rifle," until I fell asleep to the raindrops slapping against the window.

Our last day in Dublin was sunny, and we rented bicycles. It was the first time I'd driven any kind of a vehicle since leaving the States, and while it was relatively easy for me to remember that cars drove on the opposite side of the road as a pedestrian, it was much harder on a moving bike. I thought I was going to die at a particularly frenetic intersection near Trinity College, but Annie urged me on and we pedaled out past the Guinness factory.

It was raining and the water was choppy when we took the ferry back to England.

When I got back to Exeter, I bunged my gear into my room and made it to the refectory just in time for tea. I took my shepherd's pie, chips, and peas to a table where a group of my mates was sitting.

"Where the bloody hell have *you* been?" someone asked.

I told them what Annie and I had done, expecting them to be impressed. I didn't bring up our nerves of steel, allowing that to be obvious.

My friends lectured me on how stupid I'd been. I drank fourteen cups of tea while I listened to them.

"Are you *out* of your fucking *mind*? You *never* hitchhike in Northern Ireland. You could have been picked up by any fucking terrorist. Terrorists *do* sometimes pick up people and use them for cover to get back and forth across the border, you know."

I left the refectory subdued but with a massive tea buzz.

 **PISSING IN A RIVER**

Daffodils bent their yellow heads in the wind against the lush grass. The moon and stars were crisp and bright above the tall trees, and the sky was clear. I felt like I was at the hub of the universe. Bluebells lined the path. I went into the common room to watch *Top of the Pops*. Someone brought in my favorite chocolate biscuits, Digestives, and passed them to me. I was safe, and I had chocolate. Nirvana.

TRACK 8 STAY FREE

I couldn't believe it when spring term ended. I had to leave my room at uni, and I had no money. I hung around with Neil in London and Annie in Manchester, but they were broke, too. We knew I'd have to leave. Neil and Annie were going back to university in the fall, and my student visa had run out. I wanted to finish school at Exeter but wasn't allowed to work and didn't have the funding to continue there, even if Annie hid me in her room.

I couldn't quite picture myself without a place to live and working sporadically in pubs for a pittance under the table while my mates, who got government grants to go to school, went on with their lives. *If only I had found the women inside my head*, I thought. I was sure I could have stayed with them, and my life would have made sense. But now I had no plan and felt like I would be left behind by my friends. Not on purpose, but they were busy. Already I could tell how different our lives would become as they returned to their families and got ready to continue their studies and get jobs.

My goals were vague and centered around meeting the women in my head. It seemed safest if I returned to the States and finished school. I could feel the symptoms of my OCD coming back as I suddenly had no place to be and nothing to do. I didn't think I would survive as a hanger-on in my friends' lives without a life of my own. I felt myself growing weaker as a cloud of depression hung over me and my insomnia reappeared. I hated myself for choosing the safer way out, but I could tell my reprieve from mental illness was ending.

For a while, I continued to bounce between Annie and Neil. The three of us met in London in June. Annie and I went to the first-ever Lesbian Strength march. It was 1981. The march was women only, and the men stood along the route and hung out of windows cheering us on. I remember the line of women resplendent with multicolored punk hair. Blue, orange, pink, green, red, purple—we must have looked like exotic birds to anyone flying over. Afterward we went to a women-only disco in Chelsea and a punk club in Brixton with a front window full of broken TV sets.

When the club closed at two in the morning, Annie asked a policeman for directions to the motorway. When he bent down to talk to her, I got out of the car we'd borrowed from her parents, took the conical blue-and-silver constable hat off his head, put it on, stepped out into the street and directed traffic until he snatched it back. Sinking back into my seat in the car, I turned to Annie and said with satisfaction, "I was a big tit."

"That look suited you, mate," Annie said. Then we stared at each other while I wondered how I was ever going to survive in my native, alien land without her physical presence.

Before I left the country, Annie and I went on one last mission. To commemorate the impending royal wedding between Prince Charles and Lady Diana Spencer, one night we actually drove out to Althorp, the Spencer family's ancestral estate, and spray-painted "The Gays Were Here" on some pillars to protest the unfair age of consent laws for gay men. Then we ran through a dark, Northamptonshire field of tall, rain-soaked grass to dispose of the spray cans. Years later, I cried my heart out when Princess Diana was murdered.

We drove through Northampton and noticed billboards advertising a new salad dressing with the slogan "Are You Daring Enough To Try It?" We had an extra can of spray-paint in the back of the car and decided to "gay" the town. We went to every billboard we could find and wrote "Go Gay" in big, red letters under the picture of a large bottle of salad dressing pouring onto a salad. Most of the billboards sat in areas that were easy to reach and fairly deserted in the middle of the night, except for one. It was bathed in bright, scrutinizing lights in the city center. We had to climb over a railing and scramble through some bushes to reach it. It was pointless to wait for the constant traffic to die down, so we just graffitied it in front of everybody.

Annie and I arranged to meet Neil in London the night before she took me to the airport. I ate a last doner kebab. Annie said, "I can see you if you ever have a baby. It'd be sat there in its pram with you shoving greasy, repulsive pieces of kebab meat down its throat." I started crying. "I didn't mean to hurt your feelings, mate. I still love ya."

"It isn't that, you silly git."

Under the arches on Villiers Street, Charing Cross, we went to Heaven, the huge gay nightclub with beautiful neon inside and different kinds of music on each floor. Annie and I had heard that sometimes Joan Armatrading, a musician we were quite keen on, hung out there. We hit a few more pubs then walked aimlessly around London all night. At dawn, I said a tearful goodbye to Neil. I couldn't believe I was leaving him. As Annie and I pulled out in her mum and dad's car, the sky was streaked with orange, and the small milk lorries were making their deliveries. "Goodbye, milk floats." I waved sadly out my window.

We got to Heathrow, and I grabbed my gear from the back seat. I picked up Annie's bag, which was suspiciously heavy. "Give it me," Annie said. "It's just some things you might need." She unzipped my book bag and crammed in a bottle of Ribena, jelly babies, Marmite, a Mars chocolate bar because I'd said the English ones were different, a can of Newcastle Brown Ale, two packages of Chocolate Digestives, and a box of Typhoo tea bags.

"I'm really made up," I said. Annie hugged me and kissed my cheek. I smelled the rain in her hair one more time. As I made my way to International Departures, I already knew that getting on the plane would be the worst mistake I'd ever make in my life.

TRACK 9 **THE PRISONER**

For a year, I'd been a different, better version of myself, comfortable in my own brain, and content for once to be where I belonged. Though I hadn't met up with the women in my head, I'd been to the places that still held their shadows. But now that I returned to the United States, my OCD and depression slammed back into my life *hard*.

I missed the craziest things about England, like the indigenous orange-blue-and-yellow Wall's Ice Cream signs, drinking orange juice at the cinema, Cadbury's Ninety-Nines, and the way all English Kentucky Fried Chickens sold chips. I swore when I got back to Devon I was going to hug a hedgerow. But after a few years, I wasn't even communicating with Annie and Neil anymore because my incapacitating breakdowns and the shame that accompanied them made it too difficult to maintain personal relationships, especially long-distance ones.

Even though I longed to be in England, I didn't believe my symptoms would evaporate again the way they had when I'd lived in Exeter. I thought about the women in my head all the time, but they weren't present in the same way they had been. After spending a year in England without finding them, I couldn't pretend that they would suddenly appear and rescue me from myself and from being in the wrong life.

With my insomnia and noisy head, I didn't function well enough to hold down a regular job successfully. Even on a good day, I felt like anything could topple me over the edge into another serious mental breakdown, and I didn't know where to put myself for safe keeping. I couldn't maintain my sanity, but I'd learned how to maintain my grade-point average. The best option for me seemed to be staying in school, as it would give me a flexible schedule and allow me to maintain my health insurance. All my instincts had boiled down to simple survival. I got into a PhD program in literature, which offered me a teaching stipend, so halfway through my twenties, I found myself driving across the country to begin a new life just outside of Washington, DC. And that's where I stayed to save myself.

TRACK 10 **CITY OF THE DEAD**

I hadn't done anything about the war in Vietnam as a child except for scrounging for change amid the wreckage of the Bank of America building that had been blown up in my hometown. I felt very strongly that the AIDS crisis was my war and I had a moral obligation to do something about it. I joined the AIDS Coalition To Unleash Power in Washington, DC. As an AIDS activist, I punctuated my studies and teaching with arrests for acts of nonviolent civil disobedience. This did not always make me popular.

The day I attended an ACT UP demonstration at the White House, the air was crisp, and the sky was blue. After chaining myself to the White House fence, I just hung there for hours, watching tourists with their hot dogs, sodas, and ice cream bars, their maps open to historic, downtown Washington, DC. I tried welcoming them to the crack-and-murder capital of the United States, but they had come for the Jacqueline Kennedy furniture, not an ACT UP demonstration.

I didn't want to ruin the moment. After all, they'd walked past a lot of homeless people to get here. The poor slept on grates near the US Treasury and across the street in the People's Protest Park. They were everywhere, but if you planned it well and tilted your head acrobatically, you could manage to act like you didn't see them.

Even though it took all day for the police to cut us down, no one seemed to think AIDS activists hanging in front of the White House was a scenic photo opportunity. We weren't on the postcards. We were shouting, "*Act up! Fight back! Fight AIDS! The government has blood on its hands!*"

The police cut me down and I went limp, falling to the ground in a heap like I had no bones to hold me up. I was an expert at nonviolent civil disobedience. This was my fifth arrest with ACT UP. My first had been in 1987 at the Supreme Court after the second National March on Washington for Gay and Lesbian Rights. Now I dressed almost exclusively in black: heavy black shoes, black jeans, black ACT UP T-shirt, and my black ACT UP cap. The only alteration to my uniform was when I wore a white ACT UP T-shirt instead. Whatever I did, I looked like I was doing it on black-and-white television.

I made the cops carry me to the police van. I didn't blame them for getting grumpy, but we each had a job to do. Swinging between two policemen with my chin just high enough to avoid scraping the pavement, I could see the other protesters waving brilliant green-and-pink ACT UP posters. They were pictures of Ronald Reagan's face with the word "AIDSGATE" stamped across his big green forehead and had the rebellious beauty of the first Sex Pistols album. He looked like Herman from the TV show *The Munsters*. His eyes were neon pink, and the smaller text read, "Genocide of All Non-whites, Non-males, and Non-heterosexuals . . . Silence = Death." I had one of those posters hanging in my apartment, and it glowed in the dark. I used it as a nightlight.

Alone in my holding cell, I felt my heartbeat slow down. My anxiety took a vacation when I was confined, and I didn't feel depressed. I felt proud. At the university I had given up trying to explain that it was possible to be a punk, a feminist, and a lesbian all at the same time. I was tired of being treated like I was ideologically deranged.

The cops pushed a woman who was obviously high on something, probably crack, into my cell. She was wearing an unzipped, torn, white leather skirt and a fake fur coat over just a bra. She sat next to me on the metal bed.

"What did you do?" she asked.

I cleared my throat. "I chained myself to the White House fence to protest the government's policies on AIDS."

She smiled at me, nodding out.

I wasn't completely clear on holding-cell etiquette and didn't know if I should ask her what she'd done when I was pretty sure I knew. But I didn't want her to think I wasn't interested. I remembered that the politically correct term for "prostitute" was "sex industry worker."

"What are you in here for?" I asked, putting on my politest, most ingratiating smile.

She looked at me like I was totally crazy. "Baby, I'm a hooker."

TRACK 11 WHITE RIOT

The police made everyone who was going to be transferred to Central Cell Block stand up against the wall. Central Cell Block was the one place in DC that *everyone*–cops, criminals, lawyers, hookers, activists–told you not to end up. It was the dirtiest, most disgusting lock-up in the city.

The other ACT UP protesters had already been processed, and I was the only one left. A tall cop in a huge, metallic-blue cop coat turned me around to cuff me. She said, "Girl, what the *hell* are you doing here? You don't belong here."

I looked around the room. I'd never felt so white in my life. In racist DC, the prison population is mostly black. I said defensively, "I belong here as much as anyone. I broke the law. I have a right to be here." I wished I could switch myself off like a light bulb.

Later, when I related this story to an African American friend, she said, "You have the *right* to be there? They're probably still talking about you! 'Remember that white girl who said she has the *right* to be here?'" And she dissolved into laughter.

When the Central Cell Block cops arrived, a large male officer checked one man's handcuffs and bellowed, "This isn't the way we cuff people in Central Cell Block." He and his cadre took off everyone's handcuffs and put them on again *tight*.

I said to the extra-tall female officer who cuffed me, "Aren't you gonna ask me my safe word?"

All around me, people screamed for their cuffs to be loosened, but I didn't say anything. I didn't want anyone to see me squirm. The Central Cell Block cops herded about fifteen of us into a police van divided into two narrow sections by a metal partition. They crammed the men in one side and the women in the other. I slid in first along the bench, my face almost touching the wall in front of me. I pulled up my feet and slammed my monkey boots into the small, plastic window that separated me from the backs of the officers' heads in the front seat. As I did, I had a vision of the dark-haired woman in my head in her monkey boots.

The only time I saw my women these days was when I was at an ACT UP demonstration. It was the one unselfish thing I was doing. The rest of the time I focused on myself and my future "career" as a university professor, and this violated a sense of morality we shared. I thought about Gertrude Stein saying in *Lectures in America* that the writer can either serve God or Mammon. I assumed that this was true for musicians and English lit majors, too. In graduate school, I was serving Mammon.

The cops drove us into an underground parking garage and left us there. It was hot in the van, and I imagined myself dead and forgotten somewhere along the Potomac. I hadn't been able to feel my hands for a while, the plastic flex-cuffs cutting into my skin, and I worried about the blood not reaching them. I closed my eyes and tried to quell my worst OCD fear that my hands were coming off. *Dead but proud*, I assured myself. To

 **PISSING IN A RIVER**

keep myself from panicking, I often pictured myself dead rather than mutilated. I saw myself locked up and lost in the system. I thought of an old Clash song: *"I got nicked fighting in the road / the judge didn't even know / what's my name!"*

I thought about Patty Hearst locked up in a closet and raped repeatedly by the Symbionese Liberation Army. Next to that, I had nothing to complain about, and I tried to contain my claustrophobia. *Death to the fascist insect that preys upon the life of the people*, I thought, remembering an old SLA slogan. The only punk song I knew that mentioned the SLA was "The American in Me" by the San Francisco group, the Avengers. After I was sure we'd used up our entire air supply, the cops finally opened the back of the van and let us out.

I was the only white person in Central Cell Block. A huge woman behind the desk shouted at us, "You're in *my* house now." My handcuffs were removed, and I was put into a small cell. Left to myself, I evaluated the marks on my wrists and a welcoming committee of cockroaches. The paint on the bars was a filthy, peeling-off, puke green.

At least while I was in custody, I could relax because everything was out of my control. My mental problems peaked during graduate school. Instead of merely being paranoid and thinking that people were judging me all the time, people *were* judging me all the time. I was in a constant state of anxiety, and even when I stood still, I felt like I was running. My intrusive thoughts intruded even deeper into my head. And I only felt like I caught up with my real self when I was sitting in a cell. I sat on the upper metal bunk, the one without the thin, roach-stained mattress, and felt temporarily at peace.

TRACK 12 **NOBODY'S HERO**

In the midst of guilt and angst over my runaway grad-school ego and impending exams, I had to go to court for refusing to leave the office of Jesse Helms, the biggest homophobe in the Senate, until he agreed to resign. If I pled guilty to "demonstrating in a capitol building without a permit," the "unlawful entry" charge would be dropped. When it was my turn, the judge reminded me that the charge carried a maximum penalty of six months in jail and a five-hundred-dollar fine. I wondered if I could write my dissertation in jail. I had already started collecting subscription information for feminist journals that are "free to women in prison."

The judge said, "I'll give you six mo–" then paused and rubbed his head. I think he was playing with me. "No, wait. I'll sentence you to thirty days. Thirty days, execution suspended."

Oh my God! I thought, hearing the word "execution." *He can't do that.* I tried to catch my lawyer's eye. *Surely we're going to appeal this. The judge is obviously insane. He can't give me the death penalty for civil disobedience.* "Execution suspended." *Christ, I'm gonna hang by the neck until dead.* "I sentence you to thirty days suspended sentence and six months unsupervised probation." I finally understood what he was saying.

I'd never been on probation before. I couldn't get arrested again for six months or I'd automatically go to jail for thirty days, like landing on the wrong square in Monopoly. I would sit in my room listening to the Clash sing "Police on my Back." If anyone tried to arrest me, I'd have to say, "Excuse me, but *you're* fucking up *my* probation."

I was tired of living in the crack-and-murder capital. As I lay on the living room floor with my arms over my head while two armed men ran up my street from the local drug dealers' corner, I thought about where my life had taken me. I was still in America and, while I loved the challenge of literary scholarship, wasn't sure I wanted to be an academician.

But school helped me maintain my sanity. I never taught two days in a row, and my seminars were in the late afternoons and evenings. I had enough of a gap between responsibilities to recover from nights I couldn't sleep and times I was too anxious

 **PISSING IN A RIVER**

to function. This was crucial for me in managing my symptoms. And for some reason when I'm having a nervous breakdown, I read voraciously.

Being at the university allowed me to have an identity I could live with ("I'm a graduate student, not a mentally ill person who cannot hold down a full-time job"), a purpose ("I'm working on my doctorate and moving forward with my life, not stagnating in mental illness") and more time to play guitar than I would have had with regular employment. Why didn't I get a music degree instead? I didn't want to study music. I just wanted to play it.

The academic lifestyle also gave me the freedom to practice my politics. I burned American flags without worrying about being thrown out of the English department. That wasn't a violation of my probation *yet*. I burned flags at Union Station, at the Capitol, at home, and at barbecues. I lit a cigarette on a burning American flag in front of a television news camera at an ACT UP demonstration downtown, standing next to the then-director of the National Gay and Lesbian Task Force, Urvashi Vaid. Soon it wasn't enough, and I feared I'd get a flag-a-day habit.

I burned a flag in the park across the street from the White House in 1991 during a parade to show off weapons from the Persian Gulf War. It was the same year Nirvana released their CD *Nevermind*. The parade route had to be repaved because the tanks were so heavy they wrecked the road. I think it cost about a million dollars, and they only fixed the street because it went past the government buildings. The thing about Washington, DC is that you can live in the worst housing project slum—gunshots, crack houses, liquor stores, and lottery tickets—and still have an amazing view of the Capitol. At night, it gleams like clean, white bones.

I used to drive over a hill through a drug-and-gang-infested section of New York Avenue and look at the Capitol past the pink neon sign of a very dangerously situated motel. I thought of how Patti Smith had once described the nation's capital: "It's the color of fucked." This was my favorite spot because it epitomized the breach between life in the real world and the federal government. I doubted even Moses could cross that Red Sea.

Sometimes I drove through Capitol Hill to a lesbian dive called The Phase. It could be a beautiful spring day on Capitol Hill, the ritzy, rich-people area behind the Capitol, but in just one block, the carefully manicured rowhouse gardens of daffodils, tulips, crocuses, rhododendrons, and cherry blossoms ended. The brightly lit corner markets and people in expensive coats walking their small dogs were suddenly gone.

The next block was a war zone of gutted crack houses sitting in scraggly patches of black-eyed Susans, the brilliant yellow flowers growing up against cardboard windows. The abundance of liquor stores and shops pushing lottery tickets, the poor person's version of the American dream, reminded me of the Dead Kennedys song "Kill the Poor."

The day I burned the American flag at the glorification-of-the-Persian-Gulf-War-and-buried-alive-Iraqi-children parade, there were about ten of us protesting, surrounded by a million white Republicans. I dumped nail polish remover on the flag and dropped a lit match on it. I looked up in time to see a mob of angry white men running toward me. I held out my receipt, screaming, "It's my property! Burn, baby, burn!" They chased me all the way to the Metro station. Just when I thought they were going to kill me over a four-dollar piece of cloth, they turned back and threw themselves on the flag. You'd think Betsy Ross had sewn it personally.

I'd heard of "suicide by cop" before, someone who gets herself killed on purpose by forcing the police to shoot her in the commission of a crime. I wondered if I'd almost committed "suicide by Republican."

By the time I defended my dissertation, I was so exhausted by depression and anxiety I could barely function. I just wanted to be a punk musician. That was the only thought that brought me any comfort. After a brief stint in a mental hospital—that's *Dr. Crazy* to you—where I was once again improperly medicated and misdiagnosed, I fled east-coast academia and went back to California.

With my PhD in English and American literature, I was working as a telephone psychic and writing anti-Taliban songs for RAWA, the Revolutionary Association of the Women of Afghanistan. Located across the border in Pakistan, RAWA provided schools, hospitals, work programs, and food for Afghan refugees and ran secret literacy classes for women and girls inside Afghanistan. But after the terrorist attacks of 9/11, the Bush administration started bombing Afghanistan in *Operation Enduring Freedom*. I'd never thought of freedom as something to be *endured* before. And suddenly writing songs for Afghan women while I was living in the United States didn't make sense anymore. When the Patriot Act was passed, curtailing civil liberties, I made sure my passport was valid.

Before being fired from a previous job at a residential facility for schizophrenics, where hearing voices isn't such a big deal, I'd been reading through the *Diagnostic and Statistical Manual of Mental Disorders*, psychiatry's bible, trying to figure out why I was still suicidal on antidepressants. But the copy in our office was an old version. Then I got hold of the new edition in my never-ending quest to find out what was wrong with me. I'd never seriously considered OCD before because I had none of the stereotypical symptoms. I didn't wash my hands fifty thousand times a day or freak out if my possessions weren't all facing in the right direction. I was perennially disorganized and untidy. But with the fourth edition of the *DSM*, there was more of an emphasis on ritualistic *thought*, not just *behavior*, and mental acts counted as much as physical ones. People with OCD could be tortured by endless intrusive thoughts and be compelled to neutralize them by praying every waking minute. Not only time-consuming, it could be completely disabling.

I asked my psychiatrist for Prozac, which wasn't a cure but was sometimes effective in lessening OCD symptoms. Being the only psychiatrist I'd ever had who actually listened to me and valued my opinion, he gave it to me. And on the tenth day of my new regimen, I woke up and my head seemed strangely quiet. It was as sudden and as simple as that. I still had intrusive thoughts that I had to neutralize, but now I had times when I *wasn't* crushed by torpor or anxiety. It might sound ridiculous, but the sky seemed bluer. It was like coming out of an extended coma. I still had trouble falling asleep, but most nights I did sleep eventually. And I was relieved to discover, as I'd always known, that the women in my head didn't disappear with the advent of proper medication. I couldn't explain them, but they were not a symptom of mental illness. I still processed my thoughts the same OCD way, but the Prozac had taken a bit of the edge off. Even with the lingering symptoms, I felt better than I had since the year I lived in England. This was a big adjustment, and I felt like I was constantly on vacation from myself. Not in a self-hating way but in a good way. It was like someone had taken a hose and washed off the entire world.

By the time post-9/11 Christmas came around, my throat was sore from yelling at people with American flags waving out of their car windows. "You can take your flag and ram it up your ass!" I screamed inside my car. Nativity scenes were embellished with Christmas lights made into American flags, as though Jesus Christ had been born in the United States. My neighbor had a huge cross on his roof lit up in red, white, and blue, and I was mentally exhausted from having American flags shoved in my face all day long.

People of Middle-Eastern descent were randomly attacked in my town, and I don't mean my mother on her way home from

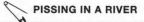 **PISSING IN A RIVER**

synagogue. Jews existed in that murky borderland between *"at least they're not Muslims"* and *"they killed Christ."* I sewed an upside-down American flag on my sweatshirt and scrawled "God Bless Afghanistan" across it, as though I had a death wish. And it was no good thinking I would simply keep my opinions to myself. I'm the kind of person who keeps on talking long after someone with any sense and normal social skills would have shut up. I'd stopped saying the pledge of allegiance as far back as elementary school. And during the Bush regime, I didn't just refuse to stand for the national anthem. Instead of sitting quietly, I threw myself on the ground and writhed with my arms stretched out in crucifixion position.

I opened up the yellow pages and found the nearest boxing studio.

TRACK 14 **LONDON CALLING**

The worst part of boxing class was that I had to watch myself in the inescapable wall mirrors. I had negative stamina. Just getting into correct boxing stance and holding up my hands in blue, sixteen-ounce gloves was enough to almost kill me. We did pushups and stomach crunches, shadowboxed, and worked the heavy bags. When the teacher wore focus mitts and I had to punch him, I pretended he was President Bush. Eventually my stance became more fluid and my punches got meaner. I never did get the hang of jumping rope, though. There was just too much of me that had to land.

I rolled the yellow hand wraps between my fingers, taping up my hands, and wrote "Sugar Rat" on a few T-shirts with permanent marker because I decided that would be my boxing name when I turned professional. After my third week, having no sense of proportion, I felt ready to take on anyone. I thought the already-in-shape people should have to wear weights so they'd have to work as hard as I did just to remain standing.

As I hit the floor, having collapsed on my face while doing pushups, I realized it was time to get the hell out of America. I was in my thirties and had the stupidest job in the world. As Guantanamo Bay opened for business and the United States government fine-tuned its acceptable level of torture, I lay awake nights wondering when the American people would rise up against their fascist government. Now that I wasn't completely exhausted from those debilitating, soul-crushing, unabridged mental breakdowns any longer, I wanted to return to England where my happiest memories and the voices in my head were from.

Even though it was expensive, I wanted to be in London because that's where the women in my head lived. I just had to figure out how to get there. And what to live on once I got there. And how to get my medication. I talked my psychiatrist into giving me prescriptions with six months of refills. But then, he said, I would either have to come back to see him or find another doctor to prescribe my meds. I called a cousin by marriage who was a doctor in Leeds. He promised to be a backup in case I had trouble filling my prescriptions, but under no circumstances would he write me out new ones when mine ran out or treat me as a patient. I wasn't terribly worried because six months seemed like a long way off. I was sure I'd figure out something, and I had my doctor in the States as a safety net. In order to enter the UK, I had to purchase a return ticket to show I intended to leave when my six-month tourist visa was up. I wasn't planning to use it, but I'd have it in case of an emergency.

To raise money, I sold my car and a few guitars, including a battered 1965 Fender Mustang with a red tortoiseshell pickguard. I sold my TV, VCR, and stereo. Everything else I packed up and stored in my dad's garage. If I lived cheaply, I could survive for six months without supplementing my income. I would earn extra cash by playing on the streets for money, never mind that I'd never had the nerve to do it before. I decided I'd be braver playing music in front of people in another country. I said goodbye to everyone at the boxing studio and promised my teacher I'd find somewhere to train in the UK. I could only carry one guitar with me on the plane, so I chose my white Gibson. My father promised to take care of the rest. Then I packed up my other most important possessions, my bootlegs. I had found someone from Britain with connections who worked in a local record store, and he managed to get me unofficial live recordings of concerts that we listed as "imports" when I purchased them.

As we drove to Los Angeles International Airport, I couldn't believe I was actually returning to England for an extended stay. I couldn't visualize what the future held for me in London, and with my OCD, uncertainty and instability were especially hard on me. But I couldn't visualize any happy endings for myself in the United States either. I was nervous but excited as I headed for international departures. I kept looking back and waving at my dad as he stood behind the security checkpoint. As I walked into the open mouth of the plane, I felt like a whale had swallowed me whole.

 **B SIDE**

TRACK 15   **WIMPY'S ARE SHIT**

I was living in a bedsit in the East London borough of Hackney. It was a cheap, furnished room in Stamford Hill with a loo, kitchenette, and faded gray-and-green wallpaper. Even though the women in my head remained reticent, the gray sheets of rain seemed to promise all good things. When I'd first arrived, I had agonized over playing in the streets for people's spare change. But if I were going to stretch out my stay longer than six months, I needed to make extra cash. Of course, according to the stamp in my passport, I was only supposed to be in the country for six months. But I didn't think that would be a problem as long as I paid my own way, committed no crime, and didn't work illegally. I didn't know exactly how immigration worked, but who would notice one extra person living in such a large city?

The first time I tried busking, I'd been so nervous I felt like horses were galloping in my stomach. Across from Dalston Kingsland railway station, I stood meekly in a corner of the Ridley Road Market, amid flower and banana stalls, tentatively plucking out chords and singing in a very small voice. I was too intimidated by the crush of people to make the requisite noise. Soon I packed up my gear and went home with less money than I had when I started, as I'd bought a Coke. The next place I tried was the Seven Sisters tube station, and that went a little better. It took me two weeks of busking to achieve my optimal volume.

Now I wasn't disconcerted by people slogging past as I stood in the mouth of the Victoria tube station. I had my white Gibson SG with the Kurt Cobain and ACT UP stickers on it, a Fender Ampcan that ran on a rechargeable battery, and my orange DS-1 distortion pedal. I strummed a weird rhythm off A and B chord variations and sang "Working for the Jihad."

> *Muhammad's fifteen*
> *gonna be a suicide bomb*
> *Johnny's fifteen*
> *goes to school with a gun*

A few people dropped copper 1p and 2p coins into my guitar case, and I nodded at them. I figured they'd like a song by an American that mentioned the gun control issue. *Yes, it's true*, I thought. *We* are *all crazy over there.*

> *Muhammad flew up*
> *to heaven on a white horse*
> *Johnny's locked up*
> *says he feels no remorse*

I switched into the ringing, open minor chords of my chorus.

> *We are martyrs one and all*
> *what does it matter anymore*
> *we are martyrs in this war*
>
> *we are martyrs one and all*
> *it could be so beautiful*
> *can't you hear the jihad calling you*

Two kind people clapped then moved on. I'd written a heavy, melodic bass line for the song and wished I could find someone to play it. As it started to drizzle, I stood in the doorway of a Wimpy bar and played "Capitalism Is My Friend." The song had a ska-like beginning that needed a rhythm section.

If only I could find a friend, I thought, *and teach her the bass lines*. Of course we'd have to find a bass and some gear. I wondered where to get those things cheap. I was thinking ahead of my reality. In reality, I was being asked to vacate my semi-dry spot by the Wimpy bar manager because I was blocking his customers from going in and out.

I put the pedal inside the pocket of my green army-surplus jacket and carried my guitar and amp into the rain. I went to the Piccadilly tube stop. There was an underground entrance to Tower Records there, and I figured that the musically inclined would pass by with leftover change. I played for about four hours, until I'd made enough money for a few days of eating and tube fare, which was expensive, then caught a bus back to my room.

TRACK 16   CATCH US IF YOU CAN

I got an ancient VCR and an even older ghetto blaster for cheap off someone flogging them in the Ridley Road Market. My room came with a bed, bed linens, comfortable chair, small settee, desk, wardrobe, and a small color TV. I also had a little two-hob cooker and mini-refrigerator. The compact bathroom had a toilet, basin, and stand-up shower. I bought a TV license and charged up a blue plastic electricity key for the pre-pay meter that supplied me with heat. And there I nestled against the warm radiators off the Amhurst Park Road among the Hasidic Jews. This area of Hackney was less rough than further south toward Dalston and Clapham. I was lucky that the building where I lived mostly housed Orthodox Jewish yeshiva students. I didn't share space with the usual mice and dysfunctional blokes. None of the flats were being used as crack houses, and prostitutes and curb crawlers didn't do a high-volume business on our street. I still heard the police sirens and helicopters every night but felt safe in my cosy bedsit.

I kept mostly to myself even though I secretly desired a modest social life, isolation being a common symptom of OCD.

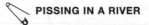 **PISSING IN A RIVER**

When I isolated myself, I wasn't involved in anxiety-provoking situations with other people that over-stimulated my brain and gave me hours of agonizing over every interaction and every little thing I'd said to anyone, wondering if I'd done something wrong. Constantly needing reassurance, that's another one.

On Sunday afternoons I stayed home religiously to watch the omnibus edition of *EastEnders*, my favorite soap opera. Sometimes I walked to the Video Exchange on Stamford Hill Road to rent videos. I found a boxing club nearby and went twice a week for four quid a session. And I did enjoy walking around London wrapped up in thoughts about the women in my head, always keeping my eyes open for them.

Now, on a drizzly afternoon, I wrapped my enormous green-and-white Exeter University scarf around my neck, buttoned up my coat over my gray, hooded Jam sweatshirt with the blue, white, and red mod circles large like a target on my chest, and went for a perambulation. I love rain on red brick and, after growing up in a postcard-pretty town—see how far that gets you when you don't fit in—filled with rich white people, I enjoyed the shabbiness and ethnic diversity of Hackney. I had hated living in a town that was so much prettier than I was. Of course London could be beautiful, but it didn't make me feel like I had to be perfect in order to live there.

I passed the turquoise "1 Nation" graffiti and went down Vartry Road, a sea of red and brown brick terraces with white lace curtains. In the background, council tower blocks rose into a white sky. I stopped for a Coke at the newsstand, then rounded the corner by the British Rail line. I went up Amhurst Park Road to the shops on Amhurst Parade where the Hasidim hung out in long, black coats. I liked the small shops in this indentation off the main road: the Hebrew Book and Gift Centre, Tasti Pizza, which delivered kosher pizza, a grocer's, kosher sandwiches, and an off-license. At the end of the parade, the windows of the flats above the shops jutted out with their pale, thin curtains. Opposite Amhurst Parade was a Turkish grocer's that always had gorgeous smells emanating from it. At the corner of Stamford Hill and Amhurst Park was the massive, dark-brick Safeway. Its letters glistened bright red in the rain. Orthodox women in headscarves wheeled their prams down the aisles. Across the big intersection between Amhurst Parade and Stamford Hill was the Boots Chemists. On Stamford Hill, I got takeaway from Spicy Wok Chinese Food/Fish & Chips, and Uncle Shloime's.

I jumped on a red double-decker bus and, even though it was only a short ride to Dalston, climbed to the upper level. I always tried to sit on one of the two front seats so I would have the most expansive, unobstructed view of the streets below. It was hard to miss the old Rio Cinema, a large, clunky-looking art-deco building on Kingsland High Street. The cinema specialized in foreign films, and I saw a depressing Iranian one called *The Circle* about how hard a woman's lot could be in post-revolutionary Iran.

Outside in the soft, blue neon glow, people sloshed briskly past me. I felt invigorated by the cold, soggy weather and walked up Stoke Newington Road to the Due South for a quiet pint. I was soaking wet by the time I reached the dark blue pub. The silver letters above the front window glittered and blurred between raindrops as I squinted to look up at them. I settled myself at the window with a warm—well, really room temperature—pint of bitter.

A really cute punk woman with spiky, medium-length black hair was sitting at a table near me with some mates. I felt immediately drawn to her in a way I didn't understand. It was more big-sisterly than sexual. But she had definitely grabbed my attention. She was wearing Doc Martens, black trousers, and a blue Nirvana T-shirt, a picture of Kurt Cobain kneeling down holding his black Strat with the "VANDALISM: BEAUTIFUL AS A ROCK IN A COP'S FACE" sticker on it that he'd smashed in Paris. The black leather jacket that hung over the back of her chair was peppered with metal and blue-jeweled studs and had a large, black-and-white fabric back patch that was a picture of the Clash up against a wall with their hands up like they were getting nicked. For some reason, she seemed familiar. Was she someone I'd gone to school with? No, she seemed too young for that. But she looked tough, in that cool, Chrissie-Hynde-like way. She looked like someone I'd like to know, and I wondered, post-revelation about animal rights, if her jacket was real leather or some cruelty-free synthetic substitute.

I wished I could say something to her, but I didn't have the nerve. I couldn't walk up to a strange woman in a gay pub and say, "Don't I know you from somewhere?" It would sound like a chat-up line, and I didn't want to pick her up. I just wanted to meet her and possibly be her friend. I tried out introductions in my head. *"Hi, I love your jacket."* My American accent sounded so obscenely pronounced in my own head I couldn't bear it. *"I have that same Nirvana shirt."* Why would I tell her that? Did I think she'd stolen it? *"Oi, wotcha, can you tell me where the bog is, mate?"* Yes, do tell me where the toilet is so I can flush myself down it. Phony English accents are nauseating. *"Hi, my name is Amanda, and I don't know anyone socially here in London. I've selected YOU, yes, lucky you, to be the first person I meet."*

It was only after the punk woman had left with her mates that I realized she reminded me of the younger woman I saw inside my head. *Shit!* My mind went numb. I felt like my heart had jumped into my throat and I was going to choke on it. I left the pub and started running, but I didn't know where I was going. I couldn't see her anywhere. I didn't know what to do. The rain had stopped. It was a big-mooned, freshly washed night. Because it was late and I was hungry, I walked back down Stoke Newington to the Istanbul Iskembecisi, a Turkish restaurant that stayed open until five in the morning. I passed a twenty-four-hour garage, a grocer's, then reached Aziziye mosque. It had two silver domes and marble tattooed with intricate blue-and-turquoise designs like flowers. The blue mosque also served as a Halal butcher, restaurant, and supermarket. I liked this part of Hackney with its synagogues and mosques. It could be dodgy late at night with gangs, guns, and drugs, but I felt safe on the main roads, which were well-lit and had lots of traffic.

I ordered falafel, chips, and a large Coke to take away. While I waited, I noticed the Kurt-shirt girl and her mates getting up from a table. When they brushed past me, I couldn't make myself say anything. I watched them from the window as they stood outside talking. Then the others went in one direction and Kurt-shirt went on alone down Kingsland High Street. I didn't know if I should charge out after her without my food and introduce myself. I froze.

When my food was ready, I splashed salt and malt vinegar on my chips and rewrapped them, the whole time thinking, *why are you wasting time?* But I knew if I caught up with her, I wouldn't know what to say. *"Am I mistaken, or did you used to visit me inside my head?"* I walked in the direction she'd gone even though it was the opposite of where I lived. I told myself I was going to get a bus on Dalston Lane and wasn't really going out of my way. But she had already disappeared from view.

I never got aggression on the High Street. The Turkish men's cafés were open all night with people sitting outside drinking coffee. Sometimes I got verbal hassle, but it amounted to nothing. I wouldn't have gone on any of the side streets. Many of those weren't even lit because the Hackney council said it had no money to buy replacement light bulbs.

I was almost to Dalston Lane when I heard what sounded like a scuffle off the main road to my left down a cut-through to the bus stop. It was safe to use during the day. There was a vegetarian restaurant that did a lot of business. But I wouldn't walk there after dark. I stopped at the mouth of the dirty, narrow side road and thought I heard somebody cry for help. Part of me wanted to run away and get help. But I knew that even if I found someone willing to come back with me, I might arrive too late. The image of the Kurt-shirted girl flashed through my mind.

I crept cautiously between the Allsorts Bargain Shop and a McDonald's thinking, *safe, safe, keep me safe.* I rounded the corner and walked alongside a deserted brick building. Near bags of rubbish behind the veggie café, I saw them. A man was shoving a woman up against the wall and ripping at her clothes. Her T-shirt was pulled up and her trousers were unzipped. I could see him trying to force his hand down her knickers. At first I didn't believe what I saw. My mind couldn't digest it fast enough and went numb with shock. No one else was on the street. In the few seconds it took me to react, the man slugged the woman in the gut and she went down on the pavement. He climbed on top of her and smacked her in the face as she resisted him.

I finally found my voice. *"Hey, you!"* I wasn't scared yet because I figured he would see me and run away. But he didn't. He just leered at me with an exaggerated attitude of entitlement like *I* was the one who was out of place. The light was dim, but as he held her down behind the row of parked cars, I could see it *was* Kurt-shirt girl. I hadn't recognized her without her leather jacket, which had been flung on the ground. I had to do something. I was still holding my takeaway. I threw my soda at his head. Ice and Coke exploded all over him. He wiped his face with his hand, looking pissed off, sticky and unfazed. *"Help!"* I shouted. "Somebody, *help!"* At that hour, no one came running. Even the McDonald's had closed for the night. But I kept jumping up and down making noise anyway. He was a medium-sized white bloke with a shaved head wearing a green bomber jacket, white T-shirt, red braces, rolled-up blue jeans, and brown Doc Marten boots with red shoelaces—the old uniform of a skinhead in the National Front. He pointed his finger at me and said, *"Shut up!* Or you're next."

I threw my bag of food at his head. He stood up and came for me, saying, "I'm gonna kick yer fuckin' 'ead in." He grabbed me, as I kicked and struggled, and threw me against a parked car with so much force I skidded across the hood and landed on the other side on my head. My hands had partially broken my fall, but I sat dazed on the pavement. Impervious pigeons scrounged around me for garbage.

I stood up slowly. Over the car, I could see that the woman hadn't got away. She was still gasping for breath after being punched in the stomach. Guiltily I felt grateful she hadn't left me there alone with him. Thinking I'd been neutralized, the man had turned his back on me and had gone back to assaulting her, jamming his hand all the way inside her knickers while she fought him.

I looked at my fingers to reassure myself, said a brief prayer for the safety of my teeth, then dizzily got into my best boxing stance and tried to remember everything I'd been taught. *Left side forward. Hands up. People who throw hooks get hit by hooks. The jab is the most-used punch in boxing.* Now he was unzipping his own trousers. "*Stop! Police!*" I screamed in desperation. "*Call 999!*" I was terrified he'd give her AIDS or kill her on top of everything else.

He jumped up, yanked up his jeans, and came after me. I'd never actually hit anyone to defend myself before. I threw a tentative jab at his jaw, and he easily knocked my hand away. Now I was scared. I knew I was in trouble. I was in way over my head, and my abdomen fluttered in panic.

Again he shoved me hard against the car. But at least my amateurish attempts to save the dark-haired punk woman were stalling his efforts to continue raping her. I reached in my pocket and slid my house key between my fingers, remembering that, according to women's self-defense tips picked up at Take Back the Night marches, it would make my fist a more effective weapon.

"You're all mouth and no trousers!" I yelled, having recently heard the expression on *EastEnders*. "I'm throwing you a wobbly!" The woman, stunned, looked at me like there was no hope in hell and we were both going to die. I broke into American. "*Don't fuck with me, motherfucker!*"

The skinhead paused. I used his second's hesitation to throw a quick right fist to his nose. The key slashed him. It was so unexpected he put both hands up to his face. I kicked him in the balls and, as he bent forward, grabbed his shoulders and brought my knee up into his ugly mug. I threw a left hook to the head and a right hook that caught him on the ear. I knew that had to sting.

"*Run!*" I grabbed the woman's hand and yanked her up off the ground, hoping she wasn't too injured to move quickly. In spite of her terror, she still had the clarity to snatch up her leather jacket before following me. *Now there's a good punk*, I thought, impressed.

We stumbled onto the main road, the woman holding up her trousers as we sprinted back up Kingsland High Street. We were so full of adrenaline, we ran all the way to Stoke Newington. "There's a cop shop up ahead," I choked out as we crossed Evering Road.

"*No.*" It was the first word she'd said to me.

"But we have to." I stopped running. "Don't we?" I looked around and didn't see him behind us. I held her jacket, and she zipped up her trousers.

She clutched my arm. "*Please.*"

I didn't have the heart to argue with her. I took her hand, and we dashed up the High Street. We passed the massive Stoke Newington police station, which looked like a big Tesco, all glass and brick, then half-jogged all the way to Stamford Hill. I took the woman to my bedsit because I didn't know what else to do.

We climbed the front steps, and I unlocked the door. We stood outside my room, gasping. "God, I've never been so knackered in my life," I said, pulling her inside.

She was doubled over, catching her breath. I sat her in the comfy chair because I was afraid she would go into shock or something, not that I was even sure what that was. Her nose and lip were bleeding.

"You're hurt," I said softly. I dipped some toilet paper—bog roll—in warm water and cleaned her up a bit. "Shit. He hit you pretty hard."

We didn't mention where else he had hurt her. I didn't know what I was supposed to do for shock, so I plugged in my electric kettle and made tea. It was the sanest thing I could think of doing. I felt responsible for her and also wanted to be a good hostess.

"Ta." She took the mug from me with trembling hands.

I looked into her pale, delicate features and said in my best Londonese, "Are you alright? Maybe we should call you a casualty."

She looked at me like I was nuts. "Maybe we should *go to casualty*?" she suggested.

"Yes, to hospital. To make sure you're alright."

"I'm alright. And you don't throw someone a wobbly, by the way. You throw a wobbly. When you're angry." She was crying, and I felt bad for her, so bad that I couldn't have arrived sooner, been a better boxer, and kept her from being traumatized.

I asked, "What's your name?"

"My mates call me Nick." She was trying hard to pull herself together and project a firm stance, but her vulnerability drew me toward her.

"I'm Amanda."

"I don't know how to thank you, Amanda."

"It's quite alright. I wanted to meet you."

Nick looked alarmed.

"God, I don't mean I was *stalking* you or anything. I just meant I saw you earlier in the pub, then at the Iskem, and I wanted to talk to you. We have the same Nirvana T-shirt," I finished weakly. *You're babbling*, I castigated myself. Christ, had it been that long since I'd had a proper, normal conversation with anyone? Nick was the first visitor I'd had to my bedsit, and I felt relieved not to be alone for once. *This is life*, I thought. *Life has come to my room.*

 **PISSING IN A RIVER**

Nick looked down at the picture of Kurt in a blue sweatshirt clutching his guitar on her chest, saw blood and seemed freaked out. I was feeling shaky myself. My legs swayed, and I sat down heavily on the bed.

"Are you gay?" Nick asked because I'd been at the Due South.

"Yes, I am," I said, and because it seemed right, "you're safe here."

She was shivering. I wanted to hold her and press my lips to her raven hair to comfort her. To say I felt close to her after what we'd been through was an understatement. And if she *were* the woman I'd known inside my head, we were practically related. But the last thing I wanted to do was violate her sense of personal space after she'd been raped. I took the duvet off the bed, and she let me wrap it around her shoulders. She was breathing fast, and I could see the beginnings of some nasty bruises on her face.

"I think I should call a doctor," I said. "Someone should look you over."

She looked up. "My best mate's sister's a GP."

"She has a jeep?" I asked, confused.

"She's a GP. She's a *doctor*," Nick enunciated carefully. She had a northern regional accent that I guessed was Mancunian because she sounded like Annie.

"Christ, *GP*." I shook my head. "Can we ring her?" Nick gave me the number, and I stepped out of the room to use the payphone in the hall. A woman answered, and I hesitated. "Dr. Jones? You don't know me. My name is Amanda. I'm calling on behalf of Nick." *On behalf of,* my mind repeated. *Who talks like that?*

"Is anything wrong?" she asked quickly.

"As a matter of fact, yes," I said awkwardly, not knowing how to explain it in the least upsetting way. "She was—assaulted. Someone—" I didn't want to use the word *rape*. "I think she should be looked at."

The woman's voice was firm and calming. "Tell me where

you are." I gave her my address. "I'll be right there." She rang off.

I felt better now that she was on her way, like I wouldn't have to make any more complicated decisions. For the first time in a long while, my heart felt light. As we waited, I remembered a sign I'd seen in a photograph of a café door in Iran: "*Sister, be quiet about yourself.*" *Like hell*, I thought.

I opened the door to a woman who looked like she was in her late thirties, or possibly early forties. "How you doing, love, alright?" she said to me. Her eyes looked worried as she quickly scanned the room behind me.

My mouth dropped open because she was gorgeous. "Alright."

She knelt in front of Nick and put down her medical bag. "Nicky, what happened?" Nick put her arms around her neck and sobbed into her coat. The woman held her. "It's alright, love. Tell me what happened." She looked up at me and said, "I'm Melissa."

I opened up my mouth but nothing came out. *Oh my God*, I thought. *Her name is Melissa. This cannot be happening.* I felt dizzy. She had shortish light-brown hair that looked invitingly disheveled and soft. I wanted to sweep back the waves from her face with my fingers. Her quick smile promised sweetness like ripe plums and showed white, even teeth. All I could think of was the romantic biblical poetry of the Song of Songs: "*Behold, thou art fair, my love; behold, thou art fair.*" But I didn't know if she'd mind my saying that her teeth were "*like a flock of ewes all shaped alike.*" She possessed the reassuring presence of the woman who'd sat beside me on the bed the night I almost tried to kill myself. And I wondered, *am I making this up or is it real?* So that I could function at all, I distanced myself from these thoughts. *She's just another person in the room*, I told myself. *You don't know her. For God's sake, try and act like a normal person.*

"I haven't met you," Melissa was saying. "Are you a mate of Nick's?"

"I'm Amanda. We never met before tonight."

"Nicky, who attacked you? It's alright, baby. You're safe."

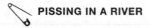 **PISSING IN A RIVER**

Melissa had Nick lie down on my bed. She covered her with the duvet and asked her where she was hurt. Then she asked me for a wet flannel. I didn't have a clean washcloth, so I wet part of a towel in warm water. She cleaned Nick's cuts with antiseptic and gently felt the bones of her face. She got two of those flashlights doctors use out of her bag. She looked into Nick's eyes and ears with them. I watched Melissa prod Nick, expertly checking for injuries. I imagined the touch of her hands was light as spring rain, precise and soothing.

"Honey, did he rape you?" Melissa asked gently.

Nick had still not articulated exactly what had happened. Now she cried harder.

"Was he—inside you?" Melissa asked in the softest voice I'd ever heard. "I have to know. You've got to tell me. Has anybody called the police?" She looked at me.

I said, "No," and stepped away to give them more privacy. Only the noises of traffic and a train passing under Amhurst Park Road reached us. Melissa stroked Nick's dark, curly hair. I looked at the street lamps outside the window.

I heard Nick wail, "But I don't *want* to go to hospital," and Melissa trying to console her.

"I promise I'll be with you the whole time. No one's going to hurt you. I'll make sure."

Melissa got up and came to me. She was wearing a yellow, pink, and green T-shirt from the punk band Chelsea under her brown, fuzzy coat. It said "Alternative Hits" and had a picture of a bloke in bright pink socks shooting up. *She's a* punk *doctor*, I thought triumphantly.

"Is she alright?" I asked, trembling because she was standing so close to me.

"I've got to take her to A and E."

"A and E?"

"Accident and Emergency. Like your emergency room in the States."

"Is her face broken?" I asked, my thoughts moving like sludge in my head.

"I don't think so, love. But she still needs to be examined. The bones in the face are very delicate and I'd like to make sure nothing was fractured. And—I have to know if she needs an internal exam. Can you tell me exactly what happened? Were you with her?"

"I was there part of the time."

"Are you hurt, love?" Her voice was empathetic, and I tried to stop shaking. I was *not* going to cry in front of this—stranger. After all, I was only a bystander. Chances were she wasn't the Melissa I'd imagined at all. Who did I think I was anyway, Zeus giving birth to Athena out of his head?

I shook my head to indicate I wasn't hurt, and Melissa asked, "Did you see what happened?"

"Most of it," I said in a raspy voice, coughing to clear my throat.

"Was she raped? Come on," she said, as I remained silent, "I need to know the details." I glanced anxiously at Nick, and Melissa put her hand lightly on my arm. "Don't be afraid to tell me."

"This guy," I said, and my voice broke. I took a breath to calm myself. "This neo-Nazi skinhead," my voice quavered, "assaulted her. I came around the corner and he was hitting her, trying, you know, to get her clothes off." I couldn't look at Melissa. I felt guilty for not stopping it sooner. "He was shoving his hand inside her knickers. He knocked her down. I was—he didn't stop. It was awful," I blurted out.

"Traumatic, was it?" Melissa said, and I nearly burst into tears at the concern in her voice. I realized then how shocked I was by what had happened. I'd thought I was handling it really well.

"And then what happened?" Melissa asked. "Did he rape her?"

"He—I think so. I mean, he didn't get his, you know, inside

her, but his hand. He got part of his hand inside her. At least—well, I don't know for sure. I assumed that it was. What would you call it?"

"I'd call it rape," Melissa said with conviction, looking me right in the eyes. "Did he get anything else inside her?"

"No, I stopped it then."

"Are you absolutely sure?"

"I'm sure."

"Alright. Tell me what you did."

Carefully I tried to describe everything with as much detail as I could remember but still left a good bit out.

"You did that?" Melissa said. "You know how to box?"

"Not really," I admitted. "I'm just a beginner. I think he was more surprised than anything else when I hit him. It stopped him long enough for us to run away." *Look at you*, I told myself. *You're having a conversation in a normal tone of voice. You're not sounding like a complete lunatic. Good going. Keep it up.*

"Well, it was very brave." She took one of my hands in hers. My knuckles were bruised and swollen. She manipulated my fingers gently. "Does this hurt?" She took my other hand. Her hands on my hands made me feel better, and I wanted her to keep holding them.

"No," I said. "I don't feel a thing." *You don't feel a thing*, I repeated to myself. *Who are you kidding?*

"You might do later. Are you hurt anywhere else?"

"I'm okay," I said, forgetting about landing on my head.

Melissa sat beside Nick again and asked her to confirm what I'd said. "Sweetie, did he actually get inside you? I know this is painful. I'm sorry. But it's better I ask you now when it's just us, right?"

I heard the soft hum of Nick's voice but couldn't make out what she said.

"Are you bleeding?" Melissa asked. "Do you know? Does it hurt a lot?" Melissa stayed there holding Nick's hand until she quieted down. Then she stood up and said to me, "Come on. Get your gear on. I'm taking you with us to A and E."

"Wait, me? Why?"

"To get your hands x-rayed. You *do* play guitar, don't you?" She nodded toward my guitar, which was leaning in the corner.

"Can't you just examine me here?" I asked, panicked at the thought of actually going outside again, let alone to the hospital, as if leaving the warmth and safety of my room would cost me way too much.

"I don't have x-ray vision." Melissa put her hand on my wrist. "Your pulse is racing. I want you examined. Listen," she said, as I balked, "I think Nick would feel better if you came with us." Her deep, ale-colored eyes were kind, and I picked up my coat.

"Are you sure you couldn't just examine us first and *then* decide whether or not we've got to go to hospital?" I tried again.

"*I'm* not going to be examining her at all. I can't perform that kind of examination here, let alone on someone I'm close to. She doesn't need to feel violated by me. I'll just be there for support."

I followed them outside and got into the small backseat of Melissa's sports car. "You've got a fab motor," I said. It was an old MGB GT in British racing green. Nick was crying a little, and no one talked on the way to hospital.

At A and E Melissa spoke to the triage nurse then disappeared with Nick. My potentially broken fingers weren't priority next to shootings and stabbings, so I was in the waiting room a while. After the nurse took me to be examined and have my hands x-rayed, I waited another eternity for the result. When I got back into the sitting area, there was no sign of Melissa or Nick. I worried that they'd gone and I would never see them again. I tried to ask the charge nurse if she'd seen them, but she was too busy to talk with me, so I parked my arse into another chair.

Melissa finally came to get me, and I could have wept with gratitude.

"Where's Nick?" I stood up.

 **PISSING IN A RIVER**

"In the car. She's been sedated. Come on, let's get you back to yours."

"Is she alright?"

"The physical damage wasn't substantial," Melissa said, as I followed her out into the cold night air. "How about you? How do you feel?"

"I'm completely fine." I held out my hands. "Nothing's broken."

"Not just that. This must've been quite traumatic for you."

I shrugged. "Whatever. I'm not the one who was attacked." I didn't even know what my feelings *were*. I still felt numb. But I wanted Melissa to think of me as courageous.

When we reached the car, Nick was hunched over in the passenger seat. I climbed in back. Melissa turned on the heat and made it nice and warm. My heart sped up as we neared my bedsit. *What am I going to do? I've got to get to know these women,* I thought. *I've got to see them again.* Melissa pulled over to the curb. I was so relieved when she invited me round for tea the following day and gave me her address in the West End, I nearly fainted dead away on the pavement. It started raining, just light slivers, as if God was shivering.

"Are you sure you're alright, love?" Melissa asked as I lingered by her window, leaning against the cold, wet metal of her car. "Do you want me to help you find someone to stay with you?"

"I told you." I smeared the drops of water on the green skin of her car roof like I was finger painting. "I'm perfectly okay." I waved goodbye as she drove off.

I lay in bed not sleeping, awash in strong emotions. I wished I had an old electric fire in a fake fireplace like the ones we'd had at Exeter instead of the more impersonal radiators. The soothing orange bars would have made good company. Now that the shock of what had happened wore off, I was aware of each swollen knuckle and every bruise. My head, neck, and arms hurt. I couldn't sleep. I spent hours with my brain on rapid fire, breathlessly repeating prayers of protection as fast as I could to neutralize the bad thoughts about rape that kept popping into my head.

I sobbed in frustration as my anxiety expanded, filling the entire room. My head pounded like a percussive bass riff. I wished Melissa would suddenly appear on the edge of the bed. My heart ached, and at that moment, I would have given anything to feel her sitting beside me, stroking my hair, though even my hair hurt. The Police song about inappropriate sexual attraction that had been so popular among the girls on my hall at Exeter when I was young, "Don't Stand So Close to Me," started playing inside my head.

TRACK 17 SHOT BY BOTH SIDES

I slept badly and awoke with the biggest headache of my life. I took a bunch of paracetamol and stayed in bed. In the late afternoon, I took another handful of paracetamol, grabbed my *London A-Z* and took the tube to Hampstead station. It was a far shout from where I lived. Outside the pubs, window boxes exploded with flowers and it was dead posh, the atmosphere far more tranquil than Hackney's. I'd been in this neighborhood before on one of my many searches for the women in my head. But of course I'd been everywhere in London. *It doesn't mean anything*, I admonished myself.

Melissa's flat was a cheerful-looking, yellow brick building on a cobblestone lane with old-fashioned street lamps and black iron posts. Before I knocked on the black door with the fancy knocker, I said some quick, urgent prayers to get them out of my system. "Melissa safe, Nick safe, me safe," I whispered because it would be my last chance to say my protective prayers out loud. For the next several hours, everything had to stay strictly in my head, and I couldn't move my lips. That was the hardest part, not moving my lips. I'm sure I wasn't always successful and seemed like a crazy person mumbling to myself.

I rapped on the door with outward confidence, though my mind was skidding everywhere, and Melissa let me in. She was in socks and green corduroy trousers, and a gray jumper over an untucked white shirt. Her eyes were an even richer brown than I'd remembered, and I felt myself dissolve into them. Melissa hung up my coat and scarf. I handed her my black bucket hat with Kurt Cobain's signature embroidered on the front in red thinking, *please be Melissa, please be my Melissa, please be my Melissa.*

Nick padded down the hall, her hair sticking up like she'd been lying down. She hugged me and held on long enough for me to rest my head on her shoulder. She smelled nice, like London in the rain. "I honestly don't know what to say. What you did—it was wicked. You saved my life." She had a black eye, swollen lip, and assorted bruises. "I thought I was going to die."

Something in the kitchen smelled gorgeous. Melissa opened up cartons of Indian takeaway and put the kettle on. "How do you take your tea?" she asked me.

"White with six sugars," I said, with as much dignity as possible. Melissa started laughing. "Ta, Dr. Jones," I murmured, as she handed me my cup.

"Please call me Melissa," she said. "And you're welcome. Sit down and have a Ruby." When I looked confused, she added, "'Ruby' means 'curry' in Cockney rhyming slang. Ruby Murray was a popular Irish singer of the fifties. I thought you'd like that." *She knows I'm an Anglophile*, I realized. I could hear a twinge of posh in her accent, but she downplayed it.

I bathed my face in the steam of my perfumed Earl Grey tea and felt my head clear for the first time all day. The hot, spicy food made all the difference. I was so tired the curry made me feel high. I felt my forehead thaw. Nick acted subdued but managed to eat a vegetable samosa, a little biryani rice, and some naan. I could tell that pleased Melissa.

"So, what are you doing this side of the pond then?" Melissa asked me. "Besides rescuing damsels, I mean."

"I hate the American flag and everything it stands for," I said then smiled to make my tone seem less heavy. "Every time I turned around in America, someone was shoving Jesus Christ and the flag down my throat. Sorry."

"My sister's name's Amanda, too," Melissa said, "but everyone calls her Jake after Jake Burns from Stiff Little Fingers. When she started playing guitar, she'd only play Fingers songs. The name just stuck."

"That's one of my favorite bands," I said eagerly. "My favorite bands are Nirvana, the Clash, the Jam, Stiff Little Fingers, Therapy?, the Pretenders, and Patti Smith."

"Spot on. Those are pretty much the same as mine. Except I'd list the Clash first and add the Ruts."

"You're right," I said. "I can't live without the Ruts either."

"I see we speak the same language."

Her approval made me feel bright and shiny inside. And Nick perked up a bit when we talked about music.

Melissa put the kettle on again and asked me, "How do you take your coffee?"

I hesitated. "White, eight sugars," I said, and Melissa looked amused. "I'm glad you're having a laugh. Why do people think it's immature to ask for lots of sugar?"

"Why don't we go into the sitting room?" Melissa suggested. "You can see my records."

The front room was airy and bright, with pale yellow walls, bright pink moldings, and white lace curtains in the window. I saw a turntable in one corner and a row of record albums that stretched along one whole side of the wall. I immediately dropped to my knees in front of them and, since my back was turned, took the opportunity to say the prayer that had been welling up inside me, putting enormous pressure on my brain. *Please let Melissa love me.* Though I recited it in silence, I felt relieved at the chance to move my lips.

"Everything by the Clash and the Jam," I announced, delightedly flipping through vinyl. She had everything, from Wreckless

Eric and Peter and the Test Tube Babies to the Vibrators and the Adverts. She had the first two XTC albums, a huge collection of Sham 69 and the Damned, the Wall's *Personal Troubles & Public Issues*, and the first Killing Joke LP. I also found the really important singles like "City of the Dead" and "The Prisoner" by the Clash, the Jam's "Dreams of Children," and Magazine's "Shot By Both Sides." "Magic," I said, "the history of punk in vinyl."

"You're into all the old British punk?" Melissa asked, smiling.

"Each new punk record that arrived from England was like manna from heaven. You have no idea how much it meant. Those fourteen songs from the original Clash album are embedded permanently in my heart. Along with *This Is the Modern World*." I had a vivid recollection of my younger self listening to the second Jam album, reading the lyrics, and staring at the pen-and-ink drawings on the record sleeve for hours, days, weeks. It was a whole new world, like somebody had opened up a window and let the air in.

"Whenever I meet someone who seems about my age," Melissa said, "I want to know—where were you in 1977?"

I knew exactly what she meant.

"Things were different then," she added wistfully. "We were the original punks. The political, intellectual punks."

"Everything new's not shite or without intellect." Nick couldn't help herself and finally got involved in the conversation. "A lot of it's got politics and ethics. Not everyone under forty has forgotten what punk means." She seemed about five years younger than I was.

"Ouch," Melissa said.

"What about American bands like Rancid, Anti-Flag, and Bad Religion?" Nick spoke up again, forgetting her pain for a moment.

"I love Rancid, as they model themselves after the Clash, but I can't listen to them endlessly," I said. "I can't get excited about most current bands. I like what they're saying, but it's not my sound."

"Yeah, I know. I'll listen to anything that reminds me of the Clash," Nick admitted. "What about AFI? Now's there's an *awesome* Yank band." Nick pronounced the word "awesome" with an American accent.

"I don't really listen to them," I said.

"Oh mate, well, you've *got* to."

"If you've got some you could lend us," I said, "I'll give them a serious listen. What about your bands I might not have heard about on my sorry side of the pond?"

"I like Capdown and Mouthwash," Melissa said. "Punk ska." When she said that I pictured her dancing. I thought she would look dead sexy.

Nick said, "I like the Mingers and Bug Central."

"I love the reissues and old bands' new releases on Captain Oi!," Melissa said. "Have you seen their catalogue, Amanda? I only let myself order from it once a month."

"Captain Oi! is my savior," I said. "I wish I could buy everything on that label, but I can't afford it."

"I like going to see bands that do animal-rights gigs," Melissa said, "like Active Slaughter, Dog on a Rope, and Smiling with Semtex. And I like to support antiracism and antifascism benefit gigs."

"I love your band Hole. And I like the Distillers," Nick said. "Brody rocks."

"First she sounded like her ex," I said, meaning Tim Armstrong from Rancid. "And now she sounds like Courtney Love from Hole. Which brings up somebody—" Of course I meant Kurt Cobain, who'd been married to Courtney Love, and his band Nirvana.

"Oh, aye," Nick said, "Kurt's magic." She smiled for the first time without wincing. "Patron saint of losers like me."

"You're not a loser and neither was he," Melissa said.

"No, really. It's okay. I don't feel bad about myself when I listen to him. Even when he's screaming, he cradles my brain gently, like it's a precious bird's egg or something."

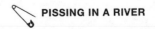 **PISSING IN A RIVER**

"That's really good," I said, impressed by her imagery. "That's exactly how it feels."

"The best band since the Clash," Melissa agreed.

"The *only* band since the Clash." I lifted up my trouser leg to show off my "Kurt" tattoo. "I'm the only lesbian I know with a man's name engraved on her leg."

"I worship at the church of Saint Kurt too," Nick confessed. "And I'm Catholic."

"I can't help it, but I get Kurt confused with Jesus," I said. "He looks so much like those racist blonde, blue-eyed renditions of our Lord."

"Yes, he fits in so well with all the other albino peoples of the Middle East," Melissa said. She and I laughed, but Nick went quiet.

"God," I said, suddenly registering the fact that she said she was Catholic, "have I upset you? I'm so sorry. My mouth is forever going off without my brain."

"No, you didn't," Nick assured me, but she had tears on her face. "I think Kurt makes a lovely Jesus. I just feel completely shattered all of a sudden."

Melissa looked at her quickly. "Are you in pain, love?"

Nick shook her head. "I should just go to bed. Am I going to see you again?" she asked me.

"Sure," I said.

"We owe her a meal at the Iskem," Melissa said. "She used her falafel as a hand grenade."

"I must've missed that," Nick said. "I was a bit out of it, me."

I shrugged. "I threw my dinner at his head to distract him. No big deal. And you've already fed me."

Nick kissed my cheek, said, "Be lucky," and went into the room where she was sleeping.

"Hang on half a mo." Melissa followed her.

Alone I thought, *keep Nick safe, keep Nick safe, please let Melissa love me*, this time keeping my mouth still, something I practiced rigorously as a survival tactic.

Melissa returned about twenty minutes later. "I wanted to tuck her in with a Valium and some pain medication."

"How is she really?" I asked.

"I sat up with her last night. And I buggered off work today and took her to see a rape-crisis counselor."

"Maybe I should go so you can sit with her." I felt bad, imagining Nick too scared to fall asleep.

"I'll check on her. She wants to try and sleep. I think she feels safe with us right outside the door."

"Was she badly hurt? Is she going to be okay?"

"She has a bit of vaginal tearing. And the bruises you can see. Of course the emotional damage is more significant. But it could have been much worse. Without your intervention." Melissa smiled. "Thank God the physical wounds will heal quickly. I'm just so grateful that I didn't have to talk to her about an HIV test or tests for pregnancy and other sexually transmitted diseases. I'm grateful to you."

"I should be getting back to mine," I said awkwardly, blushing, thinking that Melissa probably did want me to leave now that Nick had gone to bed.

"Have another cuppa before you go." Melissa got up and switched on the electric kettle.

"Ta very much."

"I'm glad you didn't bugger up your hands. You've got that lovely Gibson SG."

"You know about guitars? You're a perfect person."

"I told you, my sister's a musician. She plays with a punk band in Canada."

I could feel the effects of landing on my head returning but figured I could suppress them with another cup of tea. "What's your sister's band called? Does she have anything out I can listen to?"

"Bow Wow Mao," Melissa laughed. "She met them while they were touring the UK. They took her on as second guitar for their European tour to enlarge their sound, then asked her to stay on.

Their original guitar player quit, and now my sister writes most of their music. She keeps promising to send me a copy of their self-released CD but hasn't come across with it yet. And they're supposed to be building a website and Myspace page for the band, but I think they're on tour in Asia now."

I thought about Ann and Nancy Wilson moving up to Canada from Seattle so the men in the group could stay out of the Vietnam War. "She sounds smashing."

"She is, rather. I've got a ton of music gear upstairs. Nick and Jake are best mates. I worry about Nick now that she's gone. She doesn't trust that many people. She likes you, though. I can tell."

"Really?" My heart leaped. Then I wondered aloud, "Is she afraid of the police? Did you call them?"

"She didn't want to report it. And I'm not going to push her."

"Why? Don't you think someone should? Report it, I mean."

Melissa shrugged. "I know we're all responsible for getting rapists off the streets and that, but sometimes the whole ordeal is just too much for someone. And since it wasn't what a lot of people *still* would call a successful rape, and he didn't leave behind DNA, I doubt he would be caught or that it would be a top priority for the police. He doesn't know who she is or where she lives." She frowned, deep in thought, then tried to lighten the mood by saying wryly, "Besides, people have a nasty habit of dying in police custody in Hackney and falling down stairs when there aren't any, if you know what I mean. A bloke died just the other week in Stoke Newington station."

"Fuck me, are you serious? That's where I tried to take her."

"Well, I don't think they would have murdered you both outright," Melissa said. "I was being facetious. Except, of course, that it's true. The Plod killed a Nigerian man by kicking him in the head and strangling him in a choke hold. It was ruled an unlawful death, but no one was ever prosecuted. A Chinese woman died in custody in Stoke Newington. It helps to be nonwhite."

"That's like the States. Everyone knows you can get in trouble *driving while black*. Or even *reaching for your wallet while black*.

And don't get me started on *voting while black*. Let's just say our current president is unelected."

"Hackney cops shot a man walking home from the pub carrying a table leg in a plastic bag. They decided it was an assault rifle. It was Arthur Fowler shot dead leaving the Queen Vic." Arthur was a popular, kindly character on *EastEnders*.

"That's mad," I said, loving her accent and trying to sound like her.

"We have these special armed-response units now to cope with the rise in gun violence. The problem is they haven't got enough training. They go straight from pepper spray to guns. They haven't got intermediate weapons for mid-range violence. A mate of mine, Ivan, is a photographer. He rode with the Stokie armed-response unit and said it was terrifying, like riding with teenage boys who were all going, *'Ooh, look at us! We've got guns and a really fast car!'* Whenever they get called out, they're going to shoot something."

I thought about police saving my life when the Nazis showed up at our gay-pride march in Huddersfield in 1981, at the end of my last term in England. It was the first time the gay-pride march was held so far north. The Dibble—that's the police—had to call in reinforcements from all over northern England to protect us from the National Front skinheads who descended on us from every part of Britain. Like hairless, pale ghosts they came for us singing, "*You're gonna get yer fuckin' head kicked in.*" It was the first time I'd ever heard that song, and like a complete prat I turned to a woman next to me and said, "Oh, isn't it lovely? They're serenading us." They surged forward, and I remember people gobbing on us and the cops holding them back. Nobody carried guns then, not even the criminals, but I have no doubt I'd be dead today if it weren't for police intervention.

"I want to show you something," Melissa said, getting up and leading me past the room where Nick was sleeping. At the end of the hall, canvases and easels leaned against a door to the back garden, and I could see there was another room there off to the right.

"Do you paint?" I asked. "Can I see your work?"

"Sometime." Melissa led me into the back lounge. It had a comfortable vibe, just like the rest of her flat. There was a white carpet with colorful mod circles, pale lavender walls, a computer, shelves full of books and CDs and a nice flat-screen telly. I went directly to the CDs.

"Wire, *Pink Flag*. Eddie and the Hot Rods. Generation X. The 101ers, *Elgin Avenue Breakdown*." That was Joe Strummer's band before the Clash. Their best-known song was "Keys to Your Heart." It was anthologized on a lot of punk compilations and I was fortunate enough to have the original vinyl. I looked at the neon colors of the X-Ray Spex *Germfree Adolescents* CD then said, "You've got a CD of *Jeopardy*?"

"You know the Sound? I didn't think Americans knew the Sound."

"I have the LP from 1980. I didn't know there was a CD version."

"An online place called Renascent is reissuing everything. Now that Adrian Borland is dead." Unfortunately he had hung himself.

"'You've gotta believe in a heartland,'" I quoted from my favorite Sound song. "You've got the Equals," I said, more to myself than to her, "the Chords, and the Jolt. And you've got the Records. Shit, you've got a *ton* of Ruts I've never even *seen*." I picked up a CD of the first 999 album reissued by Captain Oi!. "Nick Cash tried to fuck me once between sets in 1979, but I refused."

"How could you resist a genuine punk star?"

"It was difficult."

"Come on, five minutes out of your life. Surely you could have accommodated him."

"Yes," I said sarcastically, "a line from a virtual stranger like 'let's fuck' always turns me on."

I flipped through some homemade CD-Rs, concerts by the

Clash, the Jam, the Pretenders with the original lineup and Patti Smith. I wondered idly if Melissa had ever listened to Patti Smith at the same time I'd been listening to her, and if that's how our thoughts got entangled so I could hear her inside my head. "Oh my God," I said.

"That's all Nick Cash wanted to hear," Melissa said.

"No, Melissa. *Heart*. You've got live Heart." I held out a concert from Boston in 1979. Something else caught my attention. "Bootlegs from Ann and Nancy Wilson's solo tour? Are you fucking kidding me? I saw them twice on that tour. It was like going to heaven. Where'd you get them? *I can't believe it*." I flung myself ecstatically onto the plush, green settee.

"I downloaded them off the Internet. I belong to several online music communities. I've always kept a spot for them in my heart. It's so liberating to be able to admit that to another old punk."

"And here I thought I was the only one. I'm a Heartmonger," I confessed. "It's the only fan club I ever joined. I can't believe we're talking openly about this. I'm so glad to have met you."

Melissa laughed. "I'm chuffed to have met you, too."

"I have one more secret. I can't believe I'm going to tell you this when I've only just met you. I listen to Oasis."

Melissa made a face. "Oh, I don't know. That's a bit dodgy."

"I know they're wankers but I love their sound. Admit it. Their sound is fab."

"Liam up-his-own-arsehole Gallagher?"

"His voice. And I love the way Noel plays guitar. Come on."

Melissa said, "I think you should have waited until we were further along in our new friendship to tell me."

"Who loves Heart?" I reminded her, and we both laughed. "Now, Jesus Christ, tell me about those Ann and Nancy solo-tour bootlegs, mate."

"My computer has a CD and DVD burner. You can make copies of anything you like. And I'm taking you to Camden Lock this weekend for bootlegs."

 **PISSING IN A RIVER**

"Only one of my favorite activities *ever*. Can I use your computer sometime to send emails to my family?" I'd been using Internet cafés, but they cost money.

"Sure," Melissa said in a fake American accent. "Sorry, that just slipped out. I didn't mean to mock you. You can't help sounding only halfway British."

"*Yet*," I insisted with confidence. "That's alright. My mates at university didn't like Americans either." I'd told her I had studied at Exeter. "But by the end of first term, no one could tell I was a Yank. I'm always at the wrong place in the wrong body." I thought about my black twin from the hospital where I was born. But through the joy I felt at being in Melissa's company, my head started to bother me again. I felt blurry, like my brain was full of lint.

I asked Melissa to play an Ann and Nancy concert and closed my eyes to listen. Nancy played her unreleased song, "The Dragon."

"I love the guitar on that," I said. "That tour was brilliant. Just Ann and Nancy on stage with tons of instruments. They're not corporate rock anymore. They played all the instruments themselves and split the lead vocals pretty much fifty-fifty. Nancy sounds great. And Ann. Well, you know our Ann." I squinted up at Melissa. "Her voice breaks my heart."

"Are you alright?"

"I'll be alright in a second."

"Do you feel ill?" Melissa sat next to me on the couch.

"I didn't get much sleep last night." I stood up shakily. "I ought to be getting back to mine." I hesitated because I didn't want to leave the scene of the Ann and Nancy bootlegs.

Melissa grabbed my arm and pulled me back down on the couch.

"Really, Melissa," I protested, "I'm alright."

"Tell me what's wrong with you."

"I'm having the worst headache of my young life." I tried getting up again.

"Hang on. Did you hurt your head?"

"Kind of," I said reluctantly. "When I tangled with that Nazi. I fell on my bread."

"You what?"

"Cockney rhyming slang." I was surprised she didn't know it. My head throbbed and I put my arm across my face. "Come on, you're the expert. Piece of bread, that's your head. China plate, that's me mate." I tried to sound more Cockney. "Plates of meat, that's your feet. Apples and pears, that's the stairs," I recited all the rhyming slang I was sure of except for "taking a butcher's," which I'd learned on *EastEnders*. Butcher's hook, take a look.

"*Loaf.*" Melissa sounded exasperated. "Your head is your *loaf*. Loaf of bread, that's your head. I'd be having a bubble at your expense, mate, if you weren't hurt. Will you please tell me what happened?"

"Bubble bath, that's a laugh," I said slowly, figuring out the rhyme. I told Melissa how I'd landed on my head.

Melissa sighed. "Why didn't you tell me this last night?"

"I forgot. Or maybe I had amnesia due to a head injury?" I suggested weakly, trying to joke her out of her sudden seriousness.

"How do you feel now?"

"Dizzy."

She left and returned with her medical bag.

"I'm alright. Really I am." I squirmed and started playing that Nick Lowe song "American Squirm" inside my mind.

"Stay still." Melissa sat next to me, holding me down. Her arms were strong and reassuring. "You've got a bloody great nasty bump on your head." She felt my head all around. "Did you lose consciousness?"

"I don't think so."

"You don't *know*, or you wouldn't *notice*?" Melissa asked. Then she lowered her voice and changed her tone. "You know, an assault of any kind can be quite traumatic. And not just for the intended victim." She opened up her medical kit and pulled out one of her flashlights.

 **PISSING IN A RIVER**

"What *is* that thing called?" I asked to cover my embarrassment at being examined by her.

"It's called an otoscope. It's for looking in your ears. Now, hush." She shined the light into my ear.

"What are you looking for?" I wanted to seem interested and intelligent instead of in pain, which I imagined would be boring to a medical doctor.

"Bleeding behind your eardrum. You've got to be careful with a head injury." She looked into my throat to check for bleeding there as well. She turned off the lamp and sat next to me in the dark. "Look here." She held up a finger and shined a bright light into my eyes. "This is an ophthalmoscope," she said before I could ask. "I'm looking to see if there are any blood vessels broken and examining your pupils. Your pupils open wide in the dark then narrow in reaction to light. If I shine a light in your eyes and your pupils don't move, that's bad. But you're fine." She turned the lamp back on and gently manipulated my neck with her cool hands. The pounding in my head got worse. I didn't know how I was going to make it back to Hackney by myself. Melissa made me lie down on the settee and I told myself I should go home to be sick in private. "Grip both of my hands and squeeze as hard as you can," Melissa said, and I was happy to do that. "Good." She brushed her finger across my palms. "Does the sensation feel the same on each hand?" She pulled off my shoes and did the same thing to my feet. Then she propped me up and tested the reflexes in my knees with a meat tenderizer. Later I found out it's more properly called a tendon hammer. "Have you got any nausea?" Melissa asked.

"I feel nauseous right now."

"Have you thrown up at all?"

"No. Can I go home?"

"Do you have someone to stay with you?"

"No."

"Shit. I want you to stay here tonight so I can keep an eye on you."

I was horrified at the thought of putting her out further. Also I needed to get back to the bedsit to take my nightly antidepressant and anti-OCD medication. If I missed a dose, I'd feel sick and achy for days afterward like I had the flu.

Melissa said, "I think you're alright but someone needs to watch you in case you start vomiting in the night or become unresponsive."

"Why?"

"To make sure you don't have a slow blood leak into your brain," Melissa said, giving me a nudge. "Satisfied?"

"Very," I said, "but I have got to go home."

"Why?"

I paused. *She's a doctor*, I thought. *I could tell her about my medication. She would know what to do. She could even write me out a prescription.* But I couldn't tell her. I didn't want her to know that about me yet. I wanted to know her better before I told her I was crazy. I decided I would either make it back to my bedsit or suffer the consequences in silence.

"You must tell me if the nausea or dizziness gets any worse," Melissa continued. "If I'm asleep, don't be afraid to knock me up."

I asked in alarm, "Knock you up *how?*"

"*Wake* me up," Melissa clarified.

"That's right," I moaned. "My head must really be bad for me to forget that expression."

"I'm sorry I can't give you anything strong enough for the pain. I have to be able to tell if you're unresponsive and confused instead of just zonked."

I struggled to get up.

"Don't be daft, mate." Melissa pushed me back into the cushions and covered me with a duvet. I closed my eyes because the pain in my head demanded it. I felt something soothing and cool. Melissa was sitting next to me, holding a wet towel on my forehead. "Relax," she said softly. "I won't let anything happen to you. You're quite nice for a septic. Septic tank, that's a Yank."

 **PISSING IN A RIVER**

Melissa got me up once in the middle of the night to check on me. She was wearing a paint-spattered Buzzcocks T-shirt that said "Orgasm Addict" for pajamas. "Listen," she said, "when you wake up, I probably won't be here but Nick will be. I want you to take it slow the next couple of days. Rest. And if anything changes, call me immediately and we'll get you in for a CT scan."

I already knew I'd give anything to be her friend. I didn't go back to sleep right away. I was wondering if Melissa was now my doctor and worried that, since she'd taken care of me, she considered me a patient and not a potential new best mate.

In the morning, there was a cup of tea on the floor near my head. Melissa had left, and Nick was in the front room. She looked like she hadn't slept. She asked if I wanted to watch a video. I thought if I ran home and took last night's medication immediately, perhaps I'd get away with having skipped a dose. But I couldn't make myself leave. We sat on the settee where I'd slept and watched a bootleg video of Nirvana in Tijuana in 1989. Kurt was in torn jeans and flannel shirt and fell frenetically on the floor every chance he got, spinning himself in a circle with his feet galloping like a wild horse. Afterward Nick said she had to go down to the job center to sign on so she'd receive her weekly giro.

"Job center? Giro?" I asked.

"I'm on the dole. Except now they call it 'job seeker's allowance.' I go down to the job center to show I'm actively looking for work, and the government sends me a cheque. If I do find anything, it's usually temporary or part time. It's hard to find anything with meaning when you don't have a *career*."

I thought about the Clash song "Career Opportunities" and said, "It's hard to find anything with meaning under capitalism. Ever think of taking up the bass?"

Nick smiled wanly. "Actually, I played a wee bit of bass when I was sixteen. Doubt I can remember any of it."

Interesting, I thought, storing that information for later.

Nick noticed me eyeing the blue-and-black badge on the lapel of her leather jacket that read "The Despair Faction," AFI's fan club, and said, "I was thinking I should get a lip ring like Davey Havok's now that my lip's swelled up anyway." He was the lead singer.

"Maybe Dr. Jones can do it. That medical degree must be good for something."

"Oh, *come on*. I'm the most easily intimidated person in the world, but even *I* don't call her that," Nick teased me.

"Are you sure you feel well enough to go out?"

"I've got to face the world sometime."

I wanted to go with her but felt really ill. When she left, I told myself, *now, go*. I was weak, and my head rang. But before I left, I looked for paper and a pen to write a thank-you note to Melissa. I didn't even know what to call her now that she was probably my doctor. *Dear Dr. Babe Gorgeous*, I thought and laughed. *There's a good start. That would be funny if I were leaving the country tomorrow forever. Dear Dr. Melissa. I can't call her that. Dear Melissa, I am desperate for your friendship and would do anything to get it. When you go to work in the morning, I'll be sitting outside your surgery. When you leave to go home, I'll be sitting in the same spot like a potted plant.* I wondered if I'd have to fall on my head again to get her attention. I tried to think of reasons being my friend would be good for *her. Dear Melissa, I am of above-average intelligence and have fairly good hygiene.* In the end, I scribbled, *"Dear Melissa, thank you for everything. You are an extremely kind person."* I left the note in the kitchen with my telephone number. I went home with a heavy heart, thinking I'd never see her again and that all her friendliness had been neutralized by my stupid head injury. I wondered what would happen if I showed up at her surgery and asked her to pierce something.

Melissa rang me that evening to see how I was feeling. I felt queasy and flu-like, but I knew that was the result of not taking

my medication properly. She told me if I felt better by the weekend, she'd take me to Camden Lock. My stomach muscles finally took a break from strangling me from inside. While I rested, I listened to Nirvana concerts that included the song "Rape Me." I played one in particular, from the Catalyst in Santa Cruz, California, June 18, 1991, because Kurt just screams and screams. It was the first time "Rape Me" was performed live. There's a lot of emotion in it.

On Saturday, I met Melissa in front of Camden Town station, and she took me to Camden Lock, the street market by the canal, to look for live-music CDs. We walked back to the Camden tube, rode the northern line all the way down to the central line, got off at Notting Hill Gate and followed the crowds to Portobello Road Market, with its brightly painted flats, pubs, and shopfronts. I bought some cheap jumpers and socks, and then we stopped at the Dub Vendor Record Shack on Ladbroke Grove to check out some reggae. It was like Chrissie Hynde had said, reggae had been the soundtrack for punk. "Look at me." I posed under the Westway. "I am the Clash!" Melissa took a photo of me with her mobile phone.

Later we met Nick at the Iskem for a meal. I felt like a fifteen-year-old boy. Melissa's beauty was distracting. Sometimes I'd have to ask her to repeat things. I wanted to hold her and stroke her sexy, tousled hair very gently. She made a kind of hush in my heart.

Nick brought her AFI CDs by my bedsit the next day and we listened to those, my best Nirvana bootlegs, and bands I was fond of that were obscure in the States like the Wall, Abrasive Wheels, and the Partisans. Soon we fell into a routine. She came to see me nearly every day. If I was out boxing, she'd sit on the outside steps and wait for me. If I went busking, I left a note on the door telling her where I'd be. Mostly we talked and listened to tunes. Like me, she was mostly involved in the worlds of books and music. She helped me write songs, and was funny and charming, as I played my guitar. I felt she was a rare person.

I wondered if I could talk her into looking for a used bass. Every time I'd brought up the idea, she said she'd be too shy to play in front of anyone anyway. She had returned to her own flat, and I offered to visit her in Bethnal Green, but she said she felt claustrophobic there. I guessed that maybe it felt too personal to her, and it was her personal space that had been violated. But she said she didn't feel like she could keep living at Melissa's indefinitely, even though Melissa had asked her to stay. She said she was feeling introverted since the attack but was comfortable around me because I'd been there.

Nick liked my stories about getting arrested for civil disobedience when I was an AIDS activist with ACT UP/DC. She gave me a long-sleeved, black-and-white ACT UP Manchester T-shirt, which I prized. "When I was in DC Jail," I said, "chatting with a woman in her cell, she told me she'd murdered her girlfriend."

"Whatever did you say?" Nick asked eagerly.

"I said, 'Oh, so you're single? Are you dating?'"

Nick started laughing.

"Not really. I didn't know what to say. Once I went to the United States Botanic Gardens and planted marijuana seeds in with the ferns then dropped dope seeds on the White House lawn through the wrought-iron fence when the guards weren't looking. It was during that stupid Just Say No to Drugs campaign. Another time, I put pink-and-black ACT UP/DC stickers—'Until There's a Cure, There's ACT UP'—on the soles of my shoes and took the White House tour. I peeled them off and stuck them to the carpet every time I bent over and pretended to tie my shoe. But the funniest thing was after the 1987 March on Washington for Gay and Lesbian Civil Rights. We'd been arrested at the Supreme Court for protesting against the sodomy statutes, and some of us refused to pay our fines. One of the women with me had given the alias Connie Lingus. In a packed courtroom, the judge referred to her as '*Ms. Lingus*' and everyone started laughing. We were each given a receipt with 'Three days in DC Jail' written on it. We were kind of depressed, thinking about

 PISSING IN A RIVER

peeing in front of an audience in the horrible prison toilet, until we happened to glance at her receipt. In proper last name, first name format, the first line read, 'Lingus, Connie.'"

Nick took me to see Rabies Babies when they played in Hackney at the Lord Cecil pub. She thought the pink-haired guitarist was cute. And we went to see Intensive Care and Deadline with Melissa. But we liked catching shows by older bands like Stiff Little Fingers best. We usually met up with Melissa once a week, and Nick and I stayed at her flat if it was late. I started carrying at least one extra dose of medication in my pocket just in case. Sometimes Nick and I had a night out at Blush, a nearby lesbian club that had a gaudy pink-and-orange sign out front and did nice veggie meals. But mostly we walked places or stayed inside because we didn't have any money, even though as the Clash song "Cheapskates" says, "*I don't like to hang about in this lonely room / 'cos London is for going out and trying to hear a tune.*"

One night we walked to the video shop and rented a film about football hooliganism. The rest of the night I couldn't stop singing, "Get yer tits out, get yer tits out, get yer tits out for the lads!" Nick was doubled over laughing. "I can't help it," I said. "It's stuck in my head now."

"Why don't you sing it for Melissa?" Nick asked. "I dare you."

I didn't get to see Melissa as often as I liked because she had a grown-up job and a busy schedule with her own circle of friends. In other words, she had a life. But Nick and I went busking, and I'll always remember her in her black jacket, carrying my plastic-wrap-covered amp against her body so it wouldn't get wet. While I played, she would entreat onlookers for coinage and clap her hands in black fingerless mitts. I had a pair of gray ones and found I could actually play with them on if I was really cold.

When I felt hesitant, I would look over at Nick and she would cock her head at me and grin, rain slanting down her face. Her presence was reassuring, and I tried out new songs that we'd written together like "Rapist Nazi, Fuck Off!" When we made enough money, we ordered pizza from Pizza Hut or Tasti Pizza, which both delivered. Or we rang up Spicy Wok on Seven Sisters Road. It did a lot of different curries like king prawn, vegetable, and mushroom. It wasn't expensive and had free delivery. The nights were getting colder, and the curries were a treat.

Nick often stayed overnight at mine, and I knew she was afraid of being alone. We slept crammed into my single bed. Lately she seemed agitated and troubled about something she wouldn't talk about. When Nick didn't appear for two consecutive afternoons, I was worried. I told myself that just because she and Melissa were my entire London social life, that didn't mean *she* didn't have other mates she'd been neglecting. I tried calling her on the phone but got no reply. I rang Melissa, but she hadn't heard from Nick either. Four days passed, then a week, and I became genuinely concerned—beyond my usual, oversensitive OCD paranoia that I was unlikable and somehow at fault. It was hard to go busking without her.

On Saturday, Melissa rang to ask if she could come round. When I opened up the door with its panes of stained glass, I was so happy to see her I had to stop myself from jumping all over her like a puppy. I'd just finished showering and I was barefoot, wearing a faded, black-and-yellow 999 tour T-shirt from the late seventies. I'd re-dyed the green portion of my hair because it looked too sallow against the bright pink. My hair was supposed to look like the fluorescent cover of the first Sex Pistols album. My tiny shower didn't drain well. My feet were green from standing in the run-off water from my hair.

Melissa gave me a quick hug. "How are you? What in God's name have you done to your feet?" She threw her black denim jacket on my bed and took off her round, blue-tinted sunglasses. When she unzipped her black hooded sweatshirt, I saw a black Angelic Upstarts T-shirt I thought suited her that said "I'm An Upstart." She didn't wait for an answer and walked around my room looking at pictures I'd stuck to the walls with Blu-Tack.

Kurt Cobain in a London launderette. Kurt lying on his back playing a Univox Hi-Flyer. Kurt in a dress.

Melissa sat on my bed and rifled through my Nirvana bootlegs. I sat next to her. She rubbed the top of my head dry with her hand and ran her fingers through my hair. "Me darlin', it's not just your feet."

I had jumped out of the shower and dressed quickly because, even though it was bright and sunny outside, my room was chilly. When Melissa had knocked on my front window, I'd run to let her in without looking in a mirror. "What is it?" I asked.

"You've got a green forehead."

"I never. Oh, go on."

"Don't believe me, mutant."

I went to the bathroom and looked in the mirror. "You can barely notice it." I pulled on a red-and-black plaid shirt, the flannel worn thin, and snapped on a green, leopard-print studded bracelet around my left wrist.

"A green forehead doesn't have to stand out to be noticeable." Melissa leaned back, crossing her ankles, her feet encased in black bovver boots. "I'm feeling dead anxious about Nick. I haven't been able to reach her all week."

"Me neither. Maybe she's out with her mates 'cause she's feeling better." Hair-dying always makes me feel optimistic.

"It's not like her not to be around at all. I've left messages. I've gone to her flat. We used to be really close when Jake was still here. They're my best mates. The three of us did everything together. Now I don't know." Her voice grew quiet. "But it isn't like her not to give me a bell when I've asked her to."

"Not one single bell?" I played with a ring on her pink-tartan bondage trousers.

Melissa eyed me suspiciously, not sure if I was taking the piss. "Sweetheart, to give us a bell means ringing up on the telephone."

"I know what it means. The dog and pony."

"The what?" She rubbed her forehead, gazing at me with eyes

the color of the sweet roasted chestnuts I bought in bags from street vendors when I was busking around St. Paul's Cathedral and the Tower of London.

"Cockney rhyming slang. I can't believe you don't know it. Dog and pony, telephone me."

"Dog and *bone*." Melissa tried not to laugh. "Dog and *bone* is the telephone."

Damn, I thought because I'd been imitating her accent. I really wanted to sound like her. Nick's Mancunian was also affecting me, and I never quite knew how my vowels were going to come out whenever I opened my mouth.

Melissa had made a list of places she thought Nick might go and asked that we split it in half and look for her.

"Isn't that a bit extreme?" I said. "Why are you so concerned? She'll think we're stalking her. She has a right to privacy."

"I know. It's a feeling I have. Like she might be reacting to what happened to her. Like she might do something self-destructive."

"Does she normally do that?" I asked.

Melissa hesitated. "She's really depressed about the rape. And she doesn't always take the best care of herself."

"Are you thinking of something in particular?"

"Another time she disappeared from my life. Even if we don't see each other, we usually talk on the phone at least once a week. I went round her flat and found her deathly ill from a really bad flu. She'd had it at least a week and could barely get out of bed to go to the loo. She wasn't eating or answering the phone. She hadn't called her clinic. I made her stay with me until she got better."

"Give me my half of the list," I said.

TRACK 19 **IN HIS HANDS**

I scoured the gay and punk clubs of East London. Then one evening, at the end of my list with no joy, I ended up in the West

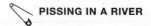

End in Chelsea near the Sloane Square tube because I'd remembered a lesbian pub I'd been to there once donkey's ages ago, an oasis in a desert of posh called Gateways. It was the oldest continuously running lesbian pub in London. I wasn't sure exactly where it had been, but I remembered which side of the street it had been on. I walked down trendy King's Road, which still had some historic punk left in it. I passed the black shopfront and green letters of BOY, the punk shop that made the neon-striped shirts Melissa sometimes wore. She'd gotten them before BOY became such a designer thing. I had a yellow leopard T-shirt from there, the only thing I could afford.

After I found the building I thought had been Gateways but wasn't, and had exhausted all other possibilities, I turned off the King's Road and went to the Chelsea embankment. I passed Vivienne Westwood's World's End, the shop that had once been the legendary SEX where the Sex Pistols were born. Knackered, I sat on a bench above the Thames, looking out at wrought-iron lamp posts strung with white fairy lights. It started to rain. I zipped up my green army-surplus jacket, put up the hood, and headed for the tube, singing the Elvis Costello song "(I Don't Want to Go to) Chelsea" under my breath. Back at mine, I rang up Melissa from the communal payphone in the entranceway outside my room. When the line beeped, I pushed in a 10p coin.

"How you doin' darlin', alright?" Melissa's familiar voice made me feel warmer and drier already. She had reached the end of her half of the list and hadn't come up with anything either. She gave me Nick's address and warned me not to walk there alone late at night because the area could be a bit dodgy. I told her I'd been there before. It was one of the areas I'd lurked in when I'd been at university looking for the people in my head.

The next day, I walked down Old Bethnal Green Road past council estates with tower blocks shooting up into the sky and peace-sign graffiti. For a change, it was damp and chilly. I was wearing a woolly gray Doc Martens beanie. It had "Dr Martens Air Cushioned Sole" and the Dr Martens cross logo embroidered in bright yellow thread in a circle on the front. I pulled it down over my cold ears and it caught on my copper-colored eyebrow ring. By the time I'd got it sorted, it was raining bullets. I walked past blackened brick terraces, past a school, and down Pollards Row. The large, bleak Westminster Arms looked like a ship against the gray sky. I found Nick's Victorian and pressed the buzzer. Melissa had told me Nick lived on the first floor facing out, so I called up to the window that was hers. I lingered in front of her building, hoping she'd come home. When I got hungry, I wandered down a desolate side street to the Sky Blue Fish Bar for cod and chips.

I didn't want to go back to my lonely room, so I drifted aimlessly around the area. I pushed open the yellow door of a pub called the Hope, but Nick wasn't inside playing on any of the fruit machines. In my head, "Pretty Green" by the Jam began to play, "*I've got a pocket full of pretty green. / I'm gonna put it in the fruit machine.*" I strolled past a faded, green shopfront that said "Holloways" next to a billboard advertising liquor and a poster proclaiming "London Flooding is a Real Danger." I turned onto Pollard Street with its corrugated metal barriers and old cars parked by the side of the road.

I roamed the streets of plain brown terraces—Quilter, Barnet, Wimbolt—their names adhering to my brain and becoming part of the legend of my quest like I was a character in an epic novel. I passed the blue sign of Imperial Van Hire, churches, dead white curtains in flat windows, so much corrugated silver fencing I thought I was inside a Coke can, more housing estates, green wrought-iron fencing around dead brown grass, and the London Picture Centre. My shoes slid on wet cobblestone roads piled with rubbish.

I moved further out of Nick's neighborhood, going all the way to Brick Lane in Banglatown. The Brick Lane Market was now closed, and I breathed in the warm, spicy smells emanating from the curry houses. I felt empty. To cheer myself up I sang "Wasteland" by the Jam under my breath. "'*Meet me on the*

wastelands, the ones behind / the old houses, the ones left stand-
ing prewar / the ones overshadowed by the monolith monstrosi-
ties councils call homes."'

It was dark, but I couldn't make myself head for home. I went down Brady Street all the way to Whitechapel and ended up at the street market on Whitechapel Road. I browsed through stalls of fruit and vegetables, clothes and household items illuminated by bare white light bulbs. Across the road, the gold letters of London Hospital were visible above the pitches. The rain slowed to a drizzle. I looked at lit-up dead chickens hanging in rows beneath green awnings. I slogged through cardboard boxes, broken wooden crates and onion sacks, pretending to be interested in grapes, oranges, tomatoes, potatoes and fuzzy pink jumpers. I watched women in saris and dresses with their blue-and-white-striped Tesco's bags hurrying toward the tube.

I huddled deeper in my coat. Too cold to loiter any longer, I took the tube all the way to Hampstead because I didn't want to go back to my room alone. By the time I reached Melissa's flat, I was almost in tears. Upset at not finding Nick and feeling so bloody lonely I ached, I hoped Melissa was home and not otherwise engaged. The lights were off in the front room and she didn't answer my knock. I argued with myself that it was ridiculous to stand outside and wait for her. I was an adult. I was being too needy.

I walked to where she kept her car and it was there. I went up the road to the Old Orleans, sat at one of the green outdoor tables and ate a small white pizza, hoping she'd stroll right past me if she were coming home on the tube. When I'd been at university, the Old Orleans had been a Pizza Pizza Express, a pretty, white building with blue neon. When it started to pour, I abandoned my table and ducked into the local pub, a tall, brown-and-white-striped brick building with "THE HORSE AND GROOM" in big gold letters on the front. I sat on a barstool in the window and drank a warm pint, continuing to watch the street. At least the pub had remained the same.

When I was too restless to sit any longer, I walked the long way round to Melissa's flat, past gray, red, and white terraces and flashy, brightly painted shops. Pretty lights glowed softly from inside and I felt very much on the outside, watching my breath turn white. It seemed gentle and quiet here, but I felt as empty as I had in Bethnal Green. Melissa still wasn't home. Exhausted from walking in circles all day, I leaned against her door. I told myself I'd only stay ten minutes, randomly deciding ten minutes, though bordering on needy, wasn't actually criminally pathetic. The rain pelted the petals off the last of the roses in her front garden. It went through me like silver darts. I moved some wet leaves around with the toe of my shoe.

I couldn't help it. I started writing a tune about Melissa.

> *I can lie like denial here at your feet,*
> *but I think you're entitled to see through me.*
> *When the angels fall I will be ready,*
> *sometimes when I look around there aren't any.*
> *When the angels fall there will be plenty,*
> *but you see right now there aren't that many.*

I'm afraid it sounded a bit like the Beatles' "Norwegian Wood."

Finally I saw Melissa coming down the lane from the tube in her long, beige raincoat. I was relieved she was alone. "Come inside, misery-guts," Melissa said, putting her key in the latch. "Why the sad face? What's happened? Did you find Nick? You'll catch your death." She closed her umbrella and I followed her into the warm flat. "Get out of those wet things." She took my parka and wool hat and hung them in the entranceway. I pulled off my gray fingerless gloves. Melissa felt my green army-surplus jumper from Portobello Road. "Love, you're soaked through. What are you doing here?"

"I wanted to see you." I hung my head in shame.

"You're freezing." She took me upstairs and ran hot water into the large bathtub. I stood there limply, morale depleted, watch-

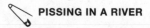

ing it fill. When Melissa went downstairs, I peeled off my jeans and black trainers and stepped into the tub. The hot water was soothing on my aching muscles. I had a bit of a scratchy throat and a headache. Melissa knocked and asked if she should come in or leave the dry clothes she'd brought me outside the door. I told her, what the hell, come in. Normally I'm squeamish about my body, but she was a doctor. She saw naked women every day without being allowed to judge them. At least that's what I told myself. Melissa perched on the rim of the tub and dipped her hand in the water. "Stay here tonight. It's raining. It's late. Why'd you want to see me?"

"To say hi."

She arched her eyebrows, waiting for me to say more. But I didn't know what to say or how *not* to say it. "I'm sorry you had to wait for me," she said finally.

"Don't be silly. It was rude of me to just barge over. You've got better things to do than look after me."

"I'm sure Nick'll turn up," Melissa said to make me feel better. "I'm probably just overreacting."

I asked, "Did you have a nice time, wherever you were?"

"I was out with Martin."

"That bloke you've been seeing?" I sounded like it was the best news I'd heard all year. It was pitiful.

"Yeah. Went for a meal then to the cinema. *Butterfly Kiss*. Weird, religious, lesbian serial-killer film."

Great, I thought, *lesbians as crazy murderers*. "Did you enjoy yourself?"

"It was alright. Had a lovely vegetable curry with pappadams and aloo matar paratha." Melissa shook her hand dry.

"Is that bread stuffed with potatoes and peas? You look nice."

She was wearing a silky, maroon-and-turquoise-striped shirt over a black-and-red Stiff Little Fingers "INFLAMMABLE MATERIAL" T-shirt. Through the picture of the cover of my favorite SLF record album, I saw the delicate arc of her breasts. She had two silver rings on her fingers. A plain band and a rose that accentu-ated the graceful way she moved her hands. She smelled good. Melissa looked surprised by my comment. "Ta, love." She pulled off her sexy, black fake-suede boots, slid off the vegan green studded bracelet fastened around her wrist with little hand-cuffs and left the bathroom. She returned and put a mug of hot tea on the plastic soap holder that stretched across the tub.

After a good long soak, I put on the black sweatshirt, blue flannel pajama bottoms and thick socks Melissa had left me to wear. Then I took the medication wrapped in cling film from my damp jeans pocket and swallowed it with the dregs of the tea. Melissa had already gone to bed. I stuck my head inside her bedroom to say goodnight. "I'm sorry I can't stay up and chat, love," Melissa said. "I've got an early start tomorrow." She was covering an extra surgery session for one of her partners who was out ill. As I turned to go downstairs, Melissa groaned, "Wait. I took the sheets off the bed."

"That's okay. I'll sleep on the settee."

"And you don't have enough blankets." She sighed. "It's cold tonight. Crawl in here with me where it's warm. There's plenty of room."

"Okay." I climbed gingerly into her bed, making sure not to crowd her. The rose-colored duvet was heavy and soothing.

She turned off the bedside lamp. "Goodnight, love." Melissa rolled over to sleep.

"Ta for the hot bath and for letting me stay," I said.

"No worries, love," Melissa murmured. In a few minutes, I heard her breathing slow down.

I stared at the back of her head. The Oasis song "Don't Go Away" was playing in my brain with Liam singing, "*Damn my education, I can't find the words to say / with all the things caught in my mind.*" Those lines stayed wedged in my thoughts because it was how I felt around Melissa. But when I wasn't paying attention, my mind played the first verse of the song as,

Cold and frosty morning, there's not a lot to say
about the things caught in my mind.
And as the day was dawning, my brain flew away
with all the things caught in my mind.

It was supposed to be *"plane"*—*"my* plane *flew away."* But when I was near Melissa, it *was* like my brain flew away, and my reaction to her beauty made me nervous. Now I held as still as possible, terrified of fidgeting and disturbing her. I held my breath and tried letting it out silently. I was afraid of accidentally moving too close to her in my sleep. *But you can clearly see she isn't bothered you're a lesbian,* I told myself. *She doesn't treat you any differently.*

Usually I repeated my prayers of protection for hours because my brain never got the message I'd completed them, like intellectually knowing I'd just eaten and remaining viscerally famished. But lying in the dark, peaceful next to Melissa's warmth, I fell asleep painlessly, my OCD more like a residue, an echo.

TRACK 20 **SAVE YOURSELF**

The blue Vespa Lounge sparkled in the rain. I looked up at its bright orange sign, sighed and went in. It was my third pub of the night. Melissa and I had looked up all the gay pubs and clubs in *Time Out.* We'd also gone on an Internet site called Gingerbeer that had up-to-the-minute information on London's lesbian scene. From the women at Gingerbeer I learned that Gateways had shut in 1985. I also discovered that the Due South, which I considered my local, had just closed.

My eyes adjusted to the Vespa's blue interior. To my utter astonishment, Nick was sitting in a corner having a pint. I slid into the chair next to her.

"Alright?"

"Alright, mate! Whatcha doin' 'ere, 'manda?" She was totally trolleyed.

"What am *I* doing here? Looking for *you. That's* what I'm doing here. Don't you know Melissa and I have been *frantic*? Where've you *been*?"

"I can't sleep." Nick's normally piercing green eyes looked dull. "I'm afraid to be alone. Where else would I be?"

"You could be with me. Why didn't you give us a ring? Melissa's worried sick about you. Why haven't you been over to see us?"

"I couldn't."

"Why not? You always have done."

"I know, but I couldn't anymore."

"But I've missed you." I reached out my hand to touch her rumpled hair, trying not to show how hurt I was.

"It's been ages and I'm still whingeing and moaning about something you can't even call a real rape. I'm not getting over it, me."

"It hasn't been that long. And it *was* a real rape. Are you fucking kidding me? Are you telling me he *didn't* violate you? Traumatize you? No, I didn't think so. Maybe we should have pressured you to report it."

"How many times can I spill my guts on your eternal shoulder of kindness? Or Melissa's? I already can't repay either of you."

"Being mates isn't about repaying," I said.

Nick pointed an unlit fag at me. "No, I find me own places to stay, me. I've got it sussed, mate."

"What are you doing?" I grabbed the coffin nail from between her fingers and tossed it on the floor. "You don't smoke."

"Give it to me." She held out her hand and looked at me with heavy-lidded eyes, not realizing I'd already thrown the cigarette away.

"How did you get like this all of a sudden? You're coming back to mine," I said.

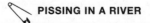

Nick ran a hand through her hair, thick and rich like Guinness stout, looking completely out of it. She rested her chin in her hands. She was wearing her black leather jacket and a torn yellow jersey that was held together with safety pins. She looked beyond mere fatigue. I stood and tried to pull her up with me by her collar. A woman joined us, setting another pint of bitter in front of Nick and sitting down cradling the other. I couldn't believe Nick was actually going to drink it. She was ready to wipe up the floor. I didn't think she'd be able to stand, let alone walk.

"Who's this?" the woman demanded.

"A mate," Nick said. "She's just leaving."

"She's not," I said firmly. "She is taking you home."

The woman rested her hand heavily on Nick's shoulder. "Go an' chat up someone else, lover." She had a Devonshire accent.

I had the feeling that Nick didn't really know this woman. Why was she talking to me like this? She seemed gruff, abrasive and, I decided, predatory. She didn't smile, and I admit I was over-protective of Nick. "I'm not chatting her up," I said, as the woman continued to eye me warily. "I'm concerned about my mate."

"Sod off," Nick muttered, morosely crumpling up an empty crisps packet in her fist. "Leave me alone."

Stung, I asked, "What's the matter with you?"

"I just can't see you right now, Amanda." Nick downed most of her pint.

The strange, raptorial woman put her arm around Nick's waist, half holding her up, and they limped out of the pub together. I grabbed at the sleeve of Nick's jacket. "You don't have to do this. Stop using yourself. Stop giving it all away." Having said that, I felt a right prat for assuming I knew what was best for her. I followed the two of them out into the rain. "You've got people who love you, you know," I shouted after Nick. "*I* love you, mate." The wolf opened her umbrella, and they huddled chummily underneath it. I stood in the open with my naked head. "Come back." I watched their figures recede.

Later I stood in front of my red-brick Victorian feeling shattered, looking at my protruding ground-floor window. The lights were on behind the yellow curtains in the basement flat as I walked up the few steps to mine. I wondered if someone nice lived down there.

I rang Melissa's mobile to let her know I'd found Nick and she could go home if she was still out looking. "What?" It was loud on Melissa's end of the line.

"Go home!" I yelled.

"Hang on, I'm walking outside."

It was only slightly less noisy so I didn't explain the circumstances. I just shouted, "Go home! I'll ring you tomorrow."

I was lying in bed not sleeping, listening to the Clash song "One Emotion" over and over again, when my buzzer rang. I turned off the CD player, pulled back the curtain and peered out. Nick was standing there, looking wet, dirty, and crumpled from the rain.

"What are you doing here?" I held the door open.

"I came to apologize." She looked awfully pale and ill.

"What's happened to what's-her-name?"

Nick shrugged. "I left when she fell asleep. I felt too restless to stay."

"Did you at least leave her a note?" I asked, still a little hurt.

"Believe me, she didn't expect one. It wasn't like that."

"What was it like then?"

"You know what it was like."

"For fuck's sake, Nick. Why'd you disappear on me?"

"I had to. Don't you see? That night. I could've got you killed an' all. I never should've gone off the main road."

I helped her out of her wet clothes and stuck her under a hot shower, getting myself soaked in the process. I dried my hair with a towel and plugged in the electric kettle. I put dry clothes in the bathroom for Nick and told her I was going into the hall to ring Melissa.

"Don't let her come over," Nick pleaded. "Not when I'm in this state."

"I need to let her know you're alright. She's really concerned about you."

Sounding half asleep, Melissa said, "Brilliant," when I told her Nick had just turned up. "Is she alright? Do you need me to come over?"

"Nah, much as I love your company. We'll pop round yours tomorrow."

Nick came out of the bathroom and I rubbed my towel over her head. I handed her a steaming mug of tea and said, "Pour that down ya, you silly git." She was shivering, and I wrapped a blanket around her. "Alcohol poisoning is a real thing, you know," I said.

Eventually, from her hesitant spurts of confession, I learned that Nick had been going out every night, getting legless and going home with strangers.

"You're not being responsible," I said. "It isn't safe."

"Not as safe as walking down the road to catch a fucking bus?" Nick asked sarcastically.

"It isn't okay to put yourself at risk on purpose."

"At risk? A woman isn't going to rape me."

"Oh, that's right, I forgot. No woman would ever put you in danger or physically harm you. That never happens in the lesbian community. Are you at least having sex with all these women safely?"

"No oral sex without cling film or an HIV test." She saluted me like a soldier.

"Well, I see it as a cry for help."

"Listen, mate. I slept with those women trying to feel safe."

"I know," I said.

After two cups of tea, Nick looked less defiant and more despondent. Her small, silver eyebrow ring and the earrings in her right ear glittered in the lamplight. "If you let me stay, I'll make it worth your while."

"You what? Sorry?"

"If you let me stay, you can fuck me," Nick said harshly.

"*Are you out of your fucking head?* Do you think that's what I want?" I nearly screamed at her. "You're fucking kidding, right?"

"Not if you don't want me to be."

"How can you do that to yourself? And how can you think so little of me? Do you really think I'd take advantage of you like that? That's really naff. What the *hell* are you thinking?"

"I can't keep coming here expecting you to take care of me. Maybe you want to have other women over."

"If I had other plans, I'd just bloody tell you," I snapped. "It's not a fucking problem."

"I couldn't show up offering fuck all."

"What a fucking naff idea," I repeated. "I can't believe you came up with it. Are you on drugs or something?"

"Only crack."

I gasped in horror, and Nick finally gave me a weary shell of a smile.

"I'm only taking the piss, Amanda," she said, but then she started to cry. "I can't live with the guilt that's inside me. I could have got you raped an' all. It was my fault. I had a few pints and thought I was bulletproof. That area's dead rough. I never should've gone off the High Street."

"That doesn't make it your fault. No one has the right to harm you."

"Summat terrible could have happened to you, d'you know wha' I mean? I can't live with it, me."

"I made a conscious decision to help you," I said. "No one held a gun to my head. I could have thought, *ugh, some bloody stupid woman has turned off the main road and got herself in trouble.* And I could've carried on down Kingsland High Street, got my bus, and left it at that. I chose to go after you. Whatever else may have happened, that was my choice and I have to live with it." I pulled the blanket more tightly around her. The room was dead frigid and I realized the radiators weren't working. My electric-

ity key had run down and I couldn't recharge it until the next day. "I could never hurt you." I ran my finger down her cheek. I could see my breath. "It's fucking freezing in here." I made Nick put on a sweatshirt and extra-heavy socks. She curled up next to me in the small bed. I put my arms around her. "I can understand why all those women want to take you home," I said, trying to make her feel better about having offered me sex. "It's not that I don't think you're attractive."

"Bollocks."

"Really." I ran my hand through her wondrous hair. "You're well fit. You're sex on legs." We both laughed. "Seriously, I think you're beautiful. And you're vulnerable. I don't want those women taking advantage of you."

"They don't scare me. Nowt scares me," Nick claimed defiantly.

In my head, I started playing the Indigo Girls song "Kid Fears."

"Was Melissa really worried about me?" Nick asked quietly.

"Yes, she bloody well was."

"Bollocks," Nick said, but I felt her body relax.

TRACK 21   **THE GHOST AT NUMBER ONE**

When I woke up, I went through the pockets of my trousers looking for dosh. I only found 50p. I went to a cash machine, got out a fiver, and ran to the newsagent's to top up my electricity key. I added money to it in one-pound increments to pay for my heat. Back at mine, I put the kettle on and let the room get a little warmer. Nick woke up as I put a cup of instant coffee on the floor next to her.

I hugged myself. "I put the heat on for a few minutes, but I daren't start turning it on during the day or my money's gonna run out. It costs a bomb." It was only autumn. We huddled over our coffees.

"Let's go to the caff," Nick said. "It'll at least be warmer there, yeah?"

We stayed in the café for several hours, drinking multiple pots of tea and eating fried eggs and baked beans on toast. Then we amused ourselves by going in some music shops and trying out expensive equipment. Later we hung out at the British Museum in the Egyptian mummy rooms.

In the early evening, we went to Melissa's flat. Nick said she was knackered and a little hungover. She went to have a lie-down, giving me the opportunity to tell Melissa what she'd done. We heard Nick listening to the Ruts on the portable CD player in her room.

"She *what?* She came *on* to you?"

"To have a place to sleep. She's been getting pissed and going home with different women every night not to be alone. She said she couldn't inflict herself on me anymore without offering something. When she said she'd have sex with me if I let her stay, I felt absolutely gutted."

"After Jake left, I don't know, something happened," Melissa said. "Nick didn't come round as much. She feels a sort of reticence around me. I don't know why."

"I think she's a little intimidated by you. Like she doesn't want to disappoint you or something. Maybe it's because you're older. And a doctor."

"So what? Do I act in a way that is off-putting? Did I suddenly become a different person now that Jake's gone? Nick's thirty-bloody-three. What am I, some historical punk artifact? She doesn't find *you* intimidating."

"*I sing on the street for money*," I reminded her sardonically. "I have no position of authority over anyone."

Melissa frowned. "Bollocks. The three of us were best mates. We went to the punk clubs together. Nick spent most nights here. It was like having another sister."

"What were you like in the early days?" I asked, imagining her dancing wildly.

"Visions of tartan skirts, bum-flaps, chains, neckties, fake leather trousers and heavy eye-makeup. And I needed less sleep than I do now."

"Do you like being a doctor?"

"I love being a doctor." Melissa was a partner in a GP practice in St. John's Wood.

"But you're a cracking artist, too."

Melissa had finally shown me some of her paintings: a devastated city smothered in American flags, President Bush eating Iraqi babies like cereal, Regent's Park in the rain. And she had beautiful sketches of Hampstead Heath and London punks. She blushed. "Well, ta. I'm glad you think so."

I heard a whiff of "Dope for Guns" coming from Nick's room. "The Iran-Contra song," I said. "What if someone bought an election and nobody cared? I voted for Jimmy Carter from Exeter on an absentee ballot, so I got to share the joy of the American democratic process with the girls in my residence hall. The results weren't particularly impressive. When they said on the BBC that Reagan had won, I kept thinking I was watching *Not the Nine O'Clock News* by mistake." *Not the Nine O'Clock News* had been my favorite television program, a comedy of fake news reports that mocked Ronald Reagan mercilessly by airing real footage of him falling over and being a complete idiot. I remembered the Ramones' song "Bonzo Goes to Bitburg" about Reagan's visit to a SS cemetery released some years later as a British single. All over Europe, he was such a figure of ridicule that my perspective was skewed and I never believed he could actually win the election.

"What were you reading at university?"

"English. That's what I've always studied."

"Not music?"

I shook my head. "I just wanted to play it, not study it."

After listening to "Dope for Guns" a few times, Nick switched to "Staring at the Rude Boys."

"Do you have that split CD?" I asked. "The Ruts and Penetration live on BBC Radio One?" It had been recorded in 1979 at the Paris Theatre in London.

"It's only one of my favorite officially released CDs ever."

"Mine, too. The only band that could have been right up there with the Clash."

"Another overdose tragedy," Melissa said because lead singer Malcolm Owen had been a heroin addict.

After "Jah War," one of the best punk-reggae songs of all time, had played for about the fifteenth time, Melissa wanted to check on Nick.

"I've been known to listen to 'Jah War' for five hours plus without stopping," I volunteered helpfully. "The Radio One version. Once I accidentally fell asleep listening to 'Maria' on that new Blondie album." I followed Melissa down the hall. "When I woke up I felt sick like I'd eaten too many sweets."

"I only listen to Blondie up until the *Parallel Lines* album," Melissa whispered.

I'd seen Blondie in Hollywood on the *Parallel Lines* tour, and the lead guitar on "One Way Or Another" was orgasmic. I'd almost been hit by a limo as I ran across the road to get a Blondie T-shirt.

Nick was asleep on top of the bed. Melissa turned off the boom box and covered her with a duvet. She brought a teapot, milk, sugar and my favorite chocolate Digestives to the front room on a tray. She set it on the wood-and-glass coffee table. "I'll be mother, shall I?"

"*My* mother?" I asked, horrified.

Melissa laughed. "That means I pour out."

"Of course it does," I said wearily, "I forgot." We sat on the settee near the window. "Once I listened to one side of the first Sex Pistols record for twelve hours straight," I confessed. "I had the turntable set on 'repeat.'"

"Which side?" Melissa asked.

 PISSING IN A RIVER

"The one with 'Anarchy in the UK' on it." I didn't volunteer the information that I'd been having a complete mental breakdown at the time.

"What's that band?" Melissa nodded at my chest. I was wearing a pink-and-black Explosion T-shirt with a picture of a woman whose head was a television set.

"The Explosion. From Boston. They're the only new punk band I really like. They model themselves after the Clash. They're very *I-hate-the-American-flag-and-everything-it-stands-for*-ish."

I had an orange guitar pick from one of their shows. I got it by crawling across the stage when the guitarist named Dave dropped it. That reminded me of the time I saw a friend I hadn't seen in years and she said, "The last time I saw you, you were crawling across the floor to get closer to Chrissie Hynde." *Man, story of my life*, I thought. I remembered kneeling in Chrissie's sweat after she'd done the same to Iggy Pop's. I like a lot of romance in my life.

"I saw them before I left the States." I sipped my Tetley's and helped myself to another biscuit. "It was the first punk gig I'd been to in ages, and I had a major identity crisis. It was an all-ages show, and most of the people there were under twenty-one. I used to know all the punks in my town who turned up at local shows. And there I was, granny punk 1977, sitting on the back left corner of the stage watching the boys stage-dive and really resenting it. It used to be me up there. The last time I stage-dove was at a Dead Kennedys concert in 1984. After that, the community center banned punk forever."

"A dark time," Melissa said. "The year the Clash broke up."

"When one male adolescent ran across the stage right in front of me and leapt off, I was sorely tempted. But then I thought, *am I too old and fat to stage-dive?*"

"Never!"

"I had a vision of myself thundering across the stage, knocking guitar players and microphone stands out of my way, and heaving myself into the crowd. And having it part like the Red Sea."

We started laughing hysterically. "I'm taking you stage-diving," Melissa gasped.

"I'll fucking *kill* myself," I protested. "I'll break a leg or crack my head open."

"That's okay," Melissa cried, "I know how to suture!"

I fell on the floor and rolled on the carpet. I was feeling really close to her then.

Melissa put an Angelic Upstarts record on her old phono-graph. I was really into them lately because of her, and I always remembered when someone introduced me to a good punk band. Like Attila the kebab seller in Manchester who'd got me into Stiff Little Fingers the year I was at Exeter and took a trip north. I'd always thought the Upstarts were a racist, fascist, skinhead band, but the opposite was true. The lead singer Mensi was actually a leader of the Anti-Fascist Action group. His lyrics ridiculed Maggie Thatcher's oppressive policies, attacked police brutality, and called for social justice. Ultra-right-wing National Front skinheads initially misinterpreted the Upstarts' leftist songs as supportive of their own cause, and when they found out their mistake, they virulently hated the Upstarts ever after. This created a lot of violence at their shows, and it confused me, seeing them surrounded by all those skinheads—not the cool, right-on skinheads against racism—who'd turned up to cause mayhem. Melissa would never go to see the Upstarts play in person because at their gigs they sometimes used the head of a real slaughtered pig wearing a police hat to symbolize police brutality, and she couldn't stand any form of cruelty to animals.

I'd borrowed a ton of CDs from Melissa: Generation X; the Skids; Slaughter and the Dogs; Sham 69; Chelsea; the Adverts; UK Subs; the Adicts; the Beat; the Redskins; the Damned; the Boomtown Rats; Johnny Moped; the Who; her entire collec-tion of the Real People, including demos, live, and unreleased

stuff; Special Duties; H-Block 101 from Australia; everything she had by the Ruts, including demos, Peel Sessions, concerts from Hamburg and Holland in 1980, Amsterdam, Strathclyde and the Marquee in 1979 and the 1978 Deeply Vale Festival. In Apeldoorn and Strathclyde, they were touring with the Damned and did a cover of "Love Song." Melissa even had a 1978 rehearsal in Bethnal Green.

I had her listening to the Dils and X from Southern California; M.I.A. from Las Vegas; the Dead Kennedys, Rancid, Romeo Void and the Avengers from San Francisco; Hüsker Dü and the Replacements from Minneapolis; Dag Nasty, Minor Threat, and Bad Brains from Washington, DC, and the first REM album.

Everything I didn't have, we found on the Internet. She played me some of her live concert videos, including the Ruts on French television and lots of Rockpalast shows. It was remarkable to see people very early on like the Pretenders, the Clash, the Jam, Patti Smith— everyone I loved. She even had a video of Patti Smith in black sunglasses performing "Hey Joe" and "Horses" on *The Old Grey Whistle Test* in 1976.

"It's late," Melissa said. "Stay the night. You can check out the sound equipment in Jake's room."

"Really? That would be ace," I said. "Are you sure it's no trouble? It *has* been getting rather parky in my bedsit, and I can't afford to heat it as much as I'd like."

We went upstairs, and Melissa sat on the edge of Jake's bed while I fiddled with a digital eight-track recorder that had sixty-four virtual tracks. "Do you realize what I could do with this?" I got excited. "I could make my own CDs." I told Melissa about my original plan to record a CD for RAWA but how I couldn't afford to pay for studio time. "This has all the digital effects you'd ever need, and you can record, mix, and master on it. Jesus fucking Christ Superstar almighty."

Melissa pulled a bed sheet off her sister's large amplifier.

"She has a Vox?" I knelt in front of it reverently. "Fuck me, I love these. It's so *Paul Weller and the Jam*. I've always wanted one." A beautiful Takamine acoustic guitar leaned in a corner. I was afraid to touch it.

"Go on," Melissa said, watching me. "You can play it."

"This is such a Nancy Wilson guitar," I said, stroking its ocher cedar top. "And I have a picture of Kurt playing one. Are you sure it's alright?"

"Jake won't mind. She told me I could do whatever I liked with the stuff in this room. She took everything she wanted with her."

"But guitars are so personal. I know what I'm like with my Gibson."

"Honestly, it's alright. She took a bunch of acoustic guitars with her. Mostly Martins, I think."

"Oh my God, you're so adorable the way you know all about guitars," I said before I could stop myself because I felt really cozy with her. Immediately I was terrified I'd both insulted her and brought up a forbidden subject, my attraction to her, but she just laughed good naturedly. I smiled with relief and knew I was going to pay profoundly later when I tried to sleep. I would go over that line again and again, wondering how I could have said it, wondering what I was going to do about my—*what*— on Melissa. Was it a crush, infatuation, lust? I knew it was deep, will-shattering, soul-crunching love. Having her sit with me like that, looking soft, sexy, and rumpled in thick blue socks and red jeans, her light hair tousled just above the collar of her red T-shirt, she looked almost accessible. And I couldn't stand being inside myself feeling the white-hot agony of my longing for her. I didn't know what to do about it, and I certainly didn't know how I was going to survive it. If only I could—in my mind I saw myself, bright like a flashbulb had just gone off, reach a hand around behind her head and pull her toward me for a sensual, gentle kiss, and I thought the pain would kill me. It was so severe I was surprised I didn't literally become unconscious.

I sat on the bed and held the Takamine in my lap. I clutched its comfortable neck, trying to get my hands to stop shaking.

It curved in the palm of my hand just right. I strummed a few chords to get hold of myself and smiled at its rich, warm tone.

"Play it some more," Melissa encouraged.

I put down the guitar, feeling self-conscious.

"Maybe sometime you'll play for me?" Melissa suggested.

I gazed shyly at my shoes. "I would love to record some songs." I had brought all the pedals I would normally use for recording with me from the States, my purple Electro-Harmonix Small Clone, orange Boss DS-1 distortion, green Ibanez Turbo-screamer and Digital Delay for those ringing, Mick Jones-like leads. I had a picture of Kurt Cobain's battered Small Clone, and he'd used the DS-1 for recording *Bleach*. "Could I even dare ask if your sister left behind a bass?"

"There's one in the wardrobe."

"No kidding? Oh, wicked. Will you really let me use this stuff?"

Melissa nodded. "Abso-bloody-lutely."

"Cheers, Melissa. I really mean it, mate."

"Which guitarists have influenced you the most?"

"Nancy Wilson, James Honeyman-Scott, Mick Jones, Kurt Cobain and Noel Gallagher," I said without hesitation. "And there's nothing like the original Pretenders line-up, with Chrissie Hynde playing aggressive rhythm guitar against James Honeyman-Scott's blistering, melodic leads and Pete Farndon's heavy, melodic bass lines."

"And you busk all day in front of strangers but you're afraid to play in front of me?" Melissa asked teasingly.

"Maybe I'll decide to care about your opinion," I said in the same joking manner.

"I'm feeling moreish," Melissa said.

"Sorry?"

"Moreish. Like you want more of something. Peckish. Hungry." She went downstairs and brought up the rest of the Digestives. "Have another bicky."

We ate biscuits and I crawled around, searching the room.

I found a sampler under the bed and a drum machine with touch-sensitive pads. "Tell me more about you and Nick," I asked. "She doesn't talk about herself."

Melissa crossed one leg over the other, getting more comfortable on the bed. She was wearing a "The Clash: Thinking Man's Yobs" T-shirt and a bright-red tartan bracelet with shiny silver studs that she liked. "Nick used to go around with a girlfriend called Emilia, whose Irish-Catholic family was not overjoyed to learn she was gay. Emilia's got a homophobic brother in London who made her life a misery. Eventually she fucked off back to Belfast. Nick was crushed."

"Oh. Gosh." Of course I'd been in Belfast that day in 1981 when Bobby Sands was elected to parliament from his H-Block, Long Kesh prison cell. I wanted to go back and see his mural on the Falls Road. "How about you?" I asked Melissa.

"How about me *what*?"

"How about you, were you in a relationship? What's your history?"

Melissa looked startled. "Well, I guess that was when I was going out with a bloke called Paul. That wasn't a great time in my life. Let's change the subject."

"How long have you been an artist? Your work's bloody brilliant."

"Donkey's years. I meant let's change the subject back to you. Are you single?"

"I am," I said eagerly. "And you? Are you and Martin serious?"

"No." She stood up, her red drainpipes bagging a little at the knees and ankles. "I'm off to bed. Play around with the sound equipment all you like."

I read instruction manuals for the digital eight-track and the sampler until I fell asleep on top of Jake's unmade bed. I was always doing that at Melissa's house, falling asleep. I'd have to give up my job as a poster child for insomnia if I wasn't careful.

When I awoke, Melissa had already left for work. I didn't mean to, but I picked up the acoustic guitar and wrote a song

 **PISSING IN A RIVER**

about her which I figured I could never sing. It was sweet I thought. But then I told myself to work on a song I could actually use.

TRACK 22 **STRICT TIME**

Ever since I'd found her in the Vespa Lounge, I'd been sticking close by Nick's side. Now it was snowing lightly, the fat flakes like white orchids, as I stood with Nick in front of Melissa's flat. I thought I could hear the snow hiss as it landed. It powdered the shrubbery, making thin twigs look like the first pear blossoms of spring. I'd gone with Nick to the post office to cash her weekly giro, and she'd taken me to the Isle of Whitby, a famous East End pub. It was freezing, but I felt insulated. Melissa answered the door in a maroon dressing gown.

"Hiya, Melissa," I shouted. "Wha'd ya know, love?"

"Where are your shoes? Don't tell me you've been running around London in the dead of winter in nothing but socks. What are you doing to her, Nick?" Melissa stepped back to let us in.

I handed her my soaking-wet sneakers. "What do you *know*, love?" I insisted at the top of my lungs.

"Hush. Get in here." Melissa grabbed my arm and pulled me inside. "Jesus Christ, you're half-drowned."

Nick sighed. "I tried to stop her."

"Melissa, I fell in the Thames," I said proudly.

"Not so much fell in as went for a bloody swim," Nick muttered.

"Are you *mad*? Why didn't you *stop* her? Don't you know it's bloody *snowing* outside?"

"I'd like to 'ave seen *you* bloody stop 'er."

"She's ice cold! And she's pissed. Come on, you. Get upstairs. Don't you know you could get hypothermia? I'm fucking serious."

"What'd ya know, love?" I said, as she led me to the upstairs bathroom.

"Yes," Melissa said, "yes. You've learnt a new expression, and you sound bloody English. Come on, get out of those wet things." She ran steaming hot water into the tub. "Get in and stay in till I get back. And don't drown," she admonished me.

"You're always sticking me in the bloody bathtub," I said grumpily.

"Hmm. How about that?" Melissa left the bathroom. The water was soothing, but I couldn't get it hot enough.

The Isle of Whitby was in Wapping, down an old cobblestone street and right on the bank of the Thames. Nick had been knocking back pints, and I vaguely remembered trying to keep up with her. We'd climbed down the back stairs so I could see the Thames up close. A few flakes of snow fell, and I felt a complete sense of oneness with my environment, like I was omnipotent—experiencing life at a revved-up rate, achieving absolute clarity. As I breathed in the sharp coldness of the air, I remembered thinking that I'd never actually touched the water of the Thames before. It seemed like the Ganges, something holy to bathe myself in.

Melissa knocked on the bathroom door. "May I come in?" She placed a cup of tea on the soap and shampoo holder.

"Ta, Melissa."

"Listen you, don't you realize—?"

"Where's Nick?"

"She's crawled into a nice, warm, sensible bed and gone to sleep. That's where she is. Listen, you can't go swimming in the Thames."

"Nick gave me her socks so I'd have dry ones," I announced.

"That was sweet of her." Melissa sat down on the closed toilet lid. I could see the soft curve of her breasts beneath her open dressing gown and the black T-shirt that said "I Wish It Could Be '77" and had a picture of two punks walking away with

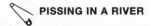

back patches on their jackets and bum-flaps attached to their belts. The band name "Special Duties" was written in blocky, different-sized punk letters. Melissa continued, "Look, I could be bloody pissed off at you."

"But you're not, are you? If you are, why are you smiling?"

"I'm not smiling. I'm grimacing." Melissa did her best to look disapproving.

"Is that a real word? Grimacing. What's a grimace? Isn't that one of those words you say out loud then wonder if it really means anything? Say it again. It's garble-nonsense."

"Will you stop, please? Being adorable is not going to work." Melissa knelt and rested her arms on the rim of the tub. Then she reached in her hand and splashed water at me. "Crikey, are you boiling yourself?" The way she left her hand hanging over the edge of the bath like that, so gracefully, the light shining off the silver ring on her finger, caused a sharp jolt of pain to run through me. I tried not to let it show in my eyes.

"The people in the pub were ever so nice. They didn't even mind me getting the floor all wet. And they were ever so good with advice, like telling me to wrap up warm and go home immediately."

"The people in the pub thought you were *mad*. And so do I. Now stay in there and drink your tea. I'll bring you something dry to wear."

I'm adorable, I thought, the words having taken this long to reach my sozzled brain.

Melissa left a pair of sweats, heavy socks, and a flannel shirt on the lid of the toilet for me. I felt happy in her clothes but still chilled. Melissa put me in her bed with a hot-water bottle at my feet, and I managed a minor tremble. "For fuck's sake, Amanda." Melissa held me against her for a minute to warm me up. "And another thing." She tucked me in again. "You can't match pints with Nick. Is that what happened?"

"I think so. I remember it being my shout, and my pints were stacking up."

"Why didn't you just buy her one and not yourself then?"

I thought about it. "That didn't make sense at the time." I didn't tell Melissa the truth, that the medications I took for my brain glitches accelerated the power of alcohol. I knew I was going to pay dearly for my drinking later. On the rare occasions I drank, I never had more than one pint. I mostly stuck with orange juice, Coke, and maybe some shandy.

Melissa made me take two paracetamol tablets and drink a large glass of water. "Go to sleep, kid. I'll be up later. No more pubs by the river for you."

I heard her laughing as she went downstairs. By this time, I was keeping a stash of medication hidden inside the Takamine's guitar case in Jake's room and wobbled down the hall to take my nightly dose with the last swallow of water. No amount of alcohol short of passing out would make me forget to do that. On my way back, I stumbled in the hallway and went down with a thud.

Melissa came upstairs and found me sitting there. She shook her head. "You're shedded."

"What?"

"It's an expression. 'My shed has collapsed taking most of the fence with it.'"

That struck me as hysterical. "My fence has collapsed!" I shrieked, rolling over on my side and resting my head on her foot. Looking down at me, Melissa pursed her lips in a way that only made her mouth seem sexier.

"Your day is over," Melissa said, grabbing my arm. "Get back to bed. And you're lucky I'm not still an A and E doc. Do you have any idea how many people come in injured on a Saturday night because they're pissed out of their brains and have fallen over? There's even a term for it. You're PFO, darlin'. Pissed Fell Over."

"What would you do?" I asked playfully.

"Give you fluids and a very stern lecture." Melissa pulled me up.

I lay in bed and crooned the first verse of "Sort It Out" by the

 **PISSING IN A RIVER**

Swedish band the Caesars in a loud, sloppy voice when Melissa went back downstairs. "'*I wanna smoke crack cause you're never coming back. / I wanna shoot speed balls, bang my head against the wall. / I wanna sniff glue cause I can't get over you. / Am I gonna sort it out?*'" I repeated it until I sang myself hoarse and then to sleep.

TRACK 23 EVER FALLEN IN LOVE (WITH SOMEONE YOU SHOULDN'T'VE)?

I noticed now that I was stricken with anxiety whenever I wasn't with Melissa. It was a startling and unpleasant new development. The anxiety came from not knowing if I was doing enough, if I was doing all I could, to make her love me. *Let Melissa love me* was in my head all the time and made it hard to concentrate. I couldn't get used to the idea that there was nothing I could do to change the way she felt. Sometimes I thought my anxiety would kill me, though I wasn't certain exactly how it would accomplish this.

With Melissa's encouragement, I used her flat as a recording studio. I downloaded royalty-free drum loops off the Internet and modified them on the sampler. Nick and I went to charity shops and outdoor markets, digging up obscure CDs I thought might contain interesting, usable beats. One of my favorites was a selection of Cuban rhythms. I didn't think anyone in Afghanistan would care if I nicked four seconds of it. I decided it would be perfect for my punk-reggae song "Holiday in Afghanistan." I lifted out a few seconds of the beat I wanted to use and recorded it onto the sampler. Then I looped it so there were no seams. I recorded this basic beat as a track on the digital recorder.

Track by track, I started adding instruments. I got out the drum machine and played along to my basic beat in real time on the touch-sensitive pads. Each pad was a different part of a drum kit, and I had thirty drum kits to choose from. I spent a few hours writing and recording a bass line with Jake's custom Fender bass that had both Precision-bass and Jazz-bass pickups.

We went to a music shop and bought a tiny, secondhand electronic keyboard for five quid. It was meant to be a child's toy, and the keys lit up pink when I played them. But it had the capacity for making different sounds like organ, jazz piano, and brass. I connected it to the digital eight-track using its headphone jack, and the recorder was so superb it sounded like real keyboards. It only had two octaves, but that was sufficient.

Late one afternoon when Nick was off with some mates, Melissa came upstairs to find me. She took off her scarf and shook out her hair, which shone in the overhead light. "I'm absolutely shagged out. Fancy taking a night off and watching a video with me?" Suddenly her tone changed. "What is it?" She looked at my horrified expression.

"You've been absolutely *fucked*?"

"What? No, tired. Shagged out is *tired*. Not shag as in fucking." She'd been on-call for after-hours care the night before, had been called out twice, and hadn't got much sleep.

"Oh. I thought you meant you'd been out with Martin."

"I'm not shagging Martin," Melissa laughed. "But if I do, you'll be the first person I tell."

I looked up at her, at the way her gray, cable-knit sweater hung on her body, accentuating her broad shoulders, and wanted to say, *don't do it. He's not good enough for you*. But how could I know that? I'd never even met the bloke.

I went out and got vegetable biryani, curry, and a few of my favorite horror films. I felt like a good scare and told Melissa she'd benefit from one, too. "Take your mind off frightening reality," I said. One of the videos I'd rented was an old one, *The Amityville Horror*, because Melissa had never seen it. James Brolin and his new wife Margot Kidder buy a possessed house in Amityville, New York. He gradually turns into one of the people who'd lived in the house previously, a man who'd murdered his entire family. Every night, he wakes up at precisely 3:15 a.m.

 **PISSING IN A RIVER**

because that's when the bloke he's turning into killed everyone with a shotgun.

We turned off the lights in the back sitting room and huddled together on the couch. Even though I'd seen *The Amityville Horror* before, it still frightened me. The demonically possessed house locked the babysitter in the closet. Melissa grabbed my arm, and I screamed. "I thought you'd seen this," she whispered.

"What's your point?" I said.

James Brolin discovered a direct passageway to hell in his basement. Melissa was almost sitting in my lap. "*God*," she yelled at the hapless family on the telly, "the walls are fucking *bleeding!* What's your first clue you should get out of the fucking house?"

After it ended, we were both terrified. "Wasn't that fun?" I asked.

"Fun," Melissa agreed. We went upstairs, and I got my hat and gloves off Jake's bed. "Where the bloody hell do you think *you're* going?" Melissa asked.

"Home," I said with false bravado.

"Are you mad? You're not seriously going out in the dark by yourself?"

I didn't like the thought any more than she did.

"You scare me to death then think you're leaving?" Melissa said. "You're staying the night or I'll never sleep. You can leave anytime after daylight."

I shrugged gratefully and turned to head downstairs to the spare bedroom. There was a telly in there I could watch if I couldn't fall asleep.

Melissa shook her head. "Uh uh. You're sleeping in here with me and we're locking the door."

As she got ready for bed, I sneaked my medication out of Jake's room and went into the loo. As I swallowed my pills with water from the tap, Melissa rapped lightly on the door. "Come in, Melissa."

"Here." She opened a cabinet and handed me a fresh toothbrush. She was wearing a clean Pretenders tour T-shirt with a picture of Chrissie Hynde and her blue Telecaster on the front.

"Oh, ta," I said. When I was done using it, I put it proudly next to hers.

In the bedroom, Melissa handed me another tour item, a gray sweatshirt that said "Pretenders" on it in pink letters, and I beamed happily at her. I carefully climbed into bed next to her, and Melissa turned out the light.

"Oh, no." I sat up suddenly. "What time is it?"

"Stop that," Melissa said. "It isn't anywhere near 3:15 a.m. yet."

"I was just asking. Oh, no!" I grabbed Melissa, and we both screamed.

"What *is* it?" She turned on the light.

"Is that James Brolin climbing up the stairs?"

"*Stop* it." Melissa shoved me. She turned off the light again.

"I thought you'd want to know," I said.

"Well, I don't. Tell Mr. Brolin to make sure the door shuts completely on his way out," Melissa murmured sleepily.

"Melissa?" I shook her.

"What?" she moaned.

"Satan wants to know if he can have a cup of tea."

"Yes," Melissa said. "Yes. Satan can have a cup of tea and even a biscuit. Alright?"

"Melissa?"

She sighed. "What?"

"Satan wants to know can he cook something in your kitchen?"

"Just so long as it isn't an animal. This is a cruelty-free zone."

"No sacrificial babies or virgins?"

"I should think not. Now go to sleep. And tell Satan to do the washing up or I'm sealing off the passageway to hell in the spare bedroom forever."

"Melissa," I said, after we'd been lying quietly a while, "do you think you'll sleep with Martin?"

 **PISSING IN A RIVER**

"What?" Her tone told me that now she was awake. "I don't know. Why?"

"No reason. Just—you don't have to."

"What makes you think I don't know that?" She sounded annoyed.

"I don't know." I knew I'd said the wrong thing. "I suppose I meant he shouldn't pressure you if you don't want to."

"What makes you think he's pressuring me? What's this sudden interest in my sex life or lack of one?"

"Do you like him a lot?"

"If I didn't like him, I wouldn't go out with him."

"Do you practice safe sex?"

"*Amanda*. What's got into you?"

"Nothing. I hope he appreciates you, that's all," I said sullenly.

"Are you trying to tell me something?" Melissa shifted around, and in the dark I saw her staring at me.

"I'm trying *not* to tell you something."

"What does *that* mean?"

"Nothing. It doesn't mean anything."

"Do you know something about Martin that I don't? Have you even met him? Look, Amanda, I'll have him fill out a questionnaire before I even *think* about sleeping with him. Happy now?"

"Overjoyed. It's a big decision."

"No, love, it isn't. It either happens or it doesn't. I'm sorry to disappoint you."

"Don't say that. You never disappoint me."

"If you're afraid I'll fall in love with him and disappear or something, I won't. Is that what's bothering you? I don't do that to my mates. Now will you please shut up and go to sleep?"

I lay there castigating myself for coming too close to saying too much.

"This is bollocks." Melissa hung up the phone after unsuccessfully trying to locate Nick for the third straight day. "I'm a little worried. What's happened? I thought you were keeping an eye on her."

"I can't exactly put her in handcuffs," I mumbled.

"Well . . ." Melissa gave me a devastatingly sexy half-smile and pain shot through my body. I instinctively put my hands to my heart. I knew she hadn't meant to upset me.

"I'll pop round her flat and see if I can find her," I offered, sinking my hands into my pockets where they couldn't get me in trouble and quickly turning toward the door.

"I'll drive you."

"Tube'll be faster." I started singing "London Traffic" from the second Jam LP *This Is the Modern World*. I grabbed Melissa's black Tom Robinson Band sweatshirt hanging in the entranceway and pulled it over my head. It had a bright yellow fist on it like the cover of his *Power in the Darkness* album.

"Invite her over for a meal. I'll get some Chinese. And for God's sake, *sing* if you're glad to be gay," Melissa called after me because the chorus of Tom Robinson's most famous song "Glad to Be Gay" begins, "*Sing if you're glad to be gay / Sing if you're happy that way*." Released as a single in 1978, it had been our anthem at Exeter in 1980. And I still had the original yellow-and-red "Glad to be Gay" badge that a woman had given me at Gay Pride in Huddersfield.

It was dark by the time I reached Nick's flat. "DYKE" was spray-painted in red by the door. I wondered if it was just a coincidence—"DYKE" for some reason being considered a universal insult—since Nick wasn't the most openly lesbian person in the world. I leaned on the buzzer. I stepped back and shouted up to her window. I hung around for a few more minutes then took the tube back to Hampstead.

I told Melissa about the "DYKE" graffiti. "You don't suppose someone left it there as a compliment?" I asked. "A sort of, well done, so you're a dyke, welcome to the neighborhood type of thing?"

"Was there a gift basket?" Melissa asked facetiously. "No, this has happened before. Now I really *am* concerned. Remember I told you Nick's ex-girlfriend has a brother in London? He's a fucking gobshite piece of filth. He blames Nick for turning Emilia *queer,* and after Emilia tore arse back to Ireland, he kept harassing Nick."

"Was Nick Emilia's first girlfriend?"

"Do you think that matters? People like that are beyond explanations."

"What did he do to her?"

"Spray-painted obscenities outside her flat until her landlady chucked her out. Got her number and rang her up all hours. Sometimes he'd be waiting for her when she came home from the pub. He totally messed her up."

I shook my head. "Why would anyone go to all that trouble?"

"He's probably just miserable about his own damn life." Melissa quoted from "Mindless Violence" by the Newtown Neurotics, *"'Mindless violence, what does it prove? / It proves you don't know the people who are shitting on you.'"*

I asked, "Did she call the police?"

"She couldn't prove he was the one doing it. They told her to change her number and ignore him. They couldn't give a toss."

"Christ, poor thing." And the first line of "Glad to Be Gay" ran through my head. *"The British police are the best in the world..."*

"The harassment stopped after she moved. Maybe Atom's tracked her down again."

"Sorry, *Atom?* His name's *Atom,* as in *Atomic?"*

"I think his real name's Adam."

I had a vision of Nick as the heroic lesbian Eve, trapped in the garden with an Adam who insisted she be heterosexual and belong to him.

For the rest of the week, when Melissa didn't have other engagements, we drove to Nick's flat in the evenings after work to see if we could find her. Melissa's hours at work had slackened off a bit as a result of hiring a new full-time partner at her practice.

I'd watch the yellow and white lights of London swirling past, the bright neon smorgasbords of Piccadilly, Kensington, and Tower Bridge. Melissa took me all round the city because she knew how much I loved it. I stared out the window at the yellow lights of St. John's Wood. I felt small and sad but also strangely happy. We passed the shiny red brick of Hampstead tube station, the circular blue-and-red underground symbols glistening in the rain. "This area's dead flash, Melissa," I said.

"I know." Melissa was blasting her favorite version of the Mano Negra song "King Kong Five" from their live album. "Our flat's been in the family donkey's years."

"You never talk about your family," I said. "Except for your sister."

"I know," she said. "Let's leave it at that."

"Do you think we should go to the police?"

"About Nick? I don't know what to do. I'd hate to get the cops involved, and I doubt there's anything they could do. She's an adult and hasn't been missing that long."

Melissa got us into Nick's flat by telling her landlady that Nick was a patient who might be seriously ill and unable to get to a phone. "Well," Melissa said as we left, having found nothing out of the ordinary, "at least we know she's not in there avoiding us."

"What if Atom's grabbed her and she's somewhere else in trouble? I think we should report her missing to the police."

"If she's missing on purpose she won't want the Met picking her up. Maybe she's in Manchester visiting some mates."

When we got home, I distracted myself by recording the guitar tracks to my song "Holiday in Afghanistan." The Vox amp gave me just the sweet crunch I wanted, and I miked in the gui-

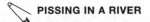

tar, tweaking it with more reverb for a bit of an aftertaste. I used my Small Clone and Digital Delay to make the rhythm guitar more chiming and the DS-1 distortion pedal for a totally biting, heavy lead. I'd got my inspiration from the Fingers' version of the Bob Marley song "Johnny Was."

I waited until Melissa went to work the next day to record the vocals because I was self-conscious about my singing. I recorded them in the loo. The acoustics were great with my voice resonating off the porcelain. To boost my self-confidence, I imagined I was Joe Strummer in that scene from *Rude Boy* when he's recording his vocals and listening through headphones so all anyone can hear is him singing a cappella.

After I mixed everything, it sounded like I'd recorded the song in a proper studio. I separated the different tracks in terms of panning, texture, and volume so I could hear each instrument and the vocals clearly even though they all blended together. I'd never heard my music sound the way I heard it in my head before.

I put new light-gauge Elixir strings on the Takamine and secretly recorded the last song I'd written about Melissa. Just two tracks, acoustic guitar and vocals. Later I went back and added a third track, a haunting, wailing riff on my electric guitar to form a melancholy harmony against the vocals. I wished I had the guts to play it for Melissa.

When Melissa rang from the clinic to invite me out with some mates, I decided against it. I was in the middle of a new song I wanted to finish. At around seven, I collected my guitar and portable amp. First I went back to mine and got the rest of my medication, since I seemed to be staying on at Melissa's indefinitely, then went out to Bethnal Green. I knew it was probably useless, but I just wanted to show my face there like I was doing something. There was no response at Nick's flat, so I walked back to the tube and busked for something to do while I waited. I figured if she was in the crowd, she'd hear me playing and we wouldn't miss each other. I strummed my guitar distractedly, scanning the people going in and out of the Bethnal Green station, ridiculously hoping to spot Nick. I stayed until I was too cold to stand around any longer, then trudged back through the dark streets to Nick's flat for a last look.

I rang her buzzer and stepped back so she could see me if she was upstairs looking out her window, afraid to open the door. A bloke was leaning against the building smoking a fag. My mental jukebox immediately dropped the needle on Patti Smith's "Land: *Horses*," and I heard her say, "The boy was in the hallway drinking a glass of tea." The rhythm of "bloke against building smoking a fag" and "boy in hallway drinking a glass of tea" were the same to me. It reminded me of Gertrude Stein talking about composition as landscape, and about all the elements in the composition having equal value. He must have noticed me staring up at her window because he said, "You a mate of hers?"

> *When suddenly Johnny*
> *gets the feeling*
> *he's being surround by*
> *horses horses horses horses*

"Sorry?" I told myself to focus.

"You one of the girls?" He took a long hit off his ciggy and chucked the dog-end into the road.

> *coming in all directions*
> *white shining silver studs with their nose in flames*
> *he saw horses horses horses*
> *horses horses horses horses horses*

"I'm sorry?" I repeated, offended.

"You lot are an abomination, you know that?"

"Are you Atom?" I got ready to tell him off, then thought better of confronting him alone in the dark. I turned and started walking back toward the tube.

 **PISSING IN A RIVER**

"Oi, I'm not through talking to you yet." He followed me.

"Sod off." *He's mad*, I thought, and I couldn't swallow my spit fast enough.

"*Oi!*" He grabbed my arm. He smelled of stale beer, like he'd washed his clothes in lager.

I yanked my arm free and shoved him. He reached for me again. I put down my guitar case and slapped his hand away. *He's a big, nasty-looking, stroppy lad*, I translated automatically in my head, pleased with myself for thinking, even under duress, in British English. That's when you really know you've mastered a foreign language. *Look at me. I'm bilingual.* I would have loved to play the hero and beat the living shite out of him for terrorizing Nick, but I didn't fancy my chances. And I had to protect my guitar.

He said, "What you need, girl, is a real man to show you how it's done."

Lovely, I thought. *I've certainly never heard* that *argument before.* "Look, mate," I said, "at least try to come up with original material."

He lunged for me unsteadily. I swung my Fender Ampcan at his head. He stumbled backward but was too alcohol inflated to be seriously dented.

"*Go Rimbaud, go Rimbaud, go Johnny go,*" Patti Smith sang in my head. I took the hint. I picked up my guitar and ran as best I could, the heavy case banging against one leg, the Ampcan against the other. Atom came after me faster than I had expected. I didn't think I could make it to a well-lit main road before he caught up with me. I sprinted into a monotone of blackness and hid behind a rubbish skip for about five minutes. Then, with no idea where I was going, I crept around the bin and went down another side street. But the Gibson hardshell case battering my leg made me loud and clumsy. I heard the sound of boots on cobblestone. I was too tired to go much farther and looked for another place to hide.

As I ran alongside a brick wall, I stumbled onto a tiny play area for kids. I clambered up on part of a metal climbing frame and looked over the wall. It was too dark to see anything below, so I figured I could hide down there. I chucked my Ampcan over the wall and hoped for the best. Then I pulled up my guitar case and tried to balance it on the wall, but something prevented it from staying there. I realized there were strands of barbed wire running along the top. I was going to give up and get down to find another way in when I heard Atom panting somewhere behind me. *Gobshite.* I put one foot on the wall and tried to heave myself up with my guitar without hurting myself. I slipped and grabbed at the wire to steady myself. "*FUCK me,*" I cursed under my breath to keep myself from screaming and letting go as I felt a jagged spike rip through my palm. *Stigmata*, I told myself, to keep calm at the sharp burst of pain, *don't worry about it. If our Lord could take it, so can you.* I managed to kneel on the wall and lower my guitar lengthwise down on the other side. I stood up and balanced my feet on either side of the barbed wire, trying to figure out how I was going to get down. I didn't feel like taking a wild, trusting leap into the open mouth of the night. But hearing the scuffle of boots, I realized it was too late, that he would see me if I didn't jump immediately. The wall was covered with a thin, slimy layer of green moss, and when I turned to jump, I lost my balance and fell instead. I felt barbed wire tear at the inside of my trouser leg, and then the ground rushed up and hit me. *Hard.* For a second, I was too stunned to feel anything. Then I felt massive relief when I realized I hadn't landed on my guitar.

As I tried to get my breath back, I became aware of a throbbing pain in my right ankle. *Oh shite*, I thought, hoping Emilia's brother wouldn't find me because I wouldn't be able to run away. I concentrated on the way the wet grass felt and lifted my head. With a shock, I realized I was looking at black, Hebrew letters. I had landed in a Jewish cemetery. *How appropriate*, I thought. *All I have to do is lie here and wait.* I was afraid to move lest I make noise. My hand burned. I decided I should remain still for at least half an hour to make sure Atom had gone. The pain in my ankle would subside, and I'd make it to a phone box. I imagined Melissa's soothing voice over the line and how nice it would feel to ride home in her warm car.

Of course it started pissing down with rain. I wondered if I should just lie on my back with my mouth open and drown myself. But the possibility of being rescued by Melissa was far too sweet to pass up. Maybe the rain would act like an ice pack from God on my swelling ankle. The freezing rain actually kept my spirits up. It was like God looking down and saying, "*Alright?*" But it was eerie lying in that place, and soon I couldn't control my shivering. All the stone inscriptions were in Hebrew so I couldn't entertain myself by reading them.

I lay in the rain and sang "Barbed Wire Love" by Stiff Little Fingers in my head until I thought it was safe to move. "*All you give me is barbed wire love . . . barbed wire love snags my jeans.*" Slowly, gingerly, I got to my feet. At first I was afraid to put any weight on my ankle, but as I hopped around looking for my Ampcan it became numb, and I found I could move about more easily. Leaning on my guitar case like a crutch, I tried to find a way out of the cemetery.

I slowly made my way to the street and found a red phone box, the old-fashioned kind that hadn't yet been modernized to allow for wheelchair access. I put my hand in my pocket and pulled out some wet, cold coins. At the flat, I got the answering machine. I tried Melissa's mobile, thinking, *please, please pick up*, with a rising sense of panic. When I heard Melissa's voice, it stirred up all the rescue fantasies I'd ever had about her. I pushed in a few coins. "Melissa, can you come get me?" *Please*, I prayed to the exacting God of OCD.

"What? Amanda? Speak up, love, I can't hear you." It was noisy on Melissa's end of the line.

"Melissa, I need your help," I shouted. "Where the fuck are you?"

"Down the disco," she yelled back. "What's wrong, love?"

"Help!" I screamed into the receiver. I lowered my head and

knocked it against the phone. I felt like I would die if she didn't leave her good time to save me.

"Hang on a mo," Melissa said calmly, and there was some shuffling about while my brain played Blondie's "Hanging on the Telephone." Then it was relatively quiet. "I'm outside. Now I can hear you."

"Melissa, I twisted my ankle. I have no idea where the nearest tube is, and I can't get home."

"What? You're hurt? What happened? Where are you?"

"I don't know where I am." Tears ran down my cheeks to mix with the rainwater, as I felt truly sorry for myself. All the most unappealing aspects of my OCD were kicking in, the need for constant reassurance, the panic, the inability not to focus on my own suffering, and I was having trouble controlling my emotions.

"Can you find a main road and get a taxi? I can meet you at the flat."

"I can't. I can't walk."

"You what? How badly are you hurt? Do you need me to call 999?"

"No," I sobbed, "fucking hell. I just need you to come get me, only I don't know where I am." I told her what had happened while my brain mocked me. *Yes, OCD is one of your more attractive mental illnesses. Um hmm. What a prize. She'll be lucky to have you. She doesn't know how lucky she is.*

"*Fuck.*" This reaction startled me, as I'd never heard Melissa sound so angry before. Then she softened her tone. "It's alright, love. Where do you think you are? Where were you the last time you saw a street sign?"

I told her I was in a phone box near a Jewish cemetery somewhere, vaguely, in the vicinity of Bethnal Green. She said that she would find me. "I've got an *A to Zed* in my car." Luckily the *London A–Z* lists burial grounds. "Don't freeze to death," she said.

"If I do, just bury me here," I said, and hung up the phone.

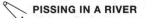 **PISSING IN A RIVER**

I stood my guitar and Ampcan in the phone box, and there wasn't room enough for me. I sat in the rain, ignoring Melissa's admonition not to freeze. I played the Clash version of Ed Cobb's "Every Little Bit Hurts" in my head.

By the time I saw the familiar headlights and then the distinctive thick, rubber bumper of Melissa's car, I was singing "I'm Not Down" by the Clash under my breath to keep warm.

Melissa pulled up and got out of her car, leaving the headlights shining on me. She bent down to examine my leg. She seemed controlled but angry. I wasn't used to seeing her like that. "I'm sorry I had to ruin your night," I said hesitantly.

"Don't be silly." Melissa untied my sodden white Converse Chuck Taylor high-top and gently felt my ankle. "Can you put any weight on it? Tell me if this hurts." She checked for point tenderness. "You have a sprain." She took off her coat and wrapped it around me.

"No," I protested, "you'll get all wet."

"Don't be ridiculous," she said firmly, rain pelting her hair and streaming down her face. "Christ, your hand." Melissa looked at my wound, which hadn't stopped bleeding. "That's quite a deep gash. It's going to need suturing." She opened her medical bag. Gently, she put on a dressing and wrapped my hand in a gauze bandage. And the phrase "the gentleness of bluebells" kept running through my head because the way she bent over me reminded me of the graceful way the heads of the bluebells leaned down from their stalks in the woods of Exeter.

Before I let her help me into the passenger seat of her car, I made her put in my guitar and amp. When she returned for me, I was singing "Behind Blue Eyes" by the Who. "*If I swallow anything evil, put your finger down my throat. / If I shiver please give me a blanket / keep me warm, let me wear your coat.*" I hoped I wouldn't get blood all over her car. Melissa once told me she'd redone the steering wheel and gearshift so there was no "tortured-screaming-dead-animal" inside.

We zipped through quiet streets with the heater on full blast. "If Nick knew he was hanging about, how could she have let you walk into that?" Melissa pounded her hands on the cruelty-free steering wheel.

"It's not her fault, Melissa. How was she to know?"

"This could have been a lot more serious than a twisted ankle."

"And stigmata," I mumbled.

"And stigmata, yes," Melissa said, and I stared at her profile to see if she was smiling. "Let's get you to A and E and have your hand sutured."

"Wait. What? You're taking me to A and E? You'll do the suturing, right?"

"The A and E doctor will do it."

"No way," I said. "No one touches me but you."

"Amanda, I'll be right there with you. It's not a complicated procedure."

"No." The weight of the whole evening came crashing down on me. "I want you to do it. I won't let anybody else touch me."

Melissa sighed. "Amanda, be reasonable."

"I will not be reasonable." I could hear my voice sounding slightly hysterical but couldn't rein it in. "No one touches me but you," I repeated.

"Calm down. Alright, I'll do it." Melissa changed direction and soon we parked behind her dark office. I rarely went to see her there because she was always so busy. She helped me to the door and went through her keys to let us in. Turning on some lights she said, "Let's get you into a consulting room."

I sat on the examining table. Melissa laid out instruments on a tray and put on sterile gloves. She held my hand and examined it in the bright light. She flushed out my wound with normal saline then swabbed the whole area with a yellowish-brown

solution she said was povidone-iodine. "How long since your last tetanus jab?"

"Just this past year when I got my London Underground tattoo and my leg got infected." I had the symbol for the tube in red on my right leg.

The corners of Melissa's mouth twitched into a half-smile as she prepared a local anesthetic. I watched her clean the surface of the ampoule with alcohol and unwrap a sterile needle. She squirted a tiny bit of liquid out of the syringe, tapping it with her finger to get out all the air bubbles. Watching her hands while she worked was soothing. Now that my hand was actually injured, I didn't freak out thinking it was going to come off. For some reason the injury made it feel more solid. Like the one psychiatrist who'd actually helped me had said, "There's a lot of stuff holding it on."

Melissa said, "This'll sting a little. Breathe in. Exhale." She gave me four quick jabs of lignocaine in my palm.

"*Ouch!*" I said. "*Ouch, ouch, OW! Fuck* me, that hurts."

"I know," Melissa said sympathetically, "I'm sorry. I knew it was going to hurt but what was I supposed to tell you? That it'll hurt like fuck? I had to give you the injection. Nothing I could say would make any difference. So I lied." She smiled at me. "I don't make that a habit."

I smiled back.

Melissa had me lie down on the table, and we waited for my hand to become numb. She sat next to me, and I could barely breathe with her so close. She reached over me to adjust a light, her breasts rubbing against my arm. I turned my head so I could watch her. Melissa pulled a curved needle with thread through both sides of my gash with a silver clamp, and I nearly jumped even though I couldn't feel it. She wrapped the thread around the clamp three times then pulled through the other end into a knot with forceps. She tied off every stitch. I wanted to say *you're beautiful when you sew* to make her laugh, but I felt a little queasy. Melissa had me lean my head all the way back against the table. "Maybe you shouldn't watch," she suggested.

"No, really," I tried to sound neutral, "it's interesting."

Melissa tied off the last stitch. "Alright?" She tousled my hair. She examined my ankle again and wrapped it in an elastic bandage. "It's just a slight sprain," she said, and I was irrationally disappointed. A minor injury seemed anticlimactic after the life-or-death drama of my harrowing escape. "Let's get you home and dry." I panicked at this until I realized she meant *her* home. She held out her arm to help me sit up so I could get off the table. I put one hand in her hand and, with the other, held onto her strong arm. She pulled me up.

In the spare room downstairs, Melissa helped me out of my soggy clothes. She elevated my ankle on some pillows and put an ice pack on it. "How's the pain?" she asked.

"It's not too bad, but I feel kind of sore all over."

"You strained your muscles when you fell."

"Cheers for fixing me up. I'm sorry I made such a fuss. Can I do without the ice? I'm freezing."

Melissa covered me with the brown duvet and sat on the edge of the bed.

"This reminds me of the time I fell off a wall in Ottery St. Mary," I said. "When I was at Exeter, a bunch of us went for Guy Fawkes night. Do you know the tradition there? Instead of just a bonfire, people run through the narrow streets carrying burning barrels of tar on their shoulders. When they can't hold onto them anymore, they heave them. It's totally mental. I'm surprised people aren't killed. I didn't want to be trapped in the crowd between the buildings with no way out, so I climbed on top of this very high wall and sat at its pinnacle. I thought I was safe there, my legs dangling well above people's heads, until one bloke lost control and flung his flaming barrel of tar directly at me. It exploded against the stone right where I'd been sitting, and I toppled off the wall backward. I crashed to the ground, pulling all the muscles in my stomach. I couldn't straighten up and had to crawl around the wall to find my mates. They helped

 **PISSING IN A RIVER**

me back on the bus. I was doubled over in agony, and they had to fetch a doctor to give me muscle relaxants." I started to laugh and held my stomach. "Ow."

Melissa adjusted the pillows behind my head. "You must be knackered. How about a nice cuppa to warm you up? Or do you just want to sleep?"

"Can't I sleep in your room? It's so fucking cold."

"I don't want you climbing any stairs tonight." Melissa heaped blankets on top of me. I stopped laughing and started to cry. "Shh." Melissa moved closer to me and stroked my hair. "You're just overwrought." I sat up and pressed my face into her breasts. I felt her arms go around me and cried harder. I couldn't tell her I was mostly crying because, with my defenses down, being near her caused me such agony. Why is love so awful?

In the midst of this, I panicked, wondering how I was ever going to sneak myself upstairs to get my medication. If it had been anyone else, I would have simply asked her to bring down my drugs. After all, the pills were in a plastic bag, not in their prescription bottles. They could be anything. But Melissa was a doctor. I was afraid she would recognize them and know what they were for. Then I saw my guitar sitting on the floor and, with a jolt of relief, remembered I had medication in the case. "Do you reckon I could have that cuppa now?" I asked to get her out of the room.

"Course you can, love."

When Melissa went into the kitchen to put the kettle on, I hopped to my guitar case then to the downstairs loo to take my pills, jarring my ankle and exacerbating the steady ache.

Melissa brought me tea and paracetamol. Then she wrapped a hot-water bottle in a towel and tucked it under the blankets on my sore stomach muscles. She pulled up a comfy chair next to the bed and sat with me. I finally dozed off thinking about how comforting it had been when she'd stretched out her arm across me to help me up. The memory of it made me feel reassured, warm, and safe.

That night I had the strangest dream. I think it was a result of what I now referred to in biblical terms as "The Fall" and of landing in a Jewish graveyard. I dreamt there was a disease called "green leaves" that made people tiny. Then I looked down at my arm and saw that my skin had darkened. The green leaves were the jungles of Vietnam, and our role in the Vietnam War made America shrink into wee nothingness. My darker skin was a statement about how rich, entitled, white kids went to college and poor, disenfranchised, black kids got sent to the front lines.

I woke up thinking about the tree of the knowledge of good and evil in the Garden of Eden and suddenly understood the book of Genesis. Good, evil. Black, white. Rich, poor. We recognize good as good because it isn't evil, and evil as evil because it isn't good. When Adam and Eve eat from the tree of the knowledge of good and evil, they create meaning through opposition. In the Torah, only God can create something without its opposite, without its shadow. But Adam and Eve can't understand good without knowing evil. They have to leave the garden in case they also eat from the tree of life and become like God. Once people have the knowledge of evil they can't be allowed to create life, each one alone, each in his own image. Adam and Eve probably weren't even different sexes in Eden. They only became that afterward to ensure that no single human being could create life by himself. The bringing of evil into this world is the creation of opposites and opposition.

Melissa was curled up in her chair asleep. My heart ached to see her there, so kind, so adorable. I shook the toe of one of her brown, black-soled baseball boots and she stirred, uncurling her legs. "Have you been here all night?" I asked. "You are unbelievably sweet."

She shivered, hugging herself. "I fell asleep. It's fucking freezing."

"Get under the covers." I pulled them back. Through the uncovered window I saw how misty it was outside in the dawn. She kicked off her shoes and crawled in next to me under the duvet. "Why were you sleeping in a chair? You know you could've climbed in with me. It's not like I would have minded."

Melissa yawned. "I was afraid of bumping your hand or your ankle and hurting you."

"You're so sweet," I repeated softly. "Melissa, I think I understand the story of creation in the Bible."

"Amanda, take the batteries out of your head and go back to sleep."

"No, really. I have to tell you before I forget. The Garden of Eden is a parable about the human condition. And the trinity is a parable about salvation. With the number three, nothing is in direct opposition to anything else. It's a triangle."

"Amanda, you're not becoming a Jesus freak?"

"No, it's a very Jewish story. Listen. In the Garden of Eden, Adam and Eve were equals. They were not opposites. And their fall from grace was, in reality, the construction of compulsory heterosexuality, which we mistakenly take for morality. Gender is only the story of how we create life. It's not supposed to *mean* anything. Men and women were created different solely for the purpose of reproduction, so that no single person could create life. Because only God can create good without evil."

"I thought Adam and Eve were kicked out of the garden because they were disobedient," Melissa said sleepily. "Because they ate from the tree of knowledge after God told them not to."

"No. They were kicked out so that they could not also eat from the tree of life and become like God, immortal creators. The reason no single human being should be allowed to create life is because we are a combination of good and evil and power corrupts us. We might only want to create life in our own image and then have power over that life. We would become little Hitlers, creating Nuremberg rallies, wanting our stamp to be on everything. It's dangerous enough when two people create a child, name it, and have power over it. Just like when Adam names all the animals and believes he now has dominion over them."

It was like the song "So Neat" on my favorite Partisans record, the 2001 EP. *"I wanna have it all / gonna make the world just like me."*

"Oh, man," Melissa said. "A theology lesson and the meaning of life without so much as a cup of tea."

"In the first story of creation, God creates male and female together, both in God's image, both equal. In the second story, God creates Adam alone, then Eve out of his rib, and gives Adam power over everything. Including Eve."

"And?"

"The men who transcribed the Bible panicked when they saw that first story. They rewrote it so Eve was not Adam's equal but created as an afterthought. The first story wasn't even supposed to *be* in the Bible but accidentally got left in the manuscript."

"And you know all of this *how?*" Melissa asked, amused by my earnest yet impossible conviction.

"Educated guess." I waved my hand to sweep away her objections. "They write that Adam's sin is having listened to the voice of his wife. And they have God say to Eve, *'I will greatly multiply thy pain and thy travail; in pain shalt thou bring forth children; and thy desire shall be to thy husband, and he shall rule over thee,'* establishing compulsory heterosexuality with one sentence to cover up the fact that Eden was *not* a heterosexual paradise."

"You make it sound like a conspiracy."

"Isn't it? Plus the two creation stories were probably written in reverse order, the second coming first, so they were obviously arranged to denigrate Eve. Do you think that means God really created Eve first?"

"Take a breath, Amanda," Melissa laughed, shutting her eyes. "You have a wonderful imagination."

"Listen. If heterosexuality were so natural, why did God have to tell them, 'Be fruitful, and multiply'? Why wouldn't it just have *happened*? If heterosexual sex were predetermined and the only option, it wouldn't *occur* to God to tell them to do that. Besides, it takes imagination to get back into Eden," I murmured, my eyes getting heavy again. "Your imagination is the only thing that's not constrained by time and space."

"Amanda, can I please go back to sleep? I promise to become your disciple later when I'm fully awake. Really, I think it's lovely that you're starting your own religion and I'm really chuffed you'd share it with me, but I'm almost unconscious. If you see a burning bush, put it out until a decent hour. By the way, I think you're probably brilliant," she confided, winking at me and rolling over to go back to sleep.

TRACK 26 HEAVEN'S INSIDE

"Anymore audiences with the Almighty?" Melissa asked first thing when she woke up. She checked the bandage on my hand and got up to look at my ankle. The swelling had gone down, and there was a bit of bruising. "How does it feel?"

"Much better today."

"It's not a bad sprain. I think you were more frightened than anything else."

I creased my brow. "Surely that's not good enough. Not after a fall like that."

Melissa smiled. "Don't worry. Your hand was sufficiently gory."

"Was it really?" I asked with some excitement.

"Oh, yes," Melissa assured me, "I nearly fainted." She leaned down and kissed the top of my head. It was a friendly kiss, the kind she always gave me. I hoped I wasn't giving off too much of a lesbian vibe. Not that there was anything wrong with my vibe, but I didn't want her to think I was asking more from her than she could give. I liked our physical closeness and wanted her to continue to feel comfortable being affectionate with me.

That night, I had a follow-up dream. I was in a tribe of people flooding out of the Garden of Eden. Only John Lennon and

I remained separate. Everyone else joined one big group that dressed the same and gave arm salutes in a scene that looked like the Nuremberg rally. I said, "When they can choose to be anything at all, why do they choose to be sheep? And they're not just sheep. They're evil sheep."

John Lennon said, "Only an evil leader wants to make over the world in his own image."

Suddenly I was alone in the middle of a mystery. I picked up a ring lying at my feet, and its inscription said I was a detective and had the same ability to seek the truth as anyone else. I had a notebook and wrote my name: *Detective!*

The only place I could go was a library with very limited space that the FBI had taken over. Entering, I realized I had wandered into hell. People were sitting on a bench suffering. They had been shrunken down to one thing, the behavior that had brought them here. This behavior now defined them. Then I noticed that not all of the people on the bench were suffering. Some people were in heaven, some in hell, but they were all on the same bench. Heaven and hell were a state of mind, not a specific location.

Then the sentence *"The images of childhood are so easily explained"* came to me, and I was suddenly surrounded by bright colors. Curtains hanging in a window were two stripes of pink and purple. I was in Israel. The colors seemed mysterious and familiar at the same time. The answer was simple. The curtains were the colors of the bathing suit I had worn as a child. I'd seen it in old photographs.

As I stood in the hot Israeli sun, an olive-skinned girl went around kissing everyone. She said, "We take things for granted. We say 'no' to living people!" We were in Jerusalem, Al-Quds, looking down at the Wailing Wall and across to the golden Dome of the Rock, Qubbat al-Sakhra, standing near a beautiful, brunette soldier sitting in the grass with her Uzi. The girl continued to go from person to person, kissing each one and saying,

"Good Shabbat." She said that the message was simple: include everyone. Notice everyone. There is no great mystery to life, but we run around endlessly searching for meaning.

TRACK 27 **THERE SHE GOES**

The telephone rang while I was upstairs looping samples, experimenting with some bhangra beats, and I had the feeling I should answer it.

"So there you are, mate," Nick said. "I was looking for you."

"I'm still recording at Melissa's. Where've you been?"

"Manchester. I'm sorry I didn't ring you. Wanna do something?"

I didn't want to tell her what had happened over the phone and asked her to meet me at the Bethnal Green station. I'd spent several days babying my ankle and wanted to go out. I rang Melissa's mobile, and she said she'd meet me at Nick's flat later.

I didn't have far to walk to reach the Hampstead tube. I took the Morden train south to Bank then changed from the Northern to the central line, which took me to Bethnal Green. Nick was waiting at the mouth of the station. She took her hands from the pockets of her leather jacket just long enough to give me a hug. She was wearing black mitts and the tips of her fingers were red with the cold. "Oi, what's happened to your hand?"

"I'll tell you over a cuppa." I wrapped the brown tweed coat I'd got at an Oxfam charity shop more tightly around myself.

"Are you limping?" Nick was wearing bright royal-blue trainers. A light snow was falling as we walked to her flat. It was hushed and beautiful even with the surrounding dilapidation. I had the Jam's "Dreams of Children" playing in my head because that song reminded me of Nick. "*Something's gonna crack on your dreams tonight. / You're gonna crack on your dreams tonight.*" I had a live version with a guitar riff during that last chorus that could break your heart. I'd recorded a song that sounded a bit like the studio version at the end, with backward guitars and keyboards fading out. I did it by playing my guitar riffs into the digital recorder using the "reverse" effect. It sounded ghostly.

The "DYKE" graffiti had been partially scrubbed off her building, leaving traces of red like a smeared lipstick kiss. Nick unlocked the door and we went upstairs. The walls of her flat were light green and lavender. There was a stereo and a crate of CDs, and the floor was lined with books on cinder-block shelves.

We settled on a blue settee with cups of tea and I looked at Nick more closely. Her eyes looked dull, heavy, and haunted like she hadn't been sleeping well.

"What, for fuck's sake, is the matter with your hand?" Nick gestured at the bandage.

I looked out the window at the tower blocks. I wasn't sure how to begin.

"Spit it out, luv."

"Don't get upset," I said, and Nick groaned. "Really. Don't."

Nick spread out her arms like she was being crucified, and I thought about my stigmata injury. Her eyes were green-gray against her brick-red jumper, which had zippers on the sleeves and a zipper going diagonally across the front. I could tell she'd sewn that one on herself by the uneven black stitching. "Nick, I got aggro from a bloke hanging round your flat."

"You what?" Nick looked alarmed.

I told her everything that had happened in the most cheerful tone I could manage without sounding like a vacant-eyed, born-again Christian talking about the Rapture that never comes when it's supposed to.

"I'll kill 'im," Nick murmured. "I am absolutely gutted."

"I'm not blaming you," I said. "It wasn't your fault."

"I saw him and just ran. I never dreamt he'd hurt anyone but me. Honestly. Are you alright now? God, I'm just so sorry. I didn't want you getting in the middle of this. That's why I scarpered."

"What were you doing in Manchester, visiting your family?"

"I visited some old mates. You know my family don't speak to me."

"What? For real?"

"Aye," Nick said gruffly. She softened her tone when she saw my confusion. "Kid, you do know me mam chucked me out of the house when she found out I was gay? I was sure Melissa would have told you."

"She didn't," I said.

"She was respecting my privacy." Nick thoughtfully fingered the punk bracelets around her right wrist, the black one with small bondage rings and the red one with silver conical studs. "Anyway, it done me head in for awhile. But not anymore." Nick played with the homemade bracelet on her left wrist, neon-pink beads, glittery blue, green, pink, and purple letters that spelled out "Punk" and a diminutive razor blade charm.

"You should have at least told Melissa what was happening. She knows your history with this Atom wanker."

"I wanted to deal with summat by myself for once. Besides, Jake's my best mate, not her. I can't just inflict myself on her now she's gone."

I stared at her in disbelief. "Has your trolley completely derailed?"

Nick shook her head. "No, luv. You mean, am I off my trolley?"

"Are you off your trolley? Don't you know that Melissa loves you?"

"Oh, aye, an' Jesus loves me and all. She doesn't need me whingeing on about some queer-bashing brother of an ex-lover. I wouldn't be in this shite in the first place if I weren't—"

"Oh, *come on*. You're not even going to *try* telling me some bollocky, rubbishy bullshit about Melissa caring what your sexuality is. That's absolute bollocks and you know it. The three of us are like family."

"You're a romantic bugger, ain't ya?" Nick said. "You hardly even know me."

"Don't fucking *say* that," I protested. "Of course I bloody know you."

Nick squinted at me. "All I know is whenever you're around me, you get hurt. Christ, if I were any kind of a mate at all I'd stay away from you. In fact, after I walk you back to the tube, that's exactly what I'll do."

"You don't mean that," I said. "Besides, Melissa's meeting me here."

"Melissa's coming here? Fuck me." Nick looked frantic. "She will fucking kill me for what happened to you."

"No one's gonna kill anybody."

Nick stood up. "It's getting dark. I'll walk you back."

"What about Melissa?"

"I ain't gonna be here, mate, am I? I can't face her."

I crossed my arms and sat immobile on the couch.

"I cannot be arsed with this." Nick sounded near tears.

"I'm not going anywhere. When Melissa gets here, the two of you can carry me out when I go limp. I wasn't a member of ACT UP all those years for nothing, you know."

"You are *not* committing an act of civil disobedience in my flat."

"*Nonviolent* civil disobedience," I corrected her.

We heard the buzzer go off.

"Well, let her in," I said. Nick didn't move. I went downstairs and opened the street-level door.

"What's going on?" Melissa followed me upstairs.

"Don't yell at her," I said.

"Don't tell me what tone of voice to use." Melissa looked more hassled than I'd ever seen her, except for the night I'd been injured. She sat on the arm of Nick's settee without removing her coat. "Have you got any idea what's been going on around here in your absence? Have you got any explanation? She could have been bloody *killed*. Why did you not *tell* us Emilia's brother had turned up again?"

"I'm sorry," Nick said, trembling. "I wish it had been me."

"That's crap," Melissa said angrily. "You know I'd be just as upset if it had been you who'd got hurt."

"I was scared," Nick said. "I never thought Atom would go after anyone but me. Why would he? If I had thought for one moment—Christ, you've got every right to hate me."

"*Hate* you? I could never hate you. Jesus, who puts these daft ideas in your head? I am not your mum. You'll not suddenly lose me, you know. I was really gutted by what happened to Amanda and pissed off you weren't here." Melissa draped an arm loosely over Nick's shoulders, and I thought her hand looked kind and full of grace.

"No, you're right. I should have warned you." Nick leaned against Melissa's damp, charcoal-gray wool coat.

"Listen. I did something you won't like," Melissa said. "I found an old address of Emilia's in Belfast. I couldn't get her number but I wrote her, telling her what's been going on."

"Fucking hell," Nick looked ill, "you told her? That is summat I cannot deal with. It took me so long to get over her. Seeing her brother brings it all back."

"She needs to know. She used to be my mate too, remember? It hurt me when she left, too. Not like it hurt you, but I felt betrayed. I should have got in touch with her ages ago, but you made me promise not to. You can slag me off all you want to, but I can't have this happening to Amanda or to you. I had to do something."

Melissa took us back to her flat and ordered in a nice curry. Nick was too upset to eat much.

"I know it's shit 'orrible," Melissa said. "But if leaving you is her way of coping with a crisis she doesn't deserve you. We probably won't hear from her anyway. And what does that say about *her*? Please have more than that."

Nick speared a pea with her fork then put it and her knife down, said, "Sorry," and went into her room.

"She was absolutely devastated when Emilia fucked off back

to Ireland. I think it was her first really serious relationship. Keep eating." Melissa pushed back her chair and went to check on Nick.

I finished my plate of curry and did the washing up. As I made the tea, I could hear them talking through the open door. "You're a sensitive person," Melissa said. "These things hit you hard. But you can stay with me for as long as you like. You don't have to cope with this on your own."

"I got so bloody depressed the last time." Nick's voice sounded shaky. "I don't want to go down there again."

I could certainly understand that. I brought in a tray with the tea. "Nicky," I sat on the edge of the bed next to her and Melissa, "I know what it's like to be too depressed to function."

"You do?" Nick asked forlornly. "My head goes black. Like a curtain being pulled down."

"I know it does," I said softly, touching her foot.

"If it gets to be too much for you to handle there *are* things we can do," Melissa said quietly. "Remember we talked about you temporarily going on some medication?"

Nick lowered her head. "You think I'm mental."

"No, I don't," Melissa said. "You're having a hard time. Everybody needs help sometimes."

"You don't," Nick accused her tremulously. "You're always so fucking well-adjusted."

Melissa patted her leg. "Oh no, love, I'm not. I have my problems like everybody else. We all have different ways of coping with them. Believe me, sometimes I need help, too. Some people just have a difficult time showing that side of themselves."

"I show it too damn much," Nick said. "I'm afraid of what you'll think of me if I fall apart."

"I couldn't give a monkey's," Melissa said firmly.

"A monkey's what?" I asked.

"It means I don't care," Melissa laughed. "For fuck's sake, Nick. I put up with this half-Yank." She gestured at me then rumpled Nick's hair playfully. "You think that I would judge you?"

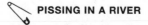 **PISSING IN A RIVER**

Telling myself to shut up, I revealed, "Nicky, I've taken psychiatric medications before."

"You have?" Nick asked.

"In the past," I said, hating myself for only telling the partial truth. But I wasn't ready to let Melissa know that what was wrong with me was permanent, that I would be on medication for the rest of my life.

We sat in the back room together and watched the Nirvana video *Live! Tonight! Sold out!* Nick and I cried through most of it because Kurt was dead. I guess Melissa reckoned it would be cathartic for Nick. It was for me too, though I'm not sure she knew that. "He's dead. Kurt's dead," I said. "I cannot believe that he's dead."

"He's been dead since 1994," Melissa said, not unreasonably.

We watched her uncut copy of Nirvana's *MTV Unplugged*, which was beautiful, and Nirvana at Reading in 1992. I loved the way Kurt started playing the guitar to Boston's "More Than a Feeling" as the introduction to "Smells Like Teen Spirit."

Nick still didn't think she could sleep, so Melissa put on *Quadrophenia*, a film based on the Who's rock opera about the mods and the rockers in Brighton. We watched videos well into the night. I was terrified of the questions Melissa would ask about my psychiatric history once we were alone. *Eventually she's going to catch me taking pills*, I thought. *Or I'm going to run out of meds completely, and she'll catch me having a nervous breakdown.* My current cache was in my Gibson case. But she never asked a thing. Instead, she tucked Nick and me into the guest bed with a hot-water bottle by our feet and kissed us both goodnight.

TRACK 28 **ENGLISH ROSE**

Melissa took me on walks to strengthen my ankle. She loved Hampstead Heath and Regent's Park. The Heath and Queen

Mary's Rose Garden were full of frost. Nick and I had both been staying at Melissa's until a mate of Nick's came down to London for a visit and she returned to her own flat. I stayed on, citing the cold weather and the urgent need to continue recording my songs.

We walked in Hyde Park one day, past the empty green-and-white-striped chairs by the water, looking at the ducks, their bums in the air as they dunked their heads to scavenge for food. The city of London was piled high all around us and I felt tranquil. I looked up at the Post Office Tower. Melissa took my hand and smiled at me. Many times she had taken my hand to warm up my fingers or in friendship, but today it felt different. I was getting a different vibe from her. Or I imagined I was. Maybe it was only my own vibe folded over on itself. I concentrated on watching my breath turn white as I exhaled and not tripping over my own feet.

I looked at Melissa in her familiar raincoat, thick-soled, black vegan creepers on her feet, and thought about what a good person she was. I had on a blue Nirvana sweatshirt, the hood pulled over my head. Melissa was a few inches taller than I was, and now she draped her arm casually across my shoulders. I tugged on the belt loop of her faded, black trousers, pulling her closer. Mist hovered over the grass, and I felt romantic. We passed a flower seller, and I stopped. I bought a bouquet with as many roses in it as I could afford and handed it to Melissa.

"This is for me?" she asked, taken aback. I nodded, nervous she might misinterpret the gesture. *God forbid she thinks I'm coming on to her.* But Melissa wasn't like that. "Cheers so much, love," Melissa said. "I can't even remember the last time anyone's given me flowers."

Then what a shit-arse Martin must be to go out with you all this time and not bring you flowers, I thought. "It's a token of my honest admiration and affection," I said rather formally, embarrassing myself.

Melissa said, "You're very sweet."

"And you're the coolest straight woman I've ever met," I said to let her know I respected her boundaries.

Melissa's eyes were gentle. "That's quite a compliment," she said finally. We continued walking, bent forward against the wind and the first drops of water. With the hood of her own black Joy Division sweatshirt pulled up, Melissa looked like a dark tulip in the slants of rain.

At the flat, Melissa put the flowers in water. "I know I'm the reincarnation of a rat," I said, having once explained to her that I was born in the year of the rat, always had rats as pets and felt a strange affinity to them. "But you are the incarnation of a rose." *Or a rain-soaked tulip,* I amended in my head.

"Come here, sweetie." Melissa gave me a hug and I felt her soft cheek against mine. "Watch you don't cut yourself on my thorns."

I laughed. "Stigmata of the highest order."

"No more stigmata for you," Melissa said firmly. She'd only just removed the sutures from my hand.

Puncture wounds reminded me of the biblical story of Abraham, and how God asked him to sacrifice Isaac, his son. Abraham had lifted the knife and God had stopped him. But Abraham had already killed Isaac in his heart. I wondered what that meant. What was God's point? Maybe it wasn't that we should do anything God tells us, but that we should have a loyalty to life, whatever life we're living, while we're here.

TRACK 29   **REUTERS**

That night, Melissa took the roses upstairs to her bedroom. As we stood on the landing, she asked, "Why did you say I was the coolest straight woman you'd ever met?"

"Because you *are* the coolest straight woman I've ever met."

She looked uncomfortable. "Usually you treat me like a person, not a category."

I looked at my feet. "I didn't want you to be upset I'd given you roses. I didn't want you to think I meant anything romantic by it. That I didn't respect your boundaries."

"First of all, I can't imagine ever being upset at a best mate giving me roses. Second, I know you respect me. I don't have any weird ideas about lesbians being predatory. And if someone, gay or otherwise, made a polite pass at me and I wasn't interested, I'd simply say so and leave it at that. I can take care of myself."

"I didn't mean to imply that you couldn't."

Melissa said awkwardly, "Do you still want to sleep in my room?"

She didn't have to ask. It had become our habit. I felt warm, comfortable and safe with her. I think she knew that and asked because something had shifted between us. I didn't know what that was, but I felt a subtle change, like one might feel a slight draught. She wouldn't want to jeopardize my feelings of safety. "I'd like to sleep with you," I said.

"It's dead cold," she agreed. "I'm being silly anyway. Why *wouldn't* you call me straight? It's how I behave. It's how I live my life. What else would you call me?" She laughed self-consciously.

"That doesn't mean I have to label you," I said.

We sat on her bed. I studied Melissa's face in the light from a street lamp that glowed faintly through the curtains. The graceful curve of her nose, her smooth skin and deep, lovely eyes. I didn't often get the chance to stare at her so blatantly because I never wanted her to catch me at it, but she had something on her mind and didn't notice. Melissa turned and brushed a hand lightly over my cheek. "Alright, love?" She sighed and lay on top of the covers. She looked at the ceiling. "Fucking hell, I feel mortified."

"What's wrong?"

"I can't believe I'm going to ask you this. When you said you didn't mean anything romantic, was it because you didn't think it would be appropriate or because you would never think of me in that way?"

My stomach began to ache. I didn't know how to reply. If I said I didn't mean anything romantic because it was inappropriate, would she think I was pathetically lusting after the unobtainable straight woman? Would she think less of me or feel sorry for me? If I said I would never think of her that way, would it reassure her or would she be insulted that I didn't find her attractive? I realized I was treating her like a stereotypical straight woman again, not giving her enough credit. She wouldn't try to trap me with a question like that. She wasn't that kind of person. She just wanted to know. But I still didn't know what to say. "I meant that I would never want to hurt you," I said. "Not for all the world."

Melissa touched my cheek again softly. "Ignore me. I don't know what I'm saying. Fucking 'ell."

"Tell me about it," I said. "I don't mind if we talk about whatever it is you don't know that you're saying."

Melissa looked pained. "The words are stuck in my throat."

"God, I know that feeling," I said.

"Listen, you know you can trust me, yeah?"

I nodded.

"I can't believe I'm going to tell you this. But you make me feel things I haven't felt in ages. I thought I'd put that part of my life away. Do you know what I'm saying? No, of course you don't because I'm not saying anything. Is it alright if I tell you this?"

Now that she'd so precisely *not* brought up the subject, I was gobsmacked. At least I thought I was. I was afraid I'd misread her. My heart shot into my mouth like an oversized cough drop and I was afraid to move. "What are you saying?"

"It isn't Martin that I'm interested in," Melissa said quietly.

Oh my God, I thought.

"I haven't been honest with myself. It's been donkey's since I've felt anything. Darlin', you're shaking. Have I upset you?"

"No," I assured her. "Sometimes I just shake for no reason."

God, I'm an idiot.

"Is it alright if I tell you how I feel? You don't have to say anything. I just want to tell you. Then we can drop it. You can tell me to shut up. I haven't felt romantic in donkey's years. I go out. I occasionally have sex. It doesn't feel like much of anything. That night you came over, pissed out of your brain, and I put you in a hot bath—I think that's when it started. I couldn't be mad at you. I felt happy being with you. When you told Nick—I know it's none of my business—about having had problems with depression, I sensed this vulnerability in you that made me want to touch you. I'm sorry I'm saying this so badly. I've never felt this way about a woman before."

"Oh my God," I said.

"But I've got no idea how you feel."

"You *know* how I feel," I said.

"No, I don't. Today the way you held my hand in the park, I thought, maybe. But then you said I was the coolest straight woman."

I groaned. "I should be shot. Why do you think I asked all those inappropriate questions about you and Martin? Why do you think I was so concerned he wouldn't appreciate you? Because I do. Because I appreciate you so goddamn much." I was so emotional I let that Americanism "goddamn" slip into my speech.

"Is it alright?" she asked. She leaned forward and gently kissed me.

Her lips on my lips made my head explode. I just stared at her. A line from my favorite Patti Smith song, "Pissing in a River," ran through my head. "*What about it, I can't live without you.*" I felt ecstasy and nausea. Finally, I managed to say, "God, you've got bottle. How can you be so calm?"

Melissa laughed. "The reason I'm calm is because I have now left my body and am watching this from the ceiling." I laughed, too. "Is this something you want to do?" she asked. "It's alright if it's not. It doesn't change the way I feel about you as a mate. You can still sleep here like before. I wouldn't—"

"You're so beautiful."

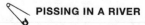 **PISSING IN A RIVER**

She looked embarrassed.

"Why would you want to?" I asked.

"Why would I want to what?"

"Sleep with me. I mean, you being so beautiful and all."

"Are you completely off your nut?"

"No. I mean, yes. Am I? I mean—what does that mean again?"

"It means calm down." Melissa smiled, creasing the delicate lines around her mouth and making me melt.

"I'm sorry. When I'm nervous, I babble like an idiot."

"I make you nervous?" She had removed her "Remember Ian Curtis" sweatshirt and wrapped her arms around me.

"Are you *kidding*? I've got to pee." I pulled free of her embrace and ran into the loo. *God, I'm such a loser. Why am I such a prat?* I cleaned my teeth an extra time while I was in the bog in case she ever felt like kissing me again.

"You're lovely," she said when I sat next to her again. She ran her hand down my cheek to my neck. And her touch made me tremble.

"You are an angel sent from heaven," I said, and we both laughed. "No, really, you are." I wondered if this would be a good time to tell her about the voices in my head. How I was sure that one of them was hers. *Oh yes, good!* I told myself. *Maybe crazy is the new sexy.*

Melissa brushed a stray lock of green hair out of my face. The unbuttoned cuffs of her shirt made her hands look even more graceful, like birds of paradise.

"The green makes your eyes look gray." Melissa ran her fingers through the pink area of my hair. She smiled, and I couldn't even think anymore.

Without warning, the incessant turntable inside my head dropped its needle on the song "It's Too Bad" by the Jam. I whispered it into Melissa's neck.

> "*Same old feeling every time I see you,*
> *and every avenue I walk I'm behind you.*

Your back is turned and your eyes are closed, girl.
You move in circles that are out of my reach now."

"I love that song," Melissa said. "What made you think of it now?"

It didn't seem like the time to say, *oh yeah, besides hearing voices, I have a twenty-four-hour jukebox in my head.* "I think you were the one I always saw in front of me. The one who was walking in the rain just out of my reach in your long, beige coat."

"That's the sweetest thing anyone's ever said to me. Why was I out of your reach?"

I wanted to say *because you started out as a voice in my head. Because you started as a hope, a wish.* I said, "Because you are the kind of person who never happens to me," stealing the idea shamelessly from Edith Wharton's novel *The Age of Innocence.*

"Oh, love," she said softly. "Am I happening to you now?"

I put my arms around her neck. She gave me a long, slow, dazzling kiss. The taste of her, that sexy mouth on mine, made me dizzy. I kissed her back hard, caressing her tongue with mine. I felt like all my life I'd been choking on salt water and now, finally, I was given fresh water to drink. We lay down, and I stroked her cheek. "Every time I see you, you happen to me all over again."

Melissa sighed. But then she said, "I'm not that special."

"Have you *met* yourself?" I practically shouted. "You *are.* I knew it from the first time I ever heard your voice. Oh God," I murmured, with her lips on mine, "you don't know, you just don't know."

"Know what?" she whispered breathlessly.

"How much I've always wanted you," I said before I could stop myself, but she didn't pull away. I held her face.

Melissa kissed me more passionately. "Can I feel your skin?"

I shrugged. "It's just skin."

She held me and pressed her mouth to my ear. "I'm sorry. Am I pressuring you?"

 **PISSING IN A RIVER**

"No, I'd love to feel your skin, too."

She put her mouth back on mine, and I simultaneously wanted to surrender myself to her completely and run out of the room to have a good cry in the toilet. She touched me softly, slipping her cool hands under my faded Nirvana T-shirt with the lyrics to "Dumb" on the back. I thought I was going to pass out. I pulled the tails of her blue-and-black shirt out of her trousers and slowly unbuttoned it. When I put my hand lightly on her breast, I felt her tense up. "What's wrong?" I whispered.

"I'm sorry." She sat up and pulled her shirt closed.

"What's the matter?" I sat up and pulled down my T-shirt, unfolding a picture of Kurt Cobain with unwashed hair on *MTV Unplugged*.

"I'm the one who started this, and I'm not ready."

I could see bright tears held back in the corners of her eyes. "That's not a problem," I said. "We're not in any hurry."

"I haven't been completely honest with you."

"You're really a man?" I suggested. *Not that it even matters at this point*, I thought.

A faint smile touched her lips. "Remember I told you I dated a bloke called Paul in the past? It wasn't as simple as that. I didn't tell you the whole truth."

I waited for her to go on, but she didn't. "Whatever it is, it's okay," I said.

"No, it's not. It sort of, well, did me in."

"Did you in *how*?"

"He–well, he––. Well." She stopped abruptly.

"Honey, did he hurt you?" *I'll fucking murder him.*

"He sort of—hit me."

"He *hit* you." The thought of anyone hurting Melissa made me want to throw up.

"I didn't fancy it anymore. I wanted to break up. But he wouldn't leave it at that. He followed me home one night. He said he wanted *closure*."

"Don't you love it when men use pseudo-feminist phrases to gain our trust?"

"And throw them in our faces," Melissa said. "I let him in. To talk. The more I tried to explain that I wanted to be on my own, the more pissed off he got. He said, '*You fucking cunt. No one does that to me.*' I told him to leave. To get out of my house."

"And he hit you?" I tried to adapt my mind to this idea.

"Yes. I tried to fight him off. He raped me," she said.

Oh, God. My stomach dropped to my knees. Even though I'd guessed where she was heading, it knocked the wind out of me. "*He raped you.*" I felt nauseous with rage and grief. "Oh, God. I'm so sorry that happened to you." I wasn't sure if she wanted me to hold her.

"I never told anyone. Not any of my mates. Not even Nick. I felt so stupid. I wanted to forget it ever happened."

"What about your sister?"

"I tried to make myself ring her up and tell her, but I couldn't. I was afraid she'd leave the band and fly home, and I didn't want her to do that, to put her life on hold for me."

"*You went through the entire thing alone?*"

"Yes. And *don't*, just *don't* feel sorry for me. That's another reason I didn't tell anyone. I don't want your pity. I am not anybody's victim. I'm still myself."

"Of course you are. What happened to that piece of filth?"

"I got a gun, and I shot him. He's buried in the garden."

My mouth dropped open.

"I'm only kidding, love," Melissa said, running her hand through my hair.

"I hope you shot him one more time for me," I said, thinking of the way Patti Smith says that in her version of "Hey Joe," the Jimi Hendrix song. "Seriously, what happened?"

"It's not something I want to talk about now." She lowered her head. "Alright?"

"Of course it's alright."

"What we were doing—about to do—brought it up for me again. I'm sorry, love."

"Don't apologize for that," I said. "How are you feeling? Are you okay?"

"I feel self-conscious, and I wish we could talk about something else."

"Oh, sure. Okay. If you could be any animal, what animal would you be?"

Melissa laughed and hit me with a pillow.

"What's your favorite color?" I held up my hands to defend myself.

Melissa grabbed me and hugged me. "You're brilliant. I'm sorry if I ruined your night."

"Do you think that's what I care about?"

"I'd rather flattered myself that you might." Melissa tried to sound jovial.

"Be serious. You know I fancy you. And I care about you. All of you."

"Don't be so mature. I can take anything but brute maturity." She smiled at me unhappily.

"You don't have to do that," I said. "You don't need to entertain me. You don't always have to be the strong one. You *can* break down, you know. You're allowed."

"I've cried enough about it already."

"You're always taking care of everybody else. You took care of Nick and me that night she was raped and you must've been feeling like crap, having it bring up crap memories for you."

I did up the buttons of her shirt, and she started crying. "You've managed it." She wiped her eyes on her shirttail. "You've made it safe enough for me to cry, and now I don't think I can stop."

"It's alright," I said.

"Don't think you've got to sit here. It could go on for hours. You've got better things to do than watch me feel sorry for myself. In fact, I'd prefer it if you didn't see me like this."

"Don't be silly," I said. "And there's nowhere else I'd rather be than here with you. Come here." I held her as rain pelted the window. "God, I never realized before how empty my arms were without you." I rested my chin on her head and rocked her. Quietly, I sang an old Dils tune called "Sound of the Rain" into her hair.

> *"I don't listen to the cops, I wish they all were dead,*
> *listen to the planes flying overhead,*
> *listen to the sound of the loss and gain,*
> *I just listen to the sound of the rain."*

I don't know why in God's name that song is comforting. But it is.

TRACK 30   JUST OUT OF REACH

"I've got to go," Melissa said. Her uncombed hair fell in front of her eyes. "You don't need to get up. I'd skive off myself if one of my partners weren't on holiday. Have a lie-in."

"I should get up," I insisted sleepily. "It's not fair I get to sleep and you don't."

"Getting up or feeling guilty about not getting up won't make me any less tired." Melissa mussed my hair. She leaned down and kissed my cheek.

In the afternoon, I stopped by her office to see how Melissa was getting on, but she was out on a home visit. I walked to an outdoor flower stall and got her a bouquet of bluebells that was half white baby's breath. It was all I could afford, not having busked regularly in a while. When I returned to the flat, I found Melissa upstairs waiting for me. She was sitting on the bed with her back against the wall.

I handed her the bouquet. "I mean it romantically this time." I lifted up her legs and sat on the bed, holding her feet in my lap,

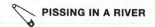 **PISSING IN A RIVER**

soothed by her black Doc Martens with their familiar rubber soles and yellow stitching.

"Oh, love. You shouldn't have," she said.

"Are you alright? You're sitting here in your coat."

"I feel vulnerable. Last night. You know. I've never really talked about it. I've not put myself in situations that would make me feel exposed. Now I've got me bulletproof coat on." She tried to smile. "I've slept with blokes since it happened, but with you it feels different. I can't hide. I can't shut off my feelings."

"I can't separate my emotions from sex either. What's wrong with us?" I said, hoping to cheer her up, but there were tears already starting in her dark, honey eyes.

"I haven't let myself feel vulnerable with anyone. Only you."

"Oh, sweetie. What about Nick?"

"Oh, you know. I feel like I have to be strong for her. To protect her."

I paused. "She'll surprise you."

"No, she won't, because I'm not going to tell her."

"I meant, what are we going to tell Nick about our relationship? Do you think she'll mind?"

"Mind?" Melissa swung her feet to the floor, sitting next to me.

"Well, she does look up to you, you know. She won't think I'm taking you away from her, will she?"

"We'll just have to make sure we never give her a reason to feel like that. Amanda, this is hard for me to say, but—"

"What is it?" I stroked her hair, brushing the stray, wavy wisps out of her face.

"Can we not tell Nick about us just now? I'm feeling—well, as I said, vulnerable. I haven't been able to be intimate, and I just—sometimes I can't bear it, thinking about the rape."

"We can tell Nick our relationship has changed without telling her about the rape."

"But what if the sex part doesn't work out and you leave? And I have to say why?"

"First of all, I'm not going anywhere. And sex is something I never expected from you anyway."

She put her head on my shoulder, and I felt the collar of my T-shirt getting damp. "Do you have another girlfriend?" she asked.

"What? You know I don't. Don't cry. I wouldn't hide that from you. Of course not. What are you thinking?"

"Last night I never even asked if you had started seeing someone else."

"I'm not."

Melissa put her hand on my cheek. "I want you to know I'm HIV-negative. I got myself tested after I was raped."

"I know you would have told me if you were HIV-positive."

"How the bloody hell do you know that?"

"I know you would never do anything to put me at risk. First do no harm." I referred to a common principle of medical ethics. "That's you all over. I got myself tested when I was in ACT UP, and I'm negative, too. I've been lucky." I brushed my hand over her slate-gray coat. It felt cool and smelled fresh, like rain-washed tarmac with just a hint of bus exhaust.

"Is it alright if we don't tell Nick yet?"

"It's just between us for now."

Melissa pulled away and dabbed her eyes with a Kleenex. "Let's forget this crap shite and go out for our tea. There's a brilliant Sri Lankan restaurant I want to take you to in Earls Court. I had the best meal of my life there."

"Is that what you want to do?"

"Yes. I'm going to wash my face and then I'm treating you to a nice meal." When Melissa came out of the loo the color was back in her cheeks and she'd changed from her work clothes into an oversized purple-and-black stripey jumper.

Back at the flat, I asked Melissa if I could still sleep with her. "Just to sleep," I said. "I like being close to you."

"I like being close to you, too."

I went into Jake's room to take my pills and put on my special blue Kurt Cobain T-shirt for sleeping in. It was a photo of Kurt in his pajamas, looking cozy and smiling, playing an acoustic guitar. When I went into the bedroom, Melissa was already under the covers. "Can I still have a kiss goodnight?" she asked, as I got in bed next to her.

"Oh my God, course you can." I moved closer and kissed her, my entire body buzzing.

"I don't know what's the matter with me," she said disconsolately as we both lay awake. "I thought I dealt with this ages ago."

"That's right," I said. "You dealt with it yesterday, didn't you?"

"You're very amusing." Melissa got up. "It's no use. I can't sleep."

"What calms you down?"

"Listening to punk music."

"Me, too." I followed her downstairs.

"Go back to bed."

"Don't be daft."

Melissa put on the Vibrators singing "Baby, Baby," and just like the song, I turned to her and said, "Baby, baby, baby, won't you be my girl?"

"Why do people think punk wasn't sweet?" Melissa asked. She put on a gorgeous acoustic version of "Baby, Baby" from the *Unpunked* album. "I have so many versions of this song it's criminal."

"You know when Knox sings, '*Aah, let me put my arms around you / just wanna use up a little of your time*'? I always thought it was, '*Just wanna use up plenty of your time.*' That makes sense especially when I think about being with you," I said, holding her hand. And Melissa blushed.

I plugged in my Gibson and wrote a song about Melissa. I wrote it to the same beat as the song "Bubblehead" by a German band called Uncle Ho, only faster, and was also inspired by "Things Are Getting Better (sic)" by the 25th of May.

In the evening, we sat in the back lounge and watched a crime drama on telly. When it ended, I said, "Have you ever noticed how whenever anyone gives a profile of a serial killer, it almost always starts, *he's a white male between the ages of twenty-five and thirty-five?*" Melissa muted the volume on the remote. I lay with my head in her lap and looked up at her in the telly-screen glow. "Why does no one ever say, *there seems to be a pattern here?*" Melissa wrapped the arms of her purple cardigan around me. She looked tired but had refused my exhortations to sleep. "I wrote a song about you today," I volunteered shyly.

"Tell it to me," Melissa said.

"Only if you go to bed."

"I'll lie down on the bed downstairs, alright?"

We got up, and after covering her with a quilt, I ran upstairs to get my guitar and the small Vox practice amp I'd found in Jake's wardrobe. Or, as I had begun to call it, "Jake's miraculous wardrobe" because so many wondrous things came out of it.

"What's it called?" Melissa asked.

"'Lipstick.'"

"Because I wear so much of it?"

"I'm glad you don't. Kissing a woman in lipstick is like kissing a crayon. Once I had a reissue lavender Danelectro guitar with lipstick pickups—single coils that look like silver lipstick tubes—and thought that made me a 'lipstick lesbian.'"

Melissa laughed as I tuned my guitar.

> *Standing in the rain wearing your sweater*
> *the angels that call after me use your name*

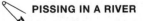 **PISSING IN A RIVER**

everywhere I go I pretend I'm walking right behind you
and you turn around
see me plain standing like a stain on the ground
in my own orbit a star a lonely satellite
without a planet to wrap her up and hold her tight
I'm watching you in my mind like you're on TV
I see you what do you see?

Streets suck me down your front door makes me drown
don't tell me the raindrops are not really angels
cause I like the way they paint your face such grace
a sweet embrace just a trace of a smile burdens your lips
the lips I want to kiss without lipstick
makes me want to drown take me down with you
I'm watching you in my mind like you're on TV
I see you what do you see?

I'm romance insomniac four a.m. I yak yak yak yak
cough syrup without the hack won't set me back
won't give the sleep I lack just a kiss one you wouldn't miss
lend me a kiss I swear I'll give it back to you
let me kiss your lips without lipstick
let me taste the rain on your hair on your coat
on your mouth on your eyelids on your cheeks
I'm standing in the rain wearing your sweater
hoping everything in my life gets better
I'm standing in the rain
take me down with you

"I'm gobsmacked," Melissa said when I finished singing and put down the guitar. "Did the angels that call after you really use my name?"

"You bet they did."

"Come 'ere," she said.

I jumped backward onto the bed. Then I draped myself over

Melissa in her pink-paisley pajama bottoms and the long-sleeved white thermal shirt that made her seem even cuddlier.

She put her arms around my neck. "You're not bored?"

"Bored?"

"With me."

"After two days? Listen. I could kiss you for a million years without needing to move on to anything else. You're the best kisser."

She rolled on top of me and put her hands beneath my head. "You're so fucking sweet." She kissed me. "Tell me more about the angels." I tugged at the hem of her shirt. She pressed herself against me and kissed me harder. I started shaking all over. "Whatever's the matter, love?"

"Nothing," I said, trying to shrug nonchalantly.

"Calm down. Take a few deep breaths."

I sat up. She took off her cardie and wrapped it around my shoulders. I couldn't stop trembling and said, "I don't know what's the matter with me. I usually don't freak out when someone kisses me."

"Ah, it's just me then," Melissa said, and I burst into tears. "Oh, God. Sorry, love. I was only taking the mickey."

"You're so beautiful, and I'm so *freaked out*." I buried my face in her breasts.

Melissa caressed my back soothingly.

"Do you know what it's like to suddenly meet the person you've wanted to meet almost your entire life and then have her—well, kiss you?"

Melissa looked confused and handed me a tissue.

I blew my nose. "It's intense. It's overwhelming. It's over-whelmingly intense."

"You've gone all white."

I said, "That's funny," because I was wearing my dark-blue "Fuck White Supremacy" sweatshirt. "Did I ever tell you I was born on the white-baby side of a segregated hospital?"

Melissa patiently waited for me to make sense, an exqui-

sitely gentle look on her face that absolutely devastated me with the terror of its beauty.

"There's things I haven't told you." I raised my head. "It's not fair of me not telling you after you've been so honest with me." I wasn't sure I should tell her what I was sure I needed to tell her. But if I didn't, I'd feel like an imposter, like she'd be kissing me under false pretenses.

"You don't have to tell me anything that makes you uncomfortable, love."

"No, I have got to tell you."

"You can tell me anything."

"It's something I never tell anyone," I said.

"I'm not just anyone."

"No," I said, "you certainly aren't." I opened my mouth to say more, but nothing came out. Finally I said, "I don't know if I can."

"You better if it's upsetting you."

I felt nauseous. "I'm afraid it's a bigger secret than listening to Heart."

"Is it bigger than listening to Oasis?" Melissa teased me.

"Unfortunately it is," I said. "My lift doesn't go up to the top floor."

"What? Where did you hear that?"

"On *Prime Suspect*," I admitted. That was a television series with the gorgeous Helen Mirren as the tough-talking Detective Superintendent Jane Tennison.

"What do you mean your lift doesn't go up to the top floor? What does that mean?"

"I have fucked-up brain chemicals," I said, not looking at her. Slowly I told her the abridged story of my psychiatric life.

When I finished, Melissa sighed and said, "Oh, love." She held out her arms to me. "Come 'ere and give us a cuddle. I'm glad you told me."

"Don't hate me," I said.

"I could never hate you."

"I wanted you to know before things went any further."

"You're afraid it would change the way I feel about you?"

I nodded strenuously. "I figured you'd be decent enough because of what you said to Nick about taking medication if she got too depressed. But I don't know how you feel personally about me doing it, basically forever, unless someone invents a cure." I looked into her eyes. "A lot of people think taking psychotropic drugs is like cheating. Even doctors. I couldn't take hearing that from you."

Melissa said, "I don't feel that way, love. How are you getting them?"

"I had a six-month prescription when I got here."

"Six months? But Amanda—" I could see Melissa trying to work out exactly how long I'd been in the country, "haven't you already been here six months?"

"I'm on my last month," I confessed. "And I guess I may as well tell you that when the drugs run out, so does my official right to be in the UK. I was only supposed to stay six months."

Melissa gasped like I'd hit her. "Fuck, love. Thank God I have a prescription pad. So in a little while, you'll be living here illegally *and* having a nervous breakdown? Do you have another doctor?"

I shook my head. "Fuck me. I always wanted to take your breath away, but not like this."

"Amanda," Melissa asked, stunned, "when were you going to tell me all this? What were you planning to do?" Her tone changed. "Are you leaving?" She looked down at her hands in her lap.

"No, of *course* I wouldn't just leave. I don't know what to do. I'm terrified of getting another shrink, and I don't even know *how* to get one. At university, I had the NHS. I can't afford private rates. And how can I sign on with a local clinic when I'll be here illegally?"

"Are you sure you weren't just gonna fuck off back to the States?" Melissa still looked hurt.

"Of *course* not." I put my arms around her, and she laid her

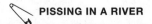

head on my shoulder. "I would never leave you. You're breaking my heart. I honestly don't know what I'm going to do. I've been in total denial. After I met you, I decided if I ran out of dosh I'd live on the street if I had to. If I had another breakdown, hopefully you'd notice and do something to help me. And maybe you'd let me sleep in your garden."

"That won't be necessary," Melissa said wryly, looking seriously unamused. "Jesus Christ, love. We've got to get you a visa extension. If you get caught living here illegally, I think they can deport you and ban you from returning. Shit. Shit. This is just a bit of a shock."

"I didn't realize staying on past six months would be a big deal. As long as I'm not working illegally or using any services, how would the government even notice me?"

"But you *do* need to use health-care services," Melissa shouted at me.

"I'm sorry."

"Let's not panic," she said, more to herself than to me. "I'll ring my solicitor. We'll contact the Home Office and get your visa extended. Then we'll sort out what to do in the long term. You can use my address. You'll say I'm responsible for taking care of you financially if you get into trouble."

"Melissa, I can't ask you to do that for me."

"Who says I'm doing it for *you*?" Melissa left the room, and I heard her on the phone. She returned and said, "I rang Harriet, my solicitor, at home. We've known each other since university, so she's an old mate. She'll get in touch with someone who knows more about immigration law and ring us back tomorrow or the next day. Now what's this about being afraid to see another psychiatrist? Tell me the truth."

"Another shrink might make me change my meds. It took ages to get the combination just right, and if they're changed one iota, I'll get really sick. Most shrinks won't just take your word for it, and every other shrink but the last one has misdiagnosed me and given me the wrong medications." Deep down,

I was somewhat proud of that, as though it meant I was an extraordinarily complex person. "And he was the only one who let me participate in my own treatment. Most shrinks assume that having a mental illness makes you stupid. *Especially* if you're female. Even the women shrinks." I fidgeted, ashamed of the whole sordid mess that was my life and barely able to meet her eyes.

Melissa said quietly, "I'll help you."

"You'll write out the scripts for me?"

"What medications are you taking?"

I hesitated. I didn't want her to know *precisely* how crazy I was.

"Amanda?"

"I hadn't really wanted to tell you."

She raised her eyebrows. "I'll tell you what I'll do. I'll just give you blank prescription forms and sign them. Then you fill in the medications and the amounts you want."

"Oh, that would be brilliant," I said.

She widened her eyes and cocked her head at me.

"Oh, you're joking."

After some stalling, I told Melissa what I was taking. I expected her to dispute me or at least say "wow" or something, but she just wrote everything down. Then she said, "Listen, I shouldn't be doing this. If I think it's necessary, I'll arrange for you to see a psychiatrist, someone I'll recommend."

"Alright," I said penitently.

Melissa still looked miserable. "Are you sure you aren't just going to leave?" She reached out a hand and tentatively touched my hair but remained apart from me.

"*No.*" I pulled her close and held her. "I wouldn't just leave you. What can I say to reassure you?"

"I know I don't really have the right to ask you for assurances. It's not like we're—committed or anything."

"Well, I've *almost* been committed," I volunteered ironically.

"We've been—dating—for all of five minutes. I know

 **PISSING IN A RIVER**

that. Don't think—" She bit her lip. "I know you don't owe me anything."

"But we were already best mates," I argued, "so of course you can ask me for things. Of course you can expect some loyalty. Would you really do all that for me? Be my doctor and my—" I stopped, afraid of saying the wrong thing or saying too much.

"Mm hmm." She put her lips on mine then asked shyly, "Do you still want me to be?"

"Yeah," I whispered breathlessly, "very much."

Melissa curled up next to me. Physically exhausted from not having slept, she dozed off. But I couldn't rest, having divulged so much. I covered her with the duvet and stroked her hair. "You know I love you, you silly git," I whispered. "Don't you?"

TRACK 32 POTENTIAL SUICIDE

Unable to sleep, I watched the glow of the moon slice the bed. Even though Melissa had been kinder and more sympathetic than I could ever have hoped, and even though she acted like *she* was the one nervous about being left, I was still scared that she would come to her senses and reject me. Melissa awoke in the middle of the night and noticed I was up. "Hiya." She smiled sleepily. "What's the matter? Can't sleep? Upset you told me?"

I nodded, and she put her arms around me.

"You should go back to sleep," I said.

"I can get up a little late tomorrow. Talk to me."

I sang from a Big Audio Dynamite song, "'On the psycho wing and I ain't done nothing.'"

Melissa grinned. "Somehow a psycho wing doesn't seem the right place for you." Her arms around me felt like heaven, and I told myself to enjoy it while I still had the chance. "Oh," she said suddenly, "you were serious."

"I guess I left that part out," I said. "It only happened once."

She scrutinized me. "You seem like the kind of person who

hid things really well. I mean, from what you've told me, you were suicidal all through graduate school and nobody twigged it. How'd you ever get caught?"

"That's it exactly," I said, impressed by her acumen. "I *did* get caught. I had a crazy lesbian therapist."

"They get you every time," Melissa said.

"The social worker at university health services suggested I see a therapist as well as a shrink for meds since I'd never tried that and I didn't understand why the antidepressants weren't working. I had to find someone off-campus, and as a graduate student on a stipend, I was always skint. There was a mental health clinic in a rough part of DC, on the Maryland border, that charged on a sliding scale according to income. My first therapist was a homophobic straight woman who said she told all her bisexual patients to become heterosexual because that's a better choice. She said she could never be a lesbian because children are too important to her. I stated the obvious fact that being lesbian does not prevent you from having children, and she said she would never raise children with a female partner because the *identification process* was all wrong."

"Oh, bloody do me a favor," Melissa groaned.

"When I pointed out her homophobia, after she'd once again assured me that I could say *anything* in that room, she threw me out of her office and told me never to come back."

"I didn't think they were allowed to do that. Don't you lot have some kind of therapeutic code of ethics or something over there?"

"Allegedly. I asked the clinic to find me a lesbian therapist, thinking, *she won't fuck me over. That* lunatic decided the noise in my head from intrusive thoughts was from multiple personality disorder. Now they call it dissociative identity disorder."

"Oh my God." Melissa tried to stifle a laugh. "I'm sorry, but that's so stupid it's almost funny. You obviously have a coherent personality."

"She wanted me to have multiple personality disorder so

she could write a paper on it. I was supposed to remember a traumatic incident from childhood, preferably incest. When I didn't, she threatened to terminate treatment because I wasn't 'trying' hard enough. So I made stuff up. And I'm a fairly strong-willed person. Anytime people say they could never be brain-washed or pressured into making a false confession, I know it's not true."

"And that's a controversial and over-diagnosed illness to begin with," Melissa said.

"One of the medications I was on, because my stupid psychiatrist believed my incompetent therapist's diagnosis, had been making me seriously ill for months. I was so weak, I could barely stand up long enough to boil water for a cup of tea or make it to therapy appointments."

"That might not have been a bad thing," Melissa said dryly.

"Eventually I stopped taking it."

"What was it?"

"Mellaril."

"That's rubbish. We call it Thioridazine over here. It's an anti-psychotic. And we don't prescribe it anymore because of its dangerous side effects. It causes odd rhythms in the heart and can be quite toxic. You were right not to take it. It's prescribed for schizophrenia only in patients who have already tried two other medications that failed. And it doesn't sound like you were psychotic or delusional anyway. I've never seen you in anything even vaguely approaching a dissociative state."

"Even though the shrink was quite happy to put me on different medication, my therapist said I was being 'difficult.' And since I refused to take Thioridazine, she was terminating my treatment. Before I left her office, she tried to make me sign a contract promising I wouldn't kill myself."

"So after driving you to suicide and throwing you out into the street, she wanted to cover her arse and continue having power over you?"

"I couldn't believe she'd just completely cut me off and didn't know what to do. She said if I refused to sign it, she was going to call the police and report me as a danger to myself and others as soon as I left her office. And when I walked out, she did."

"Fucking stupid old cow."

"The other drug I was on for my depression was in the wrong dose, so I had to cut the capsules in half and spill out half the medication."

"Why were they prescribed in the wrong dosage?"

"Fucking stupid doctor. I can't remember why. Much of that time is a badly medicated blur. But that night as I was sitting in my living room with a razor blade cutting up my antidepressants on a mirror, there was a knock on my door. And it was the police. I didn't know what to do, so I let them in. The coppers asked for me. I told them I wasn't in but that the misunderstanding with the therapist had been resolved, and they left. If only they'd stepped a foot farther into my apartment or looked over my shoulder they'd have seen a mirror, razor blade, and white powder everywhere. They would have arrested me for cocaine possession." The Oasis song "Morning Glory" played in my head, with Liam singing, "*All your dreams are made / when you're chained to the mirror and the razorblade . . .*" "If I'd been across the border in Washington, DC and black, they would've shot me. When my ex-therapist found out I hadn't been committed, she called me up and threatened me over the phone. I was so devastated by her betrayal that I agreed to check myself into a mental hospital."

"She had you right where she fucking wanted you." Melissa sounded sublimely pissed off. "Fucking vicious crazy cunt."

"Oh, she was brilliant. Totally into S/M but not just as sex roles for play. Sadomasochism as a *lifestyle*."

"Let me guess," Melissa said. "She was the sadist?"

"How'd you know?" I said.

"How the *hell* did you know about her private sexual practices?"

"She told me. Her favorite song was 'Master and Servant' by

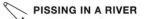 **PISSING IN A RIVER**

Depeche Mode. The Depeche Mode song I like best is 'Never Let Me Down.' I suppose that says it all."

"I can see I'm going to like her even more than I do already. I'll have her bloody license revoked. She shouldn't be allowed to bloody practice. She's a fucking bloody menace, she is. What's her fucking bleedin' number? I'll ring her up right now."

"I don't remember her telephone number," I said, chuffed at her loyalty. "But ta for the lovely thought."

"Was it bad in hospital?" Melissa brushed my pink-and-green fringe out of my eyes.

"At first. But then they kept me too drugged-up to care."

"And this was back in the 1950s?" Melissa suggested, and I thought of the Nirvana song "Frances Farmer Gets Her Revenge on Seattle" about the actress who was given a lobotomy because she didn't fit in. "How long were you in hospital?"

"Three weeks."

"Three *weeks*?"

"I'm surprised they let me out at all, except of course that they hated me, sarcasm not going over well in mental institutions. I think it implies a sophisticated intellect."

Melissa smiled. "No, you wouldn't want to be too high functioning."

"It's rather tricky. You want to present as either dramatic or catatonic. Using sarcasm as an anesthetic doesn't count as self-medicating like alcohol and drugs do. You have to prove that you're in pain. Better to spring a leaky vein in front of them. But one of the other inmates and I became friends—you know how you do when you're locked up with somebody. I have the kind of personality you have to be incarcerated with to truly appreciate. We used to empty out the fruit baskets in the cafeteria, put them on our heads, and run around the ward saying we were basket cases. They'd put us in the Quiet Room."

"Quiet Room?"

"A padded cell they'd lock you in."

"Was it a locked ward?"

"Oh, aye. There were alarms on all the doors and signs warning of the danger of '*patient elopement*.'"

"I suppose they couldn't come up with a sillier term."

"I know. For some reason *elopement* makes me think of gazelles, like they were afraid the patients would lope away across the lawn like gazelles. Once my friend got put in the Quiet Room and managed to unscrew the metal plate over the wall socket with one of her rings. Then she tried to electrocute herself by sticking her wedding ring into it."

"How apt."

"Another time she tried to throw herself out the window, but the windows there don't break," I started laughing. "She bounced off the window and back into the room with a big bruise on her forehead. She'd been in hospital a lot, and her stories were hysterical. I mean, she really cracked me up." I paused. "Is there a way to say that without sounding mental?" The old Modern Lovers tune "She Cracked" started playing in my head.

"I don't think so."

"We would sit by the Coke machine because all the drugs we took made us thirsty and tired. We weren't allowed to sleep in our rooms during the day. And we weren't allowed to doze off in the common areas either. If you looked like you were asleep, a nurse would come by, shake you and say, '*This isn't a state institution. Look sharp.*' I was so drugged I could barely hold my head up. I used to lie down on the gurney that was always parked near the Coke machine. It was in a corner where the nurses couldn't see us without making an effort. There was a sign on it that said 'Do Not Sit or Lie on Table' which, of course, I ignored. One day an orderly came over and said, 'You can't lie there.' I said, 'Why not?' He said, 'It has a specific purpose.' I said, 'Yeah, it's for lying on.' He said, 'It's not a piece of furniture.' 'Well, yeah,' I said, 'it kind of is.'"

"What happened?" Melissa asked.

"Got put in the Quiet Room again, didn't I? But the worst part was the group therapy sessions they made us endure. It was

 PISSING IN A RIVER

my idea of what a twelve-step program in hell would be like. At the first one, the counselor wrote the words *'affirmations'* and *'self-talk'* on a chalkboard and asked us what we thought *self-talk* meant. I said, *'It's the voices we hear inside our heads telling us to kill,'* and the other patients laughed. We weren't in an institution for the criminally insane, so I didn't think I was stepping on anyone's toes. He said it was the negative messages we give ourselves. Then he explained that mental illnesses were nobody's fault and that everyone was only trying to help us. He told us to say the affirmation, *'Everyone is doing his best.'* I said, *'Even when he is raping you?'* and pointed out that rape and sexual abuse caused the mental problems that put the majority of women there in the first place. Then he tried to make us say, *'I am not trapped by my past.'* My friend said, *'I'm sorry, but some of us are here with biochemical illnesses.'* And I said, *'I am not trapped by my past. I can change my genes.'* He wouldn't concede that psychiatry has been used as a tool for social control and political repression. I just wanted someone to acknowledge it, to say I was historically correct. Now that homosexuality isn't the disease anymore and homophobia is, I'm supposed to agree to be a happy, well-adjusted lesbian. But how can you be a well-adjusted lesbian in a patriarchy?"

"What does that even mean?"

"It *can't* mean," I said, thinking of Gertrude Stein's poem "Patriarchal Poetry." "'*Patriarchal poetry not in fact in fact. Patriarchal Poetry in time.*'"

"Why do you always get literary or biblical when I'm supposed to be sleeping?"

I laughed, "I don't know. But here's another story about my lesbian therapist. Once when I showed up for an appointment, two men were fighting in the clinic parking lot. As they rolled on the ground flailing at each other, I walked up and said, *'Do you know how ridiculous you look?'* But then I noticed one of them had a knife and was trying to stab the other one. I stepped in between them and kicked the knife away. I scrambled after it, and one bloke took off. The other came after me. He wanted his fucking knife back. Like I was really going to give him back his knife so he could stab someone, probably me. I ran to my car and held the driver's-side door open as a barrier between us. A group of shrinks were leaning out the window of the clinic smoking, and I shouted up to them, '*Call 911!*' That's our 999. They just gaped at me like I was mental. I screamed, '*Help! This man is threatening me!*' My therapist, Ms. Head-Up-Her-Ass, hearing the commotion, stuck her head out the window and yelled at me for disrupting her session. I held up the knife and *finally* one of the shrinks—not mine—called 911. The bloke just stood there shouting at me until the police arrived and carted him away."

"Jesus fucking Christ," Melissa said.

"Suicide by shrink," I said, and smiled.

TRACK 33 CAPITALISM STOLE MY VIRGINITY

I was awake when Melissa got up for work, having hardly slept. All night I obsessively went over everything I'd told her. And now I was apprehensive—well, scared shitless—about my visa as well.

"How you doing, love?" Melissa said, as I quietly nursed a panic attack. "How are you feeling? Alright?" Melissa sat on the edge of the bed and put her hand on my forehead.

I tried to smile, but my anxiety was pushed up against my teeth like a wave. I struggled to hold it in. I didn't want to appear too needy so early in the relationship. *Let her get used to me before I become a human barnacle,* I thought.

"Are you unwell?" She looked at me with concern. I couldn't answer because I didn't know what to say and I was trying to keep my heart from projectile vomiting out of my throat. "What's the matter?" She felt my pulse. "What are you anxious about? Calm down," she said gently, resting her hand on my head. "Everything's alright. Are you upset about what you told

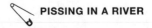 **PISSING IN A RIVER**

me last night? You needn't be. I can't talk about it now 'cos I'm late, but we'll talk when I get home, yeah? Don't worry. We're still mates. I hate to leave you like this, but I'm sorry love, I've really got to go."

When she left, I was beside myself. What did she mean *we were still mates*? I was so distraught I thought I was going to pass out. So I did the one thing I knew how to do under extreme circumstances. I went to a record shop. I took the tube to Leicester Square because that required no thought. It was on the northern line, a straight shot from Hampstead station. I walked across the road to the big Tower Records at Piccadilly where I did my underground busking. Piccadilly Circus was bright even during the day with its red, blue, and green Coca-Cola, McDonald's, Foster's, and TDK neon signs. The streets were full of black cabs, people and noise, but I was in my own lonely capsule, shut off from the world.

I spent hours looking at every single punk CD in the huge shop. That usually soothed me, but I agonized over the one perfect thing to get Melissa so she wouldn't hate me and chuck me out of her life. With my anxiety at a dangerous level, my OCD went berserk. My brain spat out intrusive thoughts faster than I could neutralize them. I would have given just about anything if I could have unscrewed my own head and taken it off for a few minutes. Was that too much to ask? It was so bad I was whispering under my breath. But I tapped my foot and pretended to be singing along with the music that was blaring throughout the shop.

I looked at *Power of the Press* by the Angelic Upstarts because it has the song "Brighton Bomb" on it, which is worth the entire price of admission. But I'd heard it on Melissa's computer and was sure she had the album. I considered the Eyes Adrift CD, which had just come out. That was the band with Krist Noveselic, Nirvana's bass player, and Curt Kirkwood from the Meat Puppets. I loved the versions of Meat Puppets tunes from Nirvana's *MTV Unplugged* concert. I'd seen Eyes Adrift perform in the States, and Krist had played his familiar black bass through a Hiwatt amp.

Krist and I had a mutual friend, Danny, who owned a guitar shop outside Seattle. I'd found Danny while shopping online for guitars. Both Heart and Nirvana bought instruments from him. He had given me a piece of red wire from a switch on the black "VANDALISM: BEAUTIFUL AS A ROCK IN A COP'S FACE" Strat Kurt Cobain had smashed. I'd had it made into a ring, which I only took off when I boxed. Danny had donated the remains of Kurt's guitar to Seattle's Experience Music Project. It had been put back together by Kurt's guitar tech, Earnie Bailey. I'd always meant to tell Nick why that guitar meant so much to me, but she'd thrown away her Nirvana T-shirt, the one with its picture, because of the blood that got on it when she was attacked.

After much consideration, I bought Melissa the Stiff Little Fingers *Complete John Peel Sessions* that had just been released and two Kurt Cobain calendars for myself. I knew Melissa would let me make a copy of the *Complete Sessions* before she kicked me to the curb, and I could use the new Kurt pictures to weep over.

As I walked back through the rounded passageways of Leicester Square station looking at graffitied MTV posters, I was so nervous my head felt numb. Melissa wasn't home. I waited upstairs for her, sitting on Jake's bed with the Kurt Cobain calendars in my lap, pretending I was looking at them when all I could see was Melissa's face. When I heard her key in the lock, my heart beat so fast I felt dizzy and shut my eyes.

"Where are you?" She came upstairs, still in her beige raincoat. "What are you doing?" Melissa took off her scarf and fingerless gloves. She sat down beside me. "I was worried about you. What have you got there?"

I looked down at her heavy black shoes and dropped the Kurt Cobain calendars on the floor. Then I put a finger tentatively on the knee of her jeans, handed her the Tower Records bag and burst into tears.

 **PISSING IN A RIVER**

"Oh my God." Melissa put aside the plastic bag and leaned toward me. "What is it, kid?"

Whenever Melissa called me "kid" it reminded me of the Pretenders song "Kid" and always sounded affectionate. I clutched at her black jumper.

"Can't you talk?" She put her arms around me, and I sobbed.

"You scared me to death this morning when you said we were still mates," I mumbled into her thick sweater.

"What? I'm sorry, love. I can't hear you. I'm not trying to make it worse." She lifted up my head with her hand beneath my chin. "Say it again."

"You scared me to death when you said we were still mates," I enunciated more carefully through my tears.

"Oh dear, is that it?" Melissa pulled her sleeve down over her hand and tried to mop my face. "I'm so, so sorry, love. Wait a minute." She untangled herself and got off the bed. "Here." She handed me a box of tissues.

I blew my nose and blinked at her. "I've got you all wet." There was a head-sized water stain on her jumper.

"This morning," she said softly. "That was me being awkward and unsure of our relationship. I don't know what our relationship *is*. I wanted to reassure you, but I didn't want to be presumptuous. I was sleepy, it was late, my brain wasn't working, and I didn't know what to say. I was afraid." She hesitated. "I was afraid of rejection, of saying something out of order, of scaring you away. What you told me last night, love. It makes fuck all difference to me."

I wiped my eyes with a Kleenex and looked at her doubtfully. "Are you winding me up?"

"*No*," Melissa said fervently. "Honestly, I couldn't give a toss. I knew I'd said the wrong thing as soon as I heard it coming out of my mouth." Melissa held me out by the shoulders so she could look in my eyes. "And I wanted to say something else, something that would signify our relationship, whatever that is. But I feel uncomfortable because I haven't been able to—well, you know. I'm so sorry that I hurt you."

I put my head on her shoulder.

"Do you want to go back to America?" she asked.

"Are you barking mad?"

"*Do* you?"

"*No*. No, no, no. I want to stay here in England even if it means sleeping in shop doorways. Just let me come in and take a hot bath once in a while."

"Stop being so dramatic and give up your bedsit and come live with me," Melissa blurted out. I was shocked into silence. "Say something."

"I'm fucking gobsmacked, Melissa."

"It'll make your money last longer. And it will look better for your visa application."

"Melissa, I would *love* to live with you, and I'm chuffed you'd ask, but—"

"But?" Melissa's eyes brightened, translucent like two warm pints of bitter.

"Melissa, I can't live off you."

Melissa started singing the X-Ray Spex song "I Live Off You."

"But I can't."

"Why shouldn't you?" Melissa insisted. "It's not even an added cost. I've already got the flat, and there's plenty of room. I won't support you. You can pay for your own food and contribute to household expenses. The only difference'll be you won't pay rent for a bedsit which you're never in anymore anyway."

My heart swelled with gratitude and joy. "But you just said you don't even know what our relationship is yet. I don't want to spoil it by moving too fast."

"We won't. You can have your own space in Jake's room, come and go as you like. Things will be exactly the same as they are now except you won't go skint paying rent, you won't be cold, and we'll be flatmates. If Harriet says it's best, will you?"

"I can't just move in with you because it's convenient. Can I? Has Harriet rung you yet?"

"Not yet. Don't you think I would have said?" Melissa rested her cheek on top of my head. "You know, love, I was really gutted by what you'd been through. And I'm a bit gutted you thought it could make any difference to me."

"Telling someone you're crazy can be a big deal," I said. "It wasn't anything negative about you."

Melissa roughed up my hair. "You're not mad. Your lift is only stuck on the ground floor, remember?"

"Aren't you going to look at your present?"

"A pressie? For me?" Melissa opened the Tower Records bag and pulled out the CD. "*The Complete John Peel Sessions*. Oh, cheers, love. Nice one. This is brilliant."

"I figured you'd let me make a copy of it," I murmured, feeling glittery inside because she liked it.

"Silly git. You won't need a copy of it. Not if you move in here with me."

That night as we lay in bed kissing, the turntable in my head played "Just the Wine" by Heart. I felt Melissa so deeply even my feet trembled. I knew she wasn't ready for sex, so I tried squashing my desire just a little. I touched her breast lightly through the material of her T-shirt and shuddered. She put her hand on my breast, and I moaned softly, unable to help myself.

Melissa felt me shifting my feet uncomfortably. "Is anything the matter, love?"

"You are so sexy I think I'm going to burst."

She blushed.

In a raspy voice, I recited what I'd heard Patti Smith say during her rendition of "Gloria" in a 1979 concert I'd recently listened to. "*'Oh, I would like to see you some morning. I would like to talk this over very sincere. Maybe we could meet in this life or after . . . There was only one layer covering the garden. I don't know when we'll get there again.'*"

Melissa sighed deeply, and I could feel her body giving way to mine, moving more deeply into me. And I thought, *we've got to get back into that garden.*

TRACK 34 OPINION

Melissa sent me to a chemist friend of hers who let me buy my drugs at a reduced rate. "And you can stop hiding them in Jake's bedroom if you want to," she called after me as I ran upstairs, and the Clash song "Drug-Stabbing Time" played in my head.

"How'd you know?" I yelled down. I had the Takamine guitar case open and I heard Melissa climbing the stairs.

"Oh, so that's where you've been keeping them," she said. "It wasn't hard to suss out." Melissa sat on Jake's bed with a note-pad and biro. "What other drugs have you tried?" she asked, crossing her legs.

"All of them."

"*All* of them?" She raised her eyebrows.

"All of them," I repeated firmly. "Ask."

Melissa began naming drugs, starting with the newer anti-depressants. I'd tried all of them. She moved through the older antidepressants, then into the antianxiety drugs and tranquillizers. I'd taken them all. When she got to the antipsychotics she said, "Now this is ridiculous. What the hell did they think you'd got?"

"Everything."

"Surely not schizophrenia?"

"When I take that standardized test, you know, the long one with eight-hundred questions like—'*are you afraid of snakes?*'—I come out schizophrenic. The report I saw on myself, after I found I had a legal right to demand it, said I was either schizophrenic, had a drinking problem, or couldn't read very well."

"I don't suppose you need to read well to get a PhD in English." Melissa's accent was a little poshed up when she was being medical. "You're moderately in touch with reality. And with the drugs you take, I'm surprised you can drink at all without getting violently ill."

"I can't." I grimaced. "Remember the Isle of Whitby? Not being able to drink *is* my drinking problem."

"You've certainly covered every dangerous and addictive sedative," Melissa said. "You've pretty much had everything except for drugs that are really meant only for full-blown schizophrenia with delusions and hallucinations. I *am* impressed. Well done, you."

"I've been writing a song called 'Empathy Death' about my Gestapo ex-therapist." I recited what I had so far.

> *I've had enough fake empathy*
> *I'll give you all of mine for free*
> *once I had a therapist*
> *now I need an exorcist*
> *my therapist was a Nazi*
> *she was Ayatollah Khomeini*
> *she was convicted for war crimes*
> *she worked for the devil*
> *but other than that I have no opinion.*

Melissa laughed. "That's you all over. It's so hard to talk to you. You never have an opinion. She's a Nazi. No, really, what was she *really* like? What do you *really* think? Don't be shy. Pick a side."

"It's a new genre. I call it 'lesbian hatecore.' You didn't realize I played 'women's music,' did you?" I laughed.

"Well," Melissa put down her notepad, "I feel absolutely convinced you've told me enough so I'm not snogging you falsely. Wha'd ya reckon?"

I said dramatically, "Take me."

Melissa pulled me down onto the bed and brushed my hair

out of my eyes with both hands as I hovered over her. As I lowered myself into her kiss, she asked, "Do you still have symptoms that bother you?"

"Mmm." I sucked her lower lip. "It's not like there's a cure, you know."

"People respond to medication differently."

"I've tried everything short of having a hole drilled in my head."

"Is there anything else you want me to know?"

"Mm umm." My whole body tingled, and I couldn't pry my lips off Melissa's mouth.

"Tell me," she whispered.

"The surgery is closed," I said, and nuzzled her soft neck and cheek as she caressed my back.

"I would never let anybody drill a hole in your head."

"That's because you're lovely."

She cradled and kissed my head.

"That's better," I said. "I had a serotonin and norepinephrine boo-boo."

"I'm glad your brain feels better."

"My problem is I get norepinephrine confused with Neo-Synephrine. That's a nasal spray."

"Yes, I know," Melissa smiled, "we have it here." She put a hand on the side of my face and moved my head into a better position then began kissing me deeply. I could feel her trembling, and the Song of Songs splashed through my head again. "You feel so good," Melissa groaned, "but I'm afraid if we take this any further, I'll shut down."

"Don't you worry about a thing, Melissa," I said, thinking, "*The song of songs, which is Solomon's.*" But out loud I said, "The song of songs, which is now mine." I only changed it slightly.

> *"Let her kiss me with the kisses of her mouth—*
> *For thy love is better than wine.*
> *Thine ointments have a goodly fragrance;*

 **PISSING IN A RIVER**

Thy name is as ointment poured forth;
Therefore do the maidens love thee."

Melissa's ringing mobile startled us. "It's Harriet," Melissa whispered, as she picked up her phone. At first Melissa mostly nodded her head vigorously. But then she started saying things like "ta very much" and "oh, that's brilliant." She rang off and stared at me in wonder.

"Well, what is it?" I demanded. "What did she say?"

"The good news is you've got to move in with me right away," Melissa said, putting her arms around me. "There's something called the Unmarried Partners rule. If we've been living together for two years as a same-sex couple, you can be granted the right to remain here. There are various ways to build up our two years of cohabitation. One way Harriet suggested is we spend six months at a time living together in each other's countries. But of course that's hard with work commitments and the cost. But we can consider it as a last resort. A student visa is another route. I know you've had about as much education as you can stand, but it's easier than leaving the country for six months. For me, anyway. We'd just have to come up with the dosh for two years of study. We're allowed to be apart for up to six months out of the two years if there's a good reason—no, me neither," Melissa said, as I violently shook my head. "We need to provide evidence of our cohabitation, but that's no problem since we've engaged a solicitor right away. The best thing is for you not to leave the country. Homophobic Entry Clearance Officers, if they suspect we're trying to build up cohabitation evidence, can refuse you reentry and deport you. If you're ever refused entry, it's going to be difficult to get you back in again. Also, since you're on a tourist visa, the ECOs can argue our relationship is evidence that you don't intend to leave, and all tourists have to show their intention of leaving when their visa's up. So just don't leave the country for any reason and don't volunteer information to immigration officials, as it's an offense to lie to them."

"And if I just stayed on illegally?"

"Some people try that, but the problem is the Home Office can say you have to return to the States and apply from there because one of the conditions of the Unmarried Partners rule is that you have to be legally in the country when you make the application. If you ask to extend your visa because you want to stay with your partner, it will probably be rejected. The important thing is for us to get your visa extended before it expires. If it does expire, you have to leave the country to reapply. If you're caught here illegally, you can be banned from returning for five years."

"Jesus, that's harsh," I said. "Did Harriet say anything else?"

"She said it's about time I fell in love, and she hopes we'll be happy."

"You're absolutely adorable," I said.

"You've got to move in with me."

"Christ, Melissa, that's a big decision. I feel like it's being forced on you. Are you sure you want to do this?"

"I wanted you to move in before we found out about the Unmarried Partners rule. Of course I'm sure. Especially if it means you can stay."

"I'm paid up at the bedsit through the end of the month," I said. "That's gives us a little time to think about it."

"As far as I'm concerned, there's nothing to think about."

"But we're jumping into being partners and bypassing all the intermediate steps. How do you know you're even going to *like* having sex with a woman? What if you change your mind?"

"Even if our relationship weren't a romantic one, I'd still say I was your same-sex partner if it meant you could stay in the country. I can't imagine my life or Nick's without you now."

"If, after some thought—I insist," I said, as Melissa started to protest. "If you still want me here, we're going to have to tell Nick about our relationship."

"Why? We can tell her it's so you can stay in the UK."

"You don't think she's going to wonder why we're suddenly

using the rule for same-sex partners? That it was the first sodding thing we came up with? She's not bloody stupid. I doubt I can officially start cohabiting with you until I'm completely out of that bedsit anyway, so you've got a fortnight to decide. You're acting like it's not, but it's a big decision. *Really*."

"I'm not going to argue with you. Jake's bedroom is now yours, so you can do what you like." Melissa put her arms around my neck. "Please recite more poetry to me. I've never had a— lover do that before."

Her use of the word "lover" made me shiver, and I said,

> *"Thy two breasts are like two fawns*
> *That are twins of a gazelle,*
> *Which feed among the lilies.*

"Or," I smiled, "to put it in my own words,

> *Thy lovely Bristols*
> *are hot as pistols."*

Bristol Cities—titties.

Melissa laughed. "You're getting really good at that. Soon you'll be a rhyming-slang dictionary."

I said,

> *"Thy lips, O my bride, drop honey—*
> *Honey and milk are under thy tongue;*
> *And the smell of thy garments is like the smell of*
>   *Lebanon."*

"Do it in your own words again," Melissa asked.

I paused.

> *Your mouth leaves honey on my tongue,*
> *And your hair smells of London.*

Your fingerprints are on my bum.
When I'm with you I am among
The lucky ones
Whom God has blessed.
I'm trembling here in your caress.

"That's bloody good for off the top of your head. Please stay," Melissa whispered.

TRACK 35 YOU'RE NICKED

Nick was sitting on my bed paging through an old gay and lesbian magazine as I sorted through my belongings. I hadn't exactly told Nick I was moving in with Melissa, just said I was bringing over some of my gear because I spent so much time there. "Six Activists Storm Helms' Office, Gay Protesters Face a Year in Jail," Nick read the headline from the August 1, 1990 issue of *Outweek* aloud. "Wait, is this you?"

"Yeah," I said.

> WASHINGTON—a band of six activists staged a raucous demonstration in the congressional office of Republican Sen. Jesse Helms of North Carolina on July 17, and each of the six may face up to one year in jail and fines of up to $600 apiece . . .

"'At 1:30 p.m.,'" Nick read, "'demonstrators entered the mail room of Helms' office in the Dirksen Senate Office Building by a back door. Once there, they used Helms' facsimile machine to transmit press releases . . .' That's quite funny."

We'd also used the phones to call newspapers and TV stations. I'd written a resignation letter for Jesse Helms, and we

 **PISSING IN A RIVER**

refused to leave until he signed it. In it, he apologized for being a homophobic bigot.

Nick was laughing. "That was in one of the gay papers here. I remember talking about it down the pub with some mates, and someone wanted to send you lot flowers across the pond." She put the magazine back in the box with other items from my arrests, like bracelets made out of discarded flex-cuffs and a summons to appear in DC Superior Court for "unlawful entry" and "demonstrating in a capitol building without a permit" from an arrest at the FDA in 1988. The bright yellow paper had my thumbprint in the corner and described my hair as "brown frizz." My jail paperwork from 1987 described my hair as "brown and blue," and my jail receipt listing the possessions taken away from me at the time of my arrest read: "orange sweatshirt, jeans, one red and one black sneaker, six earrings, gay-rights shirt, two pens, three pieces of paper, one novel, yellow police tape, two lesbian-rights buttons, six tampons, a flex-cuff."

"What's this?" Nick pulled out a 1981 issue of the British gay newspaper *Gay News* and paged through it. "Why'd ya keep this one?"

In that late May-early June issue I'd learned about the British men deported from America for being gay, which led to my arrangements to fly TWA and leaflet my own flight back to the States. There was an article explaining that the annual gay pride march was being held in Huddersfield that year to take a stand against the viciously antigay policing in the north and one announcing the first-ever, women-only Lesbian Strength march in London.

"Oh my God, is this *you*?" Nick was looking at the headline "Whistles and Hooters Greet Bullet Mayor." There was a picture of a group of protesters in front of Trafford town hall, and there I was with my sign, "No .303 for Me—Lesbian and Proud."

I looked at my much-younger self. "How the bloody hell did you *ever* recognize me?"

"You told me all about lugging your sign on the bus, you silly twat," Nick laughed.

"I forgot." I grabbed up my rucksack. "Wanna grab something? I'm ready."

"Wait a minute." Nick put all the papers in with my clothes and picked up the bag. "Show these to Melissa. She'll be dead impressed. Speaking of which, you should just stay at Melissa's permanently. If you got rid of this bedsit, you wouldn't have to busk so much."

"Well," I admitted, locking the door to my room, "she *has* asked me." We stood outside.

"You're over there all the time anyway. I want you to stay in London. I'd go spare if you ever left. D'you know what I mean?"

We stopped at a café for fried egg sandwiches and chips then got on the tube and took my things to Melissa's flat.

"Ta for helping me," I said.

Nick tucked the dark-green St. Christopher medallion she always wore into the neck of her fuzzy, black-and-gray striped jumper. She zipped up her sturdy, black cotton jacket and left to meet up with some mates.

I started Blu-Tacking the pictures I'd brought to the walls of Jake's room. The recording equipment was set up in there, and I figured I might as well make it as conducive to creative musical thought as possible. I'd photocopied and laminated black-and-white Kurt Cobain photos from Charles Petersen's book *Screaming Life* and had other pictures from Steve Gullick and Stephen Sweet's book *Nirvana*, magazines like *Rolling Stone* and the *NME* and a few gorgeous ones in neon-bright colors by photographer Michael Lavine: Kurt with Day-Glo pink hair and Kurt in a bluish tinge with a cherry-red Epiphone. I put the picture of Kurt in torn jeans, sneakers, and a flannel shirt, with his fist against his head, looking like he was having a complete mental breakdown right on the door.

I had a rare picture of Kurt playing a Gibson SG and a few of

him with Telecasters, the guitars of choice for Chrissie Hynde and Joe Strummer. There was a battered, black Telecaster with a black pickguard and a beautiful, slim, bird's-eye-maple custom neck listed at two hundred quid in one of the guitar shops I frequented, but I called it "the guitar with the thousand-dollar neck." If I could save enough money from busking, I was going to buy it.

Melissa had let me print out photographs from her computer onto photo paper, and I hung those up, too. My favorite was one I'd found of Chrissie Hynde in a blue denim jacket, PETA T-shirt, and cowgirl hat being arrested in New York City at a PETA demonstration. Her shirt said, "FIGHTING ANIMAL ABUSE ALL AROUND THE WORLD." I'd been wearing the same T-shirt the last time I'd seen her. That was the concert where I hung onto the front of the stage and she was right above me, and for two solid hours everything in my life made sense. For the encore, she'd come out with a dazzling, sparkly-gold Telecaster that was the most amazing thing I'd ever seen. Even the headstock was gold. And I had a picture of her much younger in her trademark red zipper jacket and black boots in Paris. I had a photo of Joe Strummer and Mick Jones onstage looking somberly out into the rain; the Jam performing in a downpour; Patti Smith with her wild mane of hair, now with a touch of gray; Davey Havok; Ann and Nancy Wilson; and a Who poster from Carnaby Street.

I heard Melissa at the door. When she came upstairs and looked into my room, I said, "I'm afraid you'll get sick of me."

"I won't get sick of you. What I'd like is the *opportunity* to see you enough to get sick of you." Melissa mussed up my hair.

"I brought over my Nirvana bootlegs."

"Then at least I know you're not gonna disappear," she said wryly.

"I think we ought to tell Nick about our relationship. It's too hard not telling her, and if she finds out later, she's bound to be really hurt. I feel like I lied to her today when I said you wanted me to move in but didn't say why. And I can't do that." Melissa bowed her head, the floor lamp lighting up her hair like a halo, and I continued, "I don't mean to pressure you. But you've been mates a long time, and I don't want anything coming between you. That would be devastating for everybody."

"This is going to sound daft, but I feel like if I tell her about our relationship, I'll fall apart and she'll know I was raped."

"She can't possibly know that," I said. "You're just feeling self-conscious having so many feelings resurface. And if you want her to know but don't want to tell her or can't, I'll be happy to talk to her. I will."

"You know it's not because I'm ashamed of you or anything like that, right? It's not because you're a woman. It's that we haven't—and I don't know if I can. And I feel so vulnerable, like I'll split open if I tell her."

"She doesn't have to know each intimate detail. She just needs to know we've started seeing each other romantically." I started unpacking my clothes.

Melissa picked up the copy of *Outweek*. She glanced at the magazine and gave a hint of a smile, sitting down on the bed. "I heard about this."

So you did have an inkling of me, I thought.

Jesse Helms had wanted to quarantine people with AIDS. The refrigerator in his office had a large sticker that said "KEEP THE REFRIGERATOR BEAUTIFUL," and I remember thinking, *the man who wants to put people with AIDS in concentration camps has a clean refrigerator.* My "Helms = Death" poster broke the Xerox machine when I tried to make ninety-nine copies of it and his big, fat, right-wing head got caught in the paper feed. I scattered a box of forty tampons all over his office and said I was campaigning for rights for the unfertilized. The US Capitol Police dragged us away, and I spent the afternoon handcuffed to a metal ring screwed into the wall of a police station. There wasn't much of a view, so I stared at the words engraved on the silver handcuffs, "Property of US Capitol Police," and tried making new words out of the same letters. *Type, clap, lice, lip.*

Then I tried making a sentence. *Pope foe of clit.* The officer, who was using one finger to type up my citation, asked if I knew the name of the woman on Senator Helms' staff who had phoned the police. I told him her name was Eva Braun, and he typed out the name of Hitler's girlfriend while I spelled it for him. When I was finally released, I stepped out of the police station and it was raining so hard the car alarms were going off in the parking lot. I remembered shivering in my wet sneakers and ACT UP/DC cap, drying off the black-and-white "Earn Your Attitude—ACT UP!" button pinned to my black sweatshirt.

I told Melissa how I'd been one of a group of seven ACT UP women from DC and New York who were invited to give a presentation on women and AIDS to Dr. Anthony Fauci, the director of AIDS research at the National Institutes of Health, and his staff after we got arrested there. I wanted her to know that I, too, had done something medical. I hoped she'd be impressed and think we had even more in common. "How can medical doctors, even male ones, not understand lesbian sex when they supposedly know how a woman's body works and where everything is?" I asked.

"It's a failure of the imagination," Melissa said.

I had arranged some personal items around the room to make it feel more like mine: a pin made out of a piece of green fencing that surrounded RAF Greenham Common from the Greenham Common Women's Peace Camp; my purple "Don't Do It, Di!" badge from the marriage of Lady Diana; a light blue badge that said "I HAVE BEEN CERTIFIED HANDICAPPED BY DR. RUNCIE" from the time the Archbishop of Canterbury stated that gays weren't sick, they were only handicapped; lavender, red, and yellow 999 badges; and pens from the London bookshop Gay's The Word that said, "This Pen Belongs to a Homosexual."

I glanced around the room and asked Melissa nervously, "Are you sure it's alright?"

"It's brilliant," Melissa kissed me, "and I'm so happy that you're here. Harriet was right."

"About what?" I asked.

"You know," she said.

TRACK 36   GIRL'S NOT GREY

"Nicky, I talked Amanda into moving in with me," Melissa said. The three of us were sitting in the Horse and Groom to celebrate the six-month extension of my visa. "She's in that parky bedsit, you know. I put her in Jake's old room."

"Thank God. It's about bloody time." Nick turned to me. "Now you won't have to go back to the States."

"And Nicky, your room is always there whenever you want it. But I don't think you fully understand the situation." Melissa glanced at me quickly. "Amanda could only extend her visa for another six months. You can't live in the UK more than twelve months on a tourist visa, which is what she has. But we think we've sussed a way around it. There's something called the Unmarried Partners rule. If Amanda lives with me for two years, she can apply to stay in Britain if we say we're partners. Unmarried, same-sex partners. Do you know what I mean?"

Nick nodded. "That's brilliant. I didn't know we had that here. But will there be any problem with you not being a lesbian? Should we say she's my partner?"

"Uh—" I cleared my throat, "Melissa has the financial resources and the space. She's kind of sponsoring me, you know, saying she'll be financially responsible so I won't rely on public funds. And we really have got to live together. They check. We have to provide evidence we're in a real relationship."

"Oh, I get it," Nick said quietly. She turned defensively to Melissa. "And that's a problem for you, is it? You have a problem with pretending to be gay? Is that why you both look so tense? Because if it is—"

"No, sweetheart." Melissa gripped Nick's hand reassuringly. "That's not a problem for me."

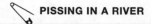 **PISSING IN A RIVER**

"So everything's alright then, yeah?" Nick looked to me for confirmation.

"We'll be living as same-sex partners," Melissa said.

Nick shrugged. "Who cares what you do if Amanda can stay? Just be openly affectionate. You already are. Are you afraid of what people will think? Your mates? Are you worried about your practice? I know it'll be hard on you, living a lie an' all that, but if it means Amanda can stay—please, Melissa, you've got to do it. Are you afraid it'll fuck up your love life? Just date that bloke you've been seeing in secret. Say it's like Romeo and Juliet or something. Make it all sound romantic and clandestine. He'll go fer it."

"You don't understand," Melissa said patiently. "I broke up with Martin. Amanda and I *want* to live as unmarried partners."

"Then it's alright. Keep your personal life private. You can do that."

"No." Melissa shook her head. "You still don't get it. We'll *be* unmarried partners. We *are* unmarried partners." Nick continued to look confused. Finally Melissa said, "Nicky, Amanda and I have been seeing each other."

"What?" Nick stared at her incredulously.

"I thought you might have guessed with Amanda spending so much time at mine."

"Wait. *What?*" Nick was utterly mystified. "What do you mean you're *seeing* each other? As in *dating*? You're not gay, Melissa, are you?"

"I'm not. I mean I *wasn't*. Not till just lately. I mean, I never was before." Melissa studied her pint of real ale. "Nicky, I can't believe this never occurred to you."

"*Me*? It didn't occur to *me*?" Nick said emotionally, rising from her seat. "Well, it didn't. I don't know what to say. I'm absolutely gobsmacked."

"I've never had these feelings for another woman before," Melissa said. "It's caught me by surprise."

"Caught *you* by surprise?" Nick said with a tremor in her

voice, falling back into her chair, her eyes reddening. "How could you not have told me?"

"I *am* telling you. This just happened," Melissa said. "This really never occurred to you?"

"No," Nick said. She looked down at her hands on the table. I saw a tear land on her wrist. "I'm going back to mine." She stood up falteringly. Melissa instinctively jumped up and put out a hand to grab her because she seemed so unsteady, but Nick stepped out of her reach.

"Hang about, you don't have to go. *Wait.*" Melissa hurriedly shrugged on her black denim jacket over the bright-red university sweatshirt she'd borrowed from me. "We'll take you."

I followed them out. We started walking up Heath Street toward the tube.

Melissa put her hand on Nick's arm. "Are you sure you want to leave it like this?"

Nick wavered, and the three of us sat down on the curb across from Hampstead station. Nick played nervously with the black zippers that zigzagged across the legs and pockets of her white trousers.

Melissa said, "We didn't mean to hurt you. *I* never meant to hurt you."

And I said hesitantly, "Is it that—do you have feelings for Melissa? For me?"

"For fuck's sake." Nick looked like she would dissolve from embarrassment.

"It's okay if you do," I said. "We can talk about it. We can talk about anything. The two of you were best mates long before I ever came along. I didn't mean to do anything behind your back."

"And I would never come between you and Amanda," Melissa said. "I know the two of you are very close."

"*Jesus.*" Nick looked so uncomfortable I thought she would burst into tears. "I can't get me head round it, can I?"

"There's nothing we can't talk about," Melissa echoed me.

"Bloody hell, I know it's got nowt to do with me." Nick looked at Melissa. "But I never thought you could be a lesbian. I always thought of you as intractably straight."

"Intractably? Well, I wouldn't go that far." Melissa slowly gave a half-smile and I wanted to kiss the delicate creases at the corners of her mouth.

"I know I should be happy for you but it's just too weird, innit?" Nick said.

"Let's go back to mine," Melissa offered.

We walked back to the flat, Nick and Melissa slightly ahead of me, as I watched Melissa's hips sway in black drainpipe trousers. The streetlight glinted off shiny silver rows of pyramid studs on her bright-red tartan belt. I heard her say, "It's really my fault. Amanda wanted to tell you straight away. It came about so suddenly. I didn't know how to handle it."

I went into the kitchen and put the kettle on. Waiting for the water to boil, I put PG Tips into three cups and hung my blue denim jacket over a chair. It had the Clash back patch Nick had given me after I'd admired hers and the upside-down American flag sewn under it, on which I'd scrawled, "Jail War Criminal Bush."

I brought the tea into the sitting room as Nick said, "You don't understand. You've been the one stable woman in my adult life. It's not that I'm sexually attracted to you, but you're not just a friend either. D'you know wha' I mean? But you've got your nice life and Amanda here. Wha'd you want me hangin' about for? I'm an emotional fucking disaster next to you. Emilia pisses off, and I fall apart. Jake leaves—I fall apart. But you're alright. You never stumble."

"Stop idealizing me," Melissa said. "It isn't fair. I don't just stumble. I fall over."

"Yeah? Well, you never show it. At least not to me." Nick opened and closed the zipper on the right leg of her trousers. "After Jake left, you seemed—distant. I thought maybe you didn't want me around as much now we were just the two of us. But then that night—when I was attacked—you really came through for me. And I thought, yeah, she really does care about me."

"Of *course* I bloody care about you," Melissa said. "Oh, honey, is that what it is? I'm sorry I seemed distant. Nothing changed in my feelings towards you. I had my own shit going on at the time."

"You never said," Nick offered glumly.

"I have a hard time showing that part of myself. It was something—personal."

For a second I thought she was going to tell Nick about the rape, and my stomach lurched. But then she said, "It had nothing to do with you. I'm so sorry I *ever* made you feel like I didn't care. That's bollocks, and it would never be true. And I'm sorry you didn't feel like you could come to me about it." She got up and sat next to Nick. "I must have really hurt you." She put out her hand to touch Nick's hair. "Can you ever forgive me?"

"Now you're taking the piss," Nick accused her.

"No, love, I swear I'm not. I'm being sincere. Please forgive me. And please stay here tonight. I'll never sleep if I don't know you're okay."

After Melissa convinced Nick to spend the night and we'd gone upstairs, I said, "I thought for a second you were going to tell her about the rape."

"No," Melissa said, and the flash in her eyes told me not to push it any further, "I wasn't."

The first sentence of Rainer Maria Rilke's *Duino Elegies* popped into my head. "*And if I cried, who'd listen to me in those angelic orders?*" And as I got into bed, softly I recited:

> "*Ah, who can we turn to,*
> *then? Neither angels nor men,*
> *and the animals already know by instinct*
> *we're not comfortably at home*
> *in our translated world.*"

TRACK 37 **GODSPEED**

Melissa had got out *The Patti Smith Masters* box set and was relaxing in the back lounge after work. She'd put on the first CD, *Horses*, and Patti Smith's lesbian rendition of "Gloria" was just ending as I came into the room. Patti's voice made me feel confessional, and I wanted to tell Melissa about the voices in my head.

"That song certainly sounds different now," Melissa said dryly, "hearing it with lesbian ears."

I sat down beside her on the settee as Patti Smith recited the introduction to the next song, "Redondo Beach," "*Redondo Beach is a beach where women love other women.*"

"That made me feel tingly and scandalized when it came out in 1975," I said. "Since we're listening to Patti Smith and she makes me want to spill my guts, there's something else I want to tell you."

"You mean besides being off yer head and listening to Oasis?" Melissa smiled at me.

"Yes. I should wait until we get to *Radio Ethiopia*. That album describes it best."

"Oh, go on." Melissa ejected *Horses* and slid *Radio Ethiopia* into the CD player.

"This might sound totally insane," I began, thinking, *what good can possibly come of a sentence that starts like that?* Even though Patti was singing, that Gang of Four song "Damaged Goods" ran quickly through my head. I inhaled deeply then let the air all out in a gush. "I have voices in my head. Or had them. Before I met you and Nick. Now I hear your voices. That's nuts already, innit? The voices are why I came to England in the first place. I came looking for the women inside my head. And I found you."

"What are you talking about?"

"A long time ago, I started hearing voices in my head."

"Did these voices come from inside or outside your head?"

"Oh, don't go all medical on me, Melissa. There were two women with British accents talking *inside* my head. Once when I was seriously suicidal, one of these women sat beside me on the bed and—"

"Wait. She sat beside you?"

"I *felt* that she was sitting beside me," I said impatiently. "She put her hand on my forehead, and the pain stopped. For several hours. You know that doesn't just suddenly happen in the middle of a nervous breakdown when your brain chemistry is completely fucked up."

"Hang on. She put her hand on your forehead? Was or was not this woman literally in the room with you?"

"I felt her hand on my forehead."

"What did she look like?"

"I had my eyes closed."

"I don't understand."

"I felt her *presence* on the bed. I felt her weight on the mattress. I don't know if you could call it *literally* or not. At first all I knew was that her name was Melissa. I recognized your voice the second I heard you on the telephone." I was convinced this was true. "And when I saw you, I knew."

Melissa stared at me. "You knew what?"

"That woman was you."

"That's not possible," Melissa said finally. "Love, I've been here the whole time."

"Have you never had even an inkling of me?"

"You said there were two. Who was the other one?"

"She was younger and had darker hair." I paused. "I was drawn to Nick the first time I saw her. She looked familiar. I knew she was the second woman. That's why I was following her that night."

Melissa said gently, "What happened to your voices after you were properly medicated?"

"*Nothing.* Those voices were *real*, Melissa. The meds can't touch them. Please don't make me see a psychiatrist."

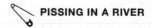 **PISSING IN A RIVER**

"I—" Melissa paused, frowning in thought. "I don't know how you expect me to respond. You say you don't hear them anymore?"

"They stopped when I met you. Now I hear your voice."

"That's either very crazy or very romantic." She sighed then said hesitantly, "It's true from the first time we met I felt comfortable around you. I let you spend the night when I'm usually far more cautious about letting someone I don't know stay in my flat. I even wondered about it at the time. But it seemed natural to take you in because you'd just rescued Nicky. Why *wouldn't* I feel that way? I guess it would have been more in character if I'd offered to drive you home or had you admitted to hospital for the night instead. I'm not normally as openly affectionate with people like I was almost immediately with you. It generally takes me a long time to open up to someone. And you know I have feelings for you I haven't had before. But isn't that called falling in love? It happens every day."

"I used to listen to this album and think of you," I said as "Pissing in a River" played on the stereo. "For a long time the voices stopped, and I missed you so much. I'd sit with my guitar and play along for hours. This was our special song. It was my way of telling you how I felt about you. That I would do anything to reach you." I heard Patti Smith sing, "*Everything I've done I've done for you / Oh I give my life for you.*"

"I don't know what to say."

"*Every move I made I move to you / And I came like a magnet for you now.*"

"There isn't anything to say. I sound nuts." I looked at her sympathetically. "I just wanted you to know. I don't want to have secrets from you."

"That's so intense."

I said, "Every move I made, I moved to you."

Melissa took off Patti Smith and put on Elvis Costello and the Attractions for "more cynicism and a little less emotion."

"I saw Elvis Costello at Exeter University," I said, to show Melissa I was oriented times three, that I had a sense of who I was, time, and place. "He was ace. He wore a suit."

"Who else did you see?"

"Oh, everyone who was around. The Tourists. Echo and the Bunnymen. The Second Stiffs Live Tour. Nick Lowe. Blurt. Ian Dury. The Jam. Any Trouble. Midnight and the Lemon Boys. I bought a badge off Glenn Tilbrook from Squeeze after they played."

"Midnight and the Lemon Boys?" Melissa asked distractedly.

"A punk band from Brighton." I still had my little black-and-yellow Midnight and the Lemon Boys badge and fond memories of dancing to them in the pub with my Exeter mates.

"Look," Melissa said, "for my own sanity, I've got to ask—are you *sure* it's not your OCD? You still have symptoms."

"This is totally different, Melissa. And I didn't just hear you. I *saw* you. I know how it sounds, but I thought I could tell you anything."

"You *can* tell me anything."

"All I know is I came looking for you, and here you are." I crossed my arms sulkily.

"Why didn't I know about you then?"

"Maybe you were busy," I snapped.

"Suspending disbelief for a moment—" Melissa began, and I glared at her, "do you think we knew each other in a past life or something?"

"Do I *know*?" I asked, exasperated. "How would *I* know? It feels spiritual. I don't know. Maybe I had a strong idea in my head of how things should be. Besides, you know if we understood absolutely everything, it would extinguish all hope. People need hope."

Melissa went silent, considering me, then finally said, "It doesn't matter how you got here. You arrived like a gift."

"I thought I was out on my arse," I said, relieved.

"Well, sanity's got a lot to answer for." Melissa ran a hand lightly over my face. "Love, I don't care if you're a nutter."

"Those are the nicest words I ever heard," I said.

TRACK 38 PRECIOUS

I felt better after telling Melissa my deepest secret. When she came home from work, I practically jumped on her, pushing her back against the door. She dropped her keys and her medical bag and put her arms around me. Shrugging off her coat, she led me upstairs.

Melissa lay on the bed and kicked off her shoes, revealing bright green-and-pink argyle socks. She caressed my face, the cuffs of her shirt undone and brushing against my cheeks. I took off my leopard punk bracelet and threw it on the floor, not wanting to impale her on the spikes. We kissed for hours then went downstairs and had our tea. Afterward, I cuddled up next to her on the couch, leaning my head against the soft black, pink, and yellow flannel of her shirt. We were watching *Maurice*, the film that had been made out of the E.M. Forster novel. He was my favorite novelist, and *Howard's End* was my favorite novel. I'd taken a tutorial on him at Exeter and kept all his books on the shelf of my residence-hall room. With limited space and in an uncharitable mood, however, I'd tossed Dickens' *Little Dorrit* out my window, and it lay all winter up against the base of the apple tree.

I was still only partially moved out of my bedsit when I got a severe flu, which I tried my best to ignore. Melissa told me to stay in bed, but after she went to work, I took the tube to Hackney. I wanted to surprise her by collecting the rest of my belongings. Slowly I rolled the pint glasses and ashtrays I'd thrown out of Exeter pub windows and collected later—having brought them all the way back from the States—into T-shirts and put them in my rucksack.

I started taking down the pictures I'd tacked to the walls of guitars I someday wanted to own—mostly printed out from eBay on Melissa's computer—but got so woozy I thought I was going to pass out. I ended up exhausted and nauseous on the unmade single bed, surrounded by photos of pink-paisley Stratocasters, blue-floral Telecasters, vintage Lake Placid and Daphne blue Strats, Jaguars and Jazzmasters with some Gibsons, Epiphones, Rickenbackers, and a few Mosrites thrown in. I rang up Melissa on her mobile and asked about the possibility of a home visit.

Melissa came to get me when the office closed. "How bad do you feel?" She put her hand on my forehead. "You've got fever." She looked around at the scattered photographs. "Is there anything else here you need right now except for your centerfolds?" She peered into the bathroom. "Don't tell me. I never noticed it before, but you don't own a hairbrush."

"Well." I shrugged.

"I asked you not to tell me," Melissa laughed. "What do you do if you get a tangle?"

"I'm not going to tell you," I said as firmly as possible given my indisposition.

"Oh, please tell me," Melissa begged. "I'm sure it's charming."

"I use a fork," I said.

Melissa collapsed across my bed in hysterics and said to the ceiling, "Bless 'er."

"Or I use yours," I said crankily. "You know I do."

"I just wanted to make sure that you flew across the ocean to start a new life without a hairbrush."

"It's not like I couldn't get one here. You *do* have hairbrushes in England, you know. I only took what I needed."

"And a hairbrush takes up the space of what, two, maybe three CDs or an effects pedal? I think you're lovely."

"Are we going or not? Or are you gonna stay here laughing all day?"

We drove out of Hackney with the Kinks playing "I'm Not

 **PISSING IN A RIVER**

Like Everybody Else." Melissa shifted gears and put her hand on mine. When the song ended, she asked me to slip *Between the Buttons*, my favorite Rolling Stones CD, into the car stereo. "I prefer old Rolling Stones when Brian Jones was in the band," she said.

"Me, too." I leaned back against the worn, comfortable seat. When the song "Miss Amanda Jones" came on, I murmured, "Amanda Jones. That'll be my name when we get married."

Melissa laughed, parking in an assigned space near her flat. She installed me upstairs in what she insisted on calling "our" bedroom, asking if she could do anything for me.

"I could murder a cup of tea."

Melissa came back upstairs, handing me a cuppa. "I put honey in it." She pressed her lips to my forehead to see if I'd got any hotter. "Poor thing. You *are* sick."

"I feel very sorry for myself," I warned her, "and very pathetic."

She went into the bathroom and came back with a white wafer of flu medication dissolving in a glass of water. "Take this. It's Co-codamol."

The wafer bubbled, spitting water out of the glass. It had an off-putting smell. I made a face. "What is it?"

"In your day it was called Paracodol." Melissa took the tea. "Drink it." I drank it as dramatically as possible and leaned against the pillows, gagging. She sat next to me. "Just relax. It'll make you drowsy." She massaged my head with her fingers.

I closed my eyes. "I'm cold," I murmured, leaning against her.

Melissa climbed over me and got under the covers, holding me against her stripey brown-and-blue shirt.

"Sometimes I get weird when I'm sick," I said.

"How will I notice?"

"Cheers, very funny. My defenses go down, and my OCD runs rampant. The intrusive thoughts and prayers for protection become so incessant they drown me."

"You have to tell me about that in more detail," Melissa said, becoming medical.

I ignored her. "And I have a jukebox going in my head twenty-four hours a day. With all the music I listen to, you'd think it would play something nice. But when I'm not paying attention, it turns demented and plays the most horribly annoying songs."

"Such as?"

"Oh, childhood songs, patriotic songs, Christmas songs. Anything that'll irritate me the most."

"What's your mental jukebox playing now?"

I paused. "'Close to You' by the Carpenters."

Melissa laughed and said, "Sorry. I know that's awful."

"Now it's singing 'America the Beautiful.' You have to move fast to keep up with it." I started singing the United States Marines song, "'*From the halls of Montezuma to the shores of Tripoli, / we will fight our country's battles on the land and from the sea.*'"

"Ouch."

"Plus, half the time it gets the lyrics wrong. One of its favorites is from the film *The Wizard of Oz*, which traumatized me as a child. '*We're off to see the Wizard, the wonderful Wizard of Oz.*' Except my mind says *gizzard*, 'We're off to see the *gizzard*, the wonderful *gizzard* of Oz.' It's maddening. '*Joy to the world, the Lord is come. / Let earth receive her King!*'"

"But you're Jewish."

"Of course I am. That only makes the Christmas songs more disturbing. If I opened my mouth and sang everything that popped into my head, you'd go spare."

"And this is going on all the time?"

"You're not going to run off to get your notepad and start writing this down, are you?"

"It's a bit important," Melissa teased me, "but I shall memorize it. And on top of this are the intrusive thoughts?"

"On top, around and underneath. And prayers for protection."

"Who are you protecting?"

"Everyone. Especially you."

"Ta." Melissa smiled. "What if I told you, as a medical doctor,

 **PISSING IN A RIVER**

that these thoughts have nothing to do with anyone's physical reality? Would you believe me?"

"Sure," I said, "but I'd keep having them anyway. We only use a tiny percentage of our brains. How can you know my brain *isn't* connected to everything in the universe?"

Melissa said, "I need to think about this more. But for now, you've done everything you need to do, and you can rest."

"Thank you," I said. "My OCD and I thank you. My OCD is a delicious combination of low self-esteem and megalomania."

"What does it feel like?" Melissa asked.

"Very *I'm-trapped-in-my-head-and-I-can't-get-out*-ish," I said.

"It sounds frustrating and painful."

"It could be worse," I mumbled, dozing off. "It *was* worse. This is like heaven."

"I'm glad. I'm sorry you still have symptoms that bother you. I wish I could do more."

"But you do. You make the mechanisms in my brain slow down. When I'm with you, I'm not tormented."

"What a lovely thing to say," Melissa said, tucking the covers in around me. "I'm all goosepimply."

TRACK 39   BRIMFUL OF ASHA

When I was well enough, we brought over the rest of my things, and I said goodbye to my bedsit. One late afternoon, I bunged my boxing gear into my white-and-green Exeter University bag and came downstairs in baggy silver boxing trunks. Melissa looked up from the book she was reading. Tagada Jones, a hardcore French band she liked, was playing on the stereo. "Well, don't you look scrummy?" She laughed as I blushed.

At boxing, I pretended the heavy bag was the president's face. Then I imagined Dick "my-daughter-is-a-lesbian-and-I'm-still-a-fucking-Republican" Cheney, Secretary of Defense Donald Rumsfeld, and Secretary of State Condoleezza Rice. I unwound my aubergine handwraps, wiped down my sweaty hair with them, and tossed them in my bag. I packed up my vinyl, hot-pink boxing gloves, and put on the fluorescent mint-green sweat-shirt on which I'd stenciled "The President's Brain Is Missing." When I'd been at Exeter, there had been a television program I liked called *Spitting Image*, which featured big-headed puppets of Ronald Reagan and Maggie Thatcher and included a regular segment called "The President's Brain Is Missing."

When I got home Dodgy, a Britpop band Melissa liked, was playing on the stereo. I referred to them as "Oasis lite" just to tease her, which really wasn't fair because I liked them and they had some great tunes like "Staying Out for the Summer." As I turned down the music to call for Melissa, I heard water run-ning in the upstairs bathroom. I got down the box of PG Tips and made two cups of tea. I tapped on the door and asked Melissa if I could come in. "I made you a cuppa." I put hers on the closed toilet lid.

Melissa was taking a shower. "Ta, Amanda." She sounded like she'd been crying.

"Melissa?" I listened to the water splash. "What's the matter?"

"Leave it, will you?" She tried to sound annoyed, but her voice broke.

"You're not alright, are you? Can I come in?"

"Do what? Oh buggery, bloody hell. Yes, come in. Why not? Bugger it."

I put my tea next to hers, swished open the shower curtain and stepped into the tub, still fully clothed in tracky bottoms, sweatshirt, and trainers.

"What are you doing?"

"What's the matter?" I asked, standing in front of her with the hot water beating on the back of my sweatshirt. She was so gorgeous I didn't think I could stand it.

Melissa started laughing and crying at the same time. "What the bloody hell are you thinking?"

I sloshed a little closer in my drowning white Chuck Taylors

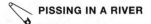

and put my arms around her slender, naked body. "Come on an' tell me what's wrong."

"I was thinking about you and me and how we haven't—you know, *haven't*. I shouldn't make remarks, like telling you you're scrummy, if I can't deliver."

I would have laughed if she hadn't been upset. "I like it when you call me scrummy. You don't have to deliver anything."

"I can't keep leading you on like that when I can't—you know."

"Honestly, Melissa, you aren't leading me anywhere I don't want to go. Will you please stop?"

"Anybody else would've gone spare by now."

"I'm not like everybody else."

"This is the first time you've seen me starkers," Melissa said thoughtfully.

"I know," I said, water running down my face. Her nipples puckered in the spray. "You've got lovely Bristols."

She lowered her eyes. I held her against my chest and heard the beautiful, melodic dirge "Ride With Me" by the Lemonheads, from when they were still a punk band, in my head. "'*Jesus rides with me*,'" I sang. I ended on the lines, "'*He's in your hair. / He'll forgive me my pain*.'" I ran my hand through Melissa's dark, wet hair. She kissed me, the shower spray drizzling between us. I could feel the warmth coming off her body like steam.

"Will you forgive me my pain?" Melissa asked.

"There's nothing to forgive."

She helped me pull off my drenched, heavy clothes.

"Ugh." I peeled off my bra. "I wouldn't give a bra the time of day if it weren't for boxing." I threw it over the shower curtain, and it made a splat on the floor. I watched the water travel in rivulets down Melissa's smooth skin. "You're so beautiful I can barely breathe."

"Stop." She looked away from me.

"Why? I'm just telling you how I feel."

"It makes me uncomfortable."

"Sweetie, face yourself. You're a very beautiful woman."

"I don't know how to respond to that."

"Just accept the compliment. It's alright to be beautiful in front of me. You don't have to be uncomfortable."

Melissa raised her eyes and took me in. "You're lovely," she whispered solemnly. I wanted to put my mouth on her breasts and gently kiss each nipple, but I didn't want to freak her out.

We got out of the tub and into her bed, snuggling under the covers. "This is the first time we've managed to be naked in bed together," I said.

Melissa joked, "C'mon, let's be having ya."

I laughed and pressed her against me. I felt her nipples touching mine and stopped breathing. Her muscles tensed so I hugged her, looking at the view of her broad, lightly-freckled back and strong shoulders.

"I'm glad you think I'm beautiful," Melissa said shyly.

"He didn't rape you because of what you look like," I said. "It's got nothing to do with you."

I held her and wondered what I would do if we ever ran into her rapist. I imagined the color running out of Melissa's face and not knowing what to do.

I remembered how in ACT UP, at one of our meetings in the old church in downtown DC, someone had asked us to do an action in solidarity with people with AIDS in prison. Some people jumped right on it but a few of us, mostly the women, were uneasy. Finally an HIV-positive ACT UP bloke stood up and said what we'd been too intimidated by political correctness to say. He had AIDS, was poor, didn't have health care, but he hadn't killed anyone. Then I said my solidarity depended on what people had actually done. It was on a case-by-case basis for me. I couldn't feel solidarity with rapists. After the meeting, we had to run to our cars because of the large rats that skittered out of the gutters and chased us across the road. And I thought about the wars we were fighting at home.

I'm sure that forgiveness is good for the soul, and I'd like

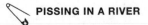

to try it sometime. But some things I'm not ready to let go of yet, and I'm not sure I'm *supposed* to let go of them. I'm still angry and can only hope that my anger continues to spur me into action. I'm still loyal to what happens here on earth, even if it means spending another forty years wandering in the desert like Moses. In sight of the Promised Land, but unable to enter.

TRACK 40 **JOE WHERE ARE YOU NOW?**

Christmas was on its inevitable way. Fairy lights dotted London. We got a Christmas tree at the Columbia Road Flower Market. It was a beautiful sight, dark-green trees and multitudes of vibrant flowers overflowing all the pitches. I particularly loved the brilliant lavenders and blues.

The Nirvana compilation CD with the studio version of Kurt's last song "You Know You're Right" was finally released. Courtney Love and the remaining Nirvanas, Krist and Dave, had been fighting over the song for years. I'd heard it on a bootleg. At the time, the only known version was from a concert in Chicago in 1993 and was referred to as "Autopilot." And Courtney had done a version of it on *MTV Unplugged*. Later I found a live, electric version of it on a website in Russia. It was a breathtaking song.

I screamed along, "'Things have never been so swell! I have never failed to fail! PAI-AI-AI-AIN!'" At first I'd thought Kurt was yelling, "I have never failed to feel," which seemed true. Melissa downloaded a copy of the video that went with the song. It looked like Kurt was performing it, even though there was no known video of him ever performing that version. He smashed his guitar. He leaped into the amplifiers. He threw himself into the drum kit. He spun himself around like a sprinkler with a spurting bottle of champagne.

I came home from busking to find Melissa looking upset in

the sitting room. "Have you heard?" she asked. "Joe Strummer's dead."

"*What?*"

"Joe Strummer. He's just died."

"He *can't* have. I don't believe it."

Joe Strummer from the Clash was our hero and the hero of the political punk movement. We rang Nick, and she came over wearing her red Brigade Rosse T-shirt, the same one Joe Strummer washes out by hand in a hotel basin in the film *Rude Boy*. Stunned, we listened to the 101ers album *Elgin Avenue Breakdown*, singing along with "Keys to your Heart" and "Motor Boys Motor." Then we played every Clash album in chronological order. On vinyl, as they were originally released. I thought my heart would crack when we listened to *Give 'Em Enough Rope*, especially during "Guns on the Roof," "Stay Free," "Cheapskates" and "All the Young Punks."

We got out Pennie Smith's classic book of excellent Clash photographs. "Remember how we used to live by this book?" I said, as we paged through it.

"To Joe, a great man of integrity," Melissa said, and we toasted him with cups of tea. We watched *Rude Boy*, *Westway to the World* and some high-quality Clash concerts Melissa had downloaded from the Internet.

We had a low-key Christmas, getting ourselves the Jam box set *Direction Reaction Creation*, the four-CD Jellyfish *Fan Club* box set and the hardcover edition of Kurt Cobain's journals. Its cover was a photo of one of Kurt's red spiral notebooks, and each page was a photocopy of the actual notebook page. I'd found Mexican *milagros* on Portobello Road, religious charms for healing and protection, and made us necklaces out of body parts like hands, feet, eyes, breasts, lips and hearts to keep us safe. I called them "OCD on a necklace."

"There's a song, reminds me of you," I said. Melissa had just come in from work and was still in her coat and scarf. I was sitting on the bed downstairs playing my guitar after a full day of busking.

"What is it? You've already told me about 'Pissing in a River.'"

"It's the Jam, 'Tales From the Riverbank.'" I sang, "*This is a tale from the water meadows / trying to spread some hope into your heart.*' You smell good," I said, as Melissa sat next to me.

"Why does it remind you of me?" she asked.

I continued singing, "*True it's a dream mixed with nostalgia, / but it's a dream that I'll always hang onto, that I always run to. / Won't you join me by the riverbank?*'"

"That reminds you of me?"

"I run to you like water runs downhill."

"I see we're feeling dead romantic today." She lay back on the bed, her coat flapping open to reveal her black V-neck jumper and the white collar of her T-shirt. I bunged myself down beside her. She pulled me on top of her and wrapped her arms around my waist. I sighed with contentment and buried my face in her shoulder. When I kissed her neck, I heard her take in her breath sharply.

She grabbed my head, the yellow-and-red, studded punk bracelet flashing on her wrist, looked intently into my eyes, and kissed me hard on the mouth. I helped her pull off her coat, and she threw her black, white, and gray scarf on the floor. As she rolled on top of me, I slipped one hand beneath her jumper and T-shirt and felt her cool, soft skin. We snogged for hours, only taking breaks to go to the loo. I felt as though I'd managed to let go of the knowledge of evil and sneak back into the elusive Garden of Eden.

I came back from the bog and noticed it was nearly midnight. Melissa was lying on the bed, her hair seductively disheveled, one hand resting on her stomach and the other behind her head. She smiled at me then sat up and pulled off her jumper, making her thick hair stick up. She was wearing a white Jam T-shirt that read "Down In The Tube Station At Midnight."

I curled up next to her with my head on her shoulder. "How'd you get to be so great?"

"That is not a serious question."

"It is. Who were you when you were growing up?"

"I was just a regular person. I don't know why you think I'm anyone special."

I looked at her upraised brows. "You know you are. You must know."

"Oh, love." She looked at me kindly. "You just wanna shag me."

"What?" I sputtered.

"You're like all the rest," Melissa teased, putting her arms around me.

"Well, you're very shaggable."

"Still?"

"Mm-hmm. Very. Always." She looked sad when I said that. "Hey," I said, sensing her intensity, "you don't have anything to prove."

"I know," she said.

I slid my hands underneath her T-shirt and felt her shoulder blades. I was a ship slipping into the water, navigating by the stars. "I feel very protective of you."

"I know." Melissa stroked my hair. "Come here, love." She pulled me closer. "Make love to me," she whispered, biting softly on my earlobe.

"Are you sure?" I asked in alarm. I'd been waiting so long for this moment. I took a deep breath and tried not to panic. "You know you can tell me to stop if you want me to, right?"

"Yeah, I do. Do you know you can tell me if this is something you don't want to do right now? I didn't mean to put you on the spot. It just came out. There's no pressure. I just—" She looked at me with a serious expression. "I ache for you. That sounds really

daft, but I do. Tonight. While we were kissing. I truly ache for you."

Ever since I'd met Melissa, my whole being had been saying, *God, you can keep all the other women. I only want this one. If you'll let me be with her forever, I'll never ask to be with anyone else.* I know eternity is a long time, but I felt I'd measured it with my heart. All my life, I'd been measuring and waiting. All this time, I'd weighed Melissa in my soul. She was the person I thought I'd only meet after I was dead and in some other, better life. I kissed her and laid my hand gently on her stomach. When I touched her breast, she gasped, "Oh, love," and held me tighter. I lifted up her Jam T-shirt and put my mouth on one of her nipples. She tasted so good and felt so amazing against my tongue. I got lost in kissing her breasts, carried away by her sounds and her breathing.

I brought my mouth back up to hers, one hand beneath her head, the other caressing her breasts. Then I ran my hand down the length of her body and rested it on the crotch of her faded black trousers. She groaned and moved against me. Listening to her gave me a sharp pleasure. I stroked her between her legs, feeling her grow wetter through the denim. I rested my hand on the button fly of her jeans and whispered, "Are you sure it's alright?"

"Yes." She kissed me hard.

"Oh my God," I whispered with her lips still on mine, "I love you so much." It felt as intense as the release of orgasm to finally be able to say that to her. Slowly I unbuttoned her jeans and slid them off her body. Then I sat her up and took off her T-shirt. I'd thought a lot about how I wanted to make love to her the first time. I wanted to make sure she stayed connected to me and didn't let her mind drift off into scary places. I wanted to take my time. I didn't know how she liked to be touched, but I wanted to be very gentle unless she signaled that she needed something else. I kissed her stomach and ran my tongue along the edges of her knickers. I touched her with my fingers through the material, making sure she was really ready before finally taking them off.

"Take off your clothes too," Melissa said hoarsely.

"I feel incredibly connected to you," I murmured. "Your skin is so soft." I kissed her shoulder. When I finally felt her clitoris with my finger, I gasped at the intensity of it. It was like putting my finger in an electric socket, only in a good way.

"Oh God," Melissa groaned, "I'm so sensitive to your touch." I moved lower. Gently, I put my mouth on her. "Oh, honey, you feel so good. Oh, God." She moaned with each caress, her clitoris under my tongue like a pebble. I knew that I would always feel its imprint there. I stroked her in a circular motion, enfolding her as her sounds became louder and more urgent. I thought I would die from pleasure when she said my name. Her hands gripped my hair.

"Oh, sweetie," Melissa said, "what are you doing to me?" She reached for my hands and squeezed them tight. I pressed myself into her, feeling her orgasm. I caressed her as she continued to come, making louder, higher-pitched sounds. I stayed where I was, kissing her, until she tugged on my head to make me stop. "Mm, love," she gasped, hugging me, "oh my God. I didn't know I could feel like that. I didn't know I could ever feel safe enough to feel like that. God, I can't move."

"You don't have to move. You don't have to do anything. I'm glad I made you feel safe." I touched then gently kissed her face. "I will never let you go."

"Was I alright?"

"You don't need to ask me that."

"But I never—" She blushed. "I was never so—vocal before. Now I've said it, I feel a right prat."

"You never have to be embarrassed in front of me. God," I said, "I am so in love with you. I never would have let this happen if I wasn't. You must know that." Melissa started to cry and nestled her face in my neck. I rubbed her back soothingly. "I love the way you sound. I love everything about you." I could feel

my eyes heavy with love when I looked at her. "You're so sweet when you come. Being intimate with you is so—intimate."

"I want to make love to you," Melissa said, drying her eyes with her fingers.

"Not now, baby." I kissed her, running my fingers through her lustrous hair. "I just want to hold you and make you feel warm and safe." As Melissa started to protest, I said, "You've been on edge for weeks. Let me do this one thing right." I stroked her hair. "Please let me hold you until you fall asleep. It would make me very happy." I pulled the blankets over her. She rested her hand gently on my face and closed her eyes. "My sweet, sweet baby," I said.

TRACK 42 GEORGE BUSH FUCK YOU

The following day, we watched George W. Bush declare war on Iraq on the telly. I taped it and wrote a song called "War Eve," integrating parts of his God-bless-America-and-all-who-defend-her-and fuck-everyone-else crap into it.

That night, I was too agitated about the war to even get in touch with my normal sexual anxieties. We were still shy around each other sexually and wanted the mood to be right. I lay in bed and could not relax. I kept thinking about my RAWA friends. Two of them had come to my town on a speaking tour of the US to raise money for RAWA. We spent an evening together so I could help them polish up a speech they were giving in front of a Jewish group the following day. I begged them to eat dinner, forcing them to look at a takeaway menu. They wanted to try chicken pizza, which turned out to be a big favorite. And I finally persuaded them to give me fifteen minutes to drive them around my city so they could at least see what it looked like. I know for a certainty this was the only time they took for themselves during their entire visit. They were twenty years old. They didn't date or fall in love. And I didn't know if they had any family left. The next time they came, I couldn't even get them to eat a chicken pizza. To me, they were true revolutionaries.

"You're all tensed up." Melissa massaged my hands, and I drifted off, thinking about the night we met and how she had held my hands in hers. She continued to press on points in my palms and fingers that sent the first warm, fragile waves of comfort through my stomach. I felt like baby Moses floating down the river about to be found. Melissa sat on the end of the bed and applied pressure to my feet. A sense of well-being flooded through me. With her strong hands, she pressed harder on my arches and toes until I was in ecstasy. I didn't realize I'd fallen asleep until I woke up the next morning.

TRACK 43 MAGAZINE

That night as we got ready for bed, Melissa put on a PETA, anti-McDonald's T-shirt, a picture of the skinned head of a cow that said "WANT FRIES WITH THAT?" And there was a sticker on it, faded by numerous washings but still clinging on, of an evil Ronald McDonald with a bloody knife and the words "Your unhappy meal is ready. McCruelty to go."

"Oh my *God*, Melissa," I said, staring at the horrible picture. "That shirt is okay to sleep in when you're alone, but *Christ*, I can't fall asleep next to that." I was wearing my tasteful Clash "I'm So Bored with the USA" T-shirt.

Melissa pulled the shirt over her head, exchanging it for one of my old ACT UP T-shirts that said "SAY IT!!! / WOMEN GET AIDS / ACT UP" in black letters. I'd started keeping my clothes in her bedroom. "I suppose you can tell it's been a while since I've really slept with someone," Melissa said a little self-consciously as she stood beside the bed.

"Are you okay?"

"I'm fine. Why do you ask?"

"A lot's been happening so fast lately—between us, the war. I worry about you."

"You don't need to worry about me."

"Christ, let *some*one worry about you. Let me take care of you."

"Amanda, I don't need to be taken care of. What's the matter with you?"

"I'm not over you being raped," I said, unable to meet her eyes. "I know it's stupid, but I feel bad I wasn't there to stop it. Or at least to help you afterwards. I can't bear it, thinking of you all alone in a kind of pain I cannot even fathom. I feel guilty you went through it instead of me."

"Why? Would you be able to handle it better than I did?" Melissa snapped.

"Are you angry?"

"Well, the subject pisses me off. I don't need to deal with *your* guilt. That's your own thing, innit?"

"I'm sorry. Please don't be mad at me."

"Kid," she said more softly, "I can be pissed off at you. It doesn't mean anything. I feel bad you had to deal with your psychiatric shite as well, you know. That isn't a pleasant thought either. But I can't make it not have happened. I can only love you now."

I blurted out, "But what about Rwanda?"

"*What*? For fuck's sake, the genocide? What's that got to do with it?"

"Remember how the United States kept calling it 'acts of genocide' instead of 'genocide' so we could pretend we weren't morally responsible to stop it? Remember how the whole world turned away and let everybody die? Remember how the surviving women were raped and infected with HIV? And what about rape in the Democratic Republic of the Congo? What about the ethnic cleansing in Bosnia?"

"Jesus, love." Melissa looked concerned. "Where's this coming from?"

"In 1994 I was completely obsessed with finishing my degree. When Rwanda happened, I wasn't even aware of it. I did nothing. All I did about Bosnia was cry. I'm doing nothing about the Democratic Republic of the Congo, and now there's genocide in Sudan. And I'm Jewish. Every Passover we think about the holocaust and say, never again. It could just as easily have been me born a Tutsi at the wrong time in Rwanda."

"But it wasn't. I don't know what you can do about that." Melissa sat next to me on the bed. "Is this what's going on in your head all the time? You went from my being raped to Rwanda in about thirty seconds."

"It's how my mind works," I said. "Don't you see the connections?"

Melissa paused. "I do."

"Welcome to the wonderful world of OCD. Or at least *my* OCD. Like many people with this illness, I am of above-average intelligence, feel an exaggerated sense of moral responsibly, and have a heightened concern with social justice. I'm responsible for everything that happens. Didn't I tell you that?"

"Yes, but I didn't understand the intensity of that aspect of it. Is that what keeps you awake at night?"

"You sound like a doctor," I said tetchily.

"I *am* your doctor." Melissa rearranged the pillows to make me more comfortable. "And your friend. And your—never mind, I don't know what I am. Have you ever gone higher on your Prozac?"

"I can't go higher on the Prozac. Besides, there's nothing wrong with seeing the connections between everything. You can't medicate away social responsibility. It's not right."

"No, but it's a problem if it stops you from functioning or sleeping. If you truly think you are the world's conscience, no wonder you can't sleep. And why not take more Prozac when you're feeling this anxious?"

I was embarrassed. "Because if I take a larger dose I can't—oh God, I can't believe we are having this conversation."

"I don't have to be the one prescribing for you," Melissa said. "You can go to another doctor. It wouldn't hurt my feelings. It's what we should have done anyway. I never should have thought—it's completely wrong."

"Please don't say that," I implored. "I'll tell you."

"But ethically—"

"Stop it. You're the most ethical person I know. Besides, the whole doctor thing, it's dead sexy, you know?" I waited for her to smile. She didn't. "I've spent enough of my life in the subdued hues of psychiatrists' waiting rooms."

"Amanda—"

"If I fall down, you bandage me up. It's natural. There's nothing wrong with it. I can tell you anything. *And* you're kind. If I go any higher on the Prozac," I said resolutely, "I can't—I can't achieve, I cannot, you know, *come.*"

"Some ginkgo biloba could help with that," Melissa said matter-of-factly.

"Really?" I moved over so Melissa could slide into bed next to me.

"Really. And you're right. Genocide is a good reason for not sleeping. You're hyperaware of connections. I just get worried about you sometimes." She kissed my ear softly and whispered, "But sweetie, I don't want to be your doctor tonight. I want to be your lover. Only I've never done this before, and I'm really nervous I'll fuck it up."

"Shit," I said, and we both started laughing, "that's so romantic."

Melissa said, "I don't want to disappoint you."

"Honey," I said, "you couldn't." And I started singing "Hey Jude" by the Beatles. "*Hey Jude, don't be afraid. / You were made to go out and get her.*'"

Melissa nuzzled my neck. "That doesn't help me."

"*And don't you know that it's just you,*'" I whispered, "*hey Jude, you'll do, / the movement you need is on your shoulder.*'"

"I don't know what the fuck that means, but ta. Our Paul's a romantic bugger. He and Linda McCartney have done so much for animal rights. I wish she were still alive."

"Me, too. Melissa, do you really want to be with me?"

"Yes, very much." Melissa's arms went around me, and I rubbed my cheek against her soft sleeve. She kissed my eyelids. "You'll tell me what you like, if what I'm doing doesn't feel good to you. And you'll tell me if you're not ready."

I immediately thought of the song "You're Ready Now" by the Manchester punk band Slaughter and the Dogs. That entire, huge last chorus started resonating in my brain, mocking me:

You're ready now / you're ready now.

Melissa was speaking to me quietly. She helped me off with my T-shirt and massaged my neck and shoulders. I started to calm down. In my head, "You're Ready Now" got less frantic. Melissa turned me over and massaged my hands and breasts. "You're Ready Now" began to sound more triumphant and less like a threat. What she was doing was so lovely I felt myself relaxing into her touch. She massaged my legs and feet. When she massaged my inner thighs, I thought I was going to die from pleasure. She slipped off my knickers, and I felt her tongue gently caress me. "You're ready now" was replaced by "oh my God." I felt her hands on my nipples. The pleasure intensified. *I am now at the hub of the universe.*

This felt way more intimate than making love with anybody else ever had. I could really feel her *loving* me as we made love. I held on tightly to one of Melissa's hands. "Oh God, Melissa," I gasped, flushed through with the sweetest feeling. I came and came again. I never did that. I pulled Melissa up beside me. "I need you here," I said.

Melissa continued to touch me. "You know I love you, don't you, love?" she whispered, and I moaned, my body responding to her words.

"Jesus, what are you doing? I can't believe you feel this good. God, Melissa." Finally I held Melissa's hand to make her stop. "Oh my God." I collapsed against her, my whole body throbbing with waves of pleasure. "Okay, okay," I said, kissing her fingers, "you've made your point. Jesus." I fell against the pillows, letting out a huge breath. "You're bloody brilliant."

"Sweetheart," Melissa murmured. She wrapped her arms around me and held me as tightly as she could.

"That's it," I said. "I belong to you. It might not be politically correct to say so, but I do. It's like *really* having sex for the first time. Nobody has ever made me feel like that. I love the way you touch me. You're so tender and sweet."

"I love the way your body responds to me," Melissa said.

I started caressing her gently. "Making love with you is like living on God," I said.

TRACK 44 **DON'T WORRY ABOUT THE GOVERNMENT**

"I feel like a proper lesbian now I've made my girlfriend come," Melissa said. She was making us a humane fry-up of eggs from cage-free chickens, baked beans, tomato, vegetarian bangers and fried bread. "You can't imagine how relieved I am."

"It wasn't a test."

"I know. And anyway, I passed."

To celebrate, I asked my dad to please ship me my made-in-Japan, silver-sparkle Fender Super-Sonic guitar, vintage black Univox Hi-Flyer with the grungiest pickups I'd ever heard, and my 1972 black Fender Musicmaster. Kurt Cobain had recorded the first Nirvana album, *Bleach*, with a Univox Hi-Flyer, and I'd had the Musicmaster routed for a humbucker, just like Kurt did with his Fenders. And I put his favorite pickup, the JB Duncan humbucker, in the bridge position.

Nick brought by the new AFI album *Sing the Sorrow* for us to hear. While she and Melissa had tea, I worked on a song I was writing called "Speaker's Corner." Speaker's Corner is at the corner of Hyde Park near Marble Arch where people with opinions stand on crates and boxes and emote. I love to go there on a Sunday and argue. It's full of loopy Christians and people who hate homosexuals. Many of the same people are there every week, year after year. When I was at university, there was a bloke called Jimmy who used to stand on a stepladder and proclaim that lesbians had driven up the price of Coca-Cola because they use the bottles to stick up their cunts.

"You sounded good," Melissa said as I came downstairs bringing my Gibson with the pink-and-black "ACT UP/DC" and black-and-white "Kurt Cobain 1967–1994" stickers on it. "What we could hear of it."

"Cheers." I rubbed my hand over the picture of Kurt's face on the sticker next to his name.

Nick said, "You ought to be performing someplace other than tube stations. You may have to." She slid a copy of that day's *Telegraph* at me. "You have to busk *legally* now. Which sort of ruins the whole point." There was an article saying how London Transport was going to require all buskers to be licensed. You had to audition to play at one of the twenty-five official pitches at a dozen stations.

"I don't know if you need to be a permanent resident," Melissa said. "And of course you don't want to call attention to yourself."

"If they're going to regulate it, what's the fun in that?" I said.

"You should start playing pubs and clubs," Nick said. "I'll bet you could get a gig for Gingerbeer's monthly barge party. And lots of places have open mics. There's a place called Club MIA in Slough that I'll bet would have you."

 **PISSING IN A RIVER**

"Money," I said. "Where will I get it?"

"The three of us will think of something," Melissa said.

"I don't suppose you need another partner in your practice?" I asked. "A literary doctor?" I sang a few lines from Kurt's song "Very Ape." "'*I take pride as the king of illiterature, / I'm very ape and very nice.*'"

TRACK 45 TWO OF US

I brought the Takamine into the back studio where Melissa was painting an extremely abstract portrait of me with my guitar. "I wrote a song for you," I said shyly.

"Not another one?" Melissa smiled and wiped her brush. "Will you play it for me?"

I suddenly felt awkward. "Okay, but don't look at me while I'm singin' it."

"What's it called?"

"'Redemption,'" I said.

Melissa turned back to her painting and I plucked out a complicated tune that started in A minor.

> *Moses don't part the Red Sea for me*
> *I'll break my own heart on the shores of the sea*
> *I'll drown on my own so call back your boats*
> *my body goes down, I hope my soul floats.*
> *Redemption is not always easy*
> *close my mouth so I don't ask for pity*
> *shut my eyes, pretend that I hold her*
> *give anything to put my head on her shoulder*
> *everything for you*
> *everything for you.*
>
> *Moses don't part my hair for me*
> *when you look in my heart I hope I'll be pretty*

if I show you my brain will you invite me
in from the rain I swear I'll walk lightly.
Redemption is not always pretty
close my mouth so I don't ask for pity
shut my ears to all the world's lies
give anything to see love in her eyes
everything for you
everything for you.

"That's beautiful," Melissa said, turning to look at me when I finished. "Do you really think of yourself that way?"

"What way?" I put down the guitar.

"That you hope you'll be pretty enough so I'll ask you in from the rain."

I lowered my gaze self-consciously. "Remember that night I waited for you outside your flat and it was raining? I think I felt like that then."

Melissa put down the brush and kissed me. "You don't need to break your own heart anymore, love," she said.

"Oh." I was barely audible. I held her against my black "SILENCE = DEATH" T-shirt with the pink triangle on the front.

Melissa squeezed me. "I love you, you know."

I rested my head against her shoulder. "I love you, too."

"I love it that you write me songs."

My face felt warm, and I sang a soppy Ramones tune I love off the *Subterranean Jungle* album, "My-My Kind of a Girl":

"When I saw you on 8th street
you could make my life complete, baby
yeah, yeah, yeah
you're my-my kind of a girl."

"Come on," Melissa laughed, "I'm serious."

I continued:

"When I saw you by the Peppermint Lounge
you were lost but you've been found, baby
yeah, yeah, yeah
you're my-my kind of a girl."

"You know what, love?" Melissa tousled my uneven, spiky hair. "I decided if I *was* talking to you inside your head somehow and was there when you needed me, then I'm glad."

I put my mouth against her ear, singing a little of the chorus to the Jellyfish song "Will You Marry Me," and kissed her.

In the back sitting room, Melissa put on Nirvana's *Nevermind* CD and fixed herself a vermouth and 7UP. I took sips from her glass as we sat together on the couch. "Lithium" was playing, and Kurt Cobain sang, *"I'm so happy cause today I found my friends, / they're in my head—"*

"Hey," I nudged her, "that's my song."

"—I'm not scared, light my candles, / in a daze cause I found God."

After "Lithium," Kurt's antirape dirge "Polly" came on, giving me a jolt. I couldn't believe I hadn't been prepared with some excuse to take the CD out before it reached that song. Nervously I said, "This album can be dead depressing if you're in the wrong mood," afraid she might be upset. "I prefer these songs live and not overproduced." I gave the sensible, musical reason to turn it off that had nothing to do with content.

"Sorry," Melissa said, getting up to change the CD. She put on "Rape Me" from Nirvana's *In Utero* CD and gave me a solemn look. My mouth dropped open, and she winked at me.

"You're a laugh riot," I said, and Melissa smiled.

I got up and put on her best bootleg of the Real People, a mod band from Liverpool that I loved. I sang along with "Feel the Pain." *"'Feel the pain, open your heart. / I'm so in love that I'm falling apart.'"*

"You're right," Melissa said, putting her arm around my shoulders as I sat back down, "mental illness *is* much funnier."

"I still wish I could track him down and kill him for you." I was only semi-joking.

"Paul? Yes," Melissa said enthusiastically, "that would make me feel ever so much better, especially when I'm visiting you in the nick. What a perfect way to be here for me." She squeezed my shoulder and kissed my cheek.

I remembered a song from a Take Back the Night march I'd gone to a long time ago in Soho.

> *Don't go out on your own tonight,*
> *you'll never get home my lad.*
> *Don't go out on your own tonight,*
> *the women are really mad.*
> *'Cos we can kick, and we can fight,*
> *and women will take back the night.*
> *Tonight's the night the women are on the rampage!*

We'd pounded our fists on the windows of the sex shops in Leicester Square. A mob of about thirty rough-looking patrons came out and stood menacingly at one end of the street. A gaggle of coppers stood at the other end. We decided to take our chances with the police, who escorted us to the tube station and made sure we got on a train.

Melissa rumpled my hair good-naturedly. "Let's go to bed and plot how we're going to kill your ex-therapists." She took my hand and led me upstairs.

TRACK 46   RETURN OF THE RAT

Once I touched Chrissie Hynde's boot with my right forefinger. The last time I'd seen the Pretenders, it had been at a really small venue. As I clung to the stage, Chrissie kicked her leg up right over my head. She danced. She told meat eaters they would get what they deserved. I was in reach of her and sublimely happy.

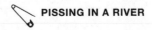 **PISSING IN A RIVER**

I never wanted to impinge on Chrissie Hynde's personal space. I remembered an article I'd read in a music paper once about Chrissie Hynde kicking out the windows of a police car with the quotation, "I don't like to be touched." Very gently, so she wouldn't notice, I touched the toe of her boot.

I was telling Melissa about it. "It was blue fake suede and very soft. I can still feel it in my mind whenever I want to. I can make love to you with this finger," I said slyly, and Melissa blushed. "Chrissie Hynde once wrote me a letter, you know."

"Chrissie *Hynde* wrote you a letter?"

"Yes, when I lived outside DC. She was in town for a PETA benefit at the Willard, a fancy hotel near the White House. I like the name because the film *Willard* is about rats. I tried to sneak in. I'd taken a photo of the Firestone Tire factory in Akron, Ohio, where Chrissie Hynde is from when I went there on a pilgrimage and put it in an envelope with a note about how her album *packed!* was released on May 21, 1990, the same day I was arrested at the big ACT UP demonstration at the National Institutes of Health. While I was waiting in the holding cell all day, I thought about how much I wanted to get that album. How I was in here, stuck in that cell, and it was out there, in the record shops. How knowing that made me feel peace of mind."

"When did you get out?"

"Later that evening."

"So you were released on the same day," Melissa said.

"What do you mean?"

"You were released the same day the Pretenders album was released. You had the same release date."

I smiled because I'd never thought of that. "I do consider it *our* album. All the PETA people were dressed in tuxedos and evening gowns. I was wearing an ACT UP T-shirt and decided if anyone asked I'd say it stood for the Animal Coalition To Unleash Pets. Chrissie Hynde was already inside, and I couldn't get in. But the security guard, Joe Turner, let me speak to a PETA representative. I gave him the envelope and asked him to give it to

Chrissie Hynde, but I didn't think he would.

"About three months later, a blue envelope fell through the mail slot in my front door with a London postmark. I didn't know anyone in London at the time, and I couldn't make out the name 'Hynde' scrawled on the back. It smelled good. Like the perfume of chilly London air. It was a three-page, handwritten letter from Chrissie Hynde. She had written:

> *I'm glad to hear you've enjoyed the music and that it's been cheering you up since 1979—It's been bumming me out since 1979!! (Not really.)*
>
> *Thank you for the "lovely" picture of Firestone Rubber Co. The place just ain't what it used to be—it's not blue collar any more . . . I'm afraid you must be a misguided youth to make a pilgrimage to Akron for any reason, let alone because of me, but I'll try to take it as a compliment & leave it at that.*

"And she'd signed it, 'love Chrissie.' I could have swooned."

I remembered when my best mates and I had driven back to Exeter from Plymouth. We'd stopped at a motorway café for a cup of tea, and we bunged all our 20p coins into the jukebox. The new Pretenders single "Message of Love" had just come out, and we punched in the buttons to make it play repeatedly. We danced to it and the other patrons left after it came on for about the twentieth time. That memory made me feel warm and safe.

Thinking about Chrissie Hynde and PETA reminded me of the pet rat I'd had after graduate school, how she used to jump on my head to wake me up and take showers with me. I showed Melissa my favorite photograph of her sitting on my red Stratocaster, looking into the camera with a soulful expression.

Melissa said, "You can see her soul pouring out through her eyes. Like there's so much of it, it won't all fit inside. Do you want another pet rat? Why didn't you say? We can get you one."

"I'm not ready."

"There's some wicked graffiti I've got to show you." Melissa

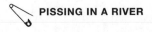

threw my denim jacket at me. It had badges from my Exeter days on the front: "The Clash" against a graphic of blue policemen, "Gays Against Nazis," "How Dare You Presume that I'm a Heterosexual?" and a black-and-white one of Chrissie Hynde's head.

I wrapped my green-and-white Exeter scarf around my neck. "Graffiti?"

Melissa put on a green anorak. "There's a graffiti artist called Banksy—he works mostly in South Bank and the East End—who has loads of rat art."

"*No*," I said. "Not rat graffiti?"

Melissa took my hand as we walked to her car in the brief, cold sunshine.

We got into Melissa's dark-green MG and motored across the bridge to South London, the Zombies blasting on the car stereo. Melissa found a stenciled picture of rats putting up a flag and taking over the city. "I'm not sure it's meant to be complimentary, but I thought you'd enjoy it." She took me through the East End. On Brick Lane, "NO WAR" was the caption, in red, for a picture of a rat holding an umbrella to protect herself from a falling bomb. Then Melissa showed me something spectacular on an overpass above Old Street in Shoreditch. A row of riot police with yellow smiley faces stretched all the way across the red-painted metal bridge with the caption, "WRONG WAR." Under the arches, posters lined the walls as we sped alongside the black taxis that reminded me of water bugs.

I put on Jefferson Airplane's "Somebody to Love." It started raining, and everything had a metallic, silver glint. I asked Melissa if we could just drive around for a while.

When we got home, I sat in the front room near the window idly watching the rain and playing "She's So High" by Blur on my unplugged Gibson while Melissa caught up on some reading. She sat in the back room, which doubled as her study, with the current issue of the *BMJ*, a medical journal of evidence-based medicine. She'd explained the difference between evidence-based and experience-based medicine to me and shown me a site on the Internet she used called "BestBETs," Best Evidence Topics. I liked to listen to her talk about medicine. I thought it was dead cool and sexy. "That's why I went to medical school," Melissa had said when I'd told her that.

I had finished my CD of songs about Afghanistan for RAWA and mailed it to Pakistan. Now I was working on an antiwar CD. The phone rang as I was plucking out "(Don't Fear) the Reaper" by Blue Oyster Cult. It was Nick. She was excited about the demo CD I'd given her with some rough versions of a few new songs. She said she was going to play it for the women at Gingerbeer to see if she could get me a gig playing on the Battersea Barge for Gingerbeer's monthly Lyrical Lounge. I started panicking immediately. "You're my new manager," I said.

When Nick arrived, she asked, "Where's Melissa?" She hung up her wet coat and scarf.

"She's in the back reading doctor stuff," I said. "Come over."

Nick pulled a folded piece of paper from her pocket. "I made a list of pubs and other places that do open mics."

"But I don't have a band," I protested.

"Solo," she said firmly. "I'll go with you everywhere you play."

Later the three of us watched news on the telly. "*There's something to be proud of*," I said as the BBC reported the Americans had bombed a children's hospital in Iraq. "That's something you won't hear on the American news. There's a media blackout on reporting anything critical of our wars. You might as well be in North Korea reading about how the Great Leader invented the toaster."

TRACK 47 TREAT ME WELL

Melissa was spending more time in her studio painting and jokingly said that post-traumatic stress was an over-achieving muse. She was using acrylics, and her dark paintings reminded

me of Vincent Van Gogh's *The Potato Eaters* because she used so much texture, and because the subject matter she selected elevated things that we weren't supposed to find culturally significant. This was especially true of her somber representations of women. When I saw *The Potato Eaters*, Van Gogh's original painting, for the first time, I realized how important it can be to see a painting in person. When I stood up close and to one side, I could see each brush stroke, the thickness and the movement of the painting.

Nick dragged me around London with my guitar. I took the battered old Hiwatt bass amp out of Jake's wardrobe, cleaned it up and finally persuaded her to practice with the bass and play with me in private. She was studying two of our favorite bass players, Bruce Foxton from the Jam and Paul Simonon from the Clash. We also listened to a pre-FM concert by the Police in Chicago, 1979 that Melissa had found because it was mad good quality and Sting was an awesome bass player. And of course we listened to Paul McCartney and the Pretenders with the original line-up.

When Nick and I rehearsed in the flat, Melissa often shut herself in her studio to paint. Lately she'd been keeping to herself more, preoccupied by a series of paintings she was working on about women and rape. I knew Nick was disconcerted by Melissa's silences and abrupt disappearances. "She's got a lot on her mind," I said, hoping to prevent Nick from taking Melissa's uncommunicative mood personally.

When we got into bed after Melissa had been working on some charcoal sketches later than usual, I asked, "Are you sure?" as she started kissing me in a sexual way. "I can just hold you."

"I appreciate the way you always treat me with such care." Melissa pulled my T-shirt over my head. "Stop looking at me like I'm going to fall apart. I'm not that fragile. I'm not gonna break. You have to stop seeing me as a victim. I don't think of you as a victim of your mental—uniqueness. I think of you as you."

"I'm sorry," I said. "I do see you as you. I know I'm working out my own issues of feeling helpless when it comes to protecting you."

"You are not responsible for something painful in my past. You can't control everything that happens. I know your OCD wants you to believe you can, and you confuse that with being a good person, but really, it's okay." She held my hands. As she kissed me gently on the mouth, loud pounding downstairs startled us.

"What the fuck is that?" I turned away abruptly. "Is someone at the door?" It had just gone half past twelve. The banging grew more insistent. Someone called Melissa's name.

"Fuck me, is that Nick?" Melissa jumped out of bed and threw on her dressing gown, tying it round her waist as she rushed down the stairs. I found my T-shirt on the floor and followed her. "Nick?" Melissa opened the front door and Nick practically fell inside. She was shaking so hard Melissa made her sit down on the floor. "What's happened? Are you hurt?" Melissa knelt beside her. The belt of her dressing gown loosened, and I could see her lush breasts, pale and smooth as driftwood caressed by the sea, as she bent forward.

Nick was almost hyperventilating but was physically unharmed. We helped her up and sat her on the bed in her room. She said that Atom had been waiting in front of her flat when she'd come home from her local at closing time.

"That fucking *gobshite*," Melissa said fiercely. "I'm not having this. You're moving in here till this is sorted. We'll get your gear over the weekend."

Nick protested, "I'll be in the way. I'll be intruding."

"No," Melissa said firmly, "you're family. And the three of us get on so well that having you here never feels like a strain. It's lovely having you here. I know I've been distracted lately." Melissa made up the bed with clean sheets. "But you belong here with us. There." She put a fresh pillowcase on Nick's favorite pillow. "You'll feel better now. Alright?"

After Nick had calmed down and we went back upstairs, I asked, "Are *you* alright?"

Melissa took off her dressing gown and got into bed. "What do you mean?"

"Uh—I don't know, a bloke stalking Nick, the threat of violence—didn't that upset you? Doesn't that bring things up for you?"

"Of course it bloody well upsets me." Melissa wrapped her arms around me. "But she's safe now, and we'll sort it out later."

"Melissa, I know you're more comfortable taking care of someone else, but I want to take care of you."

"What did I just finish telling you?" Melissa kissed me, sucking on my lower lip and running her hand seductively over my body.

I cupped my hand over her breast, gently stroking the alluring brown disc of her nipple. "Are you sure—?" I began again.

"Mmm," she murmured, "your concern is not what I need right now."

Her voice made my knees go weak even though I was lying down. I whispered, "What if Nick hears us?"

"She can't hear us downstairs at the other end of the house no matter how loud we are."

I pressed my body into hers, resting my hand between her legs. "Remember the old days when we never made love without music?"

"Oh God, yes," Melissa laughed. "How many times have I been fucked to 'White Riot'?"

"We could make love to Heart," I suggested shyly.

"Want to?" Melissa said conspiratorially.

"Yes," I said, and we both laughed.

"Which album?" Melissa asked.

"Oh, *Little Queen*. Definitely."

"Anything before or after the corporate rock period when Ann and Nancy lost their minds and had really big hair," Melissa said. I ran downstairs and brought up the first four Heart CDs.

A smile graced Melissa lips. "It's just a *Little Queen* kind of night." It was Friday, and Melissa didn't have to get up in the morning. "Mmm, that's perfect," she said as the CD played and I slid in next to her again. She kissed me and moved my legs apart with her hand. I felt myself relaxing into her touch.

"You don't have to feel like making love all the time, you know," I said, checking in with her one more time as "Love Alive" was playing, and everything was dead romantic.

"Amanda," Melissa shook me, "you're going to drive me to drink. You don't understand. I *do* feel like making love with you all the time. I get so turned on when I'm near you, or just thinking about you."

"Same here," I confessed, wondering if that was why my most intrusive OCD thought was having my hands come off. Because that's how I showed tenderness. Touching Melissa, playing guitar, typing out lyrics. I used my hands to express that side of myself, the part that felt divine.

As Ann started singing "Dream of the Archer," Melissa gave me a lingering kiss that made my whole body ache for her so much I thought I would dissolve. Kissing her shoulders, I gradually moved my hands and lips lower. She sighed deeply as she rolled over and I put my mouth on her ass and slipped my hands underneath her. "You're so lovely," I whispered.

"I want to feel you inside me, love."

Gently I slid a finger inside her as I kissed and caressed her. Her cries were as exciting and beautiful as hearing the Clash for the first time. Slowly rolling her over, I nuzzled her pubic hair and separated the lips of her labia softly with my fingers. Very lightly, I touched the tip of my tongue to her clitoris. "Oh, sweetie," she moaned.

I ran my tongue along her grooves, slowly sliding my finger back inside her as she spread her legs wider, groaning. I felt her legs quiver, and she shuddered against me with a wail. I slid another finger inside her and rocked her as her orgasms became more intense. Then I gently removed my fingers and sucked on her lightly, stroking her inner thighs until her breathing quickened again. I couldn't get enough of her. I reached my hands up to squeeze and caress her hard nipples. As I sucked her harder she exploded against me, and I felt myself coming just from feeling her pleasure.

"Oh my God," she whimpered, as I slipped a finger inside her again. "Sweetie. Oh, *Jesus*." She shivered with another wave of pleasure. I stayed inside her until she reached out both hands to pull me up next to her. "Mmmm," she sighed, trembling with an aftershock. Then she gripped me tightly as another spasm overtook her. She opened her eyes, and they were wet. She began kissing me passionately, and I felt her hot tears on my face.

"Oh, baby, I love you so much," I murmured, feeling her hands all over me like she was a Hindu Goddess with eight arms.

When we lay quietly together, I whispered in her ear, "I fancied you from the moment we first met."

She smiled. "No, you didn't. You didn't fancy me then."

"I did."

"You didn't. You were in shock anyway," she protested. "And you got knocked in the head, which is surely not the best time to know if you fancy someone."

"You looked like an angel," I said. "And when you held my hands, I didn't want you to let go."

"We held hands?"

"Well, you held my hands to see if anything was broken. And the next night, when I slept on your sofa, you had me grip your hands as hard as I could."

Melissa laughed. "I was checking to see if you were concussed, you git. Did you really like me then?"

"Oh, aye. You descended upon my bedsit and rescued us. You rubbed my head when I felt ill."

At five in the morning we went downstairs to check on Nick. We saw light from under the door, and Melissa rapped softly. "Can't sleep?" she asked, finding Nick awake, disheveled, and reading a paperback with exhausted-looking eyes. Melissa sat next to her. "Come lie down in our bed."

"That is ridiculous," Nick said. "Then I really *will* be intruding."

"Don't be silly," Melissa said. "There's nothing wrong with needing to feel safe."

We went upstairs to Melissa's big bed, and I sang "Because You're Frightened" by Magazine. I fell asleep to the metallic sound of rain on the roof and against the window and dreamed I was in junior high school again. I heard Kurt Cobain in the background screaming, *"You're in high school again. / NO RECESS!"* from his song "School." I had a crush on my Spanish teacher, Miss Digame-en-Español, but she made the class sing "My Country 'Tis of Thee" and I sang "God Save the Queen" instead. Then I sang the Sex Pistols' version of "God Save the Queen." I woke up knowing how disappointed she was in me, one of her special students, and thinking, *my mind is my refuge, the only lit café on a very dark road.* In real life, my former Spanish teacher had turned me down when I asked for her support in defeating a proposition on the ballot that would have fired all gay and lesbian teachers from the California public school system. It's stupid, I know, but I guess it really hurt me if I was still dreaming about it.

TRACK 48 **THE SEEKER**

We didn't get up until early afternoon. As we hung around the kitchen drinking cups of tea, Melissa decided Nick needed cheering up. It was such a lovely Saturday, she suggested we go to a pub by the river and said to Nick, "We'll deal with everything tomorrow." We drove out to a pleasant country pub and relaxed by the water, ate a ploughman's lunch, and watched the swans. The world was starting to blossom. I devoured my last bite of bread, cheese, and pickle.

Since the weather was warm, when we got back into the city

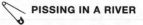

we went to Maida Vale to have tea on one of the many brightly painted boats on the canal. The boats were covered with over-flowing pots of brilliant flowers and hanging plants. I was wearing an extremely tasteful T-shirt that screamed "NAZI PUNKS FUCK OFF" in lurid red letters. I got a disgruntled look from an older couple and said, "I'm thinking of changing my name to Vivid Unpleasantness."

That night we went to a party in North London given by Melissa's friend Kate and her flatmates. The Victorian terrace was packed with sweaty people drinking and dancing on every floor and landing. While Melissa greeted mates in the kitchen, Nick and I went upstairs to the bedroom where Kate had told us to leave our coats.

The bedroom faced the street. We looked out at the yellow streetlight. I laid Melissa's dark-gray coat on a pile of outer garments on top of the bed. I unzipped and shed my black hooded sweatshirt with the white thermal-underwear lining. Underneath I was wearing a bright green T-shirt that said "ASBO" across it in big white letters. Melissa said it suited me, that I was a walking Anti-Social Behavior Order. Nick took off her black leather jacket. She was wearing a black T-shirt with a picture of Ian Dury in a green shirt and braces and "THERE AIN'T HALF BEEN SOME CLEVER BASTARDS" written across the front. She had a badge that said "I'm Not A Weekend Punk."

Nick ran into some mates on the landing. I joined Melissa in the kitchen. She was drinking lager from a plastic cup and talking to Kate. I thought she looked dead sexy in black creepers, white bondage trousers with black zippers running diagonally across the legs, and a white T-shirt with the cover of the 101ers album *Elgin Avenue Breakdown* in black. She had told me that the geezer pictured on the front was called "Metal Man" on account of he covered himself with metal. In return for his photograph, he had wanted a piece of chicken.

I walked toward Melissa, so proud to be with her I could

barely stand myself. I helped myself to a fizzy drink from a tub on the floor filled with ice, and Melissa rested her arm casually across my shoulders. It was the first time we'd attended an event with Melissa's friends as a couple. I'd met Kate and quite a few of Melissa's other mates before but not as "the girlfriend."

The DJ had a crate full of vinyl and was spinning an interesting mix of mostly late-seventies, early-eighties music. Melissa pulled me into the crowded front room to dance as the Beat's "Mirror in the Bathroom" played. We crammed into a small space by the window. Melissa swiveled her hips and held her arms over her head. "God, you're sexy when you dance," I said. "I'm crawling out of my skin."

Melissa grabbed my hands and pulled me into her rhythm. After the fast song "I Need to Know" by Tom Petty and the Heartbreakers, the DJ put on the slower "Refugee." That song had always depressed the hell out of me but not tonight. Not now that I didn't feel like I was living in exile from my own life anymore. I moved Melissa into me and put my hands on the back pockets of her trousers. With my head on her shoulder, I could see a few of her mates staring at us.

During "Needles" by Dead Man's Shadow, Melissa held me in her arms and gave me a gorgeous, lingering kiss. A woman came up and hugged her. "No Martin tonight?" she asked slyly.

Melissa laughed. "Not tonight. Not ever. Emma, this is Amanda."

"Bless you, darlin'." Emma hugged me. "It's surprising to meet you."

I laughed. "I'm as surprised as you are."

"You look happy," she said to Melissa. "Ring us." And she disappeared into the crush of bodies dancing. "Demolition Dancing" by the Ruts came on.

"Did you warn anybody that you switched sides?" I asked.

Melissa smiled at me. "Just a few."

"Aren't you worried about how your mates will react?"

Melissa spun me. "No."

"Jesus Christ. Could you possibly 'come out' any more gracefully? Couldn't you stammer just once?"

She laughed, shaking her head, tossing her hair about her face.

"Couldn't you try and hide me just a little?"

"Nope." We danced to "Roxanne" by the Police. "Is it just me, or is it getting hotter in here?" Melissa rested her head on my shoulder and kept her arms around me as the song ended.

"It's got a lot hotter," I said, breathing more rapidly.

We danced wildly to Romeo Void's "Never Say Never," jumping about with our arms flailing, taking up more space. "I haven't seen Nick in a while," Melissa said.

"She should be dancing with us," I said. "I'm gonna find her."

"I'll get some air." Melissa pushed her way slowly toward the open front door.

I got another fizzy drink from the kitchen and looked around for Nick but couldn't find her. The stairs were crammed with people talking, drinking, and smoking fags. "Sorry, cheers, sorry." I moved people out of my way. I searched all the rooms where people had gathered as the sounds of Graham Parker and the Rumour floated up. Finally I opened the door to the bedroom where we'd stashed our gear. It was dark inside. Nick was sitting on the heap of coats and scarves that lay on the bed. "There you are, mate." I sat down next to her, and she passed me her cup of lager. I took a sip. "I've been looking for ya. Come down and dance." I heard the Clash's "Safe European Home" playing now. "What's wrong?" I asked when she didn't say anything.

"Just leave me be, mate," Nick said. "I'm feeling evil, me."

"What's the matter?"

"My insides are all churning up, aren't they?"

"You're worried about Atom waiting outside your flat?"

"Yeah, well. Being stalked is lovely on the nerves."

"Come on. Let's find Melissa. She'll cheer you up."

"No, mate. I can't face all those people."

She wouldn't budge, so I went to get Melissa. She was still outside, drinking lager and talking to her mate Jane. "There's the girl," Jane said, meaning me. "Hiya, 'manda." She gave me a hug and an extra squeeze that I could tell was filled with meaning.

Melissa and I politely shoved our way upstairs with three cups of lager. I closed the bedroom door behind me, and Melissa joined Nick on the pile of coats. "Cheers," Nick said as Melissa handed her a cup.

"Dry your eyes now, love." Melissa picked up someone's scarf and mopped Nick's face with it until Nick laughed in protest, squirming and holding up her hands.

The DJ was doing a tribute to Mrs. Thatcher. First the Newtown Neurotics song "Kick Out the Tories" then the Beat's "Stand Down Margaret." We automatically sang along then got up and danced to the Redskins song "Kick Over the Statues." I laid my head on Melissa's chest and felt her sweaty T-shirt cling to her body.

After "Rock Lobster" by the B52s, the DJ took a break, leaving the B side of first Pretenders album spinning on the turntable. Of course we danced like our lives depended on it. I was looking out the bedroom window, giving it my all, becoming *one* with the Pretenders music. I felt the sweat running down my face and closed my eyes to the melodic guitar of "Private Life."

The Pretenders record was followed by "Did You No Wrong" and "Submission" by the Sex Pistols. I smiled and watched Melissa and Nick dancing close together, deep in conversation. Melissa had one hand on Nick's back and was holding Nick's hand with the other. I thought they moved together like two glorious punk angels, and I was filled with a love for them so huge I thought I would crack open. I went and put my arms around both of them.

"Tainted Love" by Soft Cell started playing, and I emitted a small cry of nostalgic excitement. "I remember dancing to that in clubs all over England with my mates. That and the Human

League's 'Don't You Want Me.' During my third term at Exeter, I attended exactly one lecture and posted in my papers from places like Edinburgh, Lake Windemere, and the Brontë house on the Haworth moors." I had loved the maroon buses of Edinburgh and the purplish moors.

Parched from dancing and out of beer, we trooped downstairs. Melissa switched to non-alcoholic refreshment because she was driving us home, but Nick and I continued drinking lager. "You know what you're doing, right?" Melissa whispered as she handed me a cup, concerned that I would make myself ill.

"I won't have too much," I said, already dizzy from the effects of medication-enhanced alcohol.

We left the party after two in the morning. We passed a kebab shop on our way to the car. I stopped and looked through the window at the spinning column of fat-dripping meat. "I'll just get chips," I said.

Melissa knew all about my love affair with greasy English food. She caught my eye and said, "If you behave yourself, I'll make you both my special bangers and mash when we get home."

"Special means healthy." I swatted Melissa's bum.

Melissa slid her finger through the belt loop of my bright-red jeans. She tugged on it, and I clomped backward in my heavy black shoes, leaning into her open coat and feeling her T-shirt still damp with sweat. "I can make you all the things you love without meat. Well, except for doner kebab. I haven't yet learned how to approximate tortured lamb meat that's been on a spit all day with flies landing on it."

Nick choked with laughter.

"Spiced meat, salad, and dressing stuffed in a pita so inebriated punters can eat it as they wobble home. What could be better?" I asked, my speech slurred.

"Did you know the doner kebab is named after the Turkish word 'dondurmek' meaning rotating roast? Mmm," Melissa said. "It was invented by a Turk called Mr. Aygun. In the UK, it's often a mass-produced elephant leg of indeterminate meat. Yummy. Some even contain pork. Definitely not *Halal*. Huge amounts of salt and saturated fat and animal species that don't appear on the label. What could be better?"

"Stop it, Melissa. You're making me hungrier."

"It's still *haram* for you," Melissa laughed. She took hold of one of my arms and Nick grabbed the other, walking me between them in the cold night air.

"Pork pie, shepherd's pie, steak-and-kidney pie," I chanted.

"I can make you all those without meat," Melissa said. They shoved me into the back seat of the car.

I leaned over the seats as Melissa drove. "Once my mate at Exeter wrote a letter to the pork-pie company complaining about a bad pork pie."

"How could she tell the pie was bad?" Melissa asked. "They're *supposed* to be rancid."

"And one day this lorry from the pork-pie people pulled up in front of our residence hall, and some blokes carried up a half-dozen crates of pork pies. We had to stack them in the hall because they wouldn't all fit in her room." I started singing "Bargain" by the Who: "'*I'd gladly lose me to find you. / I'd gladly give up all I had. / To find you I'd suffer anything and be glad. / I'd pay any price just to get you / I'd work all my life and I will. / To win you I'd stand naked, stoned and stabbed. / I'd call that a bargain, the best I ever had—the best I ever had!*'" Then I collapsed against the rear seat.

"Her voice is getting raspier," Nick said, "and her shouting is improving."

"She's uninhibited now," Melissa said. "She has to be this passionate when she's sober."

I'd been practicing singing more like Liam Gallagher. "I can hear you, you know," I said disgruntled, sitting up.

When we got home I asked Melissa to play "Bargain" on the stereo. I put my arms around her neck and said, "I'm obsessed with Pete Townshend's guitar on this."

 **PISSING IN A RIVER**

Melissa whispered back, slow-dancing with me, "That's not a secret." She winked at Nick.

I looked at her swinging hips then put on "Love Reign O'er Me" so I could belt out along with Roger Daltrey, "*Only love / can bring the rain / that falls like tears / from on high!*' I saw Ann Wilson singin' that from the front row," I said. "I could see the fillings in her teeth."

Upstairs Melissa tucked a hot-water bottle down at the foot of the bed. I pulled on a soft, clean T-shirt that said "AIDS IS KILLING ARTISTS / HOMOPHOBIA IS KILLING THE ARTS" and a dark-gray sweatshirt. Just as she was turning to go downstairs and have a cuppa with Nick, I grabbed her and whispered, "*I'd call that a bargain, the best I ever had.*"

TRACK 49   DROWNING IN THE SHALLOW WATERS OF PRESCRIBED MORALITY

On Sunday, the three of us drove to Bethnal Green in the pouring rain to get Nick's gear. Nick hadn't wanted to report Atom to the police. Melissa was slightly exasperated with her. "Well, you don't fucking have to," Melissa said. "He assaulted Amanda, too."

"He only chased me," I reminded her. "He didn't actually catch me."

"Things *are* getting better, Nick. You *can* report a gay-bashing, you know," Melissa said. "Or a gay-stalking or whatever."

"Thank you, Dr. I've-been-a-lesbian-for-all-of-five-minutes. If things were really any better, you could fucking marry Amanda here and get her bloody, bollocky citizenship."

"Bollocks," Melissa said.

They both shut up, and the only sounds were the scraping of the windscreen wipers and the rush of tires on wet pavement.

Sullenly we climbed the stairs to Nick's flat.

Melissa held an umbrella over the open hatchback as I fit in armloads of clothes and a box of CDs. Then she went upstairs to see if Nick needed any more help.

A male voice said, "Thought you'd got away from me, did you, darlin'?" And I faced the same stocky, stroppy white bloke who'd chased me off the night I'd come looking for Nick.

"What makes you think I was trying to get away from you?" I asked defiantly, immediately regretting it as I remembered I'd fucking *run away* from him the last time. "We're here. We're queer. Fuck off." The rain splashed our bare heads as we stared at each other. "Just call me Nucleus." I slammed the hatchback shut and tried to walk past him. He deliberately stood in my way. "I'm not alone this time," I said. "I've got my mates with me. You know, the champion-Rottweiler breeders." I wondered why I said inane things when my adrenaline was activated. Was adrenaline *supposed* to make you stupid?

Melissa appeared first in the doorway then Nick. "Is this him?" Melissa asked. "Is he the one?" Nick nodded. "I'm not fucking 'aving it. This is *bollocks*. I'll fucking murder him. Listen you," Melissa poked Atom in the chest with the metal point on the end of her umbrella, "if I *ever* see you round here again, I'll make you fucking sorry. Now *fuck off.*"

Atom grabbed hold of the umbrella. "Now how will *you* make *me* fuckin' sorry?" He pulled Melissa toward him.

The thought of his hands on her made me freak. "Shithead mother*fucker!*" I lunged at him and shoved him away from her. The next thing I knew, he had my arm up painfully behind my back and my face on the warm hood of the car. I couldn't see what was going on behind me, but it sounded chaotic. I heard Nick and Melissa yelling at him to let me go. The grip on my arm loosened for a second and I stumbled, trying to yank myself free. Then I was flying through the air. There was a sudden, searing pain in my shoulder, and I was sprawled out on the pavement. My whole left side seemed useless. I thought he'd broken my arm at the shoulder. I tried to sit up. It hurt so much I thought I was going to lose consciousness.

I heard someone else wail in agony. Melissa had jammed the point of her umbrella as hard as she could into Atom's leg. He fell, and Nick kicked him in the balls with her Doc Martens. I watched the neon pink letters on her belt that screamed "FUCK." Atom had curled up on the ground in a fetal position. Shouting "If you *ever* touch either of them again, I *will* fucking kill you," Melissa knelt beside me, putting her arms carefully around me.

"*Fuck*, Melissa," I said. "I think he broke my bleedin' arm."

"Easy, love." She leaned me against her and prodded me gently. "Fuck. The bastard's dislocated your shoulder."

"Put it back!" I howled. "Put it back in!" I'd seen it in films. You popped the shoulder back into place and the pain ceased immediately.

Melissa unwrapped my Exeter scarf from around my neck and carefully made a sling for my arm to keep it still. "You need to go to A and E," she said steadily. "Have you ever dislocated your shoulder before? No, I didn't think so. I want you x-rayed and medicated before anybody does anything. And I want to make sure there's no fracture."

"Fuckin' hell!"

"Honestly, you have no idea how much it would hurt if I tried to put it back in," Melissa said in an even tone. "And without a proper exam, I could cause further damage. Nicky, help me get her in the car."

I screamed as they got me to my feet and again when they put me in the front seat. I said, "*This really fucking hurts!*"

"I know, love." Melissa started the engine and shifted into first. "It's incredibly painful. Hold your arm against your body. Keep it as still as possible."

As we sped through slick streets, I told myself to stop acting like a baby. But it was agonizing every time the car stopped or went over a bump. Nick, seated behind me, held my good arm and said, "Hang in there, mate." Melissa took me to hospital where I had a bit of an excruciating wait, during which Nick tried to divert me from the pain by asking me to list every band I'd ever seen.

Through the fog of my misery, I remembered having forgotten to remember seeing Hazel O'Connor, Judy Tzuke, and Toots and the Maytals. I liked the Toots song "54-46 Was My Number" because it reminded me of being in jail. "Did I remember to tell you I patted Iggy Pop's head when he sang 'I Wanna Be Your Dog'?" I murmured absently.

When the triage nurse reached us, Melissa told her I was her patient. I had x-rays taken then lay on a trolley in a cubicle waiting for the doctor to arrive. Melissa stayed with me. I thought, *at least I'm not lying in hospital in Basra, Iraq, where there are no anesthetics or clean water because of what we've done.* Melissa must have seen the look of grief on my face because she held my hand and told me I would be all right.

The casualty doctor looked at my x-rays and examined me. It was a simple shoulder dislocation with no fractures or nerve damage. I got a jab of pethidine and Stemetil in the bum for pain and nausea while Melissa looked on sympathetically. It hadn't occurred to me until then to wonder how Melissa would handle being with me around people from her professional life. But she didn't act any differently. That shouldn't have surprised me in the slightest.

The ward sister came in to assist. They had me sit up on the gurney with my uninjured shoulder against the upright part of the bed. The doctor stood behind me and manipulated my shoulder while the nurse provided downward traction on my arm. There was a brilliant flash of pain then amazing, immediate relief. I was left with a very achy shoulder but not the wailing sort of agony I'd experienced earlier. I was given a sling to hold my arm steady, and Melissa helped me back into the waiting room.

"Alright, man?" Nick put her hand gently on my back. "You were pale as a ghost, you. I've never seen nowt like it. It was mental."

"Let's get you home," Melissa said.

Arriving at the flat, Melissa took me upstairs and put me to bed. She brought up the tea and said to Nick, "We'll bring in your gear from the car later."

"Leave it," Nick said. "I needn't stay here after all. Atom doesn't scare me anymore."

"Not now, you've kicked the crap out of him," Melissa said.

"And you. What about *you?*" Nick marveled. "You probably fractured his whole leg with your brolly. Who knew you had it in you? I mean, mate, you cry at meat."

"I know. Part of me can't believe we just left him lying there in the road. Do you suppose someone found him and took him to hospital?"

"Who cares?" Nick said. "I know. You can't stand seeing anyone in pain. You're a saint. But he was screeching like a car alarm. Someone will have found him if only to shut him up."

"You should stay here anyway until it's completely sorted," Melissa said.

"I think we just sorted it," Nick said.

"Stay."

"Alright. Cheers, Melissa."

When I felt tired, Melissa carefully arranged a pillow under my injured shoulder and sat next to me stroking my hair. As I was dozing off, I heard Melissa say, "I would have done anything in the world to keep this from happening to you," and thought something awful must have happened to me. I remember wondering what it was as I crashed into unconsciousness.

TRACK 50   I WANNA BE SEDATED

I must have cried out in my sleep because when I jerked myself awake, Melissa was beside me saying, "It's alright, love. I'm here."

"Am I still in one piece?" I cried.

"Whatever's the matter, kid? Of course you're in one piece."

"Don't let them take my arm! I need it to play guitar. Don't let them. *Please*," I begged her. My mouth was dry, and I was terrified.

"Shh, honey, you had a nightmare. Your arm is fine. All you did was dislocate your shoulder."

"Oh, God. I thought I was in hospital in Basra being operated on without anesthetic. And they—it was horrible. All those people. It's our fault."

"Calm down." Melissa knew one of my main torments was the obsessive fear that parts of my body, especially my hands, were coming off.

"But it really is happening. It really is our fault. All those people that we've killed and maimed—and we cannot make it stop. No matter what we do." I continued to weep.

"I know," Melissa said. "How's your shoulder?"

"My shoulder's okay, but my arm!" I felt a dreadful, OCD panic.

"Listen to me," Melissa said, holding my good arm securely. "Your arm is fine. You dislocated it. It is not coming off. Your arm is not coming off. I am telling you, as a medical doctor, there are plenty of things holding it on. It is not possible for it to suddenly fall off. It is not coming off now, nor will it come off at any time in the future."

I wiped my eyes and thought about Ernest Hemingway writing in *A Farewell to Arms* that the world breaks everyone, but that some grow strong at the broken places. But just thinking about the title freaked me out. *A farewell to arms, Jesus Christ! Why the hell did he have to name it that? Arms safe, hands safe, fingers safe.*

"Where are you?" Melissa asked.

"I'm right here," I mumbled, barely hearing her. I was unnerved, thinking that maybe I had to specifically mention

"thumbs." Didn't God know that in my heart when I said "fingers" I also meant "thumbs"? Couldn't God actually *see* into my heart?

"No, you're not. You're off on some other OCD plane. I can tell now, you know." She held onto me as frantic sentences raced through my head and I only saw blood spurting out where my hands should be. And it felt like being knocked down by a giant wave and churned beneath the cloudy, choppy sea, unable to breathe, not knowing which way was up to the salvation of air and sky. "Amanda, do you want me to give you something to sedate you? Has it ever been this bad before? I hate to see you in so much pain, love."

I saw her frowning with concern, and her words finally registered. I experienced a sudden, acute freak-out in my heart and blurted out, "Do you really?"

"What do you mean, *really*?" Melissa asked.

"You're always so calm." I realized how daft I sounded, but I couldn't stop myself.

"Oh, love." She kissed my forehead. "That's just my training. My first priority is to make sure you're alright and that I've done everything I can for you to keep you safe. I react afterwards." I don't know how she knew what I meant. "Love, you wouldn't really want me to fall apart instead of helping you. And who do you think is going to sit here watching you sleep?"

"You are?" I nearly wailed.

"Amanda. Look at me." She held my head with both hands, making sure that I was really seeing her. "Do you know where you are?"

"Fucking hell, of course I bloody know where I am," I snapped, offended. "Do you really react afterwards?" I was unable to let it go, which describes OCD in one sentence.

"I'll be right back." When she sat next to me again, she gave me Valium and water. "You're having a really bad panic attack. Shh." She tried to get me to lie down, but I was too agitated. "Take a few deep breaths."

Gradually, my thoughts slowed down. I still felt haunted but didn't care as much if the nightmare I was running from caught up with me. My brain felt deliciously sludgy. I scrunched down under the covers, my eyes closing. Before I fell asleep, I started dreaming out loud. "I was listening to Stiff Little Fingers in my Walkman. I'd tried to get the driver to take the prison bus through the drive-thru at McDonald's." In my mind, I was standing at the empty site of an earlier ACT UP demonstration after my release, listening to "Johnny Was" in my earphones and remembering how mad the cop driving the prison bus had been when all the other prisoners started chanting that they wanted McDonald's, too. I remember Melissa laughing softly as I conked out.

TRACK 51 **DREAM TIME**

When I woke up, the room was dark and Melissa was sleeping beside me. I shook her gently. "I had the weirdest dream. I was raped, and then the man who raped me abducted me and took me to Iraq. He made me marry him. I couldn't get away because his entire extended family was watching me to make sure I didn't escape. I was married to him for twenty years, during which the part of me that was really me went to sleep, and I became a different person. It was the only way I could survive the marriage—all the times he'd fuck me. Then you came and let me know secretly that you loved women. And I woke up and became conscious again. You had to kill him in order to rescue me. You didn't understand why I was sad. 'He was my husband,' I said. Part of me loved him. I had lived as his wife. It was like there were two of me, and you had to save me twice, first physically then mentally."

"And what did I do with you then, after I'd rescued you?" Melissa yawned.

"You brought me back with you to London where I'm recuperating nicely from my ordeal."

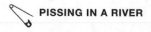 **PISSING IN A RIVER**

I fell asleep again and dreamed I was tracking a serial killer. He was dragging me up the side of a mountain on a rope. He took out a knife and slashed me in the ass. I must have shouted.

"Jesus *Christ*." Melissa sat up in bed in her black-and-white "The Only Band That Matters" Clash T-shirt. I could see the outline of her breasts and wished my arm wasn't in a sling. "You dreamt that 'cos you got a jab in the bum," Melissa said when I told her.

"I prefer to see it as a commentary on the state of the world."

"A sort of biblical commentary? As in, 'turn the other cheek?'"

"You're very entertaining."

"That's the best I can do after being screamed awake."

"Since we're supposed to drink of the blood and eat of the body, shouldn't Jesus be our Lord and Savory?"

Melissa started laughing.

"And shouldn't I talk about Jesus, my Lord to Savor?" I couldn't help myself. "And shouldn't it be father, son and holy toast? Anyway, I'm sorry I screamed you awake."

"It's not your fault," Melissa said. "Besides, you got hurt trying to protect me."

"And you stabbed a geezer in the leg for me. *You*, a professional healer," I said, pretending to be shocked.

"Don't remind me. I should've sent the police and an ambulance back for him."

"Why didn't you?"

"I was too concerned about poor you to think properly. And I didn't want to put Nick through all that. But if he turns up again, I bloody well will go to the police, and no one's gonna stop me."

"After seeing you wield an umbrella, mate, no one would dare." I sang, "*She's a Venus in bovver boots, / she's a Venus in bovver boots, / she's a Venus in bovver boots, / bloody great Doc Mar'ins, / Venus in bovver boots,*" from a song by the Nipple Erectors, Shane MacGowan's band before the Pogues. He was a raging, almost completely nonfunctioning alcoholic. There was a website dedicated to him called "When a Coma Sang."

"Do you need more pain medication?" Melissa asked.

I smiled at her. "You're so beautiful. I'll bet you were beautiful when you stabbed him with your umbrella."

Melissa laughed. "Go back to sleep."

Her breathing had slowed when I had a thought and nudged her back into consciousness.

"What? What is it? Are you alright?"

"Melissa?"

"What is it, love?"

"Is God a food group?"

TRACK 52 **RESCUE**

My arm was out of its sling, but my shoulder was still sore.

"What's the matter with Melissa?" Nick asked, as I was showing her one of my all-time favorite Nirvana CDs from Kiss The Stone in Italy. Her jeans had one black and one red leg.

"What do you mean?" I asked in a carefully neutral tone. I knew what she meant. After the initial shock of my injury wore off, Melissa returned to being distant and uncommunicative.

"She's got a lot on her mind," I said. "But look at this." I held the KTS CD *Saturday Night Sonic Attack* in front of her face. "Soundboard Nirvana from a 1990 concert in Lincoln, Nebraska." The cover was a picture of Kurt Cobain, bathed in orange light, playing a Fender Mustang and standing in front of an angel mannequin. It was taken during the later *In Utero* tour, and it looked like Kurt had wings as he stomped his sneaker on an effects pedal.

"I'm serious, mate. And stop waving that bloody CD at me." Nick held up her hands.

"I told you. She's preoccupied with an art project." Since she was working on her paintings depicting rape, I thought that was really, almost, true. "Just be patient with her. Now listen." I put on the Nirvana CD to distract her. "It has a killer version

 **PISSING IN A RIVER**

of 'Here She Comes Now' by the Velvet Underground and an intense 'Love Buzz' with extra-static guitar. You wouldn't think a show in Lincoln, Nebraska, would turn out to be one of the great ones, but it has an electric, brain-crushing version of 'Polly.' He goes up an octave and screams out the final verse. It's the most intense thing I've ever heard in my life, man."

I could tell Nick wasn't satisfied, and I felt like she was gearing up for a confrontation with Melissa that I wasn't sure I should try to stop. We went out and got some Indian for tea. Melissa came down wearing the most beautiful Clash T-shirt I'd ever seen. It was a picture of the Post Office Tower hanging over terraces and the words "LONDON CALLING" in yellow and orange. When she wore it, I just wanted to hold her.

Nick opened up the sweating, steaming food cartons, and I got out plates. Melissa pulled a sweatshirt over her head and sat down, absorbed in her own thoughts. There wasn't much conversation. Nick shot me meaningful glares across the table. I tried to signal with my own expressions that I was not in control of the situation.

Finally Nick said, "Alright. I give up. Melissa, what the fuck is going on with you? What the hell is the matter?"

"Oh, Nick," Melissa snapped, exasperated, "for God's sake, I was raped. Happy now?" She gasped, shocked by what she had just blurted out.

"*What?*" Nick froze then looked from her to me. "You *what*? You were *raped*? Oh my God."

"It didn't happen now, for fuck's sake," Melissa said, trying to sound casual. "It happened after Jake left for Canada."

"What? What are you saying?" Nick looked ill, like she'd been punched in the stomach, all the air gone out of her. My own eyes were wide with amazement, and I couldn't utter a single syllable. Melissa didn't move. Into the silence, we heard Nick say in a small voice, "Oh, God. Oh my God, no. Melissa, I'm so sorry. Why did you not tell us?"

"I don't know." Melissa's voice was resigned. "Jake had gone.

You'd broken up with Emilia. I thought you had enough on your plate."

"*Enough on my plate?*" Nick stared at Melissa incredulously.

"I didn't want you to know."

"I would do anything for you."

"I didn't want anyone to know. I wanted to forget it ever happened."

Nick said, "You must have hated me, crapping on about—"

"Don't," Melissa interjected.

"A rape that wasn't really a rape."

"Let's not do this, shall we?" Melissa replied sharply. "There isn't a hierarchy of suffering or of ways to be raped. This isn't a contest. I should have told you so you would've known I understood. That I knew how scared you were and how bad it made you feel."

"What happened?" Nick asked quietly.

"Paul raped me."

"Oh, sweet Jesus. I want to kill him."

"Me too," Melissa and I both said.

"I can't believe Jake didn't come back."

"Jake doesn't know," Melissa said. "And please don't tell her. But I wanted you to know because it's been doing my head in a bit and I didn't want you to take it personally."

"I'm so sorry." Nick looked like she desperately wanted to hug her.

"It's alright." Melissa smiled, and I could see she was trying not to cry. "I need to get some air." She pushed back her chair and rose abruptly.

"Melissa—" I got up to stop her.

"Please, just let me alone. Please." She met my eyes. "I need some time by myself. Please don't come after me." She rushed out without a coat.

I yelled from the front door, "You'll catch your death!" It was raining and windy outside.

"I cannot be arsed!" she called from up the road.

I didn't know if I should go after her or respect her wishes. Nick knelt on the settee and looked out the front window. I turned out the sitting room lights to see outside more clearly.

"There's no sign of her," I said frantically. I paced between the window and the front door. "I shouldn't have let her go."

"What were you supposed to do, hold her down? She's an adult." Nick flopped down heavily on the sofa. "Christ, I can't believe Paul raped her." She rested her face in her hands. "I just feel gutted. I can't believe I didn't know. That seriously is the worst thing I ever heard."

I waited twenty minutes. Then I couldn't stand it any longer. "I'm taking her coat and going out looking for her. I'll not have her freeze to death."

We walked up the hill then went in separate directions. Nick said she was going to check in the King William IV, a gay pub. I stuck my head inside the Horse and Groom, but Melissa wasn't in there nursing a pint. I ran toward the Heath in a panic, not knowing how I was going to find her. My green, leopard-print sneakers with the bondage straps splashed through heaps of fallen rain that seemed like so many tiny, abandoned silver shields and arrows left by a fleeing army. At least that's how I pictured it.

I saw a figure up ahead, blurry in the rain. "Melissa? Is that you?" As I came closer, I saw that it was. "Are you *mad*?" I flung her coat at her, and she put it on. The rain buttered my hair flat against my head, and I wiped water from my eyes. "Oh, Melissa." I put my hands on her face. She bent down and kissed me. I was surprised because I thought she'd be pissed off at me for coming after her. I threw my arms around her in spite of my achy shoulder. I licked the rain off her neck, and we kissed. Her mouth was warm, but she shivered. Her bright-red hooded sweatshirt that said "Joe Strummer 1952–2002" and had a picture of Joe Strummer in black against a black star was soaked completely through. "Come home," I said. And I sang to her from the song

"Morning Rain" by the Mancunian band I Am Kloot, "'*I'm the morning rain. / It's me again, / I won't go away.*'"

TRACK 53 I'M PARTIAL TO YOUR ABRACADABRA

I saw online that the Angelic Upstarts had just played a historic gig in South Shields and wondered if there was any way I could get Melissa to see them. I emailed the band through their website and explained I had a friend who loved their music but wouldn't go to any of their shows because of their use of a pig's head to represent police brutality. Gaz Stoker, the bass player who also played with Red London and Red Alert, wrote back to me. He explained that Mensi, the vocalist, got the pig's head at an abattoir and that they didn't have a pig slaughtered especially for them. It was strictly for sending an anti-police message. But I knew Melissa couldn't tolerate seeing them kick a pig's head about like it was a football.

"That was a lovely thought anyway," Melissa said when I told her. We were downstairs listening to CDs. Melissa had introduced me to the Argies, an Argentinian punk band she loved who'd been around for over twenty years and were like the Clash in Spanish, and two Clash-influenced Japanese punk bands called the Star Club and the Strummers.

Now I put on the official live Clash release *From Here to Eternity*. "You know this part?" I played "City of the Dead," waiting while Joe and Mick harmonized at the end of the first verse, "*and I wished I could be like you / Soho river drinking me down.*" "I always sing it as, '*and I went down to be like you,*'" I said. "I sang it to the people in my head to promise them I'd always be there. That I'd never let them down. I guess I'm singin' it to you."

My favorite version of "City of the Dead" was from the Agora in Cleveland, Ohio, on February 14, 1979. It had the best harmonies and the most expansive lead guitar by Mick Jones. I got it

 **PISSING IN A RIVER**

off a bloke flogging cassettes on the side of the road between the Camden Town tube and Camden Lock in 1980. I bought a bunch of Clash, Jam, and Pretenders tapes from him. He let me listen to the quality on his Walkman. That's how we did it then, before CDs and the Internet. Melissa had a copy of the same concert, with slightly better audio, from an online Clash site.

Melissa had gone out to the shops when Nick came in. Because Melissa had been honest with her about the rape, I decided I would tell Nick the truth about what had brought me to London in the first place. We sat on her bed.

"So that's why you followed me that night," Nick said after I'd told her how I thought I'd recognized her as one of my voices. "And thank God you did."

"I needed to find out who you were," I said. "I wanted to know you. I hope you don't mind."

"*Mind?* You probably saved my life that night. And it did feel like divine fucking providence when you suddenly appeared on that shite lit'le street sputtering inaccurate British idioms," Nick laughed.

"You remember that?"

"I thought you were *daft*," Nick gave me a playful shove, "fannying about, falling over that motor." We both started giggling, and I shoved her back. "I thought to meself, oh no, this daft cunt is gonna get us both killed. You daft, silly plank." Nick grabbed me and shook me affectionately. Then she threw her arms around me as I dissolved in paroxysms of laughter.

When Melissa returned, I was sitting at the computer downloading Oasis concerts. Nick had gone out clubbing with some mates, but I wanted an early night. Melissa came up behind me and put her hands on my shoulders. "Oh my God," she said, leaning her head down next to mine and peering at the computer screen, "Oasis? And bloody hell, what's this? *Pictures* of Oasis? You're saving Oasis bloody *pictures* on my hard drive?"

"I can't help it," I said. "I love them."

"You *love* them?"

"I love Liam and Noel."

Melissa looked over my shoulder at the Oasis website I was on, and read a quotation from Liam Gallagher out loud. "'*My songs are the best fucking songs in the world—I write the best fucking songs in the world.*' Lovely."

"I know they're arrogant bastards, but they play and sing so sweet."

I played her "Better Man," "Born on a Different Cloud" and "Stop Crying Your Heart Out" from a favorite concert in Finsbury Park, July 7, 2002 with brilliant sound quality. And I played her the electric version of "Don't Go Away" from a 1997 concert in Manchester, even though that song is a rip-off of the Real People song "Feel the Pain." I played her "Slide Away," "Morning Glory," "Rockin' Chair" and "I Hope, I Think, I Know."

"Influenced by the Beatles much?" Melissa asked.

"Can you think of anyone better?" I played her a stinging live version of "D'you Know What I Mean?" The lyrics, "All my people right here, right now," had always made me think of the people in my head. *My* people. I put on an early mix of "Better Man," following that with covers of the Jam's "Carnation" and the Who's "My Generation." Then I played a song Noel sang that always moved me, "Shout It Out." Finally I put on the song that had made me start listening to Oasis in the first place, a bootleg version of Noel Gallagher singing "Live Forever" by himself with an acoustic guitar.

Melissa sighed. "It's beautiful. I can't deny it."

I stood up and put my arms around her waist. "Remember that night we watched the horror video and I annoyed you by asking if you were sleeping with Martin?"

"Me? Annoyed? I don't get annoyed," Melissa laughed.

"I was lying next to you, and in my head I heard Liam singing 'Songbird.' The lines '*A man can never dream these kind of things / especially when she came and spread her wings*' really got to me. I thought of the magnitude of the gift getting to be with you would be, and I just hoped he appreciated you."

 **PISSING IN A RIVER**

"That's so sweet." Melissa touched my face. "I'm sorry I made it hard for you."

I rocked Melissa in my arms and put my head on her shoulder. "Well, all I was asking you to do was change your entire life."

We listened to "Live Forever" again. During the last chorus, instead of singing *"Maybe you're the same as me, / we see things they'll never see,"* Noel sang, *"Maybe you're the same as me, / you take two sugars in your tea, / you and I are gonna live forever."*

And Melissa shouted, "Maybe you're the same as me, you take six sugars in your tea!"

TRACK 54 WHEN ANGELS DIE

The soreness in my shoulder had dwindled to a dull ache, and I was playing guitar again. I dipped the large headstock of my Super-Sonic, swinging it around as I played "Working for the Jihad." I was using the Super-Sonic as my backup guitar and had a custom pickguard made for it out of the same pattern as the Fender pink-paisley guitars. The design was bright pink and green on a silver-sparkle background. When I put it on my guitar, it looked psychedelic and overwhelmingly glorious.

"I'm glad to see you playing again. I missed that." Melissa was curled up on the settee reading a medical journal.

Putting down my guitar, I signed onto eBay to relax and scrolled through photos of blue, solid-body electric guitars. I had an obsession with them and felt I could be trusted just to look. But I accidentally fell in love with a Lake Placid blue "Partscaster" Strat, a Mexican Standard Strat body with a vibrant finish, tortoiseshell pickguard, black pickup covers, black control knobs, Protone rosewood neck from Korea, no wear on the frets, individual tuners and pickups from a left-handed guitar. Instinctively I knew it was meant for me, so my immediate impulse was to buy it. But I didn't have enough money.

Melissa, finished with her article, stood behind me. She slid her reading glasses down her nose and peered over the top of them at the computer. "That's lovely."

I bid what I could afford, but my bid was rejected as being too low.

Nick came by around teatime to tell me I had to stop waiting for a band to come along. She put an acoustic guitar in my hands and said, "Think of yourself as The Indigo Girl."

I rehearsed my songs on the acoustic guitar and figured out ways to sing them solo that still incorporated some of my harmonic ideas. At the first pub I played in, the audience consisted of two white women in their fifties with enormous, bleached-blond hair. They wore tiny black dresses and go-go boots. Once I pulled out the chair and sat down with my guitar in my lap, I felt okay. I adjusted one microphone for my guitar and one for my vocals. I liked the way my guitar and voice came out sounding big. I hadn't let Melissa accompany me because I was too nervous, but Nick stood at the back of the pub, nodding her head in approval while I played. It felt different from busking, more on purpose, more intense.

About two weeks later, a box addressed to Melissa arrived. When she came home she said, "Open it. It's for you."

"For me?" I hopped up and down. There was another more slender box inside the first one, and it had the Fender logo on it. I pulled out a black Fender gig bag. "Oh my God," I said.

"Go on," Melissa said, smiling at me.

I unzipped the bag, and inside was my guitar in totally riveting, almost shocking, blue.

Melissa said, "It's bloody gorgeous."

"But how?" I picked up the guitar and held it in my lap. The smooth body curved into me just right.

"I knew how much you wanted that guitar. So I bought it for you."

"How much?"

"One hundred and twenty-five pounds."

"That's *good*. But—"

"Because I wanted to." Melissa put her arms around me and kissed the top of my head. "And because I could."

The neck was fast and perfect for my hands. "Playing a guitar with a great neck is like touching a beautiful woman," I said. "This plays better than those Strats that cost a bomb." And that night, I moved all three electric guitars, the Gibson SG, Super-Sonic, and Partscaster, into the bedroom.

At my second gig, I played in a pub to one person with his back to me playing darts. Finally I coaxed Nick, who had a Mick-Jones-like singing voice, into learning the harmonies to my songs. I taught her the rest of the bass lines she didn't know, and she picked them up quickly. "Shite, you're a natural," I praised her. She developed her own melodic, Pete-Farndon-early-Pretenders-esque bass style.

We started performing songs together on both acoustic and electric guitar. It was reassuring to look over at Nick, her shaggy dark hair in her face, while I played. She swung the cream-colored bass around and paced the stage in her red-and-black T-shirt that said, "ANYONE CAN BE A SEX PISTOL BUT YOU'RE ALL TOO FUCKING LAZY." I amped in the sampler for the beats, reminding myself that Echo and the Bunnymen had started out with a drum machine and Ann and Nancy Wilson had used one on their solo tour.

I loved doing my old song "Automatic Rifle Dance" with her. I'd written a melodic, beautiful bass line for it and a wild electric-guitar lead. And I wallowed in the harmonies when Nick was singing with me.

> *Get ready get ready get ready get ready*
> *get ready see you in paradise*
> *I've found everyone but Abu Nidal*
> *Hamas, Hezbollah, the IRA*
> *Loyalist Paramilitary, USA*
> *when there's a bomb in Portadown*
> *get out of town*

when bricks fly thick through the Belfast sky
hug the ground.

We put up ads for a drummer in music shops and live-music venues. Sometimes we played under different names, like Sudanese Pharmacy, Baghdad Triage, It's Raining Bastards, the Water Boarders, Hen and Radio Teeth. We had as much fun coming up with band names as we did writing lyrics together. It was heaven playing music with my best mate.

"We're in a band," I said to Nick. "That's the same as being married."

Nick smiled. "But not in a heterosexual way."

"No, of course not. Don't take anything I say heterosexually."

"And Melissa won't mind?"

"No," I said. "We have an open relationship that includes you."

After one of our sparsely attended pub gigs, a woman approached us as we were packing up our gear and asked if we needed a drummer. Nick was rolling up the guitar and bass cords while I was unplugging my effects pedals and putting them in a case. I looked up and Nick walked over. The woman looked about twenty-five, with black curls bleached to a burnt orange and dyed purple and a pierced nose.

"I'm Adele." She shook our hands soberly. "I saw your advert a while back and decided to check you out."

I pulled the black-and-white ACT UP bandana out of my back pocket and wiped my sweaty hair.

"I like your songs. Kind of feminist, yeah? Political lyrics. I'm into that. Poly Styrene is kind of my muse, like," Adele named the front-woman for X-Ray Spex. "She's kind of my archetype, you know. The archetypal feminist punk. She's also of mixed race. Like me. Somali and British."

"I don't know what your sexuality is, right?" Nick said. "But we're a lesbian band. Do you have a problem with that?"

"I'm bisexual." Adele had smooth, dark skin and high cheek-

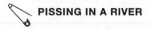 **PISSING IN A RIVER**

bones. "I don't care what you do in bed. Are you two—?" she gestured, asking if we were a couple, and Nick shook her head. "As long as personal drama stays at a minimum in the band, I honestly don't give a fuck."

Adele lived in Brixton but kept her drum kit at her mum's house in Islington because she didn't have room for it in her one-room flat. We arranged for Adele to bring over her snare drum and hi-hat cymbals to Melissa's flat the following day just to give us a taste of what she could do.

"If we play anywhere that doesn't have a PA system and have to bring our own amps, we're fucked," Nick said above the noise of the tube train as we rode home. "Your Vox amp alone will barely fit in Melissa's car. The instruments won't fit at all with us in it. We'll have to hire a van."

By the time we reached the flat, Melissa was asleep. I knew she had an early start the next morning, so Nick and I took our tea and biscuits into her room. We sat up on Nick's bed half the night talking about our show, speculating about Adele and working on some song ideas. I ended up falling asleep right there beside her.

In the afternoon, Nick and I waited for Adele to come, listening to a southern California punk band called the Scarred because Nick liked the female drummer. Adele showed up in her mum's car with her drum and cymbals. She put a silencer on her snare and a mute on her hi-hat so she wouldn't make too much noise.

We were playing in the sitting room, me on acoustic guitar and Nick with the bass turned down low. Adele smacked her snare drum and cymbals, banging out the beat to a new song I'd just written and wanted to try out called "Pour."

"It's a top fucking tune, that," Nick said when we finished. "Is it about Melissa?"

Just then Meilssa walked in and I blushed. I kissed Melissa and introduced her to Adele. Melissa went into the kitchen to get something to eat. She sat and listened to us for a while then went upstairs.

Adele was a good drummer and we quickly decided to take her on. She had the finesse of Chad Channing from the first Nirvana album. I'd always loved that album best. She could hit hard but was also delicate, and I thought she'd work well with my music. She was versatile and could play in different styles. We made plans to meet up in Islington later that week. Adele said we could practice temporarily in her mum's garage until we sorted out a proper place to rehearse.

When it got a bit late and I thought Melissa might be trying to sleep, we ended up drinking multiple cups of tea and discussing how to get a rehearsal space where we could play at full volume with the entire drum kit. Adele used to have a place in Camden Town with her old band, Menstrual Palace. *Just like the Clash*, I thought. *This is a dream. This is my dream.*

"You coming, mate?" Nick called from the door. She and Adele were going to continue their discussion of favorite tunes and rehearsal opportunities down the pub.

"Naw, you go on, mate. I'm going to spend some time with Melissa."

"Alright, luv. Be back later." She helped Adele carry her gear out to the car.

I washed up, brushed my teeth, and went into the bedroom. Melissa was reading Gertrude Stein's *The Autobiography of Alice B. Toklas*. I thought she'd like it because of the way Gertrude Stein talks about all the painters she knew, like Picasso and Matisse, and their paintings. I got in next to her.

"This part about Gertrude Stein being bored in medical school is so funny," Melissa said, putting the book on the night table. She was wearing a red-and-black flannel nightshirt. I had on a pair of knickers and my "I Was Arrested By A Lesbian Cop" T-shirt that one of the ACT UP blokes had made up especially for me and my ACT UP friend Margaret because of the way we used

to taunt the lines of riot police. "So, you've got a new drummer then? You sounded tight. I can't wait until I get to hear you loud. Nick sounds brilliant on bass and backing vocals. Are you going to start letting me come see you play? I'd really like to, you know. Or would you be too nervous?"

"I think I'll be okay now. I feel bolder with a band behind me. You look knackered."

"It was a long day." She took off her round, tortoiseshell reading glasses and rubbed her eyes.

"What's the matter?" I caressed her soft, tartan sleeve.

"Oh, I had to examine a rape victim today. Something meant for pleasure just shouldn't be used as torture."

"I just want to kiss you until all your bad feelings go away. You know, like I'm sucking out the poison after you've been bitten by a snake."

"Oh my God, you're not going to start rabbiting on about the bloody Garden of Eden again, are you?" Melissa gave me a humorous look.

"Well . . ." I shrugged, about to say something poignant about the serpent and bring up Lilith, the lesbian in midrashic literature who came before Eve and refused to have sex with Adam. But before I could, she kissed me deeply, pulling me into her lap.

"Melissa," I said, when we paused, "your latest paintings are incredible." She'd finished her series of acrylic paintings about rape. One of her paintings was a study in Gauguin-like pink, and all were unified by the thick, passionate texture of her brushstrokes. "I've been thinking about it, and if I ever get the chance to play real gigs where people actually turn up to see us on purpose, I want you to come with me."

"Well, of course, I'd love to. If I can."

"No, I mean I want you as the other act, like the support band. Not that you're in a supporting role to me or anyone. But I want people to see your paintings. It's time," I insisted, as she started to protest, "for you to show your work. And not just to me. It's brilliant, man. I mean it. And I'm not just saying that because I want to shag you," I teased her. "I want you to take a break from your practice and work as an artist for a while. You're really good, Melissa. Would you do the artwork for my albums? Even if I have to make, release, and distribute them myself?"

"That's a promise," Melissa said. Soon our knickers were on the floor. Then I was kissing her inner thighs while she shivered, and I couldn't think of anything else except moving more deeply into the center of her.

TRACK 55 GROOVY TIMES

Nick, Melissa, and I sat in the pub trying to think up a better name for the band than Star Vomit, which is what I'd called it in California. "It doesn't suit your music," Melissa said. She was wearing a dark-green sweatshirt with Patti Smith's face on it. "Star Vomit makes me think of screamo death metal or something. Your sound is melodic punk with some Britpop and bhangra thrown in. Abrasive but tuneful."

"But we're made out of the matter from the insides of stars that vomited out when the stars exploded," I explained.

"I get it," Melissa said, "but I think that the name Star Vomit is a little too off-putting."

"How about the name Sugar Rat?" I suggested. "There's a rat temple in Rajasthan, India, called Karni Mata where rats are worshipped. They're the souls of storytellers, and you bring them sweets like sugar balls."

"I rather liked that name we used for a giggle a while back," Nick said. "Hen. It reminds me of the expression 'rare as hen's teeth.' I think it's quite funny."

"It needs more of a political edge to go with your lyrics," Melissa said.

I got the pen and paper out of my back pocket. "The Shoulder Rats. To protest against animal testing." I unfolded the sheet of paper and began to write. "Ganesha Rat."

 PISSING IN A RIVER

"Extraordinary and the Renditions," Melissa said. "Sadistic Orange Jumpsuit."

"Lesbian Teacher," Nick said. "Futility Loin."

"The Dead Rapists," I said. "The Lesbian Cobains."

"I like the Dead Rapists," Nick said, glancing at Melissa.

"Except that you don't want that word staring at you from all your merchandise and literature," Melissa said.

The Mayhems. The Gender Traitors. She Sells Jesus By the Seashore. Out! Guantanamo Bay Tourism Association. Battery-Powered Halo. Oi Vey. America the Bully. Downside of the Soul. The Waterboarders. Sorry I Bombed Your Country. Lesbian Raincoat. The Democracy Pistols. Smarter Than Bombs. The Gash. Snatch. Oil Pipeline Jihad. I'm So Bored with the USA. The Breaststrokers. Democracy Through a Feeding Tube.

"I like Sorry I Bombed Your Country," I said, "but I'm afraid it's too long."

"I think anything with the word 'jihad' or any reference to terrorism will be more trouble than its worth," Melissa said, "but I do like Guantanamo Bay Tourism Association. And there's something nice about Lesbian Raincoat."

Nick looked over my shoulder at the list. "I like The Democracy Pistols."

Adele had joined us. "I'm not a full-fledged lesbian," she said, smiling, "being somewhere else on the great sexuality continuum. But I like Lesbian Raincoat. There's something reassuring about it."

"Is a real lesbian raincoat supposed to keep you dry or wet?" I laughed. "Sorry."

Nick said, "Maybe it's supposed to keep the moisture in."

"How about The Dental Dams?" Adele suggested.

"The Dental *Dames*?" I said.

"I vote for Lesbian Raincoat," Melissa said. "I think it suits your sound. The way it wraps around you. The way the rain is all-encompassing. The way it's democratic and rains on everyone."

"Yeah," Nick said, "and the way that 'Lesbian' shoves it all down everybody's throat." We all laughed.

"Cheers, then." Melissa raised her pint glass. "Here's to Lesbian Raincoat."

TRACK 56 **YOU BELONG TO ME**

Our new trio Lesbian Raincoat developed a respectable local following. Even though we'd begun by mostly performing at lesbian clubs, we were starting to gain a wider audience in the alternative community. We made extra money selling merchandise at our gigs.

Melissa had designed a logo for us, a blue raincoat, and we used it for the cover of the demo CD we recorded in Adele's mum's garage and Melissa's flat—mostly in the upstairs toilet. Melissa also designed Lesbian Raincoat badges and T-shirts. Whenever she could, she came with us to our gigs and took charge of our merchandise table. We'd started making high-quality prints of some of her paintings and sold those along with the art she had made especially for Lesbian Raincoat's posters and flyers.

By now we also had a small but efficient street team of eager young women who believed in our sound, sold our merchandise, put up posters, and helped us run our website. We called them the Fesbian Leminists after a purple T-shirt I'd had in the seventies when the words "lesbian" and "feminist" were considered so outrageous they had to be encoded. We shortened this to the Fesbians. We made them special small, dark-purple Fesbian badges. In return, they came to all our gigs for free and got free merchandise, including limited edition recordings we only made available to them. They were encouraged to post these recordings on the Internet and share them as long as they didn't sell them. Anyone posting our music for money on eBay was done. The Fesbians hung out at some of our rehearsals, which were still taking place in Adele's mum's garage in the afternoons.

I was listening to a lot of Ruts, trying to achieve that sharp, resonating Paul Fox guitar sound on a number of new songs. Nick studied "Segs" Jennings' bass playing. Sometimes we did a killer cover version of "Jah War" at our shows, and Nick and I rewrote a version of the anti-heroin song "Dope for Guns" and made it specifically about Iran-Contra. How the US smuggled arms to Iran through Israel, armed the Contras in Nicaragua, then used the supply planes to traffic cocaine into the United States.

Mostly we played in London, but sometimes on weekends we would hire a van and Melissa would drive us out to gigs in other towns. In the north we played in Birmingham, Liverpool, Manchester, Leeds, and Edinburgh. There was even some talk of us signing with an independent German label called Scratchella. The demo of my song "Working for the Jihad," which I'd posted on the Internet, had recently been released in Germany on a compilation CD by a small German label, Sterben im November, and had caught the attention of the women behind Scratchella. But Scratchella wanted us to record in Germany, and I couldn't leave the country yet. We also postponed playing in Dublin and Paris.

In the midst of all this activity, I got an email from my sister announcing she was getting married. I downloaded the attached photo of an engagement ring with a bloody great, huge, massive diamond.

"Did she tell you the name of the exploited, probably-dead African who put it on her finger?" Melissa asked dryly when I showed it to her.

"Ta for saying that. I thought I was going crazy for a minute."

"You're writing your congratulations, of course?"

"She wants me to come to the wedding."

"But you can't leave the country," Melissa said edgily, a hint of panic in her voice.

"Don't worry, love," I said. "I won't go anywhere until it's safe."

Finally, with Melissa's sponsorship, help from Harriet, and advice from the UK Lesbian and Gay Immigration Group, I managed to cohabitate with Melissa for the requisite two years and was granted indefinite leave to remain, permission to stay in the UK as her partner. Scratchella was still interested, and we made plans to record our first album in Germany, and then go on a short European tour that the label would promote. Melissa, who hadn't been on holiday in ages, arranged to take time off from work to join us.

We had about a month before leaving for Germany. "Now you can go to your sister's wedding," Melissa said.

My stomach lurched and I had a feeling of dread. "Will you go with me?"

"Can't," she said, giving me a wistful, sympathetic smile. "Not if I'm traipsing around Europe with Lesbian Raincoat."

I decided a week away from Melissa and Nick was all I could tolerate. I could already feel my OCD revving up as I contemplated spending time without them. At least the wedding coincided opportunely with Patti Smith's current American tour and I got two tickets to see her in Los Angeles. My sister wasn't leaving on her honeymoon right away, and I thought she'd go with me. I wished Melissa could come. We hadn't gone to see Patti in London at the Union Chapel in 2002 or in 2003 at the Shepherd's Bush Empire because we'd been too consumed by our own lives, as ridiculous as that sounds. But I'd downloaded those shows later on both audio and video. In Shepherd's Bush, Patti Smith called for the abolishment of George W. Bush's government and indicted him for crimes against humanity. It was her voice that got me through the Bush regime.

Carefully I picked out the CDs that would protect me on my trip and keep the plane aloft. These included live early Nirvana with Chad Channing on drums, live pre-1982 Pretenders, late-seventies Heart, and recording sessions from various Oasis

 **PISSING IN A RIVER**

albums. I was still trying to sing like Liam. Melissa drove me to Heathrow. I carried the Takamine with me in a neon-pink Dickies backpack guitar case of Jake's. I tuned down the strings so they wouldn't snap on the plane with changes in air pressure.

"How do you feel about seeing your family after all this time?" Melissa asked on the way to Heathrow.

"I don't think I can regress too far in a week," I said.

"Individuate," Melissa said, and smiled.

My OCD kicked in, telling me not to leave. Now that I was finally happy, it would be awful to die too soon. Getting on a plane seemed like I was pushing my luck. But I couldn't think of a rational reason—besides the obvious one that humans aren't meant to fly—not to get on the plane. As I said goodbye to Melissa and headed for international departures, I felt my thoughts accelerate, all the old fears rising up.

As I waited for my plane to board, I listened to Killing Joke's powerful 2003 CD, with Dave Grohl on drums, which raged against American empire building. I'd wanted an orange jumpsuit and black hood to wear on the plane to protest extraordinary rendition, Guantanamo Bay, the use of torture, and CIA black sites, but contented myself with a bright orange sweatshirt on which I'd stenciled, "America Tortures—Get It Through Your Thick F**king Head and Rise Up." I didn't spell out the word "fucking" in case there were kids on the plane. I didn't want anyone to be able to use obscenity as an excuse to tell me to take it off. With my regular anxiety and less oxygen circulating in the plane's cabin, I didn't think I'd do well with my face covered anyway. Airplanes are not good places for panic attacks. I sat and looked at the photos I'd brought along of Melissa and Nick and the three of us together and wanted to run screaming out of the airport.

My sister picked me up at LAX wearing large, assertive diamond earrings that made her whole head sparkle when she turned to talk to me. I didn't like being back in post–Patriot

Act America and immediately felt oppressed. "Don't you think you're being a little oversensitive?" my sister asked.

"Frankly, no," I said.

After over two years, everybody's American accent seemed ridiculously exaggerated, and my own accent was a source of amusement. I'd left my soul behind in England and missed Melissa and Nick so much it was a physical ache. Away from them, not hearing their voices, my OCD became more pronounced, and I looked forward to a week of ritualistic sentence repetition.

I was relieved when the ordeal of the wedding was over. Many of the guests were adorned in real furs and diamonds, and I had to keep mentally telling myself to shut up. I get uncomfortable in large herds of straight white people with money, and after two years of really coming into myself, I had even fewer adaptive social skills than usual. When the customs agent asked if I had anything to declare upon entering the United States, I should have said, "Yes, I have a really big mouth." I desperately wanted to confront the women in fur and only contained myself by imagining Melissa and Chrissie Hynde crashing the wedding with cans of red spray paint. When I say "contained myself," I mean I wasn't as bad as I should have been.

I'd never been a huge fan of weddings—government and religion in the bedroom, the traffic in women—especially if gay people didn't possess the same civil rights. I felt an appropriate wedding vow for women would be, "I do promise to be chattel." I remembered how Melissa had automatically equated my sister's engagement ring with blood diamonds and reminded myself there was a place on earth where I was considered sane.

Because my sister was still engaged with out-of-town guests for several days after the wedding, my dad, who listened to classical music his entire life and only evinced disinterest and distress when hearing rock and roll, volunteered to go to Los Angeles with me to see the Godmother of Punk so I wouldn't have to go alone. I was excited we would be sharing such an unexpected, intimate and earth-shattering experience together.

TRACK 58 ROCK THE CASBAH

It was 2004 when Patti Smith walked out onto the stage in Los Angeles. It was a real baptism into rock and roll for my father and a feeling of being born again for me. She was wearing a torn pair of blue jeans and a white T-shirt with a peace symbol she'd probably drawn on herself in black marker. There was a Palestinian flag draped over one amp and a peace symbol on the drum kit. She used every opportunity to speak out against the Bush administration and the wars in Iraq and Afghanistan. She raised her fists and didn't apologize like the Dixie Chicks and the Democrats. She played a sunburst Stratocaster and an old acoustic guitar. Oliver Ray played a Telecaster, and Lenny Kaye played a green Strat.

Patti beamed and waved. She said, "Hello, everybody! Glad to be back!" Immediately I knew I was in the presence of someone extraordinary. For me, Patti Smith was peace, love, sanity, and the restoration of American civil liberties. She looked like she had in 1975 but with some gray in her long, black, disheveled hair. She looked so much like herself I felt a big joy well up inside me. I squeezed Melissa's imaginary hand as I pictured her and Nick standing beside me. I had longed to be in Patti Smith's presence since the seventies, and being with her now was better than any of my highest expectations. Not to get weird, but she shone with an inner light, like she'd swallowed her own halo. In fact she reminded me of seeing Melissa for the first time, and I vowed to try that swallowed-her-own-halo line out on her when I got home.

Patti Smith launched into "Trampin'" with a smile in her voice, and I was intensely happy. In Patti's presence I felt safe. The loud music and her voice banished my OCD thoughts. People wanted to get up and dance, but the security guard sent them back to their seats. I desperately wanted to rush to the stage to be close to Patti but was afraid of being thrown out of the venue. The audience called out to Patti, asking her for permission to dance. Patti Smith said, "Don't look at me. Get off your fucking ass and dance if you want to. I don't got nothing to say." People shouted that the security guard wouldn't let us dance. Patti said, "One guy won't let you dance? What is he—? The strength of Gandhi? We better do what he says, or it's gonna get like Altamont here." That totally cracked me up.

I turned to my dad and said, "Gotta go!"

"Go, go," he said, smiling.

I ran to the stage, and Patti Smith knelt down right beside me to talk to the security guard. "Listen," she said, "these are my people. They won't cause you any trouble."

That's when I said, "Thank you, Patti," and touched the arm of her jacket. I didn't mean thank you for talking to the security guard. I meant thank you for everything. And while she was so close, I held onto her arm and added, "God bless you, Patti. I love you, Patti." I don't know why I said that, God bless you. I never say that. It just came out of my mouth.

Patti Smith stood up and said, "Security guy is cool. I told him that you were all harmless and they let you out just one night a year." Before she sang "Gandhi," she took off her shoes, emptied her pockets and threw yellow rose petals into the audience. They swirled around me like the pink and white blossoms in Exeter had one windy and rainy afternoon. I remembered my shoes grinding wet petals into mud and the sensation of being under God's confetti-dropping hand.

A minor-chord prologue to "My Blakean Year" put her in the mood for a spontaneous rant.

> They called out from the crowd
> tell me something
> tell me something

I got nothing to say absolutely
nothing McDonald's is gonna
sponsor be the food of the
Olympics
it's evil food
it gives our children
high blood pressure
no fucking athlete
worth his salt
would eat that sodium fat-filled food
athletes should stand together
and speak out against this atrocity
it's another kind of terrorism
McDonald's and all this fucking fast food
and all the corporations
and business
and a billion dollars worth of fucking advertising
negativity on the TV
demographic public and negative ads cost one billion
dollars
when people in Africa
can't afford their medication for AIDS
and their children are dying of starvation
and we're fucking up the infrastructure of Iraq
we're trashing Afghanistan
I've got nothing to say.

At the applause breaks between songs, I shouted for Patti to sing "Pissing in a River." But I didn't think she would. When she walked out for an encore, Patti Smith leaned over to whisper into Oliver Ray's ear, and he started plucking out the opening to "Pissing in a River" on his black Telecaster. I couldn't believe it. Lenny Kaye played the solo. She sang gently, *"What more can I do here to make this thing grow?"* Then as she snarled, *"Don't turn your back now when I'm talking to you,"* she bent right over me, her hair in my face. I felt myself melt completely into the music and disappear. It was like the revolution had happened, like bright lights were swirling all around me, like I could see everybody's halo—everyone who had one, that is. Patti Smith growled, *"What about it, I never doubted you,"* and I got a chill deep inside me.

Being in Patti Smith's presence as she performed "Pissing in a River," with guitar instead of keyboards, being close enough to get her spit on my "Rats Have Rights" PETA T-shirt was a religious experience for me. After the concert I rang up Melissa and practically screamed, "I have Patti Smith's spit on my T-shirt! I'm never going to wash it! I'm going to put it in a frame and hang it on the wall! Tell Nick!"

And Melissa said, "Love, that's perfect."

TRACK 59 HOW DEEP IT GOES

My dad drove me to LAX and we talked about Patti the whole way. As I waited for my flight back to England, I saw the newspaper headline, "Man Held as Terror Suspect Over Punk Song."

According to the article, British antiterrorism detectives stopped a flight from Durham to London and hauled Harraj Mann, twenty-four, off the plane after his taxi driver turned him in for singing along to "London Calling" by the Clash. The taxi's music system allowed Mann to plug in his own mp3 player, and he'd been playing songs for the driver from the Clash, Procol Harum, Led Zeppelin, and the Beatles.

The taxi driver became alarmed on the way to the airport when Mann sang along to the Clash lyrics, "Now war is declared, and battle come down." Another line containing the phrase "meltdown expected," he took as an imminent threat. "'He didn't like Led Zeppelin or The Clash but I don't think there was

 **PISSING IN A RIVER**

any need to tell the police,' Mann told the *Daily Mirror*." Though Durham police released Mann after questioning, he missed his flight.

As I boarded the plane, I was singing,

a nuclear error but I have no fear
'cos london is drowning and I live by the river

the avian flu is coming but I have no fear
'cos london is drowning and I live by the river

Melissa picked me up at Heathrow. I launched myself at her, almost coming out of my sneakers. "God, I missed you!" I flung my arms around her neck.

"I missed you too, baby." Melissa hadn't brought Nick along because there wasn't enough room for all three of us plus my guitar and bags in her car. "Nick's waiting at the flat."

Melissa slung my army-green, carry-on bag over her head, the strap running diagonally across her chest. She was wearing a gray hooded sweatshirt I'd got her, based on one Jello Biafra from the Dead Kennedys had worn, that said "NOBODY KNOWS I'M A LESBIAN" in big, black letters.

As we got in the car, Melissa asked, "How was it? Did you regress?"

"Patti Smith helped," I laughed. "As soon as we get home, I'm going to download a copy of the concert so we can listen to it together." I knew I'd find it on my favorite live-music tracker, which only allowed people to post music from artists who permitted taping. Patti Smith was cool that way.

Melissa had her arm around my shoulders and was playing with my hair. "I really missed you, you know?"

"Mmm, I missed you, too."

We'd been a little awkward at first but now, when I pressed my face into her body and breathed her in, I was at home. We kissed for a while before she finally pulled herself away from my embrace with a sigh and started the car.

"Wait." I reached into my bag. "I've got something for you." I'd got Melissa a signed copy of Patti Smith's new album *Trampin'* at the concert. Melissa slipped it into the car stereo and drove to Hampstead. It was so glorious to see the city again.

Nick wrapped her arms around me when I walked into the flat.

"Hey baby," I said, ruffling her hair, "I missed you." While I was away I'd perused a local record shop and finally found what I'd been wanting to give her since the night we first met. "Nicky, I've got something for you." From my bag I pulled out the same T-shirt of Kurt Cobain hugging his black "Vandalism" Strat that Nick had worn the night she was attacked and tossed out because of the blood.

The most famous appearance of that guitar was at the 1991 Reading Festival where Kurt played "Molly's Lips" with Eugene Kelly of the Vaselines. He said it was one of the greatest moments of his life. The second was at the Paramount Theatre in Seattle on Halloween in 1991. Earnie Bailey, Kurt's guitar tech, had put a Seymour Duncan JB humbucker in the bridge position for him.

"Oh, cheers, Amanda. I'm really chuffed, mate." Nick kissed my cheek.

After a second cup of tea, I said I was exhausted. Nick said goodnight, and Melissa and I went upstairs. There was so much pent-up electricity between us it was a relief to get her alone. After a week apart we were tentative, almost nervous. We knelt on the bed. I brushed my hand through Melissa's thick, chestnut hair then lifted her fresh, black "Jesus Loves The Stooges" T-shirt so I could kiss her breasts, sucking on her dark, honeyed nipples. She sighed deeply and pressed me to her. "Don't go away from me again, love," she whispered.

In Germany Nick, Adele, and I recorded the first official Lesbian Raincoat CD simply called *Out!* Adele and I added keyboards to some of the songs. Nick thumped her bass and sang backup vocals. I played all the guitar tracks and used a Jerry Jones sitar for a psychedelic lead on "Working for the Jihad." I recorded a solo, acoustic version of the song "Punishment Friday, 3:30 p.m.," which I'd written for RAWA.

Later Adele added tambourine, which was just the thing, and we donated part of the proceeds of our album—there wasn't much—to RAWA. Melissa donated the money she got selling her prints to PETA. I used my Gibson SG and blue Fender for recording. Besides Jake's Fender, Nick had found a used sunburst Epiphone Beatles Viola bass, something she'd always wanted, to add a Paul McCartney vibe to some of our songs. It was beautiful, with gold knobs and inlaid headstock, and was smaller than her Fender. Because it was hollow, it was light, and she could hear it well without being plugged in, which allowed her to practice more easily on the road and in bed.

I recorded the new song I'd written for Melissa, "Pour," with a lush guitar sound, using my blue Fender for the lead and the studio's six- and twelve-string Rickenbackers and an acoustic Martin for rhythm. Nick played a Rickenbacker bass. Adele handled all the drums and percussion. We recorded some of my older songs like "Thanksgiving Day," "Automatic Rifle Dance," and "Crawl." Adele gave a reggae-fueled percussive feel to "Holiday in Afghanistan" and "Lipstick," the first real song I'd written for Melissa.

For our European mini-tour I found a used Orange amp, made in London, and a used pedal board. I had added a white Mexican Strat with a custom lavender leopard-print pickguard to my arsenal and brought that along with my trusty white SG. I didn't use my blue Fender live because I wanted to save it just for recording. We played small venues except for a few festivals.

But we didn't play the main stages. We let it be known that we allowed people to tape our shows and post them on the Internet. We arranged with the different venues to let people in with their personal recording equipment. Playing live, we felt that once our music was released into the air, it belonged to everyone. Like the rain. It was a great first tour for us, and we learned how to coexist in a van even when we were wet and tired. Some of the Fesbians had come with us to work as roadies and manage the merchandise tables.

On the last night of our tour, we played a lesbian club in London. I put on an ACT UP T-shirt and white faux-leather punk bracelet with turquoise and silver studs. I'd also been wearing Melissa's red tartan bracelet throughout the tour for luck. Since we didn't have to conserve any energy for a next show and the stress of the tour was over, we were at our most raucous. We did wild, extended versions of "Taliban Radio Bulletin" and "Taliban Don't Dance." We ended the set with "Pour." I was aware of Melissa watching from the side of the stage—in her untucked, long-sleeved blue shirt with the black collar, pocket and cuffs, the black braces dangling over the bum of her black trousers—as I belted it out. "When you rain on me you pour . . ."

Then I ended the song the way Patti Smith finishes her live versions of "Dancing Barefoot."

> *"Oh God I fell for you.*
> *Oh God I fell for you.*
> *Oh God I feel the fever,*
> *Oh God I feel the pain,*
> *Oh God forever after,*
> *Oh God, I'M BACK AGAIN!"*

For an encore we played a smashing cover of the Clash's "Protex Blue," the lesbian version. The last thing I did was pick up an acoustic guitar and do a solo rendition of Patti Smith's "Pissing in a River."

 **PISSING IN A RIVER**

I walked off the stage with my guitar, sweaty and smiling, into Melissa's firm embrace.

It was late and I was exhausted by the time we finally packed up all our gear and got it loaded in the hired van. I was getting ready to climb into the front seat and tell Melissa to meet me back at the flat when Nick pulled me aside and told me to go home. "Really," she put her hands on my shoulders, "we can handle it. We've got the entire Fesbian crew. We don't need you. Go home with Melissa and I'll ring you tomorrow."

We kissed and said goodnight. With the strong, efficient women who were now our friends, Nick and Adele were going to drop off our equipment at her mum's garage for us to sort out later. Then they would return the van and head over to an after-hours club with their mates and the full contingent of Fesbians to celebrate. But all I wanted to do was go home.

Once we were out in the cool London air, I felt free. Melissa put her arm around my shoulders and we walked to the car in silence. I was so hoarse I could barely speak. All I wanted was a cup of tea, a nice hot bath, and *her*. Smiling, she started the car and took me to the one place where I didn't feel like an outsider.

ACKNOWLEDGMENTS

For help with research, thank you Kay Sprecher, Ivan Coleman, Simon Ottman, Micky Hillman, Karen Perizzolo, Gaz Stoker, Animal, Jake Burns, Dave Walsh, Tom Robinson, Peter Noone, the Scarred, Topper, U.K. Lesbian and Gay Immigration Group, Gingerbeer.co.uk, PETA, Keith McMahon, Brian Habes, and Adam and Coyote.

For editing help, thank you Robyn Bell for your rare, extraordinary patience and for introducing me to so much of my favorite literature. Thank you Angela Locke, Oriana Leckert, Ruth Greenstein, Roy Kesey, the women of GRiot, Nancy O'Donnell, and Riggin Waugh for teaching me so much about editing the first time around.

Thank you to my family, David, Jeannie, Devora, Pimm, and Lila.

Thank you to my friends on both sides of the pond: Rachel Folley, Michelle McCarthy, Natalie Leitner, Eric Smith, Mark Dowd, Josh Hershfield, Ursula Mahlendorf, Muriel Zimmerman, Farah Tengra, Sam Cardinell, Shinge Roshi Roko Sherry Chayat, Smashin' Kali, Doogie Plowzer, the Jessie Girls, and all my sisters in the vibrant lesbian and derby communities in and around Syracuse, New York.

Thank you Nancy O'Donnell for feeding me and making me part of your family, Mary Traynor and Crystal Doody Stryct 999 for moral support, and Paula Carey Martens for being my favorite ally.

Thank you Vicki Perizzolo for saving my stories. Thank you Robert Nagy.

Thank you Minnie Bruce Pratt, Leslie Feinberg, and Urvashi Vaid for letting me protest with you.

For musical inspiration, thank you Joshua Danyel, Miss E, and Beady Eye. Thank you Patti Smith, Chrissie Hynde, Ann and Nancy Wilson, Kurt Cobain, and Joe Strummer.

Thank you Nick Dawes at Cave Studio, Nice, France.

I am deeply grateful to Amy Scholder and Jeanann Pannasch. Thank you for giving this novel a chance. Thank you Amy for your wisdom, humor, hospitality, and kindness. Thank you Jeanann for your patience, insight, and extraordinary editorial ear. Thank you Elizabeth Koke, Cary Webb, Drew Stevens, Herb Thornby, and everyone at the magnificent Feminist Press who worked on this.

I am indebted to the Feminist Press for remaining true to its ideals of feminism and social justice, for being accessible to writers without agents, and for its commitment to non-mainstream voices.

Thank you to everyone in ACT UP/DC and ACT UP worldwide. Thank you Chelsea Manning, WikiLeaks, Edward Snowden, and all other whistleblowers and secret-information leakers, TomDispatch.com for being a vital source of real intelligence, World Can't Wait for the orange jumpsuit and all you do, PETA, RAWA, and the National Gay and Lesbian Task Force. Thank you Pussy Riot. Thank you activists, agitators, disruptors, and instigators who make people uncomfortable. Thank you to all musicians and bands that allow unofficial recording and electronic distribution of live shows not-for-profit. Thank you bootleggers for making live music available for free, preserving history, and undermining capitalism.

Thank you Jill Johnston for writing in *Lesbian Nation*: "Identity is what you can say you are according to what they say you can be."

Thank you to everyone in my chosen family I have not mentioned by name: you are all always in my heart.

The Feminist Press promotes voices on the margins of dominant culture and publishes feminist works from around the world, inspiring personal transformation and social justice. We believe that books have the power to shift culture, and create a society free of violence, sexism, homophobia, racism, cis-supremacy, classism, sizeism, ableism and other forms of dehumanization. Our books and programs engage, educate, and entertain.

See our complete list of books at
feministpress.org

THE FEMINIST PRESS
AT THE CITY UNIVERSITY OF NEW YORK
FEMINISTPRESS.ORG

PisSing in A river

a NOVEL BY LORRIE SPRECHER